PRAISE FOR THE
MORGANVILLE VAMPIRES NOVELS

"Rachel Caine is a first-class storyteller who can deal out amazing plot twists as though she was dealing cards."
— #1 *New York Times* bestselling author Charlaine Harris

"Fast-paced adventure. . . . Claire's tough-girl attitude may remind adult readers of Rachel Morgan and her world of human-vampire interactions. A tremendously popular series." — *Booklist*

"Rachel Caine's Morganville Vampires series is my all-time favorite. I love love love the characters, the town, and the surprising plots."
— *New York Times* bestselling author Maria V. Snyder

"An intriguing world where vampires rule, only the strongest survive, and romance offers hope in the darkest of hours." — Darque Reviews

"Caine's signature rapid-fire pace, plot twists, and excellent character development deliver another stellar installment to the series."
— Monsters and Critics

"Fans of *Twilight* really should check this out." — Word Nerd

"Filled with delicious twists that the audience will appreciatively sink their teeth into." — Genre Go Round Reviews

"If you love to read about characters with whom you can get deeply involved, Rachel Caine is so far a one hundred percent sure bet to satisfy that need." — The Eternal Night

"[Caine's] imagination easily tops the average. . . . Her suspense scenes, the heart of this series, crackle with vitality. . . . This series continues to provide terrific action and great entertainment." — *Kirkus Reviews*

"Fantastic." — Fresh Fiction

"Every time I think Rachel Caine can't top herself, she does."
— Fiction Vixen

ALSO BY RACHEL CAINE

THE GREAT LIBRARY

Ink and Bone

Prince of Shadows

THE MORGANVILLE VAMPIRES NOVELS

Glass Houses
The Dead Girls' Dance
Midnight Alley
Feast of Fools
Lord of Misrule
Carpe Corpus
Fade Out
Kiss of Death
Ghost Town
Bite Club
Last Breath
Black Dawn
Bitter Blood
Fall of Night
Daylighters

STORIES OF THE
MORGANVILLE
VAMPIRES

Midnight Bites

Rachel Caine

NEW AMERICAN LIBRARY

NEW AMERICAN LIBRARY

Published by New American Library,
an imprint of Penguin Random House LLC
375 Hudson Street, New York, New York 10014

This book is an original publication of New American Library.

First Printing, March 2016

For more information about Penguin Random House, visit penguin.com.

LIBRARY OF CONGRESS CATALOGING-IN-PUBLICATION DATA:

Names: Caine, Rachel, author.
Title: Midnight bites: stories of the Morganville Vampires/Rachel Caine.
Description: New York: New American Library, [2016] | 2015 |
Series: The Morganville Vampires |
Identifiers: LCCN 2015041861 | ISBN 9781101989784 (paperback)
Subjects: | CYAC: Vampires—Fiction. | Supernatural—Fiction. | University towns—Fiction. | BISAC: JUVENILE FICTION/Short Stories. | JUVENILE FICTION/Love & Romance.
Classification: LCC PZ7.C1198 Mid 2016 | DDC [Fic]—dc23
LC record available at http://lccn.loc.gov/2015041861

Printed in the United States of America
10 9 8 7 6 5 4 3 2 1

Penguin
Random
House

CONTENTS

(in order of timeline within the series)

MYRNIN'S TALE   *1*

NOTHING LIKE AN ANGEL   *9*

SAM'S STORY   *37*

GRUDGE   *45*

NEW BLOOD   *63*

THE FIRST DAY OF THE
    REST OF YOUR LIFE   *101*

AMELIE'S STORY   *127*

WRONG PLACE, WRONG TIME   *133*

DEAD MAN STALKING   *141*

LUNCH DATE   *169*

ALL HALLOWS   *175*

MURDERED OUT   *207*

WORTH LIVING FOR   *225*

DRAMA QUEEN'S LAST DANCE   *257*

VEXED   *289*

SIGNS AND MIRACLES   *313*

ANGER MANAGEMENT   *343*

AUTOMATIC   365

DARK RIDES   385

PITCH-BLACK BLUES   411

A WHISPER IN THE DARK   439

AND ONE FOR THE DEVIL   473

WELCOME BACK TO MORGANVILLE

I never thought I'd get to say that, but after receiving many, many requests for some kind of collection of all the various short stories I've written in the world of Morganville, I began to consider the idea of putting them all together—all the one-offs, exclusives, and Web stories. All the stories that were published only in certain languages or countries.

But the one thing I did *not* want to do was just give you things you could (with great effort) put together for yourself. I needed to be sure you got good stuff. New stuff.

So there are included in this anthology, thanks to the incredible generosity of my six Kickstarter backers for the Web series of Morganville, six original tales for you to enjoy. These backers have hardcover editions of these stories in a special coffee-table collection, but they've been kind enough to let me share the Morganville love with all of you, too. So where those stories appear, you'll see their names attached to them, with special thanks.

Each story has a little introduction and backstory with it, from me.

One final note: I resisted calling this *The Complete Collection*, because I don't think I'm done with Morganville yet (or it isn't done with me). Because, as you know, once you're a Morganville resident . . . you'll never want to leave.

—*Rachel Caine*

Midnight Bites

MYRNIN'S TALE

This story came about just because I wanted to know more about Myrnin for my own understanding of his character, and sometimes, the best way to achieve that is to write a character's history from his or her point of view. The character tells me what is important, and what changed, for better or worse. Discovering that Myrnin's father had some type of mental disorder was important to me, because of course when he was born, such things weren't really understood. When I was working on the draft of the first book in which Myrnin appeared, my coworker who read it said, "Oh, you've written a bipolar character, and he's actually really cool! Did you know that I take medication for that?" She went on to relate all the ways he was familiar to her. I was amazed, and honored. I won't name the coworker, for privacy, but I say now, as then: Thank you for sharing your story with me, and you know who you are. I hope Myrnin continues to make you proud.

I grew up knowing that I would go insane. My mother spared no chance to tell me so; I was, on regular occasions, walked up the road to the small, windowless shack with its padlocked door and introduced to my dirty, filthy, rag-clad father, who scratched at the walls of his prison until his fingers bled and whimpered like a child in the harsh glare of daylight.

I still remember standing there, looking in on him, and the hard, hot weight of my mother's hand on my shoulder to keep me from running, either toward him or away from him. I must have been five years old, perhaps, or six; I was old enough to know not to show any sign of distress or weakness. In my household, distress earned you slaps and blows until your tears stopped. Weakness invited far worse.

I don't remember what she told me on the first visit, but I do remember the ritual went on for years—up the road, unlocking the chains, rattling them back, shouting through the door, then opening it to reveal the pathetic monster within.

When I was ten, the visits stopped, but only because on that last occasion the door swung open to reveal my father dead in the corner of the hut, curled into a ball. He looked like a wax dummy, I thought, or something dug up in the bogs, unearthed after a thousand years of silent neglect.

He hadn't starved. He'd expired of some fit, which no one found surprising in the least. He was buried in haste, with decent rites but few mourners.

My mother attended the funeral, but only because it was expected, I thought. I can't say I felt any different.

After the burial, she took me aside and looked at me fiercely. We shared many things, my mother and I, but her eyes were brown, and mine were very dark, black in most light. That I had from my father. "Myrnin," she said, "I've had an offer to apprentice you. I'm going to take it. It's one fewer mouth to feed. You'll be on your way in the morning. Say good-bye to your sisters."

My sisters and I shared little except a roof, but I did as I was bid, exchanged polite, cold kisses and lied about how I would miss them. In none of this did I have a choice—not my family nor my apprenticeship. My mother would be relieved to be rid of me; I knew that. I could see it in her face. It was not only that she wanted fewer children underfoot; it was that she feared me.

She feared I was like my father.

I didn't fear that. I feared, in fact, that I would be much, much worse.

In the morning, a knock came at the door of our small cottage well before dawn. We were rural folk, used to rising early, but this was far too early even for us. My mother was drowsy and churlish as she pulled a blanket over her shoulders and went to see who it was. She came back awake and looking more than a little frightened, and sat on my small cot, which was separated a little from the bed in which my three sisters slept. "It's time," she said. "They've come for you. Get your things."

My things were hardly enough to fill out a small bundle, but she'd sacrificed part of the cheese, and some ends of the bread, and some precious smoked meat. I wouldn't starve, even if my new master forgot to feed me (as I'd heard they sometimes did). I rose without a word, put on my leather shoes for traveling, and my woolen wrap. We were too poor to afford metal pins, so, like my mother and sisters, I fastened it with a small wooden peg. It was the nicest thing I owned, the woolen wrap, dyed a deep green like the forest in which we lived. I think it had been a gift from my father when I was born.

At the door, my mother stopped me and put her hands on my shoulders. I looked up at her and saw something in her lined, hard face that puzzled me. It was a kind of fear, and . . . sadness. She pulled me into her arms and gave me a hard, uncomfortable hug, all bones and muscle, and then shoved me back to arm's length. "Do as you're told, boy," she said, and then pushed me out into the weak, gray predawn light, toward a tall figure sitting on a huge dark horse.

The door slammed shut behind me, cutting off any possibility of escape, not that there was any refuge possible with my family. I stood silently, looking up, and up, at that hooded, heavily cloaked figure on the horse. There was a suggestion of a face in the shadows, but little else that I could make out. The horse snorted mist on the cold air and pawed the ground as if impatient to be gone.

"Your name," the figure said. He had a deep, cultured voice, but something in it made me afraid. "Speak up, child."

"Myrnin, sir."

"An old name," he said, and it seemed he liked that. "Climb up behind me. I don't like being out in the sun."

That seemed odd, because once the sun rose, the chill burned off; this was a fair season, little chance of snow. I noticed he had expensively tailored leather gloves on his hands, and his boots seemed heavy and thick beneath the long robes. I was conscious of my own poor cloth, the thin sandals that were the only footwear I owned. I wondered why someone like him would want someone like me—there were poor folk everywhere, and children were ten a spit for the taking. I stared at him for a long moment, not sure what to do. The horse, after all, was very tall, and I was not.

Also, the horse was eyeing me with a clear sense of dislike.

"Enough of that. Come on," my new master snapped, and held out his gloved hand. I took it, trying not to tremble too much, and before I could even think, he'd pulled me straight up onto the back of that gigantic beast, into a thoroughly uncomfortable position behind him on the hard leather pad. I wrapped my arms around him, more out of sheer panic than trust, and he grunted and said, "Hold on, boy. We'll be moving fast."

I shut my eyes and pressed my face to his cloak as the horse lunged; the world spun and tilted and then began to speed by, too fast, too fast. My new master didn't smell like anyone I'd ever known: no stench of old sweat, and only a light odor of mold to his clothes. Herbs. He smelled like sweet summer herbs.

I don't know how long we rode—days, most certainly; I felt sick and light-headed most of the time. We did stop from time to time to allow me to choke down water or bites of bread and meat, or for the more necessary bodily functions . . . but my new lord ate little, and if he was subject to the needs of the body, I saw no sign of it.

He wore the cloak's hood up, always. I got only the smallest glimpses of his face. He looked younger than I would have thought— only ten years older than me, if that. Odd, to be so young and rumored to have such knowledge.

I ached everywhere, in every muscle and bone, until it made me want to weep. I didn't. I gritted my teeth and held on without a whimper as we rode, and rode, through misty cold mornings and chilly evenings and icy dark nights.

I had no eyes for the land around us, but even I could not mistake how it changed from the deep green forest to slowly rolling hills with spottings of trees and brush. I didn't care for it, truth be told; it would be hard to hide out here.

On the morning when the fog lifted with the sun's determined glare, my master drew rein and stopped us on a hilltop. Below was a valley, neatly sectioned into fields. Up the rise of the next hill sprawled an enormous dark castle, four square corners and jutting towers. It was the biggest thing I had ever seen. You could have put ten of my small villages inside the walls, and still had room for guests.

I must have made some sound of amazement, because my master turned his head and looked back at me, and for a moment, just a moment, I thought that the sunrise turned his eyes to a fierce hot red. Then it was gone, in a flash.

"It's not so bad," he said. "I hear you have a quick mind. We'll have much to learn together, Myrnin."

I was too sore and exhausted to even try to make a run for it, and he didn't give me time to try; he spurred his horse on, down into the valley, and in an hour we were up the next hill, riding a winding, narrow road to the castle.

So began my apprenticeship to Gwion, lord of the place in which I was taken to learn my trade of alchemy, and wizardry, and what men today would call science. Gwion, you will not be surprised to hear, was no man at all, but a vampire, one older than any others alive at that time. His age surpassed even that of Bishop, who ruled the vampires in France with an iron hand until his daughter, Amelie, cleverly upended his rule.

But those are tales for another day, and enough of this gazing into the mirror.

I am Myrnin, son of a madman, apprentice to Gwion, and master of nothing.

And content I am to be that.

NOTHING LIKE AN ANGEL

☽

Dedicated to Teri Keas for her support
for the Morganville digital series Kickstarter

This is the first of our original short stories in this collection, and again . . . it's a tale of Myrnin and his struggle to be the man (or vampire) that he wishes to be. It's also a story of his first encounter(s) with the lady we come to know (in *Bitter Blood* and later books) as Jesse, the red-haired bartender, whose history is intertwined with both Myrnin's and Amelie's back in the mists of time. Though Lady Grey has her own story, and maybe sometime I'll get around to telling that, too.

He'd been in the dungeon a few months this time, or at least he thought he had; time was a fluid thing, twisting and flowing and splitting into rivulets that ran dry. It was also circular, he thought, like a snake eating its tail. He'd had a cloak brooch once in that shape, in shimmering brass, all its scales hammered out in exquisite detail. The cloak had been dark blue, a very becoming thing, thick wool, lined with fur. It had kept him alive, once upon a time, in a snowstorm. When he'd been alive.

That had been one of the many times he'd tried to run away from his master. Of course, his master hadn't needed a cloak, or fur, or anything to cover him when he came looking. His master could run all day and night, could smell him on the wind and track him like a wolf running down a deer.

And then eat him. But only a little, a bite at a time. His master was merciful that way.

It was cold in the dungeon, he thought, but like his old master, he no longer bothered with the cold now. The damp, though . . . the damp did bother him. He didn't like the feel of water on his skin.

He'd been here for too long this time, he thought; his clothes had mostly rotted away, and he could see his blindingly white skin peeping through rents and holes in what had once been fine linen and exotic velvet. No telling what color it had all been, when times were better . . . dark blue, like the cloak, perhaps. Or black. He liked blacks. His hair was dark, and his skin had once been a dusty tan, but the hair was a matted mess now, unrecognizable, and his skin was like moonlight with a coppery shimmer over the top. When he had enough to eat, it would darken again, but he'd been starving a long time. Rats didn't help much, and he ached in his joints like an old, old man.

He didn't really remember what he'd done to land here, again, in the dark, but he supposed it must have been something foolish, or egregious, or merely bad luck. It didn't matter much. They knew what he was, and how to contain him. He was caged, like a rabbit in a hutch, and whether he would be meat for the table or fur to line some rich boy's cloak, he had no choice but to wait and see.

Rabbits. He'd always liked rabbits, liked their whisper-soft fur and their curious, wiggling noses and their puffball tails. He'd had a pet rabbit when he was small, a brown thing that he'd saved from the hutch when it was just a baby. He'd fed it from his own scraps and hidden it away from his mother and sisters until it had gotten too big and his mother had taken it away and then there had been rabbit stew and he'd cried and cried and . . .

There were tears on his cheeks. He wiped them away and tried to push the thoughts away again, but like all his thoughts, they had a will of their own; they scampered and ran and screamed, and he didn't know how to quiet them anymore.

Maybe he belonged here, in the dark, where he could do no more damage.

No footsteps in the hall, but he heard the clank of a key in the lock, loud as a church bell, and it made him try to scramble to his feet. The ceiling was low, and the best he could manage was a crouch as he wedged himself into a corner, trying to hide, though hiding was a foolish thing to do. He was strong—he could fight. He should *fight*. . . .

The glare of a torch burned his eyes, and he cried out and shielded them. The silver chains on his hands clicked, and he smelled fresh burns as they seared new, fragile skin.

"Dear God," whispered a voice, a new voice, a kind voice. "Lord Myrnin?" She—for it was a she; he could tell that now—put the right lilt into the name. The horror in her tone knifed into him, and for a moment he wondered how bad he looked, to engender such pity. Such undeserved sympathy. "We learned you were being held here, but I never imagined . . ."

His eyes adapted quickly to the new light, and he blinked away the false images . . . but she still shimmered, it seemed. Gold, she wore gold trim on her pale gown, and gold around her neck and on her slim fingers. Her hair was a red glory, braided into a crown.

An angel had come into his hell, and she burned.

He did not know how to speak to an angel. After all, he'd never met one before, and she was so . . . *beautiful*. She'd said a name, his name, a name he'd all but lost here in the darkness. *Myrnin. My name is Myrnin.* Yes, that seemed right.

She seemed to understand his hesitation, because she advanced a step, bent, and put something down between them . . . then withdrew to the doorway again with her torch. What she'd put there on the stained stone floor drew his attention not so much for its appearance—a plain, covered clay jar—but for the delicious, unbelievable smell radiating from it like an invisible aura. Warmth. Light. *Food.*

He scrambled toward it like a spider, opened it, and poured the blood into his mouth, and it was life, *life*, sunlight and flowers and every good thing he had ever known, *life*, and he drained the jug to the last sticky drop and wept, clutching it to his chest, because he'd forgotten what it meant to be alive, and the blood reminded him of what he'd lost.

"Hush," her voice whispered, close to his ear. She touched him, and he flinched away, because he knew how filthy he was, how ragged and beaten by his lot, where she was such a beautiful thing, so fine. "No, sir, hush now. All is well. I'm sent to bring you to safety. My name is Lady Grey."

Grey did not suit her, not at all: such a nothing color, neither black nor white, no luster or flash to it. She was all fire and beauty, and no gray at all.

Some of his memory stirred, though, gossip overheard beyond his cell by those whose lives were lived beyond this stone. *Lady Grey's become the queen. She'll not last long.*

And then, the same voices. *Lady Grey's dead—what did I tell you? Chopped on the block. That's what politics gets you, lads.*

This was Lady Grey, but Lady Grey's head had been chopped off, and hers was still attached.

He looked up, and like recognized like. The shine in her eyes, reflecting the torchlight. The hunger. The feral desire to live. She was like him, *sugnwr gwaed*, an eater of blood. A vampire. Interesting, that. He hadn't thought a vampire could survive a beheading. Not an experiment he'd ever tried. Experiments—yes, he liked experiments. Tests. Trials. Learning the limits of things.

"Lady Grey," he said. His voice sounded full of rust, like an old hinge all a-creak. "Forgive."

"No need for that," she said. "Let me see your hands."

He held them out, hesitantly, and she made a sound of distress to see the burns that were on him beneath the silver manacles. She sorted through a thick ring of keys, found a silver one, and turned it in the lock. They fell apart, slipped free, and clanked heavily to the stone floor.

He staggered with the shock of freedom.

"Can you walk, Lord Myrnin?"

He could, he found, though it was a clumsy process indeed, and his bare feet slipped on the mold of the stones. She was ruining her hems on the filth, he thought. She gave no thought to it, though, and when he reached her, she clasped him fast by the arm and gave him support he badly needed. Her other hand still held the torch, but she kept it well away from them both, which helped his eyes focus on her face, oh, her face, so lovely and well formed. A mouth made for smiling, though it seemed serious just now.

"I am sorry," he said, and this time it seemed more expert, his forming of words. "I am in no shape to entertain visitors."

She laughed, and it was like clear chimes ringing. It was a sound that made tears prick painfully. Hope could be a deadly thing here. Torturous.

"I am no visitor, and I hope this is not your home," she told him, and patted his arm gently before she took a firm hold again. "I am taking you out of here. Come."

He looked around at this narrow stone hole that had been his home for so long. Nothing in it but the scratches he'd made in the stone, half-mad words and mathematics that led nowhere but in circles.

He went with her, into air that felt fresh and new. He could hear the weak moans and cries of others here, but she ignored them and led him up a long, shallow flight of stone steps to a door that hung open.

He stepped into a guard's chamber, with a fire sizzling on the hearth and two men lying dead on the floor. Their dinner was still set on the table, and their swords lay unused in a corner. He knew these men, by smell if not by sight. They had been his captors for the past few months. They changed often, the gaolers. Perhaps they couldn't bear to be down in the dark long, to think they were as trapped as their charges.

He smelled blood in them, and it was the same as coursed through his veins, filling him with strength. Lady Grey had bled them before she'd killed them.

He said nothing. She took him to another door, more stairs, more, until there was another portal that led to a cool, clear, open space.

They were outside. *Outside.* He stopped, all his senses overwhelmed with the night, the moon, the stars, the whispering breeze on his face. So much. Too much. It was only Lady Grey's strong hand on his arm that kept him upright.

"Almost there," she promised him, and pulled him on, stumbling and clumsy with the richness of freedom, to a pair of horses tethered nearby. Dark horses, hidden in the night, with muffles around any metal. "Do you think you can sit a saddle, my lord?"

He could. He mounted by memory, feet in stirrups, reins in hands that knew their task, and followed the glimmer of the lady's dress into the darkness . . . which was, he realized, no darkness at all, to his quick-adapting eyes. Shades of blues and grays, colors muted but not hidden. The moon revealed so much . . . the castle's bulk they were leaving behind, the empty fields around it, the clean white ribbon of the road they followed. The trees closed around them quickly, hiding them, and he felt, for the first time, that he was actually free again.

He didn't know what it meant, really, but it felt good.

The ride lasted the night, and as the horizon began to take on a slow, low light, Lady Grey led him to a well-made hall—not a castle, nor yet a fortress, but something built for strength and purpose neverthe-less. He did not know the design of it, but it felt safe enough.

There were no windows in it, save for shaded slits at the very tops of the walls.

The gates parted for them as they rode to the entrance, and once inside, he realized there were men, not magic, involved: vampires like himself, dressed in plain black tunics and breeches, who had opened and then shut and barred them behind. The horses were led away without a word, off to some stables, and then they were walking into an inner keep, one built even more solid and strong, lit for vampire eyes.

"Is this yours?" he asked the lady still supporting his weight as they walked. "This place?"

"It is one place of safety," she said. "I didn't build it, nor do I own it. I suppose you might say it belongs to many. In time of need, we share our shelters." After a brief pause, she said, with what he thought might have been amusement, "You are *quite* filthy."

"Yes," he agreed. "Yes, I am."

"We'll put you right."

His angel took him to a room near the back of the stone keep—not spacious, but it had an angled slit for a window near the top, and though he had a bad moment of terror crossing the threshold, he found it had a feather bed in it, not just chains and pain. It had been so long, he wondered if he could even sleep in such a thing, but it was a terribly wonderful thing to have the chance to even think on it.

"I will arrange for a bath," Lady Grey said, and pulled a chair from the corner that he had not even seen, so blinded had he been by the bedding. "Sit here. I'll return soon." She hesitated at the door, with her hand on the latch, and he saw the compassion in her face. "I'll leave this open, shall I?"

He nodded slowly, astounded she would comprehend so easily, and watched as she disappeared silently from the room. It was a dream, he decided. A lovely dream, a wonderful thing, but it would make it all the worse when he woke up to burning chains and locks and cold, empty stones. He'd rather not dream. Not hope. It was better to live in the dark.

He closed his eyes, willing himself to wake, but when he opened them again, nothing had changed. His body ached from the ride and the stretch of muscles unfamiliar to movement; his hunger was blunted, though not truly sated yet. Surely, if it was a phantasm, he'd have imagined himself free of pain and thirst. Wasn't that the whole purpose of a dream?

He startled when Lady Grey appeared again in the doorway. She had changed her clothing to a plain pale gown, all jewelry and fine clothes put away. Over her arm, she had more clothing folded. She paused where she was, and smiled at him . . . a slow, warm thing, full of concern.

"May I assist you?" she asked him. He blinked, not certain how to answer, and then nodded, because he realized suddenly that it would be hard for him to stand on his own. Weakness was his constant companion now. He wondered if it would always be this way. *Surely not. Vampires are not so weak.*

Except he felt very weak indeed.

Her arm felt strong beneath his, and he leaned against her as they walked the short distance to what must have been set aside as a bathing chamber. Within it sat a large copper tub, big enough to submerge a full-grown man if he was so brave, and on a three-legged stool beside it sat a pile of sheets to use as windings. There was even a thick liquid of soap in a pail; it smelled like lavender. The water was warm enough to steam the chilly air.

He had his shirt—what remained of it—half off his body when he remembered his good manners, and dropped it back over his pallid skin. "Forgive me, my lady," he said. "I—am not myself."

"And little wonder of that," she responded briskly. She was binding a piece of cloth over her red hair, which was now slung in a loose braid over her shoulder. "You must have help, Lord Myrnin. I am far from shy. Disrobe."

"I—" He was utterly at a loss for words, and stared at her until her fiery eyebrows rose. She looked more imperious than any bathing attendant he could imagine. "It's not fitting that you . . . a queen . . ."

"A dead queen, well buried, and I never liked her. I've discovered quickly enough that this life gives me a freedom I never tasted before. I like it, I think." She flashed him a full, charming smile this time, and quirked one eyebrow higher. "I'll turn my back if you give me your oath not to fall and dash your head open on the stones."

"I'll try," he promised. She politely turned, and he stripped quickly, shocked at the sight of his own skin after so long but glad, so very glad, to have those stiff, evil rags off his body. Getting into the tub was a daunting challenge that he only just managed, and he raised quite a splash at the last as his feet slipped from under him to spill him into the water. It raised a gasp from him, and then a groan.

"Is your modesty protected, sir?" Lady Grey asked. She sounded as if she had difficulty keeping her laughter in check. Myrnin looked around, grabbed a small washing cloth, and draped it carefully over pertinent areas before he leaned back against the living-skin-warm copper back of the tub.

"It's not modesty," he told her as she turned. "It's politeness. I shouldn't like to shock a lady such as yourself."

"I am never shocked. Not anymore." She picked up his rags from the floor, frowned at them, and threw them into a heap in the corner. "Those we'll burn. Clean clothing will be waiting when you are done. Shall I help you scrub?"

"No!" He sat up, almost drowning the floor in a wave of water, and pulled the pail of soap closer to scoop a handful out. "No, I will manage. Thank you."

"You'll need assistance with that mange of hair," she said. "I can help with that, if nothing else."

So it was that, despite his worry and discomfort, he found himself soaking his filthy hair beneath the water, then coming up to allow her to slather lavender soap into the tangled mess and scrub with merciless strength. It took a great deal longer than cleaning the rest of him. He no longer worried about his modesty; the bubbles that formed in the water, not to mention the filth clouding the bath, protected him well enough. Lady Grey had an impressive volume of curse words for a wellborn woman, but he thought she enjoyed the challenge more than he enjoyed the sometimes painful scrubbing.

When she judged him finally fit, she rubbed his hair from wet to damp, helped him stand, and wrapped the bathing sheet around him twice to sop up the water before she helped him out. Everything felt . . . different. His skin felt surprisingly soft, like a newborn's. His hair was settling into clean waves; he'd forgotten it had that habit.

Most of all, what felt different was his own mind. Amazing that a little kindness, a little care, had settled his chaos so well.

Lady Grey was watching him with those striking, lovely eyes. He had no notion of what to say to her, except the obvious. "Thank you, my lady."

"My pleasure, my lord," she said, and curtsied just a bit. He responded with as much of a bow as he could manage in a bathing sheet. "She's spoken of you often, you know."

"She?" Myrnin paused in reaching for the black woolen breeches that she'd set out for him, and blinked at her.

"Amelie," Lady Grey said.

"Amelie?"

"Our queen. She was concerned for you, and bid me find you. It took a good slice of time, but I am pleased you're not as daft as I was told."

"Daft?"

"However, you do repeat things quite a bit."

"I will bear it in mind."

"Please do." She gave him a look he could not even begin to interpret. "Shall I help you to dress?"

"No!" He must have sounded as scandalized as she hoped, for she gave him a saucy wink and left the room, closing the heavy oaken door behind her. He almost regretted her departure. She was . . . startling. Beautiful as an angel, tempting as something a great deal farther from heaven. Had Amelie intended for him to . . . No. No, of course not.

He felt vulnerable in the empty room. It was a hard thing to struggle into the clean clothes, but once he'd fastened them up, he felt far better. She'd even given him red felt shoes, lined with fur and festively embroidered. Amelie must have mentioned his fondness for the exotic.

Lady Grey was waiting in the hallway. She took him in at a long, sweeping glance, and he bowed again. "Do I meet your approval?"

"Sirrah, you met my approval when I found you stinking and ill in a dungeon. You are bidding fair to be a heartbreaker now, though I must credit myself for the beauty of your locks." She winked at him and pulled the maid's scarf from her head as she walked down the hallway. "Come. Your mistress will want to greet you, now that you're half yourself again."

"Only half?" he murmured.

"I'll have a meal waiting when you're done. I expect that will restore you the rest of the way." She walked a few steps ahead, then turned toward him, still striding backward in an entirely unladylike manner. "Of course, restore you to *what* will be the question. Are you really a madman?"

"It depends on the day of the week," he said. "And the direction of the wind."

"Clever little madman." She turned to finish her walk with absolute precision at the doors at the end of the hallway, which she thrust open with the confidence only a queen could possibly have. "My lady Amelie, I bring your errant wizard."

"Not a wizard," Myrnin whispered as he edged past her.

"How disappointing," she whispered back, then bowed to Amelie and closed the doors, leaving him facing his old friend.

She was swathed in a dazzling white robe trimmed with ermine, intertwined most tellingly with strands of silver wire. . . . She wanted her subjects to know that she was old enough and tough enough to defeat the burning metal, and therefore them. She looked the same as always: young, beautiful, imperious. She was reading a volume, and she placed a feather in it as a marker and set it aside as he bowed to her. He assayed a full curtsy, and almost fell in rising.

She was up and at his side instantly to assist him to a nearby chair. "Sit," Amelie said. "No ceremony between us."

"As you wish, my lady."

"I am not your lady," she said. "At the least, I do not raise the color in your face the way our good Lady Grey seems to do. I'm pleased you enjoy her company. I hoped she might give you some . . . diversion."

"Amelie!"

She gave him a quelling look. "I meant that only in the most innocent sense. I am no panderer. You will find Lady Grey to be an intelligent and well-read woman. The English have no sense of value, to have condemned her so easily to the chop."

"Ah," he said, as she took her seat again. "How did she escape it?"

"I found a girl of similar age and coloring willing to take her place, in exchange for rich compensation to her family." Amelie was cold, but never unfeeling. Myrnin knew she could have simply forced a hapless double for Lady Grey to go to her death, but she was kind enough to bargain for it. Not kind enough, of course, to spare a life, but then, they were all killers, every one of them.

Even him. The trail of bodies stretched behind him through the years was something he tried hard not to consider.

"Why rescue me now, Amelie?" he asked, and fiddled with the ties on his shirtsleeves. The cloth felt soft on his skin, but he was unaccustomed to it, after so many years of wearing threadbare rags. "I've spent an eternity in that place, unremarked by you, and don't tell me you didn't know. You must need me for something."

"Am I so cruel as that?"

"Not cruel," he said. "Practical, I would say. And as a practical ruler, you would leave me where you knew you could find me. I have a terrible habit of getting lost, as you well know. Since you chose to fetch me from that storehouse, you must have a job for me." It was hard to hold Amelie's stare; she had ice-blue eyes that could freeze a man's soul at the best of times, and when she exerted her power, even by a light whisper, it could cow anyone. Somehow, he kept the eye contact. "Do me the courtesy next time of storing me somewhere with a bed and a library, Your Majesty."

"Do you really think I was the one who imprisoned you? I was not. Yes, I knew you were there, but I had no one I could trust to go to you . . . and I could not go myself. It was not until the arrival of Lady Grey I felt I had an ally who would be up to the task should you prove . . . reluctant."

"You thought I'd gone completely mad." She said nothing, but she looked away. *Amelie* looked away. He swallowed and stared hard at his clasped hands. "Perhaps you weren't so wrong. I was . . . not myself."

"I doubt that, since you are so much better already," Amelie said. Her tone was warm, and very gentle. "Tomorrow we will leave this place behind. I have a castle far in the mountains where you can work in peace to recapture all that you have lost. I am in need of a fine alchemist, and there is none better in this world. We have much to do, you and I. Much to plan."

There was a certain synchronicity to it, he found; he had been in

Amelie's company for many years, and when he left it, disaster always struck. She was, in some ways, his lucky star. Best to follow her now, he supposed. "All right," he said. "I will go."

"Then you'd best say farewell to Lady Grey and find yourself some rest," she told him. "She will not come with us."

"No? Why not?"

"Two queens cannot ever stay comfortably together. Lady Grey has her own path; we have ours. Say your good-byes. At nightfall, we depart."

She dismissed him simply by picking up her book. He bowed— an unnecessary courtesy—and saw himself out of the room. It was only as he shut the doors that he saw her guards standing motionless in the darker corners of her apartments; she was never unwatched, never unprotected. He'd forgotten that.

Lady Grey was waiting for him, hands calmly folded in a maid-enly sort of posture that did not match her mischievous smile. "Dinner," she said. "Follow me to the larder."

The larder was stocked with fresh-drawn blood; he did not ask where it came from, and she did not volunteer. She sipped her own cup as he emptied his, drinking until all the screaming hunger inside was fully drowned. "Do you ever imagine you can hear them?" he asked her, looking at the last red drops clinging to the metal goblet's sides.

"You mean, hear their screams in the blood?" Lady Grey seemed calm enough, but she nodded. "I think I might, sometimes, when I drink it so warm. Odd, how I never hear it when they're dying before me in real life. Only when I drink apart from the hunt. Is that normal, do you think?"

"Whatever is normal in this world, we have no part in it," he said. "How long was I in the dark, my lady?"

"Ten months."

"It seemed longer."

"No doubt because it was so congenial."

"You should have stayed for the formal procession of the rats. Very entertaining; there were court dances. Although perhaps I imagined it in one of my hallucinations. I did have several vivid ones."

She reached across the table and wrapped her long, slender fingers around his hand. "You are safe now," she told him. "And I will keep my eye on you, Lord Myrnin. The world cannot lose such a lovely head of hair."

"I will try to keep my hair, and my head, intact for you." She'd kept her hand on his, and he turned his fingers to lightly grip hers. "I am surprised to find that you accept Amelie's orders."

Lady Grey laughed. It was a peal of genuine amusement, too free for a well-bred young woman, but as she'd said, she'd buried that girl behind her. "Amelie asks favors of me. She doesn't order me. I stay with you because I like you, Lord Myrnin. If you wish, I'll stay with you today, as you rest. It might be a day of nightmares for you. I could comfort you."

The thought made him dizzy, and he struggled to contain it, control it. His brain was chattering again, running too fast and in too many wild directions. Perhaps he'd overindulged in the blood. He felt hot with it. "I think," he said finally, "that you are too kind, and I am too mad, for that to end well, my lady. As much as I . . . desire comfort, I am not ready for it. Let me learn myself again before I am asked to learn someone else."

He expected her to be insulted; what woman would not have been, to have such a thing thrown in her face? But she only sat back, still holding his hand, and regarded him for a long moment before she said, "I think you are a very wise man, Myrnin of Conwy. I think one day we will find ourselves together again, and perhaps things will be different. But for now, you are right. You should be yourself, wholly, before you can begin to think beyond your skin again. I remember my first days of waking after death. I know how fragile and frightening it was, to be so strong and yet so weak."

She understood. Truly understood. He felt a surge of affection for her, and tender connection, and raised her hand to his lips to kiss the soft skin of her knuckles. He said nothing else, and neither did she. Then he bowed, rose, and walked to his own chambers.

He bolted the door from within, and crawled still clothed between the soft linen sheets, drowning in feathers and fears, and slept as if the devil himself chased the world away.

As he rode away that night in Amelie's train of followers, he looked back to see Lady Grey standing like a beacon on the roof of the stone keep. He raised a hand to her as the trees closed around their party.

He never saw her return the salute . . . but he felt it.

Someday, he heard her say. *Someday*.

He didn't see her for another three hundred years. Wars had raged; he'd seen kingdoms rise and fall, and tens of thousands bleed to death in needless pain over politics and faith. He'd followed Amelie from one haven to the next, until they'd quarreled over something foolish, and he'd run away from her at last to strike out on his own. It was a mistake.

He was never as good when left to his own devices.

In Canterbury, in England, at a time when the young Victoria was only just learning the weight of her crown, he made mistakes. Terrible ones. The worst of these was trusting an alchemist named Cyprien Tiffereau. Cyprien was a brilliant man, a learned man, and Myrnin had forgotten that the learned and brilliant could be just as treacherous as the ignorant and stupid. The trap had caught him entirely by surprise. Cyprien had learned too much of vampires, and had developed an interest in what use might be made of them—medical for a start, and as weapons for the future.

Confessing his own vampire nature to Cyprien, and all his weaknesses, had been a serious error.

I should have known, he thought as he sat in the dark hole of his cell, fettered at ankles, wrists, and neck with thick, reinforced silver. The burning had started as torture, but he had adjusted over time, and now it was a pain that was as natural to him as the growing fog in his mind. Starvation made his confusion worse, and over the days, then weeks, the little blood that Cyprien had allowed him hadn't sustained him well at all.

And now the door to his cell was creaking open, and Cyprien's lean, ascetic body eased in. Myrnin could smell the blood in the cup in Cyprien's hand, and his whole body shook and cramped with the craving. The scent was almost as strong as that of the hot-metal blood in the man's veins.

"Hello, spider," Cyprien said. "You should be hungry by now."

"Unchain me and find out, *friend,*" Myrnin said. His voice was a low growl, like an animal's, and it made him uneasy to hear it. He did not want to be . . . this. It frightened him.

"Your value is too great, I'm afraid. I can't allow such a prize to escape now. You must think of all there is to learn, Myrnin. You are a man with a curious mind. You should be grateful for this chance to be of service."

"If it's knowledge you seek, I'll help you learn your own anatomy. Come closer. Let me teach you."

Cyprien was no fool. He placed the cup on the floor and took a long-handled pole to push it within reach of Myrnin's chained hands.

The red, rich smell of the blood overwhelmed him, and he grabbed for the wooden mug, raised it, and gulped it down in three searing, desperate mouthfuls.

The pain hit only seconds later. It ripped through him like pure lightning, crushed him to the ground, and began to pull his mind to pieces. Pain flayed him. It scraped his bones to the marrow. It ripped him apart, from skin to soul.

When he survived it, weeping and broken, he became slowly aware of Cyprien's presence. The man sat at a portable desk, scratching in a small book with a feather pen.

"I am keeping a record," Cyprien told him. "Can you hear me, Myrnin? I am not a monster. This is research that will advance our knowledge of the natural world, a cause we both hold dear. Your suffering brings enlightenment."

Myrnin whispered his response, too softly. It hardly mattered. He'd forgotten how to speak English now. The only words that came to his tongue were Welsh, the language of his childhood, of his mother.

"I didn't hear," Cyprien said. "Can you possibly speak louder?"

If he could, he didn't have the strength, he found. Or anything left to say. Words ran away from him like deer over a hillside, and the fog pressed in, silver fog, confused and confusing. All that was left in him was rage and fear. The taste of poisoned blood made him feel sick and afraid in ways that he'd never imagined he could bear.

And then it grew worse. Myrnin felt his arms and legs begin to convulse, and a low cry burst out of his throat, the wordless plea of a sick creature with no hope.

"Ah," his friend said. "That would be the next phase. How gratifying that occurs with such precise timing. It should last an hour or so, and then you may rest a bit. There's no hurry. We have weeks together. Years, perhaps. And you are going to be so very useful, my spider. My prized subject. The wonders we will create together . . . just think of it."

But by then, Myrnin could not think of anything. Anything at all.

The hour passed in torment, and then there were a few precious hours of rest before Cyprien came, again.

The day blurred into night, day, night, weeks, months. There was no way to tell one eternity from the next. *No time in hell,* Myrnin's mind gibbered, in one of his rare moments of clarity. *No clocks. No calendars. No past. No future. No hope, no hope, no hope.*

He dreaded Cyprien's appearances, no matter how hungry he became. The blood was sometimes tainted, and sometimes not, which made it all the worse, of course. Sometimes he did not drink, but that only made the next tainted drink more powerful.

Cyprien was patient as death himself, and as utterly unmoved by tears, or screams, or pleas for mercy.

Time must have passed outside his hell, if not inside, because Cyprien grew older. Gray crept into his short-cropped hair. Lines mapped his face. Myrnin had forgotten speech, but if he could have spoken, he would have laughed. *You'll die before me, old friend,* he thought. *Grow old and feeble and die.* The problem was that on the day that Cyprien stopped coming and lay cold in his grave, Myrnin knew he would go on and on, starving slowly into an insanely slow end, lost in this black hole of pain.

And finally, one day, Myrnin became aware that Cyprien had *not* come. That time had passed, and passed, and the darkness had never altered. Blood had never arrived. His hunger had rotted whatever sanity he had left, and he crouched in the dark, mindless, ready for whatever death he could pray to have . . . until the angel came.

Ah, the angel.

She smelled of such pale things—winter, flowers, snow. But she glowed and shimmered with color, and he knew her face, a little. Such a beautiful face. So hard to look upon, in his pain and misery.

She had keys to his bonds, and when he attacked her—because he could not help it, he was so hungry—she deftly fended him off and gave him a bottle full of blood. Fresh, clean, healthy blood. He gorged until he collapsed on the floor at her feet, cradling the empty glass in his arms like a favorite child. He was still starving, but for a precious moment, the screaming was silent.

Her cool fingers touched his face and slid the lank mess of his hair back.

"I find you in a much worse state this time, dear one," said the angel. "We must stop meeting like this."

He thought he made a sound, but it might have been only his wish, not expressed by flesh at all. He wanted to respond. Wanted to weep. But instead he only stayed there, limp on the ground, until she pulled him up and dragged him out with her.

Light. Light and color and confusion. Cyprien dead on the stairs, the cup of poisoned blood spilled into a mess on the steps next to his body. The bloodless bite on his neck was neat, and final.

There was a book in his pocket. *That book.* The book in which he'd recorded all of the torture, the suffering. Myrnin pointed to it mutely, and the angel silently slipped the book from Cyprien's body and passed it to him. He clutched it to his breast. And then, with the angel's help, stamped his foot down on the wooden mug to smash it into pieces.

"I killed him for you," the angel said. There was tense anger in her voice, and it occurred to him then that her hair was red, red as flame, and it tingled against his fingers when he hesitantly stroked it. "He deserved worse." She stopped, and looked at him full in the face. He saw her distress and shock. "Can you not speak, sir? At all? For me?"

He mutely stared back. There was a gesture he should have made, but he could not remember what it would be.

She sounded sad then. "Come, let's get you to safety."

But there was no safety, out in the streets. Only a blur of faces and shrieking and pain. A building burned, sending flames jetting like blood into the sky, and there was a riot going on, and he and his angel were caught in the middle of it. A man rushed them, face twisted, and

Myrnin leaped for him, threw him down on the rough cobbles, and plunged his fangs deep into the man's throat.

As good as the fresh blood his angel had delivered had been, this, *this* was life . . . and death. Myrnin drained his victim dry, every drop, and was so intent on the murder of it that he failed to see the club that hit him in the back of the head, hard enough to send him collapsed to the paving. More men closed in, a blur of fists and feet and clubs, and he thought, *I escaped one hell to suffer in another*, and all he could do was hug the book, the precious book of his own insanity and suffering, to his chest and wait to die.

But then his angel was there, his fiery angel. She needed no sword, only her own fury, and she cleared them from him. She was hurt for it, and he hated himself that he was the cause of her pain, but she drove them back.

The head wound must have sparked visions, because he saw himself, a different self, sober and sane and dressed in brilliant colors, and he saw himself in an embrace with his angel—no, his Lady Grey, his savior; he remembered her name now. He remembered that much, at least.

The book was gone. He did not know where he'd put it. But somehow it didn't seem so important now. He had her. *Her.*

The vision vanished, and then Lady Grey turned to him, with something strange in her wide eyes as she helped him to his feet.

"Come, my lord," she said. "Let us have you out of this place."

Escape was difficult to achieve, but she changed from her blood-spattered gown and wrapped him in layers of heavy clothes, then hired a carriage to rush them out of London. The streets were unsafe around them, and he was, he admitted, not the most pleasant of companions. The filth on him had been unnoticeable when he was locked away, but now, with the clean smell of the countryside washing through the windows, and Lady Grey in her neat dress seated across from him, he knew he stank horribly. As neither of them breathed to live, though, it was a tolerable situation. For now.

But in addition to the filth, he was also given to fits, and he knew they distressed her. Sometimes he would simply leave his body while it thrashed hard enough to snap his bones; sometimes, the fit came as a wave of terror that drove him to cower in the footwell of the coach, hiding from imaginary agonies. And each time such things came to devour him, she was there, holding his hand, stroking his foul and filthy hair, whispering to him that all was well, and she would look after him.

And he believed her.

The trip was very long, and the fits passed slowly, but they lessened in intensity as his vampire body rejected Cyprien's poisons from it; he slept, drank more blood, ate a little solid food (though that experiment proceeded less well), and felt a very small bit better when the carriage finally rocked to a stop at the ruins of an ancient keep set atop a hill.

"Where are we?" he asked Lady Grey, gazing at the old stones. They seemed familiar to him. She looked at him with a sudden, bright smile.

"That's the first you've spoken," she said. "You're getting better."

Was he? He still felt hollow as a bell inside, and yet full of darkness. At least there were words in him now. Yes. That was true.

"You will remember this place," she said. "Come. It looks worse than it is."

She must have paid the driver off, or bewitched him, because the coach thundered off in a cloud of dust and left them in the moonlight beside what seemed a deserted pile of tumbledown walls . . . and then he blinked, and the ruins wavered like the shimmer of heat over sand, and rebuilt into what the keep would have been, in its prime. Small but solid.

And he *did* know it. He'd visited it often in his dreams, trapped in Cyprien's cells.

"I remember," he said. "I had a bath."

"And you'll have another, for all our sakes," Lady Grey said, and linked her arm in his. "Can you walk?"

"Yes," he said. His voice sounded rusty and uncertain, but his will was strong, and he put one clumsy foot before another as she walked him forward. The gate opened as they approached, and servants bowed them in.

One of them, a tall, lean man, approached and said, "Shall I take him and see him presentable, my lady?"

Myrnin shrank back. He couldn't help it. The man wasn't Cyprien, but he seemed to be, in that moment, and he clung to Lady Grey's arm like a fearful child. She understood, he thought, for without a flicker, she said, "No, I will attend Lord Myrnin for a while. Draw a bath, as hot as can be done. He'll need a long soaking. Fetch him clothes, too."

The servant—vampire, not human, Myrnin realized—drew away and went to do her bidding. Lady Grey walked him into the dark hallways, and for some ill reason Myrnin felt safer in the gloom than he had in the light. He'd adapted to the shadows, he thought. So many years in the dark, it had seeped into him and stained him.

"This happened before," he said to her, as they walked. "Didn't it?" Things blurred when he tried to focus on them. Everything blurred and shook, except for her. She was a still, steady, glowing constant, and he kept his gaze on her.

"You were imprisoned before, yes, but not so unkindly as this time. But you are improving already," she said, and smiled. In the darkness, it was as if the sun had come out, but it was a kinder sun, one that warmed instead of burned. "I've been searching for you for almost ten years, when word came that you'd gone missing. How did this happen to you?"

"I trusted."

"The man I killed?"

Myrnin nodded. Just the thought of Cyprien, the impartial, cool interest in the man's face, made him shiver again. He'd known cruel men before; Amelie's father, Bishop, had been one such, with no regard for the living or the vampires who came after them. Death had been just another tool to him.

Cyprien hadn't given him the kindness of death.

"He was my friend," Myrnin whispered, and tears welled up in his eyes, and rolled down his face in a cold trickle. "My fellow seeker."

"Then I should have killed him much more slowly than I did. If I'd known . . . well. Done's done. Now, come and sit awhile until your bath is hot."

She sat him on some impossibly soft cushions, and he leaned his head against the pillows and slept a little, or at least thought he did, until her soft, strong hands roused him and moved him to his feet. He thought it was a dream. It seemed a dream, a sweet one, with the smell of roses in the air and the air skin-warm and damp, and her hands stripping away the layers of things he'd worn for so long.

Someone—Lady Grey, he realized—helped him into the feverish heat of the bath, and bathed him like a child. This wasn't like the last time, when he'd had enough of his wits to be ashamed for his lack of dignity and modesty; he'd left all that behind. Madness had stripped him far more naked. He sat passively while she scrubbed him, back and front, and poured slow torrents of soapy water over his head to clean it, too.

It was all done in strangely comfortable silence, until she finally said, "Well, I think you look more yourself now, Lord Myrnin." The water had gone cold, and it was black with grime. "Stand up." He obeyed her, not thinking of anything really, and flinched only a little when she poured buckets of more hot water over him to sluice away the lingering filth.

Then he stepped out onto the warm stone floor, blinked down at himself, and realized for the first time that he truly was nude as the day he'd been born, and Lady Grey, fully dressed, was standing in front of him with an upraised bath sheet.

Her gaze was level and calm, and she smiled a little. "Oh, don't be ashamed. I wasn't the Virgin Queen, by any stretch."

He grabbed for the bath sheet, almost overbalanced, and she had to help him wrap it around his body. Of a sudden, his knees went weak, and he sagged in her arms. She carried him to a low couch and draped him in another layer of warmth, combing his damp curls from his face so that he could see her as she bent closer.

"Poor dear man," she whispered, and her eyes were so warm, so gentle. He could see the girl she'd once been, before kings and fear and death. "What was done to you, down there in the dark?"

"Terrible things," he whispered back, and tears blurred the sight of her. His voice trembled uncontrollably. "Terrible things. But they're done now. Why do you bother? Why save me? I'm nothing. I'm a fool and I'm *broken!*" His voice rose on that last, raw and savage, and he hated himself for it all, for his foolish trust, his weakness, his madness, his continuing and pointless existence.

"You are not nothing. You are not a fool." Lady Grey's hand moved from his forehead to touch his chin, and turn his face toward her. She looked fierce now, more queen than girl. Less kind but even more lovely. "And what's broken can be mended stronger than ever."

"How can you be sure?"

"Oh, I'm sure." She gave him a secret, slow smile. "I've seen it. You may call it a vision, if you'd like. But I promise you, your future is worth the struggle. You must reach for it, Myrnin."

"I'm . . . so tired." Tired enough to weep with it. He felt raw and new and fragile.

"Then rest," she said. "And tomorrow, you will begin again."

"You won't . . . leave me?"

"Not until you're ready."

He choked on the tears, then managed to say, "You . . . you have become my saving angel, you know."

"Oh, dear Myrnin," Lady Grey said, and put her hand on his cheek. "I am *nothing* like an angel. And someday . . . someday, I hope that you'll know that very well."

She pressed her lips to his, a soft whisper of sweetness, and then she sank down next to him, and put his head in her lap, and hummed him into a deep, deep sleep.

And he wasn't afraid.

SAM'S STORY

)

I know what you're thinking. I KNOW! Why? Why did I do ...
Okay, I'll avoid spoilers, but I hear the question a lot. Well, this story
doesn't answer that, unfortunately, but it does show a little bit of
Sam's history and character. I do plan to write, in detail, a story of
Sam and Amelie, and how their romance came to be ... but I'm not
quite ready yet. This is a little piece of character study that I did to
help understand Sam in my mind—who he was, what he felt, how he
related to the other characters around him.

And if you're asking WHYYYYY ... I can only say that Sam
told me it was the right thing to do. Would I do it again? Probably
not, because at the time, I didn't know that we'd continue Morganville for so many more books, and reach so many more readers. But
choices get made, and there's no going back. I think Sam would say
that, too.

I don't know where to start, but I guess I'll start at the beginning, as boring as it is.

My name is Sam Glass—Samuel Abelard Glass, to my mother when she was annoyed.

I was born in 1932, a Depression-era child who grew up to be a World War II teen and a postwar adult. I turned eighteen in 1950, which in Morganville meant that I had to choose to either align myself with a vampire Protector, as my parents had before me, or strike out on my own without any kind of guarantees.

I'd like to say I was brave enough to do that. I wasn't. I signed the contract, got the bracelet, and life went on as normal, at least in terms of this town, where vampires are a fact and living with them is a challenge everybody faces.

I started at the local college, Texas Prairie University, and when I was nineteen, I met Melinda Barnes, and I fell in love. She was a lovely girl, bright as a star, and things went fast. Too fast, maybe. At twenty, I found myself with a wife, and a baby on the way. My parents had passed on, so I had inherited the family home, one of the big Founder Houses in town. Melinda was dreaming of a houseful of kids, and as she got bigger every month with the child we'd made, I thought about it, too. I didn't know if it was the right thing to do, having kids in Morganville, but I'd made the choice, and Melinda was so happy. . . .

And then something went wrong, badly wrong, while I was in the waiting room at Morganville General Hospital's maternity wing. In those days, fathers were expected to sit and wait, or pace and wait, or worry and wait. I paced, wondering how many hours I had left to go, wondering whether those shrieks I could hear from beyond the doors belonged to Melinda. Feeling guilty and anxious and scared.

When the doctor came out, he came slowly, and the look on his face told me all I really needed to know.

Melinda had died in childbirth. They'd managed to save my son, though that had been close, too.

Married at twenty, a widower with a baby at twenty-one. We got by, me and Steven. I'd been terrified of having a baby to tend, but he won me over right away, the first look I had at his big china-blue eyes. So beautiful. I'd never understood what it felt like to really belong so completely to someone else, but little Steven became my world.

I wasn't all on my own, of course—in the 1950s, nobody trusted a young man to properly raise a child on his own. I had plenty of help from the local busybodies—and some of it was welcome, I admit.

One day, I had a visit from the Founder.

I had never met Amelie, but I expected someone old, dry, chilly. Instead, she was beautiful, and quiet, and when she smiled, the world lit around me. It was a courtesy visit, a condolence call to acknowledge my loss and meet the newest member of the Glass family. She didn't mean it to be anything more. Neither did I.

Instead, we became friends. Tentative friends, well aware of the huge gulf between us, but I sensed how lonely she was, and she could see the same thing in me. I was alone in the world, with Steven depending on me, and I suppose I was overwhelmed, too. Her kindness—and it was kindness, as strange as that might sound, considering who she was—seemed like water in the desert to me.

She began to drop by more often, helping with Steven, leaving her bodyguards at the door or dispensing with them altogether. With me, Amelie could shed the thousands of years and remember what it was like to be human. To simply . . . be.

By the time my boy turned three, I was in love with her. Not the kind of flash-point love I'd felt with Melinda; that had burned fast, and faded. This was different, longer, richer. I knew it was stupid, impractical, impossible, but I could see, in unguarded moments, that she felt the same.

It might never have been anything more than a phantom, a dream that neither of us could acknowledge, except that Edgar Bryan went insane.

Old Edgar had never been one of the town's saner residents; he'd been bounced in and out of mental treatments for years, and most knew to avoid him when he was "in a mood." I don't know how it happened, exactly, but I earned a reputation as a reasonable man, someone who could help calm down a bad situation; I'd dealt with more bar fights than I could remember, and even a few political arguments between humans and vampires.

When Edgar went around the bend, the first person they called was me. In fact, I got to the Barfly Tavern before the police, although I could hear the sirens wailing across town. Edgar had barricaded himself in a back room, along with six hostages, after he'd gone crazy and accused half the town of being out to get him.

It was already a killing matter by the time I got there. One of those he took hostage was a vampire—a young one, not nearly as capable of protecting herself as most of the others. And I knew her. Her name was Marion—she was so quiet and shy she barely registered as a vampire at all.

When Edgar started waving his Buck knife around at one of the bartenders, Marion stood up and stepped in between them. She had to, by Morganville's rules—she owed the girl Protection. I wasn't there, but I heard she was brave. She trusted that being a vampire was enough to protect her, because nobody could be that crazy.

Only Edgar was, and he killed her.

In Morganville, that meant that Edgar's time was up; he was going to die for that, most likely in a medieval, horrible way. There was nothing I could do for the dead vampire, but I could try to get the other five people out without losing more of them to Edgar's ravings.

It took all night, but I convinced Edgar to let the rest of them go—and it was a good thing I did. Amelie showed up before dawn, with her entourage, just as I took the last of them out to safety, while Edgar agreed to lay down his knife for good.

He snapped completely at the sight of her—maybe knowing that his life was over anyway. He went straight for her, screaming. If I'd been thinking at all, I'd have known that he couldn't hurt her; she had guards, and she was far stronger and faster than he was.

But I wasn't thinking. All I could see was Amelie, and the knife, and that horrible sight of poor Marion in the back room with her head lying two feet from her bloodless body.

So I played the hero. You can guess how that ended—with Edgar's Buck knife buried so deep in my guts that the tip sliced through my spinal cord. It didn't matter. All that mattered was that I'd stopped him before he got to Amelie.

I didn't see what happened to Edgar, which I suspect was a blessing. I closed my eyes for a while, and when I opened them again, my head was lying in Amelie's lap, and she was staring down at me with an expression of completely unguarded grief on her face.

There were tears in her eyes. Tears. That meant something, something so huge I couldn't even put a name to it.

Before I could, I went away again.

The next time I came back, I was . . . different. It felt quiet inside, so very quiet, and yet I could hear everything, feel everything so intensely. Amelie's cool fingers against my face, like silk and marble.

I tasted salt on my lips. Salt and copper.

Blood.

Amelie hadn't made a human into a vampire in a hundred years in Morganville. But she'd done it to me. She'd done it to save me, for my son's sake—or so she told me. But she knew, and I knew, that it was something else.

I blamed her at first. It was hard to understand the life—if you can call it life—that vampires lead, the cravings, the impulse to violence and cruelty. I'd never been a cruel man. It sickened me to find that in myself, and I fought hard to beat it down. Stay the kind of person I'd been in life. Be a peacemaker.

I tried to stay away from Amelie. Being around her awakened all kinds of emotions in me—and the stronger the feelings, the harder it was to control my worst impulses. Amelie kept me at arm's length, rightly afraid that she and I would make each other too open, too vulnerable, and after what seemed like an eternity, I spent whole days at a time without feeling out of control and desperate.

But I missed her. I missed her all the time.

I was a terrible father in those years, but Steven turned out better than I deserved. He grew up strong and wild, and not a bit afraid of me, even when the black moods came over me. I suppose his love helped keep me the person I wanted to be, in the end.

At eighteen, Steven refused to sign a contract, and more than once, I was forced to come to his rescue when he got on the wrong side of one vampire faction or another. A few years later, he fell wildly in love with a girl from out of town, Rose, and within a year after that, they were expecting a child. I'd been a father, a widower, a dead man, a vampire. . . . Being a grandfather seemed too much, suddenly.

But just like when I'd held Steven in my arms for the first time, holding my grandson, Michael, on the day of his birth seemed to fill that empty space inside. Love hadn't changed for me. I still loved my family. I still wanted desperately to protect that small, beautiful life.

Michael Glass. He was my grandson, but as I watched him grow, watched him settle into a kind, thoughtful, gifted boy with loving parents to guide him, he felt more like my own child. And I tried to give him the guidance I hadn't been able to give Steven. From time to time, it even felt like I succeeded.

Amelie—Amelie and I are complicated. I love her; I know that. I would do anything for her, anything at all, and that's dangerous to her as well as me. So we keep our distance, for the most part. She has to play the ice queen, especially now that Oliver's in town and pressing her for control, and I understand that. I make her vulnerable.

I hate being her weakness.

When she turned Michael, I agreed with her decision, but I hated that, too—seeing his mortal life end, and my grandson being dragged headlong into this world of ancient politics and power. I wanted to protect him. I always thought that I could protect him from everything, but not even a vampire can promise that.

Not even a vampire should, in Morganville.

One thing about it, though: I don't feel as alone.

Selfish as that is, I can't tell you what it means to me.

GRUDGE

☾

I wrote this story again as a kind of backstory exercise. . . . This one was done to get on paper the story behind the death of Shane's sister, Alyssa, and his family's flight from Morganville, which was such a pivotal event in his life. I also wanted to see who Michael, Shane, Eve, and Monica were before and after those events, and before they met Claire—because even though Claire is the main character of the Morganville series, relationships between the other characters formed long before she arrived.

So here, in its entirety, is the story of that night told mainly from Shane's point of view.

"Heads up," Michael Glass said, and jerked his chin at something over Shane's shoulder. "Incoming."

Shane didn't even need to look. Michael's expression said it all—the kind of amusement only a best friend can have when your life is about to hit a brick wall. And there was only one brick wall who'd be walking toward him during the break between classes. (Well, two, but he didn't think Principal Wiley was out to get him this week. So far.)

"Oh, hey, Shane!" said a girl from behind him. He already knew it was coming, but the voice still gave him cold chills. She was just being so nice. It was completely weird. "Funny running into you here."

Shane slammed his locker door, spun the lock, and turned to face Monica Morrell, the crown princess of Morganville High School— at least in her own mind. And he wasn't really all that sure she was wrong, which sucked. He didn't like her. In a big way, actually. But she did have power, and power was important everywhere in Morganville . . . even in English class.

"What, in the same hallway we both walk every day?" he asked. He managed to keep most of his sarcasm out of it, though. "You need something?" He was hoping he was giving off enough *not interested, go away* vibes to drive off a dozen Monicas, but from the glow in her eyes and the smile on her face, she was definitely not picking up the clue phone. She'd gotten some tanning thing done, and he had to admit, Monica was beautiful, in that predatory mean-girl kind of way. The kind that owed more to product than personality.

She stepped up very close, close enough he could smell the expensive perfume she'd drenched herself in, and dropped her voice to a low purr. "I definitely need something," she said. Monica was his age, sixteen going on seventeen, but she acted like she'd jumped over the teen years and straight to being some oversexed middle-aged cougar. Not that he had anything against oversexed middle-aged cougars; he'd take one of those over Monica any day. "Let's find someplace quiet and discuss it."

Somewhere behind him, Michael—who was unconvincingly sorting through books at his own locker, killing time and shamelessly gawking—made a choking sound. *Shut up, man,* Shane thought, but he couldn't look away from Monica. She was too dangerous. "Yeah," Shane said slowly. "About that. I'm—I've got class." And he tried to back up and move around her.

She got in his way. Her smile stayed on, and stayed bright, but he saw a little flicker of impatience in her eyes. "Oh, come on. Since when is Shane Collins concerned about class?" she practically cooed. And before he could stop her, she came at him, backed him up against the lockers with a bang that attracted the attention of the fifty or sixty MHS students currently in the hallway, and . . .

And then all of a sudden she was all over him, hands in the wrong places, sliding up under his shirt, and she was kissing him, and for a long second his body was mostly saying, *Mmmm, girl, warm,* before his brain yelled, *Monica!* and the whole thing went very wrong.

Shane grabbed her by her shoulders and shoved her back. Hard. Monica stumbled, shock all over her pretty face, and for a second he saw genuine hurt . . . but only for a second.

Then it was anger, turned up to eleven.

"Oh, sorry—didn't know you were gay, Collins! I should have known you and Glass—"

"Hey!" Shane said sharply. "Back off." Because she was already drawing a crowd, and there was nothing Monica liked better than a stage for her personal drama. Michael slammed his locker door, and when Shane glanced over at him, he saw that his friend's face had gone very still. Michael could get really cold when he wanted, but the last thing he needed right now was Michael weighing in, especially when Monica was bound to push buttons. "Walk away. Look, I'm already doing it." And he did, shouldering his backpack and pushing past her in the general direction of his next class.

Monica followed. "That's it? You're just going to walk away?" Her voice carried so well she really should have been a drama queen. "So you get me to do all those awful things and then you pretend like it never happened?"

"Make up your mind, Monica—either I'm a perv hookup artist or I'm gay," Shane said, and kept walking. "Pick one."

"You're a walking social disease. I don't have to pick anything!"

"Certainly don't have to pick me," he said, and flashed her a grin and a finger on the way into his classroom. "Not interested."

And he figured, in his innocence, that it probably would blow over by the end of school.

Wrong.

There was no sign of Monica, or any of her posse, lurking around for Shane when school ended, which he figured was a good thing. Michael had headed off to practice guitar, as he did pretty much every day; Shane, on the other hand, was all about the slacking off, preferably someplace not his own house, but in a pinch that would do. Today, he thought he'd walk his sister, Alyssa, as far as the front door—because he was a good brother, mostly—and then see what kind of trouble he could find in one of the game shops, preferably the one that let him play for free, as long as he bought a game once in a while. His mom would gripe, because he probably wouldn't show for dinner; his dad wouldn't much care, because, like on most nights, he'd probably wind up at the bar and end up not caring about much.

Alyssa would care, but she was a big girl now, and she'd just have to get over it, the way Shane had gotten over all of the crap that came along with being a Morganville inmate.

He loitered outside the junior high gym until his sister came out—a leggy, willowy girl with a face that was going to be beautiful when it finally gave up the baby fat. For now, she looked . . . sweet.

And deeply amused.

"What?" Shane stayed slumped against the concrete wall. She slumped next to him and crossed her arms. Out on the grass field, the Morganville High Vipers football team was making an effort to look tough. Not very successfully.

"You," Alyssa said, and laughed. She had a nice laugh, when it wasn't directed at him. "I hear you got all up Monica's nose today."

"She did it first," Shane said. "She was all over me in the hall. I guess you heard that, too."

"Hands down your pants?"

"What? No!" His ears were turning red. He didn't even want to have this conversation with his kid sister. "It wasn't like that."

"So what was it like? Did she kiss you?"

Yes. "Kinda."

"Tongue kiss?"

"Shut up, Lyss."

"Because tongue kissing Monica would probably give you some dire germs."

"I'm not kidding—shut up!"

Alyssa made a rude noise, but she let it go, pushed off the wall, and started walking with long, easy strides. She was wearing gym clothes—gray shorts, a T-shirt Shane personally felt was too tight, and cross-trainers with little footie socks. She was sweet, and shy with everybody but Shane, it seemed like. "So, after the thing we won't discuss, I heard you punched her."

"Do you really think I'd punch a girl?"

"Well, it's Monica."

"No. I pushed her off me, that's all. Then she—"

"Wait," Alyssa said, and turned backward as she walked, facing him. She was basically the only person Shane had ever seen who could walk backward as fast as forward. It was weird. "Let me guess. She said—uh—you were gay?"

Huh. "Yeah."

"Well, that's her go-to insult for anybody who doesn't drool over her like a total perv. Did she go to level two?"

"You tell me."

"Did she Myspace bomb you yet?"

Shane blinked. "No."

"Wow. Bet she did. Bet everybody who owes her a favor has gone out and trashed your page." Alyssa executed a perfect twirl and fell back in step, walking forward. "Next thing she'll try to get her big brother to arrest you or something."

Richard Morrell was newly hired on at the Morganville Police Department. Shane didn't know him well, but any Morrell was bound to be worse than he expected. "Great," he said. "Just what I need, a record."

"Tough guy," Alyssa said, and sent him a brilliant, sly grin. "Race you."

"I'm a tough guy. I don't run."

"Loser!" She stuck her tongue out at him and set off, long legs flying, her long brown hair whipping like a flag behind her. It was hot still in Morganville—fall wasn't making itself felt yet—and heat shimmering off the pavement made it look like she was running through water.

"Crap," he sighed, and kicked it up to a jog, just to keep her in sight.

Today was a fairly typical day—nobody on the streets, doors and windows closed even during the day. And nobody lurking, at least visibly, to snatch Alyssa off the street. Shane didn't worry so much about pervs in Morganville—although he was pretty sure they existed—as about vampires.

Because it was just a fact of life. Morganville had vampires. And he and Alyssa were both wearing bracelets—leather, with an embossed symbol—that identified them as being minors under the Protection of a vampire named Sullivan. Not that Sullivan was worth much. For a vamp, he did a crappy job of intimidating people, or taking care of them, or even just showing up when he was supposed to. Maybe he was a drunk, like Shane's dad was. Who knew?

All Shane knew was that he despised the vampires, and when he turned eighteen, he was not going to sign up with one of the undead bloodsuckers. He was going to live free, live fast, and die young.

Speaking of which . . . "Lyss! Slow down!" Because she was pulling so far ahead now he could hardly see her at all. She waved, jogged backward, and then sprinted around the corner.

He was maybe fifteen feet behind her when something rushed at him from the mouth of a dark alley, and dragged him into the shadows. Shane let out a surprised yelp and immediately tried to get himself on his feet, but whatever was pulling him, it was strong, and fast, and he was off-balance.

A kick hit him in the ribs, and he rolled into a ball. *Lyss*, he thought, in despair. *Keep running.* If she looked back and didn't see him, she might come back. She might get hurt.

He couldn't let that happen.

Someone yanked his head back, and he felt sharp nails digging into his scalp. The perfume wave hit him a few seconds later, sickly sweet and familiar, and then Monica Morrell smiled nastily down into his face and said, "I forget—where were we? Oh, this is Brandon. He's my Protector." She put her free hand on the vampire standing next to her, the one holding Shane's left arm in a viselike grip. Brandon had that dark, broody thing going, all black leather and pale attitude, and he looked like he really couldn't give a crap about Shane or Monica, and ripping Shane's arm out of its socket was just another day at the office. "He wants you to apologize."

Shane gritted his teeth against a wave of pain from his shoulder, which was complaining it wasn't supposed to bend that way. "I'm sorry you're a vicious skank," he said. "I'm sorry I didn't punch you when I had the chance. How's that?"

Monica's fingernails dug deep enough in his scalp to cut, and she shook his head side to side, miming a no like he was her puppet. "Not what I was looking for, you jerk. Apologize. Now. And ask me out."

"Ask you out? Are you out of your freaking mind? Ow!" Because that had made her nails really dig in. "Do you really think we're going to hit it off, you crazy—"

"I didn't say I'd say yes," she said. "Fine. If you won't apologize, then you're just going to have to be a tragic cautionary tale for all the rude people. Brandon?"

She said it with a kind of bratty assurance, and she even snapped her fingers, as if she had the vampire right where she wanted him. Shane could have told her—without even knowing Brandon at all, except to avoid him—that she'd just made a serious mistake.

"What?" Brandon asked softly, and Shane felt the pain in his arm start to retreat. Brandon had let go of him. "Are you calling a dog, you spoiled little girl? Because dogs bite."

Monica, who'd been lost in her own sleazy sense of victory, suddenly snapped back to reality, let go of Shane's hair, and stepped back, looking very, very alarmed. "I didn't mean—I'm sorry, Brandon. I just wanted—"

"I said I'd do you this favor," Brandon said, with emphasis on the word *favor.* "I'm finished now. You should put some thought into how you're going to pay me back."

And he turned and walked off into the shadows, avoiding the sunlight, heading who knew where.

Shane rolled up to his feet. He was tall, and even if he still felt awkward in his body, he knew he wasn't a pushover. And Monica— Monica wasn't even a big girl.

He didn't threaten her. His heart was pounding, and he saw red, and he wanted nothing more than to make her pay for scaring him that bad, but . . . he couldn't. He just stared at her for a long, hostile moment, then said, "Leave me alone, bitch," as he turned and walked away, heading for the sunlight.

At the end of the alley, he saw a tall girl's shadow, hovering uncertainly near the entrance. Lyss. She'd come back, which was stupid. "Go!" he yelled at his sister, and waved her off. "I'm fine! Go on!"

Behind him, he heard Monica Morrell say, in an ice-cold whisper, "Nobody does this to me, Collins. Nobody."

He swung around, intending this time to scare the hell out of her, but . . . she was running the other way. Chasing after her pissy vamp boyfriend, maybe. Not that Shane cared.

He got to the end of the alley. Alyssa was standing there, looking wan and scared and suddenly younger than twelve. "What happened?" Her eyes were big and round. "Shane, you've got dirt all over—"

"It's nothing," he interrupted, and put a hand on her shoulder to move her off down the sidewalk, fast. "Let's just get home."

Home wasn't that much of an improvement, but after having run into Monica—violently—Shane didn't feel real good about letting Lyssa stay home alone. Mom was out doing mom-things—he didn't really know what—and Dad, well. Dad would be over at one of the two bars, pounding back boilermakers and pretending like life was good.

"I thought you were going to the game shop," Alyssa yelled from behind her closed bedroom door as she changed clothes. "You don't have to babysit, you know! I'm not a kid!"

"You are, and I do, and shut up," Shane said. "I'm opening a can of SpaghettiOs. Better hurry up."

She made a vomiting noise, which made him grin. He went downstairs and, true to his word, opened up the can, microwaved the SpaghettiOs, and started wolfing them down. When Lyss finally showed, he tossed her the can opener. "Make yourself something."

"Wow, you are some babysitter. Why don't you just tell me to go play in the street?"

"Not nearly exciting enough. Make yourself something and I'll play you on Super Mario Bros. Winner gets to pick dessert."

"Twinkies!"

"I said winner, loser."

Lyssa popped a spoon in her mouth and crossed her eyes at him, poured soup into a bowl, and stuck it in the microwave.

Two hours later, he'd lost at video games, Lyssa had her Twinkie, and somehow they ended up watching bad movies. Mom called. She was stuck at work. Not too surprising; she ended up staying late a lot these days. Probably couldn't deal with Dad, who of course still hadn't shown up. Shane put on a DVD—one of those Pixar movies Lyss loved, and he secretly did, too, although it probably wasn't cool—and she fell asleep halfway through it. He let it finish, then nudged her with one foot.

"Hey," he said. "Go upstairs, sleepy butt. You've got school tomorrow."

She stretched and yawned. "So do you!"

"Yeah, but I'm in charge, so I get to stay up. Go on."

"You suck, Shane."

"Do not make me come over there."

She made a show of being too tired to run up the stairs, and crawled up them on her hands and knees, which was funny and odd, and as soon as she was gone, Shane picked up his cell and told Michael about Monica.

Michael was worried. Yeah, he was, too, kinda. Plus, Alyssa was probably right—his Myspace page was going to be a mess.

Shane decided to worry about that in the morning. For now, there were language, violence, and nudity warnings on HBO.

Sweet.

He fell asleep on the couch, just like Alyssa had. When he woke up, HBO was running boxing, and it was really late. Mom and Dad still weren't home. Shane yawned, considered watching boxing, and decided to wander upstairs instead.

That was when he smelled smoke, halfway up the stairs.

For a second he thought, *Somebody's barbecuing*, and then, stupidly, *What, at midnight?* And then he smelled more smoke, and saw it, a pale white haze in the air, and the smoke detectors started going off with loud whooping shrieks upstairs.

Oh God.

Shane ran the rest of the stairs. The smoke was thicker at the top, choking and rancid; it tasted like burning plastic, and before he knew it, he was on his hands and knees, crawling instead of running. The air was better there. He could hear something crackling now, and that had to be the fire, fire—Alyssa was in her room and he had to get to her. . . .

"Lyss!" He banged on her closed door, yelling and coughing, then rose up to his knees to try to open it. He couldn't. The knob burned his hand, and the paint on the door was blistering, smoke pouring out from underneath like water on a sinking ship. "Lyssa!"

He had to try. He had to save her.

Shane fell onto his back, gasping for air, coughing constantly, and pulled both his legs back for a last effort at a kick. He hit the doorknob, and the whole door shuddered, then flew back on its hinges.

A ball of flame erupted out at him, and he rolled, feeling his clothes catch fire. He had to keep rolling to put it out, and then he crawled back. Alyssa's door was open. He had to get to—

Somebody grabbed him by the feet and started dragging him backward. "No!" he screamed, or tried to; he couldn't breathe—it felt like his lungs were stuffed with wet cotton. "No, Lyssa—"

It was his father. Frank Collins dragged him out to the stairs, then collapsed in a coughing heap, sucking whatever air remained near the floor, and rolled Shane down the steps. Shane barely felt any of it. The world was taking on dark, glittering edges, and his chest hurt, and none of it meant anything because he had to get to his sister. . . .

His mother was there, too, grabbing his arms and dragging. His dad made it down and helped.

They dragged Shane outside, and suddenly there was all this air, and he began coughing and vomiting black stuff and shaking and crying, and oh my God, Lyssa. . . .

His dad grabbed him and shook him. "Why didn't you get her?" he yelled, right in Shane's face. "She was your responsibility!" He was slurring his words, so drunk he could hardly stand up.

Shane couldn't help it. He laughed. There was something terrible about it. Something broken.

His mother was trying to go inside. The firefighters and cops were there now, and they stopped her and brought her back. She sat down on the wet grass with Shane and rocked him back and forth as their house turned into an orange, flickering bonfire against the cold black sky, as their Morganville neighbors—and even some of the vampires— came out to watch.

And then Shane looked up, and he saw Monica Morrell and her two BFFs, Gina and Jennifer. They were standing at the edge of the crowd, closest to where Shane sat, and Jennifer looked horrified and fascinated by the fire—but Gina and Monica were staring straight at Shane.

Monica held up her hand. She had a Bic lighter, and she flicked the wheel and showed him the flame. Then she made a little finger-and-thumb gun and shot it at him.

Shane heaved himself up off the grass and went for her, screaming, raving, crazy, and not caring at all about the rules, about whether she was a girl, about anything, because if she'd done this, if she'd . . .

Somebody stopped him. The face didn't register with him for a long couple of seconds, but then he saw it was Michael, grabbing on, and then Monica's brother, Richard, the cop.

"She killed her!" Shane screamed, and felt his knees go out from under him, because saying it had made something awful become horribly real. "She killed Alyssa!"

Michael hadn't realized, Shane saw; his friend's face went white, and he looked at the house, and whatever he said, Shane couldn't hear it over the violent pounding of his heart. He tried to get up. Michael stepped back, but Richard Morrell kept him down.

"Shane!" Richard was yelling, and shaking him, but all Shane could see was Monica's face over her brother's shoulder. She wasn't smiling anymore. In fact, she looked as pale as Michael, and now she was staring at the house, too.

Like she hadn't known.

Like she hadn't thought.

Shane kept screaming, and fighting, until Richard finally rolled him over and put him in handcuffs, but even then, Richard's hand on his back was only there to keep him down.

To keep him from doing something insane.

Monica, you stupid bitch.

She hadn't known. She hadn't realized Alyssa was still in the house. And Shane didn't care. He didn't really care about anything anymore.

By the time the fire was out, Monica was gone.

Time passed. Things happened. Shane didn't much care, still; he felt numb, even days later. He felt numb when he picked through the wreckage of the house, looking for something that hadn't been destroyed. Looking for something of his sister's.

The cops brought him in, along with his parents, and gave them the dog and pony show. Terrible accident, faulty wiring, no reason to believe . . .

It was bullshit. Shane knew it. Big cover-up, because Mayor Morrell's precious baby girl just couldn't be a killer. Wouldn't be right.

Sometime in there, his dad got screaming drunk and his mom started taking Valium and still, Shane really didn't care. He sat alone, mostly. He thought about nothing. He just . . . existed. They were stuck in some crappy motel room with borrowed clothes and no money and no home, and Lyssa was gone. So what did any of it matter anyway?

Michael kept coming over; he kept trying to talk, trying to get Shane to think about something else. And that was cool and all, but Shane just couldn't even care about Michael, either. He guessed Michael knew. He saw the pain in his friend's face, the confusion, but none of it touched him.

He just wanted people to leave him the hell alone.

He was out buying a pizza—they never ate anything else these days, when the three of them remembered to eat at all—when he saw Monica Morrell outside the store. She was with her brother, the cop.

Shane put the pizza down on the counter and walked outside.

Richard got in the way, fast. "No," he said, and put a hand flat on Shane's chest. "Listen to her. Just listen."

Monica looked bad. Worse than Shane had ever seen her. She wasn't pretty; her face was puffy and red, her eyes swollen, like she'd been crying for days. Her hair was stringy and unwashed. She looked miserable.

He didn't care. He wanted to hurt her, and it took everything he had inside—everything he had left—not to deck Richard and go after her, right then.

But somehow, he stood there, numbed, waiting.

"I didn't know," she said. Her voice was muffled, and her nose was running. She was crying again. "I'm sorry. I'm really sorry. I didn't know."

"She didn't do it," Richard said, staring into Shane's face. For a Morrell, he didn't look like a complete jerk, but again, Shane just couldn't care. "My sister did not do this. Understand? She was trying to piss you off, and she pretended she'd started the fire. She didn't know Alyssa was in the house. She wouldn't have done that. She didn't torch your house. It was an accident."

Shane laughed. It was a dry, empty sound, and he saw Monica flinch, like he'd hit her. "Oh, man," he said. "You really don't know her at all, do you?"

Richard's face turned hard. "I know this," he said. "You come near my sister, and this is going to get ugly. You want your parents to lose another kid?"

Shane didn't answer. He looked past Richard, at Monica, and made a little gun out of his finger and thumb.

Then he silently fired it at her.

Then he went back, got his pizza, and went to the motel, where the world was still dying in slow motion.

Two days later, Michael's grandfather Sam Glass arranged for them to get out of Morganville. Shane didn't know how, didn't know why, didn't care. His father was sober enough to drive, for a change. His mother—he didn't know what his mother was doing anymore.

They drove past the borders of Morganville, and it occurred to Shane that maybe this was Richard's way of keeping Shane away from his sister. Well, it had worked. They were out of town, and heading . . .

"Where are we going?" Shane asked. It was the first thing he'd said in hours.

His dad said tightly, "Nowhere."

And he was right about that.

NEW BLOOD

☾

Dedicated to Samantha Monical for her support
of the Morganville digital series Kickstarter

Here is our second original story for this collection, and in a way, it's an outside look into the last story you read. This is about Eve and Michael, and life before and after the fire at Shane's house. I really enjoyed getting to write from Eve's point of view; she's tremendous fun, and looks at things from angles I hadn't considered before—especially her relationship with her brother. This story has it all: sweet romance, evil Monica, sinister Bloodmobile, and yet another view of the Collins family disaster.

Samantha, to whom this story is dedicated, requested a story from Eve's point of view specifically, so you can definitely thank her for this one!

The flyer Eve Rosser was handed on the way out of class was candy-colored pink, with a big red cartoon heart on it— typical February crap. She glanced at it, shoved it in her black Dracula notebook, and forgot about it. February was lousy with stupid Valentine-themed stuff. This would be a flyer for a band bake sale, or a drama-sponsored dance, or something equally dumb that had no relation to actual Valentine's Day. She was hoping for a bake sale, though. At least there might be cookies.

Morganville High wasn't huge, but it was crowded; too many loud, proud students all jammed into ancient hallways built too small. Tough swimming upstream to her locker, but one thing about being Morganville's resident Weird Girl: people tended to give her personal space. Unlike some of the poor kids she saw getting slammed face-first into lockers. Bullying might be a problem in other places, but it was a way of life here. You were a predator, or you got eaten. The kids who were getting locker facials weren't at the top of the food chain, and they were trying hard to settle for being invisible.

Eve didn't consider herself a predator, but she always made sure *everybody* saw her. Hard to ignore her rice-powder makeup, black eyeliner, funky black hair, and generally Hot Topic–worthy outfits. Today's combo featured heavy combat boots, skeleton tights, a red mesh poufy skirt, and a tight black top. Distressed leather jacket, natch. Being Morganville's only Goth had its benefits.

Halfway down the hall, Shane Collins spotted her and waved her closer. He towered over most of the crowd, so he always found it easy to see her; given he was well over six feet, the basketball coach was always pestering him to join the team, but Shane wasn't a joiner—more of an avoider. Eve had that in common with him. As she got closer, she saw he was talking to Michael Glass, her own personal rock-star crush. Michael was Shane's best friend and, without any doubt at all—at least in Eve's mind—the hottest guy in Morganville.

Eve's steps slowed a little, because her heart had sped up. Just the sight of Michael did that to her . . . made her feel light inside, a little giddy, a little terrified. He was just so . . . yeah. *That.*

Ironic that he was just about the only person in school who didn't seem to really notice her, despite all the careful, time-consuming work she put into it. Not that Michael ignored her—he looked at her; he smiled; he said things. But not the *right* smiles. Not the *right* things. He always seemed to be thinking of something else.

As she came closer, Michael's deep blue eyes fixed on her, and again, she wondered what was really going through his head under that mop of blond hair. He was good at not showing it, and although he smiled at her, it wasn't a warm *Hey, gorgeous, can't wait to get to know you better* sort of thing. It was just a smile, to a person.

She smiled back. It probably looked awkward.

Shane wasn't happy. She could tell by the tense lines of his face that he was upset about something. Pretty much a normal day, then. Her morning horoscope had said, *Take today's terrific personal energy in a positive direction—ask out that hot babe you've been admiring from afar, or impress your boss with initiative.* She imagined Shane's horoscope read more like,

Today you're going to be funny and awesome, but also angry about something dumb. Because that would be his every-single-day horoscope.

"Did you see this?" he demanded, and waved a pink paper in her face. She grabbed it from him and glanced at it. Yep, cartoon heart right on top.

"Everybody got one," she said, and shoved it back. "Good morning, Drama Queen. What have you got against Valentine's Day? Oh, except the total lack of girlfriend."

"Are you flunking English, Club Dead?" He was staring at her like she'd grown fangs or something. She was pretty sure she hadn't.

"What? No! Of course not. It's kind of my mother tongue. Be pretty embarrassing to fail."

"Breaking news, then, Vampira, your reading comprehension sucks. It's not a V-Day flyer."

She grabbed it away and looked it over, this time carefully. Pink paper, check; red heart, check . . . with a drop of blood dripping from the point at the bottom of that heart.

The text below read SHOW US SOME LOVE. . . . GIVE BLOOD!

"Seriously?" she said, and then at a higher pitch, *"Seriously? A blood drive? In Morganville?"*

"Keep reading," Michael said. His gaze on her was steady, and she wished for the eleventy millionth time it was more . . . something. God, he was so cute she almost forgot about the paper in her hand. Almost. She managed to pull her attention back to it.

The *Bloodmobile* was coming. That evil black beast was coming here, to Morganville High, for a blood drive organized by . . . "Seriously?" she blurted again, and laughed. Because if there was anything the MHS Spirit Leaders—aka the cheerleaders—were known for, it was for being a showcase for Monica Morrell, the mayor's daughter, and generally useless otherwise. At sixteen, the same age Eve and Shane were, Monica was already a world-class brat, maturing into full-on bitch. "Why in the hell are our cheerleaders running a blood drive? Is Monica trying to bathe in the blood of the innocent *again?*"

"She's standing right behind you, by the way," Michael said. Yes. Of course she would be. Eve turned to see Morganville's Most Likely to Succeed by Climbing over the Bodies of Others staring at her from a distance of, like, two feet. Her girlfriends were attached to her shoulders like bat wings. All gorgeous, all glossy, but of course Monica was the glossiest and gorgeous-est. She was also, by virtue of those insanely tall pumps she had on, the tallest. Those looked painful.

Eve still topped her by an inch or so, though. Score.

"Who allowed you to have an opinion, emo freak?" Monica asked, and gave Eve a scorching head-to-toe look. "Somebody needs to nine-one-one the fashion police, because that's a felony."

"I really wish you *would* call, because I'm pretty sure this is a hooker-shoe-free zone. Also—news flash, you really need to stop taking style tips from people with sex tapes." Eve said it with all the warm concern she could manage, which only made Monica angrier, of course. If they'd been alone in the locker room, or even in front of a bunch of girls, Monica would probably have slapped her, and then it would have been *on*, but Shane loomed at Eve's back, and Michael, though not as hair-trigger on temper, was definitely tense.

Monica was mean. She wasn't stupid. She gave Eve a clear *Later, loser* look, and tossed her shiny hair. "For your information, the blood drive's for Morganville General Hospital. Not for the blood bank."

"You got that in writing somewhere? I mean, somewhere that doesn't include your contract with your dark lord, Satan," Shane said. "Because you doing something just out of the goodness of your heart sounds about like . . . Wait, what's the word I'm looking for? Oh, right. Bullshit."

Monica made a kissy face at him, and he made a retching sound. Eve thought she might have been the only one to see the flash of hurt that raced through Monica's expression. *God,* she thought, stunned. *Tell me the Queen Bitch doesn't have a total crush on Shane Collins!* That would be . . . wrong. And also dangerous, because as far as Eve could tell, Shane wouldn't even consider a hate-you makeout with Monica, much less anything else, and Monica didn't take rejection all that well.

"Don't forget the sign-up sheet in the cafeteria," Monica said to all of them, but her attention was totally focused on Shane. "I want to see all of you strapped down and giving it up."

Now Eve felt like vomiting, too, given the way Monica seemed to roll that around on her tongue. It was a welcome relief to hear Michael say, "Don't you have some fifth graders to menace, Monica? It's getting boring now."

"Watch it, Glass," Monica's bestie, Gina, said, and leveled a really well-manicured finger at him. "You can't talk to her that way."

"Yeah? Wait until you see how I talk to you," Michael shot back, and slammed his locker door. Funny. Shane was all instant violence . . . explosive, but quick to be over it. Michael got mad slow, but he burned a long time, and everybody knew when that tone came into his voice, it was time to back the hell away. "Clear off. Now."

Gina might have pushed, but Monica knew better; she grabbed her friend's arm and shoved her forward, moving with the flow to the other end of the hall. It was first lunch; the smell of overdone meat loaf and waterlogged vegetables was starting to sour the hallway. "They're heading for the cafeteria," Eve said to the boys. "What say you to tacos?"

"I say yea," Shane said, and held up his hand for a slap. When she went for it, he yanked it too high for her to reach. "Too slow and too low."

She punched him in the stomach——not hard, just playing——and he let out an exaggerated *woof* and bent over, still holding up the hand. She slapped it. "I can always cut you down to size, Shane," she said. "Come on. Primo *comida* awaits."

The taco stand a block away from the school—brilliantly, it just read TACOS in big red and yellow letters—was crowded with teens and adults alike, but Shane shouldered his way up and ordered while Eve and Michael grabbed a small table that had just been abandoned. He came back balancing a bag and three sodas. The bag held nine tacos and about half a gallon of hot sauce, which was a smart move on Shane's part. They all loved hot sauce.

Lunch didn't require a lot of chitchat, at least for the first two tacos apiece, and then Shane mumbled around a mouthful of shell and spicy beef, "You think the blood drive's legit?"

"Hell no," Michael said. "There's got to be something going on there. Monica Morrell never did a nice thing in her life unless there was something in it for her."

"Well, they're using the Bloodmobile," Eve pointed out as she slathered more hot sauce on her taco. She liked them gruesome. "That alone tells you the vamps have a stake in it. Pun intended, by the way, because I am awesome like that."

Michael gave her a smile. A genuine smile, one that made her tingle inside and out. She smiled back, and for a second—a beautiful, amazing second—it felt like they were really communicating.

Then Michael looked away at Shane and said, "What would the vamps get out of a blood drive for the hospital?"

"Maybe they're planning on having some kind of cocktail party fund-raiser, and we're providing the drinks."

"Ugh," Eve said.

"So I take it neither of you will be signing up on the donation sheet," said Michael.

"What idiot would volunteer for blood donations in this town, anyway? We have to do it from eighteen on by law. I'll enjoy my last couple of years of needle-free existence, thanks."

"I'd do it," Michael said. He didn't put any particular emphasis on it, but Eve caught her breath as if he'd gut-punched her, and didn't dare look at him for a few seconds. "I mean, if the hospital really needed it. But this still sounds sketchy as hell to me, mainly because Monica's involved."

I just called him an idiot. Michael Glass. An idiot. The most gorgeous boy in town. Who's the idiot now, idiot? Eve bit back the urge to babble out some crazy explanation, like *I would, too—I didn't mean it—I would totally give blood for sick babies.* Which would be true, but sounded desperate.

"Maybe one of us should, you know, investigate it," Eve said, before she could think too hard about what she was saying. "Sign up, get on the bus, check it out."

"No frigging way," Shane said. "I'm crazy, but I'm not that—"

"I'll do it," she rushed on, before she could think it over. She wanted to—what? Make up for what she'd said? Well, she was doing it by being a total victim-in-training, which wasn't smart, but at least it made Michael give her a long, very serious look.

"I don't think that's such a good idea," he said slowly. "Not alone, anyway. If you're doing it, you need backup. I'll go with you."

"Together?" Oh, God, was there any other way to make herself sound like a total fool today? "I mean, we're blood donor buddies?"

"Yeah," he said, and smiled slowly enough that it made her swallow. Hard. "Together. Okay with you?"

"Sure," she said, and tried to pretend like it hadn't just been the pinnacle of her life, right there. "Whatever."

She floated through the rest of school, and the walk home, even though she didn't see Michael again the entire time. For the first time,

she really, really wanted a best friend to blurt out all her excited feelings to, but she'd long ago decided that no Morganville girls were to
be trusted with valuable intel like that. She'd been burned too many
times. Hell, once upon a time, she'd thought Jennifer—now one of
Monica Morrell's wing-girls—was a good friend. Granted, that had
been elementary school, but betrayal still stung.

Her good feeling faded fast when she got home, because her dad was
already there. If he was home early, it meant he'd quit work early, and
stopped off at the bar, and worse, they'd already cut him off. Eve paused
at seeing his car in the driveway, and thought about heading away again,
but this time of year dark came fast, and she didn't want to be out
roaming at night. Sure, technically, she was underage and *should* be free
from predatory vamps, but nobody in Morganville trusted that kind of
thing.

She compromised and headed around back, creeping low past the
living room window, and made it to the back porch. The door was
locked, of course, but she keyed herself in, eased the door closed
behind her, thumbed the lock back on, and . . . ran right into her dad,
who was standing at the refrigerator, grabbing another beer.

He glared at her, and she froze, hesitating between rushing past
him and trying to pretend all this was sitcom-normal.

"About time you dragged your ass home," her dad said, and popped
the top on his beer. He was swaying a little, which meant he was only
an hour or two of steady drinking from falling down and leaving them
alone the rest of the night—but it was a dangerous couple of hours. "I
had to pick your damn brother up from school. He got in trouble
again. Didn't I tell you to keep an eye on him?"

There was no point in explaining, again, that it was pretty tricky to
keep an eye on a junior high student while actually attending high
school across the street, so she said nothing. He drank two big, quick
mouthfuls, then set the beer down on the painfully clean kitchen

counter. Her mom kept it spotless, all the time, because if she didn't . . .
well. If she didn't.

"What did he do?" Eve asked. It was vital, at this point, to keep
Dad talking. It was also important to try to ease away, one small step
at a time, to keep distance between them and angle for the hallway so
if she had to run, she could.

"Smarted off to some teacher," he said. "And then he pulled a
knife when she tried to march him to the principal's office. Stupid
kid. Don't know where he gets this stuff."

Eve knew. She couldn't believe her dad didn't. "Did he hurt anybody?"

"Why the hell would you say that? No, of course he didn't. The
kid's stupid, not crazy. I brought him home and tanned his ass for
him. He won't be sitting down for a week." That brought on another
drink from the can, but he returned it to the counter, and his mean,
narrow eyes stayed on her. "I told you to watch him, didn't I?"

"Dad—"

"Don't you *Dad* me, and when are you going to grow up and stop
painting yourself up like some damn clown?" He charged at her, but
there was a kitchen chair in the way, and he bumped into it. Eve
skipped past and down the hall, not running but walking fast and
hard. She took the right turn to the end of the hall, where her room
faced her brother, Jason's. His door was shut, and she didn't hesitate;
she opened her own door, stepped in, and shut it softly, then clicked
the dead bolt lock she'd installed herself when she was twelve. It
wasn't just on account of her dad, but times like these, it helped.

She dumped her book bag on the bed and turned to stare at the
closed door. For fifteen seconds, it was quiet. Twenty. Twenty-five.

And then, a fist hit the door with a bang. Just once, hard enough to
make the whole thing jump and shiver, but the lock held tight. He
rattled the knob.

"Ingrate!" her dad yelled, and she heard him kicking another door. Jason's. *Oh God.* But she'd helped Jason make his room a fortress, too, and pretty soon she heard her father wandering off toward the kitchen to rescue his forgotten beer.

Eve sank down on her bed, weak at the knees, and reached over for her stuffed gargoyle. She hugged him hard for a while, then reached out and picked up the walkie-talkie from her bedside table. She turned it on. "Earth to Uranus," she said. "Come in, Uranus."

Static crackled, and even the comfort of her unconditionally loving stuffed animal felt a little empty, until she heard her brother's voice come through the speaker. "My call sign's Charon, dumbass. In case you forgot."

"That's just a moon, not even a planet." She let a second or two go by, and then said, "You okay, Jase?"

"Like you care." There was a dull resentment in Jason's voice. He was younger than she was, but in some ways he was also way older. And harder. "Anything that takes the heat off you, right?"

"I didn't even know he was here! What the hell, Jase, you pulled a *knife?*"

"So what? I like knives."

All of Eve's good intentions shriveled, because she knew he did. He'd shown her one six months ago, a long, wicked thing, and he'd cut her with it. Accidentally, he'd said. She hadn't been so sure. Still wasn't. Jason . . . something had broken in Jason, and she didn't know how to fix it. It made her feel awful and hollow inside.

"How bad did he get you?" she finally asked.

"It won't show."

"Shit . . ." It felt bad sitting here, separated, not knowing what to say. Not knowing what to do. "I wish—"

"You wish you had a spine, Sis? You wish you could stand up to the old man? Don't worry about it. Next time he raises a hand to me, I'll break it off. Count on it."

Just like that, he was off the radio. She tried him again, but he didn't answer. Eve slowly stretched out on her bed, pulled a *Nightmare Before Christmas* blanket over herself when the chills set in, and tried to think about what to do. Call the cops? Yeah, she'd tried it. Mom had shut that down right at the door, and nobody was going to listen to bad-kid Jason and his weird Goth sister anyway. Not like the cops in Morganville ever really cared too much.

She was half-asleep when her mother knocked on her door and told her dinner was on the table. Eve rolled out of bed, took her hair out of the pigtails, and shook it down around her face so it mostly covered her eyes—her go-to strategy for dealing with her family—and got ready to endure dinner. Dad would be passed out, so it'd just be a silent affair anyway; Jason would be simmering with rage, Mom would be checked out on a mental vacation, and the meal would be horrible. *So not looking forward to creamed corn and Spam.*

Eve heard a sound at the window, and turned, thinking it was a branch, or maybe—insanely—Michael Glass trying to get her attention.

Instead, a vampire smiled at her from the other side of the window. Brandon. Eurotrash sleek, a chin sharp enough to cut. He looked completely normal just now. A completely normal Peeping Tom, looking in like he wanted to leap through the glass and do terrible, terrible things to her.

Eve bit back a scream. If she yelled, Brandon would be gone in the next instant like a bad dream, and it might even rouse her dad from his alcoholic slumber. Besides, Brandon couldn't get in. Not without an invitation, which she damn sure wasn't going to give. *I'm still underage, you asswipe,* she thought as she yanked the curtains closed to shut him out. *You don't have any right to try to get me.* Not that age mattered much to Brandon. He'd been creeping on her since she was twelve. It still made her feel sick and anxious, but she didn't let it get to her. Not much, anyway.

When she peeked out, he was gone. Probably his idea of a joke. *Ugh.* If she complained about it, he'd say he was patrolling the property; he was, after all, their ink-on-contract family Protector. Nothing she could do about it. Like so much else wrong in her life.

Dinner was, as she'd predicted, silent. Jason picked at his food, staring sullenly down; his hair was hanging in his face, just like Eve's, and although their mom chattered on about nothing, and ignored everything really going on, neither of them said a word beyond a grunt or a one-word answer. When they were done, Eve carried the dishes into the kitchen and washed them. Jason dried. They worked in silence, and when she glanced over, she saw Jase was keeping an eye on the couch in the living room, where their dad was passed out with beer cans on the floor around him.

They were careful not to clatter anything too loudly.

It was a weird fact of life that after all that adrenaline, all that fear, all that strain, Eve fell asleep within seconds once she was in bed. She rarely had nightmares. Maybe bad dreams weren't really necessary when you lived one in real life. . . . But she thought she was having one when she woke up to the sounds of sirens and a flickering glow that wasn't sunrise filtering through the curtains. She got up, pulled on her black fuzzy bathrobe, and pulled the fabric back to stare outside.

There was a house on fire about six blocks away, blazing, shooting flames into the sky. The clock read two in the morning, and she had a sick feeling that whoever had been in that place might not have gotten away safe. The fire department was already there; she could see the fire trucks and the flashing lights.

There was a knock on her bedroom door. Eve answered it, and

found her mother standing there in her own bathrobe. Without asking, Mom pushed past and went to the window.

"Yeah, sure, come on in," Eve said. She closed the door and deadbolted it again. "I just woke up. Do you know whose house it is?"

Her mother stared at the fire with dry, empty eyes for a moment, and then said, "It could be Mildred Klein's house—she lives over on that block. Or the Montez family."

Eve knew Clara Montez, and the name hit her hard. Clara was a junior this year. Pretty and quiet and smart. She had an older brother who'd already graduated, and a sister in junior high, and another one still in elementary school.

Eve grabbed her cell phone from the table and checked contacts; Clara was in her list, and she quickly called. She clutched the phone anxiously while she watched the flames tent higher over the burning bones of the house in the distance.

"It's not me," Clara said instantly. She sounded breathless and excited. "It's the Collins house! Gotta go!"

Eve must have made some kind of a sound, because the next thing she knew, her mother was holding her by the shoulders, asking her what was wrong. Eve's hands were shaking. She looked back at the fire, heart pounding, mouth dry. *Collins.*

It was Shane's house burning.

"I have to go," she said, and tore free of her mom's grasp to start yanking things out of drawers. She didn't care what she came up with—mismatched underwear, a torn pair of sweatpants, a Powerpuff Girls T-shirt. Whatever came out of the drawer, she pulled on. Her mother was talking, but it was just noise. Eve looked at her phone. Another call had come in. This one was from Michael. She checked the voice mail. "It's Shane," he said. "His house is on fire!" The call cut off. She could hear the roaring flames in the background.

It was like a kick to the gut that just kept kicking. She didn't know what to do, what to say, what to ask . . . and finally slipped on shoes. They might have been slippers. She didn't really care.

When she tried to stand, her mother grabbed her by the shoulders and held her in place.

"No!" her mom said, too loudly. "Eve, you're not going out there!"

"Mom," Eve said. "That's the Collins house. *Shane's* house."

"I don't care whose house it is! You can't go out there!"

Eve shook free and left the room. She hesitated, looking at Jason's door, then kept going. She heard her dad snoring away as she passed her parents' bedroom. Mom continued to follow her, still arguing, but quietly now; nobody wanted to wake up Dad.

Eve went to the hall closet, pulled up a loose floorboard, and found one of the carved sharp-pointed stakes she'd hidden there. She grabbed her black hoodie and threw it on; it would hold the stake in the pocket without trouble. Her mom's complaints had changed tone, more of the *Why do you have that? Don't you know what kind of trouble you could get us into?* sort of rhythm now, which Eve also ignored.

She was out in the dark before the *Don't blame me if you get yourself killed* chorus kicked in, and headed at a run for the fire.

She was about a block away when someone stepped out of the dark into her path, and she yelped, flailed to a stop, and pulled the stake out of her pocket. The shadow stepped into the shallow pool of light from a streetlamp, and she recognized her own brother. "Jason! Jesus, what are you doing out here? Are you crazy?"

"Are you?" he asked. He seemed perfectly at home in the dark, all night-stalking black clothing and bad attitude. "I'm out here all the time. I know how to get around."

"Are you insane? You're too young to be out on your own——"

"You heading for the fire?" he interrupted, and she caught her breath and nodded. "Then stop wasting breath and come on."

They jogged the rest of the way together, and Eve wanted to ask Jason why he went out at night, what he did when he was out here, but the answers sounded like something she really, really didn't want to know. Besides, her stomach was all in knots thinking about Shane and his family, and as they came closer to the fire, it got worse. The stink of the smoke became horribly real, for one thing; it wasn't like a pile of wood you burned in a fireplace. It had an acrid, searing stench to it. Burning plastics, cloth, foam, paint . . . all the things that made a building into a home, going up in black, bellowing clouds.

The Collins house was a total loss already. The fire department was really piling water on it to keep it from spreading to other nearby homes, and the heat was intense as Eve got closer. She could feel it battering at her skin like a physical force. The police had set up barriers, and she crowded up against one with a bunch of neighborhood people, some still in pajamas and bathrobes; she spotted the Montez family huddled together, watching in horrified fascination. There were some vampires lurking, but like the humans at the barricades, they were just gawking. Bloodsuckers liked to keep their distance from fire.

"What happened?" Eve asked Mrs. Montez. The older woman had her hair up in curlers under some kind of net bag, and a pink robe wrapped around her plump body. "Do you know?"

Mrs. Montez shook her head. "People say it was set, that fire. I don't know."

"Did everybody get out?" Eve was straining to see Shane, or his little sister, Alyssa, or their parents, but she couldn't spot anybody.

"Not the little girl. She didn't." Mrs. Montez shook her head in somber regret, and Eve caught her breath. The night, for all the heat and cinders, felt suddenly very cold. *Alyssa?* No, that couldn't be right. It just couldn't. There was some mistake. Mrs. Montez just didn't know, that was all. She was just . . . mistaken.

And then, on the other side of the barricades, Eve caught sight of a face she knew. Soot-stained, pale, but achingly familiar. Michael Glass. He was standing helplessly off to the side, watching the fire with wide, empty eyes. Nobody was paying him any mind, though a police officer was nearby. She supposed they were keeping him there as some kind of . . . witness?

Eve didn't think about what she intended to do; she just ducked under the barricade and ran straight for Michael. He saw her coming at the last second, and somehow managed to get his arms out just in time for her to hit him in a fierce, full-bodied hug.

He held on to her just as tightly, and she breathed in the smell of the smoke that clung to him, the sweat, the electric burn of fear and grief. She knew, somehow. From the shaking strength of his arms around her, she knew Mrs. Montez hadn't been wrong.

Alyssa Collins was dead.

"Shane?" She managed to mumble it out, and he heard her, even over the roar of the fire. She felt his face against her hair, and then his skin against her cheek as he turned his head. Incredibly warm. Scratchy, from the beard that was growing in a little. "Is Shane okay?"

"He made it out," Michael said. She expected him to let go of her then, but he didn't. Maybe they both needed the support. "His dad dragged him. Shane was still fighting to get—get to Alyssa."

"But he couldn't reach her?" Eve said, because she could tell it was hard for him to say it. "Oh my God, Michael. He couldn't get to his little sister. He must be so wrecked. . . . Where is he?"

"With his parents," Michael said. "I guess the cops wanted to talk to them about how the fire started. Not that there's much doubt about it."

There was a low, angry tone to that, and Eve pulled back a little and looked at him. "What?" she asked, and his blue eyes got very hard, very focused.

"Monica," he said. "Shane told me he saw her out here with a lighter. The bitch burned his house. She killed Alyssa."

"No!" Eve couldn't help blurting it out. "She couldn't have . . . Oh my *God*. I never thought—I mean, she's a horrible, awful person, but . . ."

"She's leveled up from horrible to a damn murderer," Michael said. "To killing a *kid*. And odds are good nobody's going to do a damn thing about it. They'll probably say it was bad wiring or some bullshit, and the mayor's precious daughter won't even get a slap on the hand."

That was harsh. It was probably also really, really true, and it made Eve want to throw up. She couldn't get her head around it. Alyssa, gone? Alyssa was in junior high. A cute, funny girl who would have grown up to be a sassy woman, who should have been able to do all the things that Eve was still experiencing—have her first boyfriend, her first kiss, her first love.

But Lyss would never get those things, and it was so hard to imagine.

There was a giant rush of sound from the house, and big timbers collapsed, still burning. The walls caved in. Flames shot so high it looked as if they were scorching the stars above, but the fire didn't warm Eve anymore. Her hands felt icy, and she needed the heat of Michael's body against hers. He must have felt the same, because he held on, and there was no distance between them. No barriers.

The two of them stood like that until the flames began to die down, and the crowd started to disperse, and night took darker hold around them. The cops hadn't bothered them, but now Detective Hess came striding over, grim-faced, to talk to Michael.

That meant they had to separate, and it hurt; it physically ached in her to see Michael standing so alone, with that pain still etched into his face.

Hess asked questions, but there wasn't much that Michael could answer. He'd seen the fire in the distance, realized it might be his friend's house, and gotten here in time to see Shane pulled out of the burning front door by his dad. Nobody had been able to get inside after that; it was too dangerous.

Unspoken in that, Eve realized, was that Michael had probably tried. Or worse, had been forced to hold Shane back from rushing back in to die. How hard would that have been for him, to do that?

"Okay," Detective Hess finally said, and closed up his notebook to slip it in his jacket pocket. He seemed weary and beaten by the whole thing, or maybe just by being a lifelong Morganville resident. "Thanks for your help, Michael. I'll be in touch if we have more questions."

Michael hesitated and said, "Did Shane already tell you about Monica?"

Detective Hess paused in the act of turning away. "Why don't you tell me about it?"

"He saw her outside. She had a lighter. She was flicking it and smiling. Pretty easy to draw that picture."

"Pretty easy to draw the wrong one, too," Hess said, and gave Michael a long look. "Did you see her? See her set the fire?"

"I believe Shane." Michael's voice was even, but the muscles in his face and shoulders were tense.

Hess nodded and finally faced Eve. "You, Miss Rosser? When did you arrive?"

"I saw the fire from my house," she said. "I came to see if everybody was okay."

"You're friends with Shane as well; is that right?"

Eve nodded. She realized she didn't even look like herself just now—hair down and limp around her face, no makeup, ratty random clothing. "I don't know how to help him through this."

"It's a terrible thing," Hess agreed. "Not much anybody can do right now. Anything more you can add, either one of you? Anybody you know of who would have had a reason to do something like this to the Collins family?"

"Nobody," Eve said. "I mean, his dad's not the nicest guy, but . . ."

She spread her hands helplessly. It was setting in, the reality of what had happened to her friend, his sister, his whole family, and she felt sick to her stomach and none too steady. "No. Just . . . take a look at Monica."

"Why do you think she'd do a thing like this?"

Eve didn't have an answer, but Michael finally did. "I wasn't going to say this, but I guess I should. Shane and Monica kind of got into it this afternoon at school. She came on to him and he told her to back off. She didn't take it too well."

"Wow," Eve said. "Seriously? She . . ."

"Tried to stick her tongue down his throat? Yeah. He made it pretty clear it was never going to happen, and she got . . . angry."

Hess raised his eyebrows a little and took out his notebook to make a note, but Eve didn't think he looked convinced.

"Maybe she didn't mean it to go this far," Eve said. "I hate to try to excuse the Queen of Stupidly Mean, but maybe she only meant to scare him and it got out of control . . . ? I can't believe she really set out to kill anybody."

"If she was even here at all, which isn't proven except on Shane's word," Hess said, and closed his notebook. "I'll look into it. If it was Monica Morrell, I'll arrest her. But you two, keep your mouths shut about this. I don't need the town going vigilante. Monica's not that popular in the first place with certain . . . classes of people."

Meaning Eve's class—the wrong-side-of-the-tracks, poverty-level kind of people. Eve nodded, unwillingly. Detective Hess was a good guy—she knew that—but she also knew that nobody who worked for the town of Morganville could be considered exactly impartial. The mayor—Monica's dad—had his job not because he was popular but because the vampires had picked him for it, and they would keep him in power as long as he did what they wanted. The cops enforced rules that didn't really apply to people like Monica, with position and favor from the bloodsuckers. There were two levels of humans in Morgan-ville, and Eve knew where she, Michael, and Shane really stood: at the bottom.

Whatever Hess promised, she didn't have much hope Monica would ever see the inside of a jail cell, even if they caught her on cam-era setting the fire.

Michael watched the cop walk away, and Eve's attention stayed riveted on his face. Just for this one moment, she felt it was okay to stare, openly, without feeling like she was somehow invading his pri-vacy. They still felt connected—and they were, she realized. Some-how, she'd never let go of his hand.

And then he let go. It was a gentle sort of release, a regretful slide of his hand down her arm, but then the contact was gone, and she felt . . . alone. Really, really alone, even with the crowding of firemen working the dying fire. Even with the police cars flashing lights. Even with the gaggle of neighbors still gossiping at the barricade.

"You should get home," Michael said. "I can't believe you came out alone in the dark, Eve. You know better than that. I'll walk you back."

"No," she said. "No, you don't have to look after me, and besides, your house is only a few blocks away in the other direction. I'll be okay. Really. Look, I'm wearing vampire Kryptonite." She flashed her leather bracelet, which was what minors got to wear to show they had family Protection from the more predatory Fang Gang set; Michael had his on, too. His, she suspected, was slightly more legit. Protection from her family's Protector, Brandon, wasn't exactly reliable.

Michael, knowing this, was shaking his head. He waved over one of the cops—a pale vampire dude Eve didn't recognize, with eerie light blue eyes—and asked if she could have a ride home. The cop didn't object, just impatiently waved Eve over to a waiting police cruiser.

She turned back to Michael. "I— Please tell Shane . . ."

"I know," he said. "I will. Get home safe, Eve."

That was all. No great declaration of feelings, nothing she could put her finger on, but there was a tone in his voice, a gentleness, that made her think maybe, maybe . . . And then she felt horrible even thinking it, because, *Jesus*, talk about bad timing. Shane's sister was dead, and she was obsessing about whether Michael Glass liked her. What a horrible person she was.

As she joined the cop at his car, she saw her brother, Jason, lurking in the shadows near the barricade, and urgently gestured for him to come with. He shook his head and vanished. No police rides for Jason; well, she should have seen that coming, probably.

The bad news, though, was that the vampire cop giving her a ride had a partner. A human partner, which ordinarily would have been *good* news, at least personal-safety-wise.

That partner was, however, Richard Morrell. Monica's big brother.

Richard opened the back door of the cruiser for her as she approached, and she couldn't tell anything at all from the utterly blank expression on his face. He wasn't bad-looking, for an older guy, but he was definitely dangerous. A Morrell with a badge and a gun? Nightmare waiting to happen. She fully expected trouble.

Sure enough, when the car started, with the vampire cop driving, Morrell turned back to look through the barrier at her. It occurred to her that this might have been the all-time worst idea ever, because she was locked in a cage with doors that didn't open except from the outside, but she tried not to panic. At least outwardly.

"I heard someone saw my sister at the scene," Morrell said. "Is that true?"

"I wasn't here," Eve said. "I got here later."

"That wasn't what I asked. Did someone see Monica here when the fire started?"

Eve shrugged. She sure wasn't going to rat out Shane Collins, not to a Morrell. Let him find out on his own; he wouldn't have any problems doing that.

Richard Morrell shook his head and turned face forward. "Look, Eve, I know you're going to find this hard to believe, but I'm not your enemy," he said. "I'm trying to find out how much trouble my sister's gotten herself into. If she did this, I'll be happy to put handcuffs on her . . . but I don't think she did. She's not a good person, but she's not *that* bad."

It sounded like the kind of explanations she and Shane traded back and forth about their fathers. *He's not that bad. Sure, he gets a little crazy, but you know, just when he's drinking.* It was the coping mechanism of someone trapped in a dangerous relationship, according to all those self-help books she checked out of the library. It had never occurred to her until then that someone like Richard Morrell might feel the same—but why wouldn't he? His arrogant dad was probably a pig to live with, and his sister had grown up an entitled bitch made in Daddy's adoring image. Maybe Richard was the odd one out, just trying to be normal.

She'd given up the idea of that a while ago, being normal. Who wanted *that*? Sure, it meant you blended in, but personally, she felt like there was a hell of a lot more safety in being seen. Especially in a town where the number of missing persons kept going up. She'd never just vanish. People would notice.

Eve cut the thought off, because it was entirely possible that she *might* just vanish by accepting this ride tonight. She shut her mouth and watched the streets glide by. Empty sidewalks. No cars on the road. Most of the houses completely dark, except for security lights. Some dogs barking. Morganville was deeply creepy in the dark with that vast, cloudless Texas sky curving overhead with its blanket of white stars.

And then the car pulled up to the curb of her house. Richard Morrell got out and opened her door. He even offered her a hand out, but she didn't take it. He could be okay, but she wasn't prepared to concede it yet.

"Want me to walk you to the door?" he asked her. She shook her head. The last thing she needed was for her dad to wake up and see cops with her in the middle of the night. God. That would be the start of a very unpleasant conversation that would end in tears.

"I'll be fine," she said, and hurried off around the house to the back. She wondered about Jason, but like he'd said, he was out at night all the time. Going out to look for him, or waiting around in the dark for him, was victim-stupid behavior. Maybe, as a big sister, she should have been more worried, but Jason . . . Jason always just looked after himself. Had since he was ten. It made her feel horrible that she was okay with that, but Jason wasn't . . . wasn't quite normal. And she was afraid of him, sometimes.

She let herself in and tiptoed to her room. Her dad was still snoring like a chain saw, thank God, and her mom was in bed, too, so Eve locked herself into the Fortress of Solitude with real relief. She undressed and slid into bed, realizing only then how exhausted she felt, body and soul.

Her hair reeked of toxic smoke, but even that couldn't keep her awake for long.

Her dreams were of fire.

Eve tried Shane the next day but got no response at all; it was possible his phone had been lost in the blaze, she supposed. She called Michael, who said he hadn't seen Shane since the cops had loaded the family into a car. The news spread around town that Alyssa's body had finally been recovered from the ruins of the house, and a quiet, private funeral was held a few days later. Eve wasn't invited. She knew only because Michael had been there.

When she saw him at school the morning after the burial, he told her that Shane was gone.

"Gone?" she repeated, horrified. Michael looked . . . lost. Shaken, as if he couldn't believe it, either. "What do you mean, *gone*? You don't mean—" She couldn't help but think that *gone* was the word people used for *dead* when they weren't brave enough to say it outright. Had he offed himself?

"No, God. He's alive," Michael said, and leaned in closer to her against the lockers. It was rush hour in the school hallway again, so that might have been partly just the pressure of the chattering crowd, but she didn't think so. It felt . . . deliberate. Like he was making a safe space for just the two of them. "I mean he and his parents got the hell out of Morganville last night. Somebody helped them. I don't know how, or who, but they're . . . gone."

"Jesus," she breathed, and grabbed his arm. "Do you think they're going to get away with leaving like that?"

"I have no idea," he admitted. "Depends on whether the Founder let them go, but my gut feeling was they were on the run. So I don't know. I hope they'll be okay."

"Can you call him?"

"No phones," he said. "They went dark. I don't think we're going to see him again, Eve."

"Maybe that's a good thing?" she said. "I mean, maybe out there he can find something else. Something happy that's not—this." She meant Morganville, and Michael understood. She knew he did, and their eyes met and held.

"I'd like to believe there's still something happy here," he said, and her heart lurched, then sped up. He couldn't mean that the way she wanted to take it. He couldn't. And as she obsessed over it, he hurried right on. "Speaking of unhappy things, though, Monica wiggled off the hook. Said she was nowhere near the Collins place when it went up, and got her friends to back her up on it. So if she did it, she's definitely going to get away with it."

That made Eve's blood beat faster in her veins, and she wanted to punch something. Someone. As she stared off into space, she realized she was staring straight at a pink poster with a cartoon heart on it.

She smiled slowly, and pointed. Michael followed her gesture to look at the poster.

"I say we find out what Monica's got going with this blood drive crap," she said. "It's today, right? Maybe we can ruin her day some other way, Michael. Are you in?"

"Are you kidding?" He gave her a smile, a full one, and it was glorious. It was also a little crazy. "I'm all in. Got to look out for each other now, right?"

"Right," she said, and tried to control the rush of heat that came over her. "Right."

Signing up for the blood drive was suspiciously easy; there were only about ten names on the list, and four of them had been crossed off. Rude comments were written about the remaining six, which might or might not be valid. Eve boldly scrawled her name and Michael's at the bottom, just as Gina, Monica's BFF / attack dog, came up to grab the sheet off the board. She was dressed for a party, not school, but that was the typical look Monica's gang went for. Always ready for the camera, not so much for the tests.

Well, Eve probably spent as much time at the makeup table, to be fair, but she felt the results were *much* more valid. And besides, she studied. Occasionally.

"Seriously?" Gina said, and speared Eve with a scorching look. "*You're* giving blood? That's bullshit."

"I help babies," Eve said frostily. "And, you know, old people.

Who need blood. Like, you know, normal people do, which I suppose doesn't include you."

Gina gave her one of her patented bitchy, half-crazy smiles. The glitter in her eyes was more like the light off the edge of a razor than humor. "*Normal?* That's hilarious, Necro Girl. I don't think they take donations from freaky pervs who want to sleep with dead people and probably already have some rank disease."

Michael stepped up. That was all, just took one simple step forward, and he met Gina's eyes. The stare held for a few long seconds, but Michael didn't blink. He seemed so *quiet* that it made all the hubbub and roar of the normal school hallway seem to fade into absolute silence.

Eve held her breath. Michael didn't fight; he rarely even got into arguments. But there was something like steel inside of him that just . . . didn't . . . bend.

Gina's brittle edge hit it and shattered, and she looked away with a sneer. "Whatever, not my problem. Take it up with the bloodsuckers on board. Who knows? Maybe you'll never make it out. That would improve our landscape."

She flounced off with the paper clutched in one hand. Michael watched her go, then took in a slow breath and relaxed.

Eve punched him in the shoulder. "Damn, boy, you scary," she said. "I had no idea."

"I live in Morganville," Michael said, and flashed her a warm, fast grin that just about broke her heart. "Scary comes standard-issue, right?"

He walked off, in the direction Gina had gone, and after pausing to really appreciate that Michael Glass—*Michael Glass*—had stood up for her, Eve dashed off in his wake.

The Bloodmobile was parked outside in the school lot, and it stood out like a sleek, black-painted shark. The bold red blood drop on the side looked real and fresh, and nauseatingly three-dimensional. For the first time, Eve had the thought that it might be a terrible idea to go inside there voluntarily. Legend said that sometimes people didn't come out.

Maybe it ate them.

She caught up to Michael at the rickety metal steps just as he was reaching for the handle of the door. "Michael . . ."

He knew where she was coming from; she could tell from the smile he gave her. "We're okay," he said. "I don't know about you, but I'd rather do something than just—pretend. I'm doing this for Shane."

For Shane. Eve took in a deep breath and nodded. She hoped it looked resolute.

Then they were inside the dark belly of the beast.

Which was . . . surprisingly well lit, and filled with plush donation chairs that looked more like fancy recliners than terrifying instruments of torture . . . though the built-in restraints looked less than reassuring.

All the couches were empty, and there were two attendants standing quietly, watching as Eve hesitantly walked down the narrow aisle. "Um, hi?" she said. "I'm on the list?" There was no way she could manage to make that a declarative statement. She cleared her throat and tried again. "I mean, I hear it's for a good cause; is that right?"

"Smooth," Michael murmured behind her, and she caught herself in a frantic giggle and turned it into a fake cough that turned real, and distressingly deep. One of the attendants—the taller woman with short, neatly trimmed dark hair—opened up a cooler and took out a bottled water, which she handed Eve. Eve popped the cap and drank frantically, and the cough finally stopped tickling her throat.

"Morganville General is low on plasma and platelets," the woman confirmed. She didn't sound very concerned about it, and Eve began to think that the lighting in this bus was more about making everyone's skin look falsely pink than being reassuring. Because she was starting to think both of the lab coats were vamps. "Why don't you take the couch on the right, dear."

"Aren't you supposed to do some kind of test first, or questionnaire, or . . ." Eve had Googled that part. She knew how it was supposed to go.

"We've got an in-seat system," the attendant said. "No waiting."

Michael moved up closer behind Eve, and despite everything, she couldn't help but notice how deliciously *warm* he was. She pressed back against him. It wasn't deliberate, but she just found herself touching him, and it felt so good.

He didn't move back, either.

"Want me to go first?" he asked Eve. She turned her head and looked at him; at this extremely close distance, his blue eyes were even more stunning than usual, and for a second she couldn't think what the answer to that question would be. Or even that there was a question. It wasn't until the corner of his mouth quirked a little (because he knew exactly what she was thinking, dammit—she could tell) that she jerked herself out of her trance and straightened up to stop leaning on him.

"No," she said, with as much dignity and courage as she could manage. (It wasn't much.) "I'm okay. I mean, you only need a pint, right?" A pint seemed like what donations were supposed to be. According to Google.

"We'd of course much prefer a larger donation," the chilly lady said, with a smile that didn't seem like a smile at all. More like she'd studied what smiles meant.

"Yeah," Michael said. "Can we talk to someone in charge about that? I have a cousin who works at Morganville General. Seems like they actually don't need extra blood right now. I checked."

That was a record-scratch moment, and Eve was caught just as off guard by it as the vamps. *Could have told me that,* she tried to eye-communicate to Michael; she wasn't sure if she just looked scared, though. She felt scared, but Michael . . . looked totally calm. She didn't want to assume she could read him that well, but she thought he was trying to silently tell her, *I've got this.*

The vampires in charge of the Bloodmobile hadn't expected any lip from mere high school humans, she could tell; the one that had been talking to her seemed annoyed, but the other one, the leaner, Asian one, seemed more amused. "All right," he said. "So if you know the blood's not for the hospital, why show up? Most of you have better survival skills."

"I've got excellent survival skills," Eve said. "Want to see me run away screaming?"

"I'm not in the mood for fast food." Wow, a vampire with a sense of humor as sharp as his teeth. She could almost appreciate that. "You're in no danger, I promise. Yes, the blood's being put to another use. Research."

"Research," Michael repeated. "Want to explain what that means exactly?"

"No."

"Then how do Monica and her Mean Girl posse come into it?" Eve cut in. "Because they're definitely getting a cut, right? Not of the blood, because, ew, I don't think they swing that way."

The female vampire walked away to flip through some paperwork. The male Asian vamp crossed his arms and gazed at her with thoughtful intensity, which made her way more nervous. "The mayor's daughter receives a fee for each donor she secures," he said.

"You have an entire town full of donors already," Michael pointed out. "Why this? Why the high school?"

"The blood of children is different from that of adults. We'd rather have the donors very young, but your age group is a compromise we can accept."

Creep. Eeeeee. Eve swallowed and looked at Michael. This time, she hoped what she was sending was *Let's just get out of here now.* Monica was getting a bounty for lining up her classmates for the needle. That was really all they needed to know, because as social ammunition went, it would fire pretty well.

But Michael wasn't done. She was starting to recognize that look in his eyes, and it worried her. "What kind of research are you talking about? What are you trying to do, breed a better class of cow? Or are we just not as tasty anymore?"

The vampire exchanged a lightning-fast look with his colleague, and Eve felt the mood change. Michael had said something that made them worried.

"Perhaps you should come with us for better answers," the friendlier vamp said, although he was far from friendly now. "Please. Sit down. We're finished here, anyway."

The female vamp moved to the front of the vehicle and got in the driver's seat. Eve bolted for the exit, but *of course* the other vamp was there ahead of her, a blur in her vision for an instant and then, *bam,* right in the way. She skidded to a halt, bracing herself on the padded donation chairs on either side, and stared at him as he slowly smiled. No fangs, which was nice, but it still gave her a solid chill.

"Get out of the way," Michael said, coming up behind her. She moved, but he wasn't talking to her. "Let us out. Now."

"Sorry," the vamp said. "Can't do that. You have a few too many questions to—"

The door behind him suddenly opened, and the vamp almost toppled backward, which would have been funny as hell, but he caught himself and whirled around to face the newcomer—a man dressed in a smothering trench coat, hat, gloves, and sunglasses.

"Sorry," said Michael's grandfather, Sam Glass, in the mildest possible tone. "Am I interrupting something? I came to get my grandson."

Sam Glass was a vampire—a young one, hence all the layers. Without them, he was eerily like Michael in a lot of ways—curling hair that he wore a little shaggy and long, a strong and gorgeous face, the same ocean blue eyes. His hair was more red than blond, and he looked physically to be maybe late twenties . . . but damn, if it wasn't clear they were related. Brothers, maybe.

But Sam Glass had died long ago, and it was all a weirdly complicated family situation at Glass Christmas dinners.

Sam was the youngest vamp of Morganville by a long stretch, but rumors were he was also a favorite of Amelie's, and nobody messed with what the Founder liked without risking a painful lesson.

So the Asian guy in charge of the Bloodmobile faked a smile, bowed slightly, and moved out of the way. His eyes tracked Sam as he entered and gestured to Michael. "Come on, kid," Sam said. "Time to go."

"Not without Eve," Michael said. "Sam, I can't leave her."

Eve couldn't read Sam's expression, and his eyes were hidden behind the sunglasses, so she just didn't know what he was thinking about that. She hoped she didn't look as terrified as she felt, because if Sam decided Eve didn't much matter, well . . . she expected this to be her last ride before a well-padded coffin.

"Sure," Sam said. "You were coming to dinner tonight, weren't you, Eve? I'll give you a ride home so you can get ready."

"Thanks, sir," she whispered. Her mouth was very dry, and her hands were shaking.

Michael put his arm around her and guided her to the exit. Sam gave her a hand down the stairs, and the warm leather of his gloves felt almost like human skin. That gave her another instinctual shiver. She decided she liked the heat of Michael's touch much better.

Sam folded up the stairs to the Bloodmobile's door and shut it, and they all watched as it glided away, sleek as a barracuda. Then Michael's grandfather hustled them into the shade, stripped off his hat and glasses, and said, "Are you both insane, or just stupid? Why would you go in there if you didn't have to?"

"Good question," Eve said, and laughed. It was hysterical laughter, and she clapped her hands over her mouth to try to shut it off. The giggles kept escaping, and she had to blink hard to keep tears from leaking, too. "Seemed like a good idea at the time . . . ?"

"We wanted to know why Monica was strong-arming our classmates for blood donations," Michael said. "Do you know?" That was . . . blunt. Edging in on aggressive, Eve thought.

Sam gave his grandson a steady look, then changed the subject. "Leave the mayor's daughter alone, Michael. She's not worth your time. People like that self-destruct, or they change, but it's up to her, not you."

"She's done a lot of damage," Michael said. "What about what she did to Shane and his family?"

"I'm sorry about your friend, but he and his parents are gone now. They're out of Morganville. Stop thinking about revenge and start thinking about your future, kids."

"Oh, I have," Michael shot back. "I'm getting the hell out of this place as soon as I can. I already talked to Mom and Dad about it. They're planning to move—didn't you know? They've already applied and gotten exit papers to go to the East Coast so Mom can get her surgery next year. And once I'm eighteen, I'm gone."

"I know about your parents," Sam said. "I support their decision. Yours, I'm not so sure. Morganville is all you know, Michael. You have no idea how hard the world outside can be for a kid on his own."

"I'm not a kid," Michael said. "Stop calling me one, *Grandpa*."

He pushed off and walked away into the school, leaving Sam standing there. Eve felt weirdly awkward, and she reached out to pat the man's arm just a little. "Sorry," she said. "He, ah, probably didn't mean that. He's just upset."

"I know," Sam said. "It's not easy for him, with a sick mom; losing his best friend only makes it that much worse. I'm glad he still has you."

"Has me? Uh . . . I'm just . . ." Eve scrambled for some kind of definition for what she was. "A friend."

"He needs friends," Sam said. There was a distant, sad look in those blue eyes now, but he still smiled at her. "We all do. What I said to him goes for you, too, Eve. Leave Monica Morrell alone."

"The question is, how do I get her to leave *me* alone?"

He shook his head, put on his hat and sunglasses, and went out into the sun, walking fast.

Eve winced at the bright stab of sunlight, and went into the school. Michael was nowhere to be found . . . but later, she found a note stuffed into her locker. She opened it carefully; Monica and her buds were always writing hate mail. But this just read simply *THANKS*, and had a little guitar drawn at the bottom . . . and she knew it was from him.

"Love notes?" Monica's voice came from right over her shoulder, and Eve almost tore the paper in half as she convulsively shivered. She turned, banging into the lockers hard enough to leave a bruise, and shoved the note back into the depths of her book stash. "Who's it from, Stinky George? Has to be somebody from the bottom of the loser pile."

Leave Monica alone. She almost heard Sam's voice in her ear, but what did he know, really, about being a girl trapped in a high school hallway with someone who ate the weak alive?

Eve turned, looked Monica full in the face, and said, "George might be bath-challenged, but he's smarter than you, and he can always take a shower. You'll always be as dumb as a supersized bag of stupid."

Monica threw a punch. Eve bent her knees, dropping fast, and the punch went high and smacked hard into the metal of the locker door. Something snapped with a muffled sound, and Monica let out a choked, disbelieving cry of pain as she reeled backward. It was only then that Eve realized neither of her normal backup singers was with her. Just Monica Morrell. Alone.

Eve took a step in as Monica cradled her broken hand to her chest, big eyes filling with tears of pain. She did feel a stab of empathy— just a little. She did remember how it felt, getting hurt. She'd been hurt plenty.

"Word of advice," Eve said. She suddenly realized that she was taller than Monica, and she felt stronger than her, too, as Monica flinched. "Stay away from Michael Glass. You hurt his friend. He's not going to forget."

Eve slammed her locker, whirled the combo lock, and walked away. Monica yelled something at her, but Eve just responded with a quick middle finger and no look back.

This time, she understood the yell plenty. "I'm going to make you sorry!" Monica said. "You pervy skank! Brandon's *my* Protector, too! Just wait till you turn eighteen, bitch—he's going to make you pay!"

Well, crap, Eve thought as she stiff-armed the exit, adjusted the backpack on her arm, and started the walk home. *I guess I should have thought of that.*

She was never going to let Brandon get a fang into her. Never.

Not even if she had to tear up his contract and throw it in his face and run for her life.

She was imagining what that might be like when Michael Glass fell in beside her. He was carrying his guitar in a soft case strapped to his back, and had a distinct lack of books. Then again, he was a smart guy; he probably didn't need to study nearly as hard as she did.

Her heart did that guilty flutter thing again when he joined her.

"Sorry about bugging out like that," he said. "I've got a gig at Common Grounds. Want to drop in?"

"Sure," she said, as casually as if it didn't mean everything in the world to her. "Why not?"

She could worry about the future later.

THE FIRST DAY OF THE REST OF YOUR LIFE

This was my very first Morganville short story, published in Charlaine Harris and Toni L. P. Kelner's fantastic collection *Many Bloody Returns*. Because when Charlaine Harris asks you whether you'd like to contribute a story to an anthology that has the theme of "vampires and birthdays," you definitely say yes to that.

I realized that I had the perfect birthday to discuss: Eve's eighteenth, on which she had to make the choice to either be a good little Morganville resident, sign her Protection agreement, and fit in . . . or be Eve. I think you already know the answer, but it's fun getting there.

A little factoid—the Glass House address is a combination of the numbers of my first dorm apartment in college and a book by Stephen King: 716 Lot Street (as in *'Salem's Lot*).

Eighteenth birthdays in Morganville, Texas, are usually celebrated in one of two ways: one, getting totally wasted with your friends or, two, making a terrifying life-or-death decision about your continued survival.

Not that there can't be some combination of the two.

My eighteenth birthday party was held in the back of a rust-colored Good Times van, circa way before I was born, and the select guest list included some of Morganville's Least Wanted. Me, for instance—Eve Rosser. Number of people who'd signed my yearbook: five. Two of them had scrawled *C YA LOSER*. (Number of people I'd wanted to sign my yearbook? Zero. But that was just me.)

And then there was my best friend, Jane, and her kid sister, Miranda. Jane was okay—kind of dull, but seriously, with a name like Jane? Cursed from birth. She did like some cool things, other than me of course. Wicked eighties make-out music, for instance. Black Phoenix Alchemy Lab perfume, particularly from the Dark Elements line, although I personally preferred the Funereal Oils.

Miranda—a tagalong to Jane—was a kid. Well, Miranda was a weird kid, who'd convinced a lot of people she was some kind of psychic. I didn't invite her to the party, mostly because I didn't think she'd be loads of fun, and also she wasn't likely to bring beer. Her BPAL preferences were unknown, because she didn't live on Planet Earth.

Which left Guy and Trent, my two excellent beer-buying buddies. They were my buddies because Guy had a fake ID that he'd made in art class and Trent owned the party bus in which we were ensconced. Other than that, I didn't know either one of them that well, but they were smart-ass, funny, and safe to get drunk with. Guy and Trent were the only gay couple I actually knew, gaydom being sort of frowned upon in the heartland of Texas that was Morganville.

We were all about the ironic family values.

The evening went pretty much the way such things are supposed to go: guys buy cheap-ass beer, distribute to underage females, drive to a deserted location to play loud headbanger music and generally act like idiots. The only thing missing was the make-out sessions, which was okay by me; most of the guys of Morganville were gag-worthy, anyway. There were one or two I would have gladly crawled over barbwire to date, but . . . that was another story.

Jane bought me a birthday present, which was kind of sweet, especially since it was a brand-new mix CD of songs about dead people. Jane knows what I like.

I was still a mystery to Guy and Trent, though. Granted, Morganville's a small town, and all us loser outcast freaks had a nodding acquaintance, but . . . Goths didn't much mix with other identity groups. The Goth population was even smaller than the few gays, given the town's prominent undead demographic. They have no sense of humor.

Oh, I forgot to mention: vampires. Town's run by them. Full of them. Humans live here on sufferance, heavy on the "suffer."

See what I mean about the ironic family values?

I could tell that Guy had been trying to think of a way to ask me all night, but thanks to consuming over half a case of beer with his Significantly Wasted Other, he finally just blurted out the question of the day.

"So, are you signing or what?" he asked. Yelled, actually, over whatever song was currently making my head hurt. "I mean, tomorrow?"

Was I signing? That was the Big Question, the one all of us faced at eighteen. I looked down at my wrist, because I was still wearing my leather bracelet. The symbol on it wasn't anything people outside Morganville would recognize, but it identified the vampire who was the official Protector for my family. However, I was no longer in that select little club of people who had to kiss Brandon's ass to continue to draw breath.

I also would no longer have any kind of deal or Protection from any vampire in Morganville.

What Guy was asking was whether I intended to pick myself a Protector of my very own. It was traditional to sign with your family's hereditary patron, but no way in hell was I letting Brandon have power over me. So I could either shop around to see if any other vampire could, or would, take me, or go bare—live without a contract.

Which was attractive, but seriously risky. See, Morganville vampires don't generally kill off their own humans, because that would make life difficult for everybody, but free-range, non-Protected humans? Nobody worries much what happens to them, because usually they're alone, and they're poor, and they disappear without a trace.

Just another job opening at the Chicken Shack fry machine.

They were all looking at me now. Jane, Miranda, Guy, and Trent, all waiting to hear what Eve Rosser, Professional Rebel, was going to do.

I didn't disappoint them. I tipped back the beer, belched, and said, "Hell no, I'm not signing. Bareback all the way, baby! Let's live fast and die young!"

Guy and I did drunken high fives. Trent rolled his eyes and clicked beer bottles with Jane. "They all say that," he said. "And then there's the test results, and the crying. . . ."

"Jesus, Trent, you're the laugh of the party."

"That's life of the party, honeybunches. Oh, wait, you're right. Not in Morganville, it isn't."

"Boo-ha-ha. Is that funny at all in other vans in town?" Jane asked. "Because it's not so funny in here, ass pirate."

"You should know, princess, as many vans as you've bounced around in," Trent shot back.

"Hey!" Jane tossed an empty bottle at him; Trent caught it and threw it in the plastic bin in the corner. Which, I had to admit, meant that Trent could hold his liquor, because he led the field in ounces consumed by a wide margin. "Seriously, Eve—what are you going to do?"

I hadn't thought about it. Or, actually, I had, but in that what-if kind of way that was really just bullshit bravado . . . but now it was down to do or don't, or it would be when the sun came up in the morning. I was going to have to choose, and that would rule the rest of my life.

Maybe I shouldn't have gotten quite so trashed, given the circumstances.

"Well, I'm not signing with Brandon," I said slowly. "Maybe I'll shop around for another patron."

"You really think anybody else is going to stand up and volunteer if Brandon's got you marked?" Guy asked. "Girl, you got yourself a death wish."

"Yeah, like that's news," Jane said. "Look how she dresses!"

Nothing wrong with how I was dressed. A skull T-shirt, a spiked belt low on my hips, bike shorts, fishnets, black and red Mary Janes. Oh, maybe she was talking about my makeup. I'd done the Full-on Goth today—white face powder, big black rings around my eyes, blue lips. It was sort of a joke.

And also, sort of not.

"It doesn't matter," said a small, quiet voice that somehow cut right through the music.

I'd almost forgotten about Miranda—the kid was sitting in the corner of the van, her knees drawn up, staring off into the distance.

"It speaks," Trent said, and laughed maniacally. "I was starting to think you'd just brought the kid along to protect your virtue, Jane." He gave her a comical flutter of his eyelashes. I coveted his long, lush eyelashes.

Miranda was still talking, or at least her lips were moving, but her words were lost in a particularly loud guitar crunch. "What?" I yelled, and leaned closer. "What do you mean?"

Miranda's pale blue eyes moved and fixed on me, and I wished they hadn't. There was something really strange about the girl, all right, even if her rep as the town Cassandra was exaggerated. She'd known about the fire last year that had burned the Collins family out; she'd even known—supposedly—that Alyssa Collins would die in the fire. The girl had a double helping of weird, with creepy little sprinkles on top.

"It doesn't matter what you decide to do," she said louder. "Really. It doesn't."

"Yeah?" Trent asked, and leaned over to snag another beer from the Coleman cooler in the center of the van floor. He twisted off the cap and turned it over in his fingers. I admired the black polish on his nails. "Why's that, O Madame Doom? Is one of us going to die tonight?" They all made hilariously drunken *ooooooooh* sounds, and Trent upended the bottle.

"Yes," Miranda whispered. Nobody else heard her but me.

And then her eyes rolled up in her skull, and she collapsed flat out on the filthy shag carpet on the floor of the van.

"Jesus," Guy blurted, and crawled over to her. He checked her pulse and breathed a sigh of relief. "I think she's alive."

Jane hadn't moved at all. She looked more annoyed than concerned. "It's okay," she said. "She had some kind of vision. It happens. She'll come out of it."

Trent said, "Damn, I was starting to get worried it was the beer."

"She didn't have any, moron."

"See? Serious beer deficiency. No wonder she's out."

"Shouldn't we do something?" Guy asked anxiously. He was cradling Miranda in his arms, and she was as limp as a rag doll, her head lolling against his head. Her eyes were closed now, moving frantically behind the lids like she was trying to look all directions at once, in the dark. "Like, take her to the hospital?"

The Morganville hospital was neutral ground—no vampires could hunt there. So it was the safest place for anybody who was, well, not working at full power. But Jane just shook her head.

"I told you, this happens all the time. She'll be okay in a couple of minutes. It's like an epileptic seizure or something." Jane looked at me curiously. "What did she say to you?"

I couldn't figure out how to tell her, so I just drank my beer and said nothing. Probably a mistake.

Jane was right—it took a couple of minutes, but Miranda's eyes fluttered open, blank and unfocused, and she struggled to sit up in Guy's arms. He held on for a second, then let go. She scrambled away and sat in the far corner of the van, next to the empty bottles, with her hands over her head. Jane sighed, handed me her beer, and crawled over to whisper with her sister and stroke her hair.

"Well," Trent said. "Guess the emergency's over. Beer?"

"No," I said, and drained my last bottle. I was feeling loose and sparkly, and I was going to be seriously sorry in the morning—oh, it was morning. Like, about three a.m. Great. "I need to get home, Trent."

"But the night's barely late-middle-age!"

"Sunrise in three hours. I don't want to meet Brandon drunk off my ass."

"Might improve—okay, fine." Trent shot me a resentful look, and jerked his head to Guy. "Help me drive, okay?"

"You're driving?" Guy looked alarmed. Trent had downed lots of beer. Lots. He didn't seem to be feeling it, and it wasn't like we had far to go, but . . . yeah. Still, I didn't feel capable, and Guy looked even more bleary. Jane . . . Well, she hadn't been far behind Trent in the Drunk-Ass Sweepstakes, either.

And letting a fourteen-year-old epileptic have the wheel wasn't a better solution.

"Not like we can walk," I said reluctantly. "Look, drive slow, okay? Slow and careful."

Trent shot me a crisp OK sign and saluted. He didn't look drunk. I swallowed hard and crawled back to sit with Jane and Miranda. "We're going home," I said. "Guess you guys get dropped off first, right? Then me?"

Miranda nodded. "Sit here," she said. "Right here." She patted the carpet next to her.

I rolled my eyes. "Comfy here, thanks."

"No! Sit here!"

I looked at Jane and frowned. "Are you sure she's okay?" And made a little not-so-subtle loopy-loop at my temple.

"Yeah, she's fine." Jane sighed. "She's been getting these visions again. Most of the time they're bullshit, though. I think she just does it for the attention."

Jane was looking put out, and I guess she had reason. If Miranda was this much fun at parties, I could only imagine what a barrel of laughs she was at home.

Miranda was getting more and more upset. Jane gave her a ferocious frown and said, "Oh, God. Just do it, Eve. I don't want her having another fit or something."

I crawled across Miranda and wedged myself uncomfortably into the corner where she indicated. Yeah, this was great. At least it was going to be a short drive.

It was what was waiting at the end of it that I was afraid of. Brandon. Decisions. The beginning of my adult life.

Trent started the van and pulled a tight U-turn out of the high school parking lot. There were no side windows, but out of the back windows I saw the big, hulking thirties-era building with its Greek columns fading away like a ghost into the night. Morganville wasn't big on streetlights, although there were a crapload of surveillance cameras. The cops knew where we'd been. They knew everything in Morganville, and half of them were vampires.

God, I couldn't wait to apply for my paperwork to get the hell out, but in order to do that, I needed an acceptance letter to an out-of-state university, or waivers from the mayor's office. I wasn't likely to get either one, with my grades and 'tude. No, I was a lifer, stuck in Morganville, watching the world go by.

At least, until somebody cut me out of the herd and I became a Snack Pack.

Trent was driving faster than we'd agreed. Not only that, the van was veering a little to the side of the road. "Yo, T.!" I yelled. "Eyes front, man!"

He turned to look back at me, and his pupils were huge and dark, and he giggled, and I had time to think, *Oh shit, he's not drunk—he's high,* and then he hit the gas.

Miranda's hand closed over my arm. I looked at her, and she was crying. "I don't want them to die," she said. "I don't."

"Oh Jesus, Mir, would you stop?" Jane said, and smacked her hand away. "Drama princess."

But I was looking at Miranda, and she was staring at me, and she slowly nodded her head.

"Here it comes," she said, and transferred the stare to her sister. "I'm sorry. I love you."

And then something bad happened, and the world ended.

I walked away from the smoking wreckage. Staggered, actually, coughing and carrying the limp body of Miranda; she was alive, bleeding from the head but still alive.

My brain wouldn't bring up anything about Trent, Jane, or Guy. Nothing. It just . . . refused.

I walked until I heard sirens and saw flashing lights, and dropped to my knees, with Miranda in my lap.

The first cop on the scene was Richard Morrell, the son of the mayor. I'd always thought that even though his family was poisonous, he was kind of a nice guy; he proved that now by easing Miranda out of my arms and to the ground, cushioning her head gently to keep it from bumping against the pavement. His warm hand pressed on my shoulder. "Eve. Eve. Anybody else in there?"

I nodded slowly. "Jane. Trent. Guy." Maybe I'd been wrong. Maybe I'd imagined all of that. Maybe they were about to crawl out of that twisted mass of metal and laugh and high-five. . . .

Too much imagination. I imagined dead, bloody bodies crawling out of the wreck, and swayed. Nearly collapsed. Richard steadied me. "Easy," he said. "Easy, kid. Stay with me."

I did. Somehow, I stayed conscious even when the ambulance drivers wheeled the gurneys past me. Miranda was taken first, of course, and rushed off to the hospital with flashers and sirens.

They didn't bother hurrying for the others. They just loaded the black zippered bags into one ambulance, and it drove away. The fire department hosed down the wreck, and it smelled like burned metal and reeking plastic, alcohol, blood. . . .

I was still kneeling there on the pavement, pretty much forgotten, when Richard finally came back, did a double take, and looked grim. "Nobody came to get you? From your family?"

"You called them?"

"Yeah, I called," he said. "Come on. I'll take you home."

I wiped my face. The white makeup was almost gone, and my skin was wet; I hadn't even known I was crying.

Not a mark on me.

Sit here, Miranda had told me. *Right here.* Like she'd known. Like she'd picked me over her own sister.

I couldn't stop shaking. Officer Morrell found a blanket in the back of his patrol car and threw it around my shoulders, and then he bundled me in the back and drove me the five miles back home. All the lights were on at my parents' house, but it didn't look welcoming. I checked the time on my cell phone.

Four a.m.

"Hey," Richard said. "It's the big day, right? Time to grow up, Eve. I'm sorry about your friends, but you need to focus now. Make the right choices. You understand?"

He was trying to be kind, as much as he knew how to be; must have been hard, considering the asshole genes he'd been given. I tried to think what his sister, Monica, would have said in the same situation. *What a bunch of trashed-out losers. They shouldn't be in our cemetery. We've got a perfectly good landfill.*

I knew Monica too well, but that wasn't Richard's fault. I nodded to him numbly, gave back the blanket, and walked up the ten steps from the curb to my parents' front door.

It opened before I reached for the knob, and I was facing Brandon, the family's vampire Protector.

"I've been waiting for you, Eve," he said, and stepped back. "Come in."

I swallowed whatever smart-ass remark I might normally have given him, and looked back over my shoulder. Richard Morrell was looking through the window of the police cruiser at me, and he gave a friendly wave and drove off. Like I was in good hands.

You know every stereotype of the romantic, brooding vampire? Well, that's Brandon. Dark, broody, bedroom eyes, wore a lot of black leather. Liked to think he was badass, and what the hell did I know? Maybe he was.

I hated his guts, and he knew it.

"Honey?" Mom. She was hovering behind Brandon, looking timid and nervous. "Better come inside. You know you shouldn't be out there in the dark."

Dad was nowhere to be seen. I bit my tongue and crossed the threshold, and when Brandon closed the door behind me, it was like the cell slamming shut.

"I was in an accident," I said. Mom looked at me. We didn't look much alike, even when I wasn't Gothed up. . . . She had fading brown hair and green eyes, and I took after Dad's darker looks. I sometimes thought maybe this was some kind of play, and Mom was an actress, and not a very good one, playing the role of my mother. She phoned in her performance.

"Officer Morrell called," she said. "But he said you weren't hurt. And you know, we had a guest." She smiled at Brandon. My skin tried to crawl off my bones.

"Three of my friends were killed," I said.

"Oh dear!"

"Once more with feeling, Mom."

"Any of mine?" Brandon asked casually. I gritted my teeth, because I wanted to scream and hit him, and that wouldn't have done me any good at all.

"N-no," I managed to stammer. "Jane Blunt, Trent Garvey, and Guy—" What the hell was Guy's last name? I wanted to cry now. Or keep crying. "Guy Finelli."

Brandon smiled. "Sounds as if Charles had a bad night." Charles being a rival vamp. I knew he was the Protector for Jane's family. I hadn't known he'd been responsible for one or both of the others. Charles was just the opposite of Brandon—a bookish little man, soft-spoken and mild until you pushed him. Not a bad choice, if I had to go shopping for Protectors, I supposed.

God, I hated this. I wanted this over.

"Let's just do it," I said, and walked down the hallway to the living room. Predictably, Dad was parked in his recliner with an open beer, probably working on his usual six-pack. He was a bloated vision of my future—two hundred and fifty pounds, sallow and grim and full of rage and resentment he couldn't fling anywhere but around here, in the house. He managed the biggest local bar, which of course was owned by Brandon. All nice and tidy. Brandon owned the mortgage on the house. Brandon owned the notes on our cars.

Brandon owned us.

And now Brandon was smiling at me, all sleek and horrible with those hungry, hungry eyes, and he was taking a folded, thick sheaf of papers out of the pocket of his long black coat.

"You only wear that thing because you saw it on TV," I said, and snatched the paperwork from him. I read the first bit. *I, Eve Evangeline Walker Rosser, swear my life, my blood, and my service to my Protector Brandon, now and for my lifetime, that my Protector may command me in all things.*

This was it. I was holding my future in my hands, right here.

Brandon held out a pen. My father tore his attention away from the glowing escape of the television and took a sip of beer, watching me with dead, angry intensity. My mother looked nervous, fluttering her hands as I stared without blinking at the black Montblanc the vampire was holding out.

"Happy birthday, by the way," Brandon said. "There's a signing bonus. Ten thousand dollars."

"Guess I could bury my friends in style with that," I said.

"You don't have to worry about that." Brandon shrugged. "Their family contracts cover that sort of thing."

Mom sensed what I was thinking, I guess, because she blurted, "Eve, honey, let's hurry. Brandon does have places to go." She encouraged me with little vague motions of her hands, and her eyes were desperate.

I took a deep breath, held the crisp paper in both hands, and ripped it in half. The sound was almost drowned out by my mother's horrified gasp, and the sound of the beer can crushing in my father's hand.

"You ungrateful little freak," Dad said. "You disrespect your Protector like that? To his face?"

"Yeah," I said. "Pretty much just like that." I ripped the contract in quarters, and threw it at him. The paper fluttered like huge confetti, one piece landing on his shoulder until Brandon calmly brushed it off. "Fuck off, Brandon. I'm not signing with you."

"No one else will take you," he said. "And you're mine, Eve. You've always been mine. Don't forget it."

My Dad got out of his recliner and grabbed my arm. "You're signing that paper," he said, and shook me like a terrier shaking a rat. "Don't be stupid!"

"I'm not signing anything!" I screamed, right in his face, and took Brandon's expensive pen and stomped on it with my Mary Janes until it was a leaking black stain on the floor. "You can be slaves if you want, but not me! Not ever again!"

Brandon didn't look angry. He looked amused. That was bad.

Dad shoved me and sent me reeling. "Then you're gone," he said. "I won't have you in my house, eating my food, stealing my money. If you want to go out there bare, then do it. See how long you last."

I was stunned, at least a little; he'd never done that before, even though he'd never really loved me. I backed away from him, into Mom. She got out of the way, but then, she always did, didn't she? She had all the backbone of a balloon.

She avoided my eyes completely. "You'd better go, honey," she said. "You made your choice."

I turned and ran down the hall to my room, slammed the door, and dragged my biggest suitcase out from under the bed. I couldn't take much, I knew that; even taking a suitcase was risky, because it slowed me down. But I couldn't wait for dawn; I had to get out of here now, before Brandon stopped me. He wasn't supposed to use compulsion on me, but that didn't mean he wouldn't.

Or that my parents wouldn't. For my own good, of course.

I filled up the bag with underwear, shoes, clothes, a few mementos that I couldn't leave, just in case Dad decided to load the barbecue grill with my belongings the minute I was out the door. I left the family photos. Mom and Dad weren't fond memories, and neither was my brother, Jason, who was better off in jail, where he was currently rotting.

I went out the back door, since Brandon was still talking to Mom and Dad in the front, and dragged the suitcase as quietly as possible across the backyard to the alley. Alleys in Morganville are freaky at night, and wildly dangerous, but I didn't have much choice. I hurried, bouncing my suitcase over rough, rutted ground and past foul-smelling trash bins, until I was on the street.

And I realized I had no idea where to go. No idea at all. All the friends I'd had were dead—dead tonight—and I couldn't even really grieve about that; I didn't have time. Lifesaving had to come first, right? That was what I kept telling myself.

Didn't help me carry that giant boulder of guilt on my back.

Cabs didn't run at night, because cabbies knew better, and besides, there were only two in the whole town. No bus service. At night, either you drove or you stayed home, and even driving was dangerous if you were un-Protected.

I could go to the local motel for the night, the Sagebrush, but it was a good twenty-minute walk, and I didn't think I had twenty minutes. Not tonight. I'd officially forfeited Brandon's Protection when I'd ripped up that paper, and that meant I was an all-you-can-suck buffet until I got somebody to take me in. Houses had automatic Protection. Any house.

Michael.

I don't know why I thought of Michael Glass, but all of a sudden I had a flashback to the last time I'd seen him, playing guitar in Common Grounds, the local hot-spot coffee shop. I'd gone to high school with Michael, crushed hard on Michael from a distance, and semistalked him after he graduated, attending every single gig he'd landed in Morganville. He was good, you see. And a sweetheart. And little baby Jesus, he was hot. And he had his own house.

I knew the Glass House. It was one of the historic homes of Morganville, all gently decaying Gothic elegance, and Michael's parents had moved out on waivers two years ago. Michael lived there all alone, as far as I knew.

And it was only three blocks away.

I had no idea if he was home, or if he'd be stupid enough to let me in when I was running for my life, but it was worth a try, right? I broke into a jog, the wheels of my suitcase making a whirring, grating hiss on the sidewalk. The night felt deep and dark, no moon, only starlight, and it smelled like cold dust. Like a graveyard. Like my graveyard.

I thought of Trent, Guy, and Jane, in their silent black bags. Maybe they were in cold metal drawers by now, filed away. Lives over.

I didn't want to be dead. I didn't.

So I ran, bumping my suitcase behind me.

I didn't see a soul on the streets. No cars, no lights in windows, no shadows trailing me. It was eerily quiet outside, and my heart was racing. I wished I had weapons, but those were hard to come by in Morganville, and besides, I had nosy parents who trashed my room regularly looking for contraband of all kinds. Being under eighteen sucked.

Being over eighteen wasn't looking so great, either.

I heard the hiss of tires behind me, over the puffing of my breath, and the low growl of a car engine. I looked back, hoping to see Richard Morrell following me in the police car, but no such luck; it was a nondescript black sports car with dark-tinted windows.

Vampire car. No question.

Two more blocks.

The car seemed content to creep along behind me, tires crunching over pavement, and I had plenty of panic time to wonder who was inside. Brandon, in the back, almost certainly. But Brandon wouldn't be the one to fang me, although he'd probably take his turn before I was dead. He had people to do that for him.

The suitcase hit a crack in the sidewalk and tipped over, dragging me to an off-balance halt. I saw a light go on in one of the houses I was passing, and a curtain twitch aside, and then the blinds snapped shut and the lights flicked off. No help there. But then, in Morganville, that wasn't unusual.

I wasn't crying, but it was close; I could feel tears burning in my throat, right above the terror twisting my guts. *This was your choice*, I told myself. *You couldn't do anything else.*

Right now, that wasn't much comfort.

Up ahead, I saw the looming bulk of the Glass House—one more block to go. I could make it, I could. I had to. Jane and Trent and Guy were gone. I owed it to them to live through this.

The car sped up behind me as I crossed the street to the next corner. Four houses to go, all still and lightless.

There was a porch light on in front of 716, and it cast a glow on the pillars framing the porch, picked out the boards in the white fence in front. There were lights on inside, and I saw someone pass in front of a window.

"Michael!" I screamed it, and put everything into one last sprint. The car eased ahead of me and pulled in at the curb with a squeal of brakes, tires bumping concrete. A door flew open to block the sidewalk, and I gasped, picked up my suitcase, and tossed it over the fence. It weighed about fifty pounds, but I managed to toss it anyway. I grabbed the rough whitewashed boards with their sharp tops and vaulted over, got my shirt caught on the way and ripped it open. No time to worry about that. I dragged my suitcase over the night-damp grass and yelled his name again, with even more of an edge of panic. "Michael! It's Eve! Open the door!"

They were behind me. They were right behind me. I knew it, even though I didn't dare look back and they made no sound. I could feel it. I felt something grab the suitcase, nearly twisting my arm out of the socket, and I let go, stumbling against the porch stairs. The house stretched above me, gray and ghostly in the dark, but that porch light, that was life.

Something caught my foot. I screamed and kicked, fighting to get free. My searching fingers scratched at the closed wood of the door, and I tasted dust again. I'd been close, so close. . . .

The door opened, and warm yellow light spilled out over me. Too late. I tried to grab for a handhold, but I was being yanked backward . . . and I could feel breath on the back of my neck. Cold, rancid breath.

Something flew over my head and slammed into the vampire pulling on me, knocking him flying. I crawled back toward the door and got a hand over the threshold.

Michael Glass grabbed my hand and dragged me inside with one long pull. My feet made it over the line just a fraction of a second before another vampire slammed into the invisible barrier there.

Brandon. Oh, damn, he was angry. Really angry. Vampires usually didn't look like movie vamps—they were all about the fitting in—but right now he clearly didn't care. His eyes had turned bloodred, and his face was whiter than I'd ever made mine. And I could see fangs, fangs a viper would have envied, flicking down from their hiding place to flash in menace.

Michael Glass didn't flinch. He looked pretty much as I remembered him, only . . . better, somehow. Stronger. Tall, built, golden hair that waved and curled surfer-style. He had blue eyes, and they were fixed on Brandon. Not afraid, but wary.

"You okay?" he asked me. I nodded, unable to say anything that would really cover how I felt. "Then get out of the way."

"Huh?"

"Your legs."

I pulled them in, and he calmly shut the door in Brandon's face. I sat there on the wooden floor, knees pulled in to my chest, and tried to slow my heart down from triple digits. "God," I whispered, and rested my forehead on my knees. "That was close."

I heard the rustle of fabric. Michael had crouched down across from me, back to the opposite wall. He was wearing some comfortable old jeans, a faded green cotton shirt, and his feet were long and narrow and bare. "Eve?" he asked. "What the hell was that?"

"Um . . . my eighteenth-birthday present." I was shivering, and I realized my skull shirt was displaying a whole lot more bra than I'd ever intended. Kind of a plunge bra. Victoria's Secret. Not so much of a secret right now. "Brandon's pissed."

Michael rested his head against the wall and looked at me with narrowed eyes. "You didn't sign."

I shook my head, unable to say much about that.

"You can stay until dawn, but you need to go then. You got someplace to go?"

I just looked at him miserably, and I felt tears starting to bubble up again. What had I been hoping for? Some white knight hottie to save me? Well, I wasn't going to get it from Michael. He hadn't even come outside to get me; he'd just thrown a chair or something.

Still, he'd opened the door. Nobody else on this street had, or would have.

"Okay," Michael said softly. He stretched out a hand and awkwardly patted me on the knee. "Hey. You're okay, right? You're safe in here. Don't cry."

I didn't want to cry, but that was how I vented, and boy, did I need to vent. All the fury and grief and rage and confusion just boiled up inside, and forced their way out. I was shaking, sobbing like a punk, and after a couple of shaking breaths I felt Michael move across to sit next to me. His arm went around me, and I turned toward his warmth, soaking his shirt with tears. I would have told him everything then, all the bad stuff . . . the van, my friends, Brandon. I would have told him how Brandon gave my dad a pay raise when I was fifteen in return for unrestricted access to me and Jason. I would have told him everything.

Lucky for him I couldn't get my breath.

Michael was good at soothing; he knew not to talk, and he knew just how to touch my hair and how to hold me. It wasn't until the storm became more like occasional showers, and I was able to hiccup steady breaths, that I realized he had a clear view down my bra.

"Hey!" I said, and tried to artfully tuck the torn edges of my shirt under the strap. Michael had an odd look on his face. "Free show's over, Glass."

Trent would have snapped back some snazzy insult, but not Michael. Michael just looked uncomfortable, and edged away from me. "Sorry," he said. "I wasn't——"

Well, if he wasn't, I was offended. I gave good bra: 34B.

I raised my eyebrows.

Michael held up his hands in surrender. "Okay, yeah. I was. That makes me an asshole, right?"

"No, that makes you male and straight," I said. Was it wrong I felt relieved? "I just need to change my— Oh, damn. My suitcase! It's still out there——"

Michael got up and walked down the polished wooden hallway. The house felt warm, but strange—old and, despite the big open rooms, kind of claustrophobic. Like it was . . . watching.

I loved it.

The living room was normal stuff—couch, chairs, bookcases, throw rugs. A guitar case lying open on a small dining table, the guitar lying abandoned on the couch as if he'd put it down to see what the trouble was out in the yard. I'd heard Michael play before, though not recently. People had said he'd given it up . . . but I guessed he hadn't.

Michael pulled the blinds and looked out. "It's on the lawn," he said. "They're going through it."

"What?" I pushed him out of the way and tried to see for myself, but it was all just a black blur. "They're going through my stuff? Bastards!" Because I had some lingerie in there that I seriously wanted to keep private. Well, maybe share with one other person. But privately. I yanked the cord on the blinds and moved them up, then unlocked the window and threw up the sash. I leaned out and yelled, "Hey, ass-holes, you touch my underwear and——"

Michael yanked me back by my belt and slammed the window shut about one second before Brandon's face appeared there. "Let's not taunt the angry vampires," he said. "I have to live here."

Deep breaths, Eve. Right. Suitcase not as important as jugular. I sat down in one of the chairs, trying to get hold of myself and not even sure who that was anymore. Myself, I mean. So much had changed in five hours, right? I was an adult now. I was on my own in a town where being alone was a death sentence. I'd made a very bad enemy, and I'd done it deliberately. I'd been disowned by my own family, not that they'd been much of a family in the first place.

"Need a roommate?" I asked, and tried for a mocking smile. Michael hesitated in the act of reaching for his guitar, then settled in on the couch with the instrument cradled in his lap like a favorite pet. He picked out random notes, pure and cool, and bent his head. "Sorry. Bad joke."

"No, it's not," he said. "Actually—I might consider it. You and me, we always got along in school. I mean, we didn't know each other that well, but——" Nobody had known Michael really well, except his buddy Shane Collins, but Shane had bugged out of Morganville with his parents after his sister's death. Everybody had wanted to know Michael, but he was private. Shy, maybe. "It's a big house. Four bed-rooms, two baths. Hard to manage it by myself."

Was he offering? Really? I swallowed and leaned forward. My shirt was coming loose again, but I left it that way. I needed every advantage I could get. "I swear, I'm good for rent. I'll get a job somewhere, at one of the neutral places. And I clean stuff. I'm a demon with cleaning."

"Cook?" He looked hopeful, but I had to shake my head. "Damn. I'm not so great at it."

"You'd have to be better than me. I can screw up the recipe for water."

He smiled. He had one of those smiles—you know the ones, the kind that unleash lethal force on girls in the vicinity. I couldn't remember him smiling in high school. He was probably aware that it might cause girls to faint, or unbutton clothes, or something.

"We'll think about it until tomorrow night," he said. "Pick any room but the first one—that's mine. Sheets are in the closet. Towels are in the bathroom."

"My suitcase—"

"After dawn." He was looking down again, picking out a sweet, quiet melody from the strings. "I've got someplace I have to go before then, but you'll be safe enough just going out to get it and coming right back inside. I don't think Brandon's pissed enough to hang around in the sun."

Hopefully. Some vampires could, and we all knew it, but Brandon seemed more of a night person. "But—you'll come back, right?"

"I'll be back by dark," he promised. "We'll talk about the rent then. But for now, you should—" He looked up. His gaze reached the level of my chest, fixed, and then lowered again. The smile this time was directed at the guitar. "Put on a new shirt or something."

"Well, I would, but all my shirts are in my suitcase, getting molested by Brandon and his funboys." I flipped a finger at the window, in case they were watching.

"Get something out of my closet," he said. I thought he was playing something from Coldplay's catalog now, something soft and contemplative. "Sorry about staring. I know you've had a tough night."

There was something so damn sweet about that, it made me want to cry. Again. I swallowed the impulse. "You don't know the half of it," I said.

This time, when he looked up, his gaze actually made it to my face. And stayed there. "I'm guessing bad."

"Real bad."

"You'd tell me if I was a friend, right? And not just some guy whose door you randomly knocked on in the middle of the night?"

I thought about Jane, poor sweet Jane, my best and only real friend. Trent and Guy, who probably had been destined for nothing but still had been, for tonight at least, my friends. "I'm not so good for my friends," I said. "Maybe we ought to just call you a really nice stranger." I took a deep breath. "I lost three friends tonight, and it was my fault."

He kept looking at me. Really looking. It was a little bit hot, and a little bit disconcerting. "Then would you talk to a really nice stranger about it? For"—he checked his watch—"forty minutes? I need to leave before sunrise, but I want you to be okay before I do."

It took only thirty minutes to tell him about the Life and Times of Me, actually. Michael didn't say very much, and I felt so tired afterward that I hardly knew it when he got up and went into the kitchen. I must have dozed off a little, because when I woke up, he was kneeling next to my chair, and he had a chocolate brownie on a plate. With a semi-melted pink candle sputtering away on top.

"It's a leftover," he warned me. "Two weeks at least. So I don't know how good it is. But happy birthday, anyway. I promise you, things will get better."

They just had.

AMELIE'S STORY

A brief vignette, and one that I wrote mainly to understand Amelie and Oliver's relationship. This was written very early on, between *Glass Houses* and *The Dead Girls' Dance*. It was also before I'd thought about Bishop, or even much about Myrnin, although I already had the broad strokes of his character in mind. This little scene was written to help me understand how these very long-lived, somewhat disinterested characters would see these teenagers who'd defied them . . . and it also gives us a bit more about Shane's father, since I was beginning to write that book and had a feeling for what was coming.

The characters changed over time, developed more depth and richness and personality, but I think the outlines are there in this story, and the sense of their long view of things.

This was originally posted as part of the Captain Obvious "hidden content" on the Morganville Web site.

Outside, nightfall had truly come, and it was a glorious darkness.

Amelie stood, one hand holding back the heavy velvet of the draperies, and watched the streetlights of her town blink on one after another. A faint circle of safety for the humans to cling to, an important illusion without which they could not long survive. She had learned a great deal about living with humans, over the past few hundred years.

More than about living with her own kind, she supposed.

"Yes?" She had heard the tiny whisper of movement behind her, and knew one of her servants had appeared in the doorway. They never spoke unless spoken to. A benefit to having servants so long-lived: one could reasonably expect them to understand manners. Not like the children of today, sparking as bright as fireflies, and gone as quickly. No manners. No sense of place and time.

"Oliver," the servant said. It was Vallery; she knew all their voices, of course. "He's at the gates. He requests a conversation."

Did he? How interesting. She'd thought he'd slink off into the dark and lick his wounds for a year or two, until he was ready to play games with her again. He'd come very near to succeeding this time,

thanks to her own carelessness. She could ill afford another occur-
rence.

"Show him in," she said. It was not the safest course, but she
found herself growing tired of the safe road. There were so rarely any
surprises, or strangers to meet.

Like the surprise of the children living in her house on Lot Street.
The angelic blond boy, with his passion and bitterness, woven into
the fabric of the house and trapped there. Or the strange girl, with her
odd makeup and odder clothing. Or the other boy, the strong one,
quick and intelligent and wishing not to seem so.

And the youngest, oh, the youngest girl, with her diamond-sharp
mind. Fierce and small and courageous, although she would not know
the depths of her abilities for years yet.

Interesting, all of them, and that was a rarity in Amelie's long,
long eternity. She had been kind to them, out of no better reason than
that. She could afford to be kind, so long as it risked her nothing in
return.

Oliver deliberately made noise as he approached her study, a gesture of politeness she appreciated. Amelie turned from the window
and sat down in the velvet-covered chair beside it, arranging her skirts
with effortless grace and folding her hands in her lap. Oliver looked
less harassed than he had; he'd taken time to bathe, change, compose
himself. He'd tied his gray curling hair back in the old style, a subtle
sign to her that he was willing to accommodate her preferences, and
he was perfectly correct in his manners as he bowed to her and waited
for her to gesture him to take a seat.

"I am grateful to you for the opportunity to speak," Oliver said as
he settled himself in the chair. Vallery appeared in the doorway with a
tray and two silver cups; she gave him a slight nod, and he delivered
them refreshment. Oliver drank without taking his eyes from her. She
sipped. "I thought we had an agreement, Amelie. Regarding the book."

"We did," she said, and sipped again. Fresh, warm, red blood. Life itself, salty and thick in her mouth. She had long learned how to feast neatly on it. "I agreed not to interfere with your . . . searches. But I never agreed to forgo the opportunity to retrieve it myself, if the chance presented. As it did."

"I was cheated."

"Yes," she agreed softly, and smiled. "But not by me, Oliver. Not by me. And if you should consider taking your petty revenge on the children, please remember that they are in my house, under my sign of Protection. Don't make this cause for complaint."

He nodded stiffly, eyes sparking anger. He put his cup back on Vallery's tray. It rang empty. "What do you know of the boy?"

"Which boy?"

"Not Glass. The other one. Shane Collins."

She raised one hand in a tiny, weary gesture. "What is there to know? He is barely a child."

"His mother was resistant to conditioning."

Amelie searched her memory. Ah, yes. Collins. There had been an incident, unfortunate as such things were, and she had dispatched operatives to see to the end of it when the elder Collins had taken his wife and son and left Morganville. "She should be dead by now," she said.

"She is. But her husband isn't." Oliver smiled slowly, and she did not care for the triumph in his expression. Not at all. "I have a report that he returned to town only an hour ago, and went straight to the house where his son is staying. Your house, Amelie. You are now sheltering a potential killer." She said nothing, did nothing. After a long moment, Oliver sighed. "You cannot pretend that this is not a problem."

"I don't," she said. "But we shall see what develops. After all, this town is a sanctuary."

"And the children?" he asked. "Are you extending your Protection to them even if they come after vampires?"

Amelie sipped the last of her blood, and smiled. "I might," she said.

"Then you want a war."

"No, Oliver, I want the right to make my own decisions in my own town." She stood, and Oliver stood, too, as if drawn on the same string. "You may go."

She went back to the window, dismissing him from her thoughts. If he was inclined to dispute his dismissal, he thought better—possibly because Vallery was not the only servant she had within a whisper's call—and he withdrew from the field without surrender.

Amelie folded her hands on the warm wood of the window ledge and stared at the faint glow of moonrise on the horizon.

"Oh, children." She sighed. "Whatever shall I do with you?"

She was not in the habit of risking her life or position. Especially not for mere humans, whose lives blinked on and off as quickly as the streetlights below.

If Oliver was right, she would have little choice.

WRONG PLACE, WRONG TIME

)

Another free-on-the-Web story under the Captain Obvious hidden content, I wrote this story to give a little shading and understanding to Richard Morrell, Monica's (exasperated) older brother. We first met him in *Glass Houses*, and I took a liking to him immediately—it's not easy being the son of the most corrupt human in Morganville while also being the brother of the most outrageous, selfish bully. Add to that a real desire to do some good in the world and help protect his fellow Morganville residents, and you've got a man who has a hard day ahead of him.

But one thing's for certain: Richard does love his sister. He knows her flaws, but that doesn't mean he won't go to the wall for her—and even compromise his ethics from time to time.

This is about to be a very bad day to be a criminal in Morganville.

Richard Morrell looked at the man sitting across from him—shaking, pale, covered in blood that the ambulance attendants had sworn wasn't his own—and said, "Let's start at the beginning. Tell me your name." He kept his tone neutral, because he wasn't sure yet which approach to take. The guy looked too shaky to push really hard, and too paranoid to take well to friendliness.

Businesslike was apparently the right course, because the man blinked at him, ran a blood-smeared hand across his sweaty forehead, and said, "They're dead. They're dead, right? My friends?"

"Lets talk about you," Richard said, very steadily. "What's your name?"

"Brian. Brian Maitland."

"Where are you from, Brian?" Richard smiled slightly. "I know you're not from around here."

"Dallas," Maitland said. "We were, y'know, just passing through. We thought, *Jeez, it looks like such an easy score,* y'know? No big deal. We weren't going to hurt anybody. We just wanted the money."

"One thing at a time, Brian. What are your friends' names?"

"Joe. Joe Grady. And Lavelle Harvey. Lavelle—Lavelle's Joe's girl. I swear, Officer, we were just passing through. We thought—we saw the bank open after dark, we thought—we figured—"

"You figured it would be an easy score," Richard said. "You said. So what happened?"

"I, uh—" Maitland seemed to vapor-lock. Richard motioned over one of the two cops standing in the corner of the room—the human one—and asked for coffee in a low voice. He waited until the steaming Styrofoam cup was in Maitland's big, bloody hands before prodding him again.

"You're safe now," Richard said, which really wasn't the truth. "Tell me what happened at the bank."

Maitland sipped at the coffee, then gulped convulsively, not seeming to care that it was hot enough to raise blisters. His eyes had that terrible distance to them, something Richard was way too familiar with.

"There was this girl," he said. "Pretty little thing, cashing a check at the teller window. Joe took the guard, Lavelle covered the couple of people in the lobby, and I grabbed the girl."

"Describe her," Richard said.

"I don't know, pretty. Brunette. Had a mouth on her—I'll tell ya that." He shook his head slowly. "She kept telling me we were in the wrong place, wrong time, wrong damn town. Pissed me off. But she was right."

He gulped more coffee, eyes darting nervously from Richard to the night visible in the barred window of the room. He hadn't once looked at the cops standing behind him. Richard figured he was blocking it out, the knowledge that one of them might not be entirely human.

"This girl," Richard said softly. "What did you do to her?"

"Nothing," Maitland said, and then corrected himself. "Okay, I hit her. Just to shut her up. And then Joe shot that guard, and somebody triggered the security alarms. These bars came down at the door.

We couldn't get out. Why the hell would they want to keep us inside the bank, with the customers? Ain't the whole point to get us outside? Don't you people know nothing about security?"

"You said Joe shot the guard. What happened then?"

"The guard——" Maitland's voice went tight, and then silent. He shook his head. There were tears standing in his damp eyes. "It ain't possible, man. I saw him go down. Joe put four bullets right in his chest, and he wasn't wearing no vest. I saw the blood." Maitland choked down his fear. "And then he got up. I never seen anybody do that. Sure, you see guys on drugs or something who just don't really know they've been shot——they can go for a while before they fall down, but it ain't like they're normal, y'know? This was just some working guy. He shouldn't just——get up like that."

Maitland started to shiver again, and gulped more coffee. When he put the cup down, it was empty. Richard motioned for a refill, and waited. Maitland didn't seem to need prodding now. He wanted to get it out.

"Joe, he emptied the gun, but the guard just kept coming. I was watching them, so I didn't see what happened to Lavelle, but I heard her start yelling. And then she just——stopped. Joe——that guard, there was something wrong with him, man——I don't know——it was like he was possessed or something, like, call-the-exorcist wrong. His eyes got all red, and he——he . . ." Maitland looked down. "You wouldn't believe me."

Richard sat back in the straight-backed chair, eyes half-closed, and said, "The guard bit your friend in the throat and drank his blood."

"Um . . ." Maitland seemed surprised. "Yeah. Just like that. And then he, uh . . ."

"Broke his neck."

"Yeah."

"Same thing happened to Lavelle, right?"

"Yeah. One of those bank people, the teller I guess, she was . . . like the guard. Y'know, wrong. And then the girl—"

"The one you hit."

"Yeah, that one. She said I was going to die, and she laughed. I was gonna shoot her, but the guard, the one that had Joe's blood all over him, he . . . he grabbed me from behind and threw me across the room. I landed on Lavelle." Maitland hid his face in shaking hands. "I thought I was next."

There was a knock on the door. Richard nodded his permission, and the vampire cop stationed next to it turned the knob. In walked Richard's sister, Monica Morrell.

Richard tried hard not to react, but his heart kick-started to a much faster beat, and fury pounded hot in his temples. She looked awful— and he knew how much that meant to her. She'd been treated at the hospital, but she'd never forgive them for letting her out in public with bloody, matted hair and an unflattering bandage over the whack in her skull. Her skin was pale, and there were dark circles under her eyes. No makeup. The blouse was designer, and it was destroyed—ripped and stained.

One of her arms was in a sling.

Richard kept his seat, kept his expression blank, and said, "Monica, is this the man who hurt you?"

Monica came around to Richard's side of the table, close enough to touch. Not that they touched. "Yeah," she said. "That's the son of a—"

"See? She's okay. You're okay, right, lady?" Maitland interrupted her, almost manic in his desire to get her on his side.

Monica hissed like a cat, and her eyes burned with pure fury. Richard reached out and put a hand on her uninjured wrist—just a light hold, nothing that would set her off. He knew his sister well enough to know how much force he could get away with.

"You're going to die," Monica said. "Just like your friends. Sucker."

"Take her outside," Richard said to the vampire cop. "I'll talk to her later. Put her in my office."

Once Monica was gone, the air seemed still and far too warm. Maitland felt it, too, and kept wiping sweat from his forehead.

"Look," he blurted. "I screwed up, okay? But it wasn't my idea. I was just . . . It was Joe. Joe said it would be an easy score, and look what happened—Joe's dead. Lavelle's dead. You want to lock me up, fine. Just . . . don't lock me up here. Not in this town, okay? There's something wrong here. I want to go back to Dallas. Hell, send me to Huntsville, anywhere but here, okay?"

Richard shrugged. "Your lawyer is here," he said. "I think you'd better talk to him before you say anything else."

"But . . . I don't want a lawyer! Look, I just want to confess. Send me off to prison, please, just not—"

Richard stood up. He leaned over the desk, hands flat on the warm surface, and stared right into Maitland's face. "You hurt my sister," he said. "And that blows your one chance for ever leaving this town alive."

Maitland's mouth opened, and he tried to speak, but nothing came out. Richard pushed back, walked out of the interrogation room, and joined Oliver on the other side of the glass. The vampire was standing silently, arms folded, watching Maitland through the one-way window. His eyes were glowing a very faint red in the darkness.

"Does he really have a lawyer?" Oliver asked.

Idle curiosity, Richard thought. It wouldn't matter a hill of beans to him.

"Sure. Jessie Pottsdam."

Oliver laughed, and Richard saw the flash of fangs in the dim light. "You really should never be underestimated, my boy," he said. "One day, you're going to make this town a very fine mayor."

Richard, still expressionless, stared through the glass at Maitland.

The two cops had followed him out, and now Jessie Pottsdam was going into the room, looking every inch the lawyer he was. Crisp black suit, white shirt, carefully knotted red tie. Expensive shoes and leather briefcase.

Jessie smiled down at his client, and his eyes glowed bright red.

Maitland screamed. Oliver reached over and switched off the speaker. "I don't believe we need to observe the rest," he said. "Justice is swift."

Richard watched anyway, sickness twisting at his stomach. *It has to be done.* The man was a liar; he would have killed everyone in that bank, including Monica.

It's justice.

It didn't really feel that way.

DEAD MAN STALKING

This story was first published in the BenBella Books anthology *Immortal*, edited by none other than P. C. Cast, so if you want to read some other killer YA vampire tales, go in search of it! You won't be disappointed.

I decided to do an action-oriented story from Shane's point of view. There was a running joke at the time that I should throw some zombies into Morganville, and while I didn't succumb to the temptation in the books, I veered into it here . . . in a way. We get to visit some great Morganville locations, fight some zombies, and find out where Michael has disappeared to—and what Shane's father has been doing just beyond the town's borders that might change everything.

This story is set sometime after Michael's transformation to full vampire, but not long after; Shane's still getting used to the idea that his best not-a-vamp friend has switched sides. There's a little bromance, and a lot of Frank Collins.

I *might* have been thinking just a little bit about the iconic *Buffy the Vampire Slayer* episode "The Zeppo" . . . but only in the undead football player sense. And yes, I quoted the eighties movie *Buckaroo Banzai*. Guilty as charged.

L iving in West Texas is sort of like living in hell, but without the favorable climate and charming people. Living in Morganville, Texas, is all that and a take-out bag of worse. I should know. My name is Shane Collins, and I was born here, left here, came back here—none of which I had much choice about.

So, for you fortunate ones who've never set foot in this place, here's the walking tour of Morganville: It's home to a couple of thousand folks who breathe, and some crazy-ass number of people who don't. Vampires. Can't live with 'em, and in Morganville, you definitely can't live without 'em, because they run the town. Other than that, Morganville's a normal, dusty collection of buildings—the kind the oil boom of the sixties and seventies rolled by without dropping a dime in the banks. The university in the center of town acts like its own little city, complete with walls and gates.

Oh, and there's a secluded, tightly guarded vampire section of town, too. I've been there, in chains. It's nice, if you're not looking forward to a horrible public execution.

I used to want to see this town burned to the ground, and then I had one of those things—what are they called, epiphanies? My epiphany was that one day I woke up and realized that if I lost Morganville and everybody in it . . . I'd have nothing at all. Everything I still cared about was here. Love it or hate it.

Epiphanies suck.

I was having another one of them on this particular day. I was sitting at a table inside Marjo's Diner, watching a dead man walk by the windows outside. Seeing dead men wasn't exactly unusual in Morganville; hell, one of my best friends is dead now, and he still gripes at me about doing the dishes. But there's vampire-dead, which Michael is, and then there's dead-dead, which was Jerome Fielder.

Except Jerome, dead or not, was walking by the window outside Marjo's.

"Order up," Marjo snapped, and slung my plate at me like a ground ball to third base; I stopped it from slamming into the wall by putting up my hand as a backstop. The bun of my hamburger slid over and onto the table—mustard side up, for a change.

"There goes your tip," I said. Marjo, already heading off to the next victim, flipped me off.

"Like you'd ever leave one, you cheap-ass punk."

I returned the gesture. "Don't you need to get to your second job?"

That made her pause, just for a second. "What second job?"

"I don't know, grief counselor? You being so sensitive and all."

That earned me another bird, ruder than the first one. Marjo had known me since I was a baby puking up formula. She didn't like me any better now than she had then, but that wasn't personal. Marjo didn't like anybody. Yeah, go figure on her entering the service industry.

"Hey," I said, and leaned over to look at her retreating bubble butt. "Did you just see who walked by outside?"

She turned to glare at me, round tray clutched in sharp red talons. "Screw you, Collins—I'm running a business here. I don't have time to stare out windows. You want something else or not?"

"Yeah. Ketchup."

"Go squeeze a tomato." She hustled off to wait another table—or not, as the mood took her.

I put veggies on my burger, still watching the parking lot outside the window. There were exactly six cars out there; one of them was my housemate Eve's, which I'd borrowed. The gigantic thing was really less a car than an ocean liner, and some days I called it the *Queen Mary*, and some days I called it *Titanic*, depending on how it was running. It stood out. Most of the other vehicles in the lot were crappy, sun-faded pickups and decrepit, half-wrecked sedans.

There was no sign of Jerome, or any other definitely dead guy, walking around out there now. I had one of those moments, those *Did I really see that?* moments, but I'm not the delusional type. I had zero reason to imagine the guy. I didn't even like him, and he'd been dead for at least a year, maybe longer. Killed in a car wreck at the edge of town, which was code for shot while trying to escape, or the nearest Morganville equivalent. Maybe he'd pissed off his vampire Protector. Who knew?

Also, who cared? Zombies, vampires, whatever. When you live in Morganville, you learn to roll with the supernatural punches.

I bit into the burger and chewed. This was why I came to Marjo's—not the spectacular service, but the best hamburgers I'd ever eaten. Tender, juicy, spicy. Fresh, crisp lettuce and juicy tomato, a little red onion. The only thing missing was . . .

"Here's your damn ketchup," Marjo said, and slid the bottle toward me like a bartender in an old Western saloon. I fielded it and saluted with it, but she was already moving on.

As I drizzled red on my burger, I continued to stare out the window. Jerome. That was a puzzle. Not enough to make me stop eating lunch, though.

Which shows you just how weird life in Morganville is, generally.

I was prepared to forget all about Jerome, postlunch, because not even Marjo's sour attitude could undo the endorphin high of her burger, and besides, I had to get home. It was five o'clock. The bottling plant was letting out, and pretty soon the diner would be crowded with adults tired from a hard day's labor, and not many of them liked me any better than Marjo did. Most of them were older than me; at eighteen, I was starting to get the *Get a job, you punk* stares. I like a good ass-kicking, but the Good Book is right: it's better to give than to receive.

I was unlocking the door to Eve's car when I saw a reflection behind me on the window glass, blocking the blazing westerly sun. It was smeared and indistinct, but in the ripples I made out some of the features.

Jerome Fielder. What do you know, I really had seen him.

I had exactly enough time to think, *Dude, say something witty,* before Jerome grabbed a handful of my hair and rammed me forehead-first into hot metal and glass. My knees went rubbery, and there was a weird high-pitched whine in my ears. The world went white, then pulsed red, then faded into darkness when he slammed me down again.

Why me? I had time to wonder, as it all went away.

I woke up sometime later, riding in the backseat of Eve's car and dripping blood all over the upholstery. *Oh, crap, she's gonna kill me for that,* I thought, which was maybe not the biggest problem I had. My wrists were tied behind my back, and Jerome had done some work on my ankles, too. The bonds were so tight I'd lost feeling in both hands and feet, except for a slow, cold throb. I had a gash in my forehead, somewhere near the hairline, I thought, and probably some kind of concussion thing, because I felt sick and dizzy.

Jerome was driving Eve's car, and I saw him watching me in the rearview mirror as we rattled along. Wherever we were, it was a rough road, and I bounced like a rag doll as the big tank of a car charged over bumps.

"Hey," I said. "So. Dead much, Jerome?"

He didn't say anything. That might have been because he liked me about as much as Marjo, but I didn't think so; he didn't look exactly right. Jerome had been a big guy, back in high school—big in the broad-shouldered sense. He'd been a gym worshipper, a football player, and the winner of the biggest-neck contest hands down.

Even though he still had all the muscles, it was like the air had been let out of them and now they were ropy and strangely stringy. His face had hollows, and his skin looked old and grainy.

Yep: dead guy. Zombified, which would have been a real mind-freak anywhere but Morganville; even in Morganville, though, it was weird. Vampires? Sure. Zombies? Not so you'd notice.

Jerome decided it was time to prove he still had a working voice box. "Not dead," he said. Just two words, and it didn't exactly prove his case because it sounded hollow and rusty. If I'd had to imagine a dead guy's voice, that would have been it.

"Great," I said. "Good for you. So, this car theft thing is new as a career move, right? And the kidnapping? How's that going for you?"

"Shut up."

He was absolutely right—I needed to do that. I was talking because, hey, dead guy driving. It made me just a bit uncomfortable. "Eve's going to hunt you down and dismember you if you ding the car. Remember Eve?"

"Bitch," Jerome said, which meant he did remember. Of course he did. Jerome had been the president of the Jock Club and Eve had been the founder and nearly the only member of the Order of the Goth, Morganville Edition. Those two groups never got along, especially in the hothouse world of high school.

"Remind me to wash your mouth with soap later," I said, and shut my eyes as a particularly brutal bump bounced my head around. Red flashed through my brain, and I thought about things like aneurysms, and death. "Not nice to talk about people behind their backs."

"Go screw yourself."

"Hey, three words! You go, boy. Next thing you know, you'll be up to real sentences. . . . Where are we going?"

Jerome's eyes glared at me in the mirror some more. The car smelled like dirt, and something else. Something rotten. Skanky homeless unwashed clothes brewed in a vat of old meat.

I tried not to think about it, because between the smell and the lurching of the car and my aching head, well, you know. Luckily, I didn't have to not-think-about-it for long, because Jerome made a few turns and then hit the brakes with a little too much force.

I rolled off the bench seat and into the spacious legroom, and, ow. "Ow," I said, to make it official. "You learn that in Dead Guy Driver's Ed?"

"Shut up."

"You know, I think being dead might have actually given you a bigger vocabulary. You ought to think of suggesting that to the U. Put in an extension course or something."

The car shifted as Jerome got out of the front seat, and then the back door opened as he reached in to grab me under the arms and haul. Dead he might be; skanky, definitely. But still: strong.

Jerome dumped me on the caliche white road, which was graded and graveled, but not recently, and walked off around the hood of the car. I squirmed and looked around. There was an old house about twenty feet away—the end of the pale road—and it looked weathered and defeated and sagging. Could have been a hundred years old, or five without maintenance. Hard to tell. Two stories, old-fashioned and square. Had one of those wraparound porches people used to build to catch the cool breezes, although cool out here was relative.

I didn't recognize the place, which was a weird feeling. I'd grown up in Morganville, and I knew every nook and hiding place—survival skills necessary to making it to adulthood. That meant I wasn't in Morganville proper anymore. I knew there were some farmhouses outside the town limits, but those who lived in them didn't come to town much, and nobody left the city without express vampire permission, unless they were desperate or looking for an easy suicide. So I had no idea who lived here. If anyone but Jerome did, these days.

Maybe he'd eaten all the former residents' brains, and I was his version of takeout. Yeah, that was comforting.

I worked on the ropes, but zombie or not, Jerome tied a damn good knot and my numbed fingers weren't exactly up to the task.

It had been quitting time at the plants when I'd gone out to the parking lot and ended up roadkill, but now the big western sun was brushing the edge of the dusty horizon. Sunset was coming, in bands of color layered on top of one another, from red straight up to indigo. I squirmed and tried to dislocate an elbow in order to get to my front pocket, where my cell phone waited patiently for me to text 911. No luck, and I ran out of time anyway.

Jerome came back around the car, grabbed me by the collar of my T-shirt, and pulled. I grunted and kicked and struggled like a fish on the line, but all that accomplished was to leave a wider drag path in the dirt. I couldn't see where we were going. The backs of Jerome's fingers felt chilly and dry against my sweaty neck.

Bumpity-bump-bump up a set of steps that felt splinter-sharp even through my shirt, and the sunset got sliced off by a slanting dark roof. The porch was flatter, but no less uncomfortably splintered. I tried struggling again, this time really putting everything into it, but Jerome dropped me and smacked the back of my head into the wood floor. More red and white flashes, like my own personal emergency signal. When I blinked them away, I was being dragged across a threshold, into the dark.

Shit.

I wasn't up for bravado anymore. I was seriously scared, and I wanted out. My heart was pounding, and I was thinking of a thousand horrible ways I could die here in this stinking, hot, closed-up room. The carpet underneath my back felt stiff and moldy. What furniture there was looked abandoned and dusty, at least the stuff that wasn't in pieces.

Weirdly, there was the sound of a television coming from upstairs. Local news. The vampires' official mouthpieces were reporting safe little stories, world events, nothing too controversial. Talk about morphine for the masses.

The sound clicked off, and Jerome let go of me. I flopped over onto my side, then my face, and inchwormed my way up to my knees while trying not to get a mouthful of dusty carpet. I heard a dry rattle from behind me.

Jerome was laughing.

"Laugh while you can, monkey boy," I muttered, and spat dust. Not likely he'd ever seen *Buckaroo Banzai*, but it was worth a shot.

Footsteps creaked on the stairs from the second floor. I reoriented myself, because I wanted to be looking at whatever evil bastard was coming to the afternoon matinee of my probably gruesome death. . . .

Oh. Oh, dammit.

"Hello, son," my dad, Frank Collins, said. "Sorry about this, but I knew you wouldn't just come on your own."

The ropes came off, once I promised to be a good boy and not rabbit for the car the second I had the chance. My father looked about the same as I'd expected, which meant not good but strong. He'd started out a random pathetic alcoholic; after my sister had died—accident or murder, you take your pick—he'd gone off the deep end. So had my mom. So had I, for that matter.

Sometime in there, my dad had changed from random pathetic drunk to mean, badass, vampire-hunting drunk. The vampire-hating component of that had been building up for years, and it had exploded like an ancient batch of TNT when my mother died—by suicide, maybe. I didn't believe it, and neither did my dad. The vampires had been behind it, like they were behind every terrible thing that had ever happened in our lives.

That was what I used to believe, anyway. And what Dad still did.

I could smell the whiskey rising up off him like the bad-meat smell off Jerome, who was kicked back in a chair in the corner, reading a book. Funny. Jerome hadn't been much of a reader when he'd been alive.

I sat obligingly on the ancient, dusty couch, mainly because my feet were too numb to stand, and I was trying to work circulation back into my fingers. Dad and I didn't hug. Instead, he paced, raising dust motes that glimmered in the few shafts of light that fought their way through smudged windows.

"You look like crap," Dad said, pausing to stare at me. I resisted the urge, like Marjo, to give him a one-fingered salute, because he'd only beat the crap out of me for it. Seeing him gave me a black, sick feeling in the pit of my stomach. I wanted to love him. I wanted to hit him. I didn't know what I wanted, except that I wanted this whole thing to just go away.

"Gee, thanks, Dad," I said, and deliberately slumped back on the couch, giving him all the teen attitude I could. "I missed you, too. I see you brought all your friends with you. Oh, wait."

The last time my dad had rolled into Morganville, he'd done it in a literal kind of way—on a motorcycle, with a bunch of badass motorcycle buddies. No sign of them this time. I wondered when they'd finally told him to shove it, and how hard.

Dad didn't answer. He kept staring at me. He was wearing a leather jacket with lots of zippers, faded blue jeans, sturdy boots. Not too different from what I was wearing, minus the jacket, because only a stupid jerk would be in leather in this heat. Looking at you, Dad.

"Shane," he said. "You knew I'd come back for you."

"Yeah, that's really sweet. The last time I saw you, you were trying to blow my ass up along with a whole building full of vampires, remember? What's my middle name, Collateral Damage?" He'd have done it, too. I knew my dad too well to think anything else. "You also left me to burn alive in a cage, Dad. So excuse me if I'm not getting all misty-eyed while the music swells."

His expression—worn into a hard leather mask by wind and sun—didn't change. "It's a war, Shane. We talked about this."

"Funny thing, I don't remember you saying, 'If you get caught by the vampires, I'll leave you to burn, dumbass.' But maybe I'm just not remembering all the details of your clever plan." Feeling was coming back into my fingers and toes. Not fun. It felt like I'd dipped them in battery acid and then rolled them in lye. "I can get over that. But you had to go and drag my friends into it."

That was what I hated the most. Sure, he'd screwed me over—more than once, actually. But he was right—we'd kind of agreed that one us might have to bite it for the cause, back when I believed in his cause.

We hadn't agreed about innocent people, especially my friends, getting thrown on the pile of bodies.

"Your friends, right," Dad said, with about a bottle's worth of cheap whiskey emphasis. "A half vampire, a wannabe morbid freak, and—oh, you mean that girl, don't you? The little skinny one. She melted the brains right out of your head, didn't she? I warned you about that."

Claire. He didn't even remember her name. I closed my eyes for a second, and there she was, smiling up at me with those clear, trusting eyes. She might be small, but she had a kind of strength my dad wouldn't ever understand. She was the first really pure thing that I'd ever known, and I wasn't about to let him take her away. She was waiting for me right now, back at the Glass House, probably studying and chewing a pencil. Or arguing with Eve. Or . . . wondering where the hell I was.

I had to get out of this. I had to get back to Claire.

Painful or not, my feet were functional again. I tested them by standing up. In the corner, Dead Jerome put aside his book. It was a battered, water-stained copy of *The Wonderful Wizard of Oz*. Who did he think he was? The Cowardly Lion? The Scarecrow? Hell, maybe he thought he was Dorothy.

"Just like I thought, this is all about the girl. You probably think you're some knight in shining armor come to save her." Dad's smile was sharp enough to cut diamonds. "You know how she sees you? A big, dumb idiot she can put on a leash. Her own pet pit bull. Your innocent little schoolgirl, she's wearing the Founder's symbol now. She's working for the vampires. I sure as hell hope she's like a porn star in the sack for you to be betraying your own like this."

This time, I didn't need a knock on the head to see red. I felt my chin going down, my lungs filling, but I held on to my temper. Somehow.

He was trying to make me charge him.

"I love her, Dad," I said. "Don't."

"Love, yeah, right. You don't know the meaning of the word, Shane. She's working for the leeches. She's helping them regain control of Morganville. She has to go, and you know it."

"Over my dead body."

In the corner, Jerome laughed that scratchy, raspy laugh that made me want to tear out his voice box once and for all. "Could be arranged," he croaked.

"Shut up," my dad snapped without taking his eyes off me. "Shane, listen to me. I've found the answer."

"Wait—let me guess—forty-two?" No use. Dad wasn't anywhere near cool enough to be a Douglas Adams fan. "I don't care what you've found, Dad, and I'm not listening to you anymore. I'm going home. You want to have your pet dead guy stop me?"

His eyes fixed on my wrist, where I was wearing a bracelet. Not one of those things that would have identified me as vamp property—a hospital bracelet, white plastic with a big red cross on it.

"You wounded?" Not, of course, was I sick. I was just another foot soldier, to Dad. You were either wounded or malingering.

"Whatever. I'm better," I said.

It seemed, for just a second, that he softened. Maybe nobody but me would have noticed. Maybe I imagined it, too. "Where were you hurt, boy?"

I shrugged and pointed to my abs, slightly off to one side. The scar still ached and felt hot. "Knife."

He frowned. "How long ago?"

"Long enough." The bracelet would be coming off in the next week. My grace period was nearly over.

He looked into my eyes, and for a second, just a second, I let myself believe he was genuinely concerned.

Sucker.

He always had been able to catch me off guard, no matter how carefully I watched him, and I didn't even see the punch coming until it was too late. It was hard, delivered with surgical precision, and it doubled me over and sent me stumbling back to flop onto the couch again. *Breathe,* I told my muscles. My solar plexus told me to stuff it, and my insides throbbed, screaming in pain and terror. I heard myself making hard, gasping noises, and hated myself for it. Next time. Next time I hit the bastard first.

I knew better, though.

Dad grabbed me by the hair and yanked my head back. He pointed my face in Jerome's direction. "I'm sorry, boy, but I need you to listen right now. You see him? I brought him back, right out of the grave. I can bring them all back, as many as I need. They'll fight for me, Shane, and they won't quit. It's time. We can take this town back, and we can finally end this nightmare."

My frozen muscles finally unclenched, and I pulled in a whooping, hoarse gasp of air. Dad let go of my hair and stepped away.

He'd always known when to back off, too.

"Your definition of . . . the end of the nightmare . . . is a little different . . . from mine," I wheezed. "Mine doesn't include zombies." I swallowed and tried to slow my heart rate. "How'd you do it, Dad? How the hell is he standing here?"

He brushed that aside. Of course. "I'm trying to explain to you that it's time to quit talking about the war, and time to start fighting it. We can win. We can destroy all of them." He paused, and the glow in his eyes was the next best thing to the look of a fanatic with a bomb strapped to his chest. "I need you, son. We can do it together."

That part, he really meant. It was sick and twisted, but he did need me.

And I needed to use that. "First, tell me how you do it," I said. "I need to know what I'm signing up for."

"Later." Dad clapped me on the shoulder. "When you're convinced this is necessary, maybe. For now, all you need to know is that it's possible. I've done it. Jerome's proof."

"No, Dad. Tell me how. Either I'm in it or I'm not. No more secrets."

Nothing I was saying was going to register to him as a lie, because I wasn't lying. I was saying what he wanted to hear. First rule of growing up with an abusive father: you cope; you bargain; you learn how to avoid getting hit.

And my father wasn't bright enough to know I'd figured it out.

Still, some instinct warned him; he looked at me with narrowed eyes, a frown wrinkling his forehead. "I'll tell you," he said. "But you need to show me you can be trusted first."

"Fine. Tell me what you need." That translated into *Tell me who you need me to beat up.* As long as I was willing to do that, he'd believe me.

I was hoping it would be Jerome.

"Of everybody who died in the last couple of years, who was the strongest?"

I blinked, not sure it was a trick question. "Jerome?"

"Besides Jerome."

"I guess—probably Tommy Barnes." Tommy was no teenager; he'd been in his thirties when he'd kicked it, and he'd been a big, mean, tough dude even the other big, mean, tough dudes had given a wide berth. He'd died in a bar fight, I'd heard. Knifed from behind. He'd have snapped the neck off anybody who'd tried it to his face.

"Big Tom? Yeah, he'd do." Dad nodded thoughtfully. "All right, then. We're bringing him back."

The last person on earth I'd want to bring back from the grave would be Big Tommy Barnes. He'd been crazy-badass alive. I could only imagine death wouldn't have improved his temper.

But I nodded. "Show me."

Dad took off his leather jacket, and then stripped off his shirt. In contrast to the sun-weathered skin of his arms, face, and neck, his chest was fish-belly white, and it was covered with tattoos. I remembered some of them, but not all the ink was old.

He'd recently had our family portrait tattooed over his heart.

I forgot to breathe for a second, staring at it. Yeah, it was crude, but those were the lines of Mom's face, and Alyssa's. I didn't realize, until I saw them, that I'd nearly forgotten how they looked.

Dad looked down at the tat. "I needed to remind myself," he said.

My throat was so dry that it clicked when I swallowed. "Yeah." My own face was there, frozen in indigo blue at the age of maybe sixteen. I looked thinner, and even in tattoo form I looked more hopeful. More sure.

Dad held out his right arm, and I realized that there was more new ink.

And this stuff was moving.

I took a step back. There were dense, strange symbols on his arm, all in standard tattoo ink, but there was nothing standard about what the tats were doing—namely, they were revolving slowly like a DNA helix up and down the axis of his arm, under the skin. "Christ, Dad—"

"Had it done in Mexico," he said. "There was an old priest there— he knew things from the Aztecs. They had a way to bring back the dead, so long as they hadn't been gone for more than two years, and were in decent condition otherwise. They used them as ceremonial warriors." Dad flexed his arm, and the tattoos flexed with him. "This is part of what does it."

I felt sick and cold now. This had moved way past what I knew. I wished wildly that I could show this to Claire; she'd probably be fascinated, full of theories and research.

She'd know what to do about it.

I swallowed hard and said, "And the other part?"

"That's where you come in," Dad said. He pulled his T-shirt on again, hiding the portrait of our family. "I need you to prove you're up for this, Shane. Can you do that?"

I gulped air and finally, convulsively nodded. *Play for time,* I was telling myself. *Play for time; think of something you can do.* Short of chopping off my own father's arm, though . . .

"This way," Dad said. He went to the back of the room. There was a door there, and he'd added a new, sturdy lock to it, which he opened with a key from his jacket.

Jerome gave me that creepy laugh again, and I felt my skin shiver into gooseflesh.

"Right. This might be a shock," Dad said. "But trust me, it's for a good cause."

He swung open the door and flipped on a harsh overhead light.

It was a windowless cell, and inside, chained to the floor with thick silver-plated links, was a vampire.

Not just any vampire. Oh no, that would have been too easy for my father.

It was Michael Glass, my best friend.

Michael looked—white. Paler than pale. I'd never seen him look like that. There were burns on his arms, big raised welts where the silver was touching, and there were cuts. He was leaking slow trickles of blood on the floor.

His eyes were usually blue, but now they were red, bright red. Scary monster red, like nothing human.

But it was still my best friend's voice whispering, "Help."

I couldn't answer him. I backed up and slammed the door.

Jerome was laughing again, so I turned around, picked up a chair, and smashed him in the face with it. I could have hit him with a powder puff, for all the good it did. He grabbed the chair, broke the thick wood with a snap of his hands, and threw it back at me. I stumbled, and would have gone down except for the handy placement of a wall.

"Stop. Don't touch my son," my father said. Jerome froze like he'd run into a brick wall, hands working like he still wanted to rip out my throat.

I turned on my dad and snarled, "That's my friend!"

"No, that's a vampire," he said. "The youngest one. The weakest one. The one most of them won't come running to rescue."

I wanted to scream. I wanted to punch somebody. I felt pressure building up inside, and my hands were shaking. "What the hell are you doing to him?"

I didn't know who he was, this guy in the leather jacket looking at me. He looked like a tired, middle-aged biker, with his straggly graying hair, his sallow, seamed face, his scars and tats. Only his eyes seemed like they belonged to my dad, and even then, only for a second.

"It's a vampire," he said. "It's not your friend, Shane. You need to be real clear about that—your friend is dead, just like Jerome here, and you can't let that get in the way of what needs to be done. When we go to war, we get them all. All. No exceptions."

Michael had played at our house. My dad had tossed a ball around with him and pushed his swing and served him cake at birthday parties.

And my dad didn't care about any of that anymore.

"How?" My jaw felt tight. I was grinding my teeth, and my hands were shaking. "How did you do this? What are you doing to him?"

"I'm bleeding it and storing the blood, just like they do us humans," Dad said. "It's a two-part spell—the tattoo, and the blood of a vampire. It's just a creature, Shane. Remember that."

Michael wasn't a creature. Not just a creature, anyway; neither was what Dad had pulled out of Jerome's grave, for that matter. Jerome wasn't just a mindless killing machine. Mindless killing machines didn't fill their spare time with the adventures of Dorothy and Toto. They didn't even know they had spare time. I could see it in Jerome's wide, yellowed eyes now. The pain. The terror. The anger.

"Do you want to be here?" I asked him, straight out.

For just that second, Jerome looked like a boy. A scared, angry, hurt little boy. "No," he said. "Hurts."

I wasn't going to let this happen. Not to Michael, oh, hell no. And not even to Jerome.

"Don't you go all soft on me, Shane. I've done what needed doing," he said. "Same as always. You used to be weak. I thought you'd manned up."

Once, that would have made me try to prove it by fighting something. Jerome, maybe. Or him.

I turned and looked at him and said, "I really would be weak if I fell for that tired bullshit, Dad." I raised my hands, closed them into fists, and then opened them again and let them fall. "I don't need to prove anything to you. Not anymore."

I walked out the front door, out to the dust-filmed black car. I popped the trunk and took out a crowbar.

Dad watched me from the door, blocking my way back into the house. "What the hell are you doing?"

"Stopping you."

He threw a punch as I walked up the steps toward him. This time, I saw it coming, saw it telegraphed clearly in his face before the impulse ever reached his fist.

I stepped out of the way, grabbed his arm, and shoved him face-first into the wall. "Don't." I held him there, pinned like a bug on a board, until I felt his muscles stop fighting me. The rest of him never would. "We're done, Dad. Over. This is over. Don't make me hurt you, because, God, I really want to."

I should have known he wouldn't just give up.

The second I let him go, he twisted, jammed an elbow into my abused stomach, and forced me backward. I knew his moves by now, and sidestepped an attempt to hook my feet out from under me.

"Jerome!" Dad yelled. "Stop my—"

The end of that sentence was going to be *son*, and I couldn't let him put Jerome back in the game or this was over before it started.

So I punched my father full in the face. Hard. With all the rage and resentment that I'd stored up over the years, and all the anguish, and all the fear. The shock rattled every bone in my body, and my whole hand sent up a red flare of distress. My knuckles split open.

Dad hit the floor, eyes rolling back in his head. I stood there for a second, feeling oddly cold and empty, and saw his eyelids flutter.

He wouldn't be out for long.

I moved quickly across the room, past Jerome, who was still frozen in place, and opened the door to the cell. "Michael?" I crouched down across from him, and my friend shook gold hair back from his white face and stared at me with eerie, hungry eyes.

I held up my wrist, showing him the bracelet. "Promise me, man. I get you out of here, no biting. I love you, but no."

Michael laughed hoarsely. "Love you, too, bro. Get me the hell out of here."

I set to work with the crowbar, pulling up floorboards and gouging the eyebolts out for each set of chains. I'd been right; my dad was too smart to make chains out of solid silver. Too soft, too easy to break. These were silver-plated—good enough to do the job on Michael, if not one of the older vamps.

I only had to pull up the first two; Michael's vampire strength took care of yanking the others from the floor.

Michael's eyes flared red when I leaned closer, trying to help him up, and before I knew what was happening, he'd wrapped a hand around my throat and slammed me down, on my back, on the floor. I felt the sting of sharp nails in my skin, and saw his eyes fixed on the cut on my head.

"No biting," I said again, faintly. "Right?"

"Right," Michael said, from somewhere out beyond Mars. His eyes were glowing like storm lanterns, and I could feel every muscle in his body trembling. "Better get that cut looked at. Looks bad."

He let me up, and moved with about half his usual vampire speed to the door. Dad might not let Jerome have at me, but he wasn't going to hold back with Michael, and Michael was—at best—half his normal strength right now. Not exactly a fair fight.

"Michael," I said, and put my back against the wall next to him. "We go together, straight to the window. You get out—don't wait for me. The sun should be down far enough that you can make it to the car." I gathered up a handful of silver chain and wrapped it around my hand. "Don't even think about arguing right now."

He sent me an *Are you kidding?* look, and nodded.

We moved fast, and together. I got in Jerome's way and delivered a punch straight from the shoulder right between his teeth, reinforced with silver-plated metal.

I intended only to knock him back, but Jerome howled and stumbled, hands up to ward me off. It was like years fell away, and all of a sudden we were back in junior high again—him the most popular bully in school, me finally getting enough size and muscle to stand up to him. Jerome had made that same girly gesture the first time I'd hit back.

It threw me off.

A crossbow bolt fired from the far corner of the living room hissed right over my head and slammed to a vibrating stop in the wooden wall. "Stop!" Dad ordered hoarsely. He was on his knees, but he was up and very, very angry. He was also reloading, and the next shot wouldn't be a warning.

"Get out!" I screamed at Michael, and if he was thinking about staging a reenactment of the gunfight at the O.K. Corral, he finally saw sense. He jumped through the nearest window in a hail of glass and hit the ground running. I'd been right: the sun was down, or close enough that it wouldn't hurt him too badly.

He made it to the car, opened the driver's side door, and slid inside. I heard the roar as the engine started. "Shane!" he yelled. "Come on!"

"In a second," I yelled back. I stared at my father, and the moving tattoo. He had the crossbow aimed right at my chest. I twirled the crowbar in one hand, the silver chain in the other. "So," I said, watching my father. "Your move, Dad. What now? You want me to do a cage match with Dead Jerome? Would that make you happy?"

My dad was staring not at me but at Dead Jerome, who was cowering in the corner. I'd hurt him, or the silver had; half his face was burned and rotting, and he was weeping in slow, retching sobs.

I knew the look Dad was giving him. I'd seen it on my father's face more times than I could count. Disappointment.

"My son," Dad said in disgust. "You ruin everything."

"I guess Jerome's more your son than I am," I said. I walked toward the front door. I wasn't going to give my father the satisfaction of making me run. I knew he had the crossbow in his hands, and I knew it was loaded.

I knew he was sighting on my back.

I heard the trigger release, and the ripped-silk hiss of wood traveling through air. I didn't have time to be afraid, only—like my dad—bitterly disappointed.

The crossbow bolt didn't hit me. Didn't even miss me.

When I turned, at the door, I saw that he'd put the crossbow bolt, tipped with silver, through Jerome's skull. Jerome slid silently down to the floor. Dead. Finally, mercifully dead.

The Wonderful Wizard of Oz fell facedown next to his hand.

"Son," my dad said, and put the crossbow aside. "Please, don't go. I need you. I really do."

I shook my head.

"This thing—it'll only last another few days," he said. "The tattoo. It's already fading. I don't have time for this, Shane. It has to be now."

"Then I guess you're out of luck."

He snapped the crossbow up again.

I ducked to the right, into the parlor, jumped the wreckage of a couch, and landed on the cracked, curling floor of the old kitchen. It smelled foul and chemical in here, and I spotted a fish tank on the counter, filled with cloudy liquid. Next to it was a car battery.

DIY silver plating equipment, for the chains.

There was also a 1950s-era round-shouldered fridge, rattling and humming.

I opened it.

Dad had stored Michael's blood in bottles, old dirty milk bottles likely scavenged from the trash heap in the corner. I grabbed all five bottles and threw them one at a time out the window, aiming for a big upthrusting rock next to a tree.

Smash. Smash. Smash. Smash . . .

"Stop," Dad spat. In my peripheral vision I saw him standing there, aiming his reloaded crossbow at me. "I'll kill you, Shane. I swear I will."

"Yeah? Lucky you've already got me tattooed on your chest, then, with the rest of the dead family." I pulled back for the throw.

"I could bring back your mother," Dad blurted. "Maybe even your sister. Don't."

Oh, God. Sick black swam across my vision for a second.

"You throw that bottle," he whispered, "and you're killing their last chance to live."

I remembered Jerome—his sagging muscles, his grainy skin, the panic and fear in his eyes.

Do you want to be here?

No. Hurts.

I threw the last bottle of Michael's blood and watched it sail straight and true, to shatter in a red spray against the rock.

I thought he'd kill me. Maybe he thought he'd kill me, too. I waited, but he didn't pull the trigger.

"I'm fighting for humanity," he said. His last, best argument. It had always won me over before.

I turned and looked him full in the face. "I think you already lost yours."

I walked out past him, and he didn't stop me.

Michael drove like a maniac, raising contrails of caliche dust about a mile high as we sped back to the main highway. He kept asking me how I was doing. I didn't answer him, just looked out at the gorgeous sunset, and the lonely, broken house fading in the distance.

We blasted past the Morganville city limits sign, and one of the ever-lurking police cars cut us off. Michael slowed, stopped, and turned off the engine. A rattle of desert wind shook the car.

"Shane."

"Yeah."

"He's dangerous."

"I know that."

"I can't just let this go. Did you see—"

"I saw," I said. "I know." *But he's still my father*, some small, frightened kid inside me wailed. *He's all I have.*

"Then what do you want me to say?" Michael's eyes had faded back to blue now, but he was still white as a ghost, blue-white, scary-white. I'd spilled all his blood out there on the ground. The burns on his hands and wrists made my stomach clench.

"Tell them the truth," I said. If the Morganville vampires got to my dad before he could get the hell out, he'd die horribly, and God knew, he probably deserved it. "But give him five minutes, Michael. Just five."

Michael stared at me, and I couldn't tell what was in his mind at all. I'd known him most of my life, but in that long moment, he was just as much of a stranger as my father had been.

A uniformed Morganville cop tapped on the driver's side window.

Michael rolled it down. The cop hadn't been prepared to find a vampire driving, and I could see him amending the harsh words he'd been about to deliver.

"Going a little fast, sir," he finally said. "Something wrong?"

Michael looked at the burns on his wrists, the bloodless slices on his arms. "Yeah," he said. "I need an ambulance."

And then he slumped forward, over the steering wheel. The cop let out a squawk of alarm and got on his radio. I reached out to ease Michael back. His eyes were shut, but as I stared at him, he murmured, "You wanted five minutes."

"I wasn't looking for a Best Supporting Actor award!" I muttered back.

Michael did his best impression of Vampire in a Coma for about five minutes, and then came to and assured the cop and arriving ambulance attendants he was okay.

Then he told them about my dad.

They found Jerome, still and evermore dead, with a silver-tipped arrow through his head. They found a copy of *The Wonderful Wizard of Oz* next to him.

There was no sign of Frank Collins.

Later that night—around midnight—Michael and I sat outside on the steps of our house. I had a bottle of most illegal beer; he was guzzling his sixth bottle of blood, which I pretended not to notice. He had his arm around Eve, who had been pelting us both with questions all night in a nonstop machine-gun patter; she'd finally run down, and leaned against Michael with sleepy contentment.

Well, she hadn't quite run down. "Hey," she said, and looked up at Michael with big, dark-rimmed eyes. "Seriously. You can bring back dead guys with vampire juice? That is so wrong."

Michael almost spat out the blood he was swallowing. "Vampire juice? Damn, Eve. Thanks for your concern."

She lost her smile. "If I didn't laugh, I'd scream."

He hugged her. "I know. But it's over."

Next to me, Claire had been quiet all night. She wasn't drinking—not that we'd have let her, at sixteen—and she wasn't saying much, either. She also wasn't looking at me. She was staring out at the Morganville night.

"He's coming back," she finally said. "Your dad's not going to give it up, is he?"

I exchanged a look with Michael. "No," I said. "Probably not. But it'll be a while before he gets his act together again. He expected to have me to help him kick off his war, and like he said, his time was running out. He'll need a brand-new plan."

Claire sighed and linked her arm through mine. "He'll find one."

"He'll have to do it without me." I kissed the soft, warm top of her hair.

"I'm glad," she said. "You deserve better."

"News flash," I said. "I've got better. Right here."

Michael and I clinked glasses, and toasted our survival.

However long it lasted.

LUNCH DATE

☾

I rarely wrote stories from Claire's point of view, mainly because she's the main character in the books, so it seemed redundant to have her take the lead in the shorts, too. But I did enjoy it from time to time, such as in this short story (free on the Web site) that just gives us a taste of the romance building between Claire and Shane. This is set in that late-romance period somewhere around *Feast of Fools* when things are hot . . . but not yet reaching the boil that they would in *Carpe Corpus.*

One of Shane's many terrible jobs is featured, which is always fun for me. Poor Shane. Poor bosses.

L unch was always an iffy proposition at the Glass House. Some days all of Claire's housemates were in; most days nobody was. Some days, there was food in the fridge. Most days, not. Claire had made a fine art out of scrounging up crackers and cans of soup. Her favorite was cream of tomato. Yum.

She was slurping up her soup, alone as usual, when she heard a thump from upstairs. Odd. She knew for a fact that Eve was at her job on campus, and Michael was off teaching guitar lessons. Shane . . . Well, she never knew for sure where Shane would be, but she'd looked for him before making lunch and there hadn't been any sign of him.

Not another visitor through the portal. Honestly, having one of those mystic doorways in the house was getting to be a royal pain. "Grand Central Station," Claire said, then sighed and gulped down the rest of her lunch before dumping the bowl in the sink and heading upstairs. The house was a comfortable mess, but it was slowly creeping toward the *Oh my God, who lives here?* kind of mess, so she'd have to get on everybody's case to do a little picking up. Just to show she wasn't immune, she picked up a stack of books she'd left on the dining table and carried them upstairs with her.

Once she'd dumped the books on top of—well, all the other books she'd been meaning to find a shelf for, Claire grabbed the miniature baseball bat Shane had bought her—aluminum, but electroplated in silver. Good for vampire-whacking, should the need come up. It was surprisingly heavy.

The thump came again. Not, as she would have thought, from Amelie's private room upstairs, or from the attic.

It was coming from Shane's room.

Claire took a firm grip on the bat, and flung open the door. "Freeze!" she yelled. Stress made her voice sound too high, like the squeak of a little girl on helium. Embarrassing. And not intimidating.

There was a half-naked man standing in the middle of Shane's room.

Oh.

Shane, in his underwear, tried to get into his jeans so fast he staggered and tipped over onto the bed. "Hey!" he protested. "What is it with girls busting in on me when I'm getting dressed? Out!"

Claire couldn't help it—she burst out laughing. It was ridiculously funny, the way he was rolling around on the bed trying to wiggle into those jeans, and also—well, yeah. Hot.

She lowered the bat and turned her back. "Sorry. I heard noises. I thought—wait. Girls, plural? Somebody else busts in on you besides me?"

She heard the bed creak, clothes rustling, and he said, "Well, yeah. Eve kind of walked into the bathroom once while I was in the shower. Which is when I got rid of the clear shower curtain and got the dark one."

"Eve's seen you naked?"

"Um—behind a sheet of plastic with water all over it? There's no safe answer to this, is there?"

Claire turned, unasked. He was just pulling on his old gray T-shirt. "Not really," she said. "Anyway. Why are you changing clothes?"

Shane tried for an innocent look, which didn't go well on his face. "Got bored?"

"Shane, I've never seen you change clothes in the middle of the day, ever. You were gone when I got up, and you just got back. What happened?" Because she was thinking the worst. She supposed that the worst in places other than Morganville probably had something to do with him seeing another girl. Here, she was assuming he'd gotten blood all over himself.

He thought about lying to her; she could see it flash across his face. But then he sighed, shook his head, and opened up the closet door. He took out a plastic bag and held it out toward her.

Inside were his Nike cross-trainers, a pair of worn blue jeans, and a shirt that might have once been red, a hundred washings ago. And they stank. Claire pulled back with a choking sound. "What the heck is that?"

"You know how I said I was going to get a job?"

"Yeah?" She found she was holding a hand over her nose and mouth, and her eyes were watering. "What does that have to do with anything?"

"I got a job . . . at the city dump. Raking garbage. Hey, did you know there are seagulls out there? Kind of far from the ocean. Anyway, they have showers in the locker room, so I took one before I left, but I forgot to bring a change of clothes." He tied off the bag and pitched it into his closet. "Also, I've decided to look for a better job."

"Good idea." He looked so completely annoyed at the idea of another job search that Claire couldn't stop the giggles that boiled up.

"You laughing at me?"

"Kinda, yeah."

Shane lunged for her. She squealed and dodged, and made a mock swing at him with the bat. He caught it easily in one hand, and pressed her up against the wall.

Oh.

"How do I smell?" he asked her, very low in his throat. She felt her whole body tingle in response.

"Good." That didn't quite cover it. She took a deeper breath. "Great, actually."

"Glad to hear it." He brushed her lips with his, very lightly. "Let's be sure. Take a nice, deep breath."

She took one. "Maybe a little hint of old diapers."

"Hey!"

She kissed him. He certainly didn't taste like old diapers. He tasted like cinnamon and spices, and his lips were soft and hot under hers, and she forgot all about the bat in her hand until it hit the floor with a heavy thunk.

"You taste like tomato soup," Shane murmured. "I came home to get lunch, you know."

"Well, get your own."

"Maybe later."

Claire took in another deep breath—he really didn't smell at all like old diapers—and pushed him back. She was nowhere near strong enough to do that, if he didn't want to be pushed, but he obligingly stepped back. "Now," she said. "And you're doing your own laundry, stinky. Don't even think about asking."

"Would I do that?" He did the puppy-dog thing with his eyes.

He totally would.

And she knew, as they went downstairs, that she really didn't mind that at all.

It must be love, she thought, and handed him a can of tomato soup.

ALL HALLOWS

What goes together better than Morganville and Halloween? Morganville, Halloween, Eve, Shane, a sinister stranger at a rave . . . This short story was originally printed in the *Eternal Kiss* anthology, edited by Trisha Telep, and I was delighted to write it. Michael's a vampire, and Eve's desperately in love and trying to make that Romeo-Juliet thing work.

Miranda delivers another of her eerie prophecies, which hasn't quite come true . . . yet? *But who knows?* More Morganville stories yet to be told.

I always wanted to put the Glass House gang in full costume; we got to do a little with *Feast of Fools*, but I wanted to see what they'd wear if they picked the costumes themselves. Not sure it's a total surprise, but it was a pleasure.

Dating the undead is a bad idea. Everybody in Morganville knows that—everybody breathing, that is.

Everybody but me, apparently. Eve Rosser, dater of the undead, dumb-ass breaker of rules. Yeah, I'm a rebel. But rebel or not, I froze, because that was what you did when a vampire looked at you with those scary red eyes, even if the vampire was your hunky best guy, Michael Glass.

None of them were fluffy bunnies at the best of times, but you really did not want to cross them when they were angry. It was like the Incredible Hulk, times infinity. And even though my sweet Michael had been a vampire for only a few months, that just made it worse; he hadn't had time to get used to his impulses, and I wasn't sure, right at this second, that he could control himself.

Controlling myself seemed like the least I could do.

"Hey," I breathed, and slowly stepped back from him. I spread my hands out in obvious surrender. "Michael, stop."

He closed those awful, scary eyes and went very, very still. Eyes closed, he looked much more like the Michael I'd grown up around— dreamy, with curling blond hair in a surfer's careless mop around a face that made girls swoon, tall and not just when he was onstage playing guitar.

He still looked human. That made it worse, somehow.

I tried to decide whether I ought to totally back off or stand my ground. I stayed, mainly because, well, I've been in love with him since I was fourteen. Too late to run now, just because of a little thing like him being technically, you know, dead.

I wasn't in any real danger, or at least, that was what I told myself. After all, I was standing in the warm, cozy living room of the Glass House, and my housemates were around, and Michael wasn't a monster.

Technically, maybe yes, but actually, no.

When Michael's eyes opened again, they were back to clear, quiet blue, just the way I loved them. He took another breath and scrubbed his face with both hands, like he was trying to wash something off. "I scared you," he said. "Sorry. Caught me by surprise."

I nodded, not really ready to talk again quite yet. When he held out his hand, though, I put mine in it. I was the one in black nail polish, rice-powder makeup, and dyed-black hair; what with my fondness for Goth style, you'd think that I'd have been the one to end up with the fangs. Michael was way too gorgeous, too human to end up with immortality on his hands.

It hurt, sometimes. Both ways.

"You need to eat something," I said, in that careful tone I found myself using when speaking about sucking blood. "There's some O neg in the fridge. I could warm it up."

He looked mortally embarrassed. "I don't want you to do that. I'll go to the clinic," he said. "Eve? I'm really sorry. Really. I didn't think I'd need anything for another day or so."

I could tell that he was sorry. The light in his eyes was pure, hot love, and if there was any hunger complicating all that, he kept it well hidden deep inside.

"Hey, it's like being diabetic, right? Something goes wrong with your blood, you gotta take care of that," I said. "It's not a problem. We can all wait until you get back."

He was already shaking his head. "No," he said. "I want you guys to go on to the party. I'll meet you there."

I touched his face gently, then kissed him. His lips were cool, cooler than most people's, but they warmed up under mine. Ectothermic, according to Claire, the resident scholarly nerd girl in our screwed-up little frat house of four. One vampire, one Goth, one nerd, and one wannabe vampire slayer. Yeah. Screwed up, ain't it? Especially living in Morganville, where the relationship between humans and vampires is sometimes like that between deer and deer hunters. Even when vampires weren't hunting us, they had that look, like they were wondering when open season might start.

Not Michael, though.

Not usually, anyway.

He kissed the back of my hand. "Save the first dance for me?" he asked.

"Like I could say no, when you give me that *oh baby* look, you dog."

He smiled, and that was a pure Michael smile, the kind that laid girls out in the aisles when he played. "I can't look at you any other way," he said. "It's my Eve look."

I batted at his arm, which had zero effect. "Get moving, before you see my mean look."

"Scary."

"You bet it is. Go on."

He kissed me again, gently, and whispered, "I'm sorry," one more time before he was suddenly gone.

He left me standing in the middle of the living room of the Glass House, aka Screwed-Up Frat Central, wearing a skintight, pleather catsuit, cat ears, and a whip. Not to mention some killer stiletto heels. Add the mask, and I made a superhot Catwoman.

The costume might have been the reason for Michael's shiny eyes and out-of-control hunger, actually. I'd intended to push his buttons for Halloween. . . . I just hadn't intended to push them quite that hard.

I heard footsteps on the stairs, and Shane's voice drifted down ahead of him. "Hey, have you seen my meat cleaver—holy shit!"

I turned. Shane was standing frozen on the stairs, wearing a lab coat smeared with fake blood and some gruesome-looking Leatherface mask, which he quickly stripped off in order to stare at me without any latex barriers. What I was wearing suddenly felt like way too little.

"Eve—jeez. Warn a guy, would you?" He shook his head, jammed the mask back on, and came down the rest of the stairs. "That was not my fault."

"The leering? I think yes," I said. And secretly, that was pretty cool, although, hey, it was Shane. Not like he was exactly the guy I was hoping to impress. "Totally your fault."

"It's a guy thing. We have reactions to women in tight leather with whips. It's sort of involuntary." He looked around. "Where's Michael?"

"He had to go," I said. "He'll meet us at the party." No reason to tell Shane, who still couldn't quite get over his anti-vamp upbringing, that Michael had gone to snag himself a bag of fresh plasma so he wouldn't be snacking on mine. "Seriously, do I look okay?"

"No," Shane said, and flopped down on the sofa. He put his heavy boots up on the coffee table, sending a paper plate with the dried remains of a chili dog close to the edge. I rescued it, gave him a dirty look, and dumped the plate in his lap. "Hey!"

"It's your chili dog. Clean it up."

"It's your turn to clean."

"The house. Not your trash, which you can walk your Leather-faced ass into the kitchen to throw away."

He batted his long, silky eyelashes at me. "Didn't I tell you that you look great?" Shane said. "You do."

"Oh, please. Chili dog. Trash. Now."

"Seriously. Michael's going to have to watch himself around you. And watch out for every other guy in the room, too."

"That's the idea," I said. "Hey, it was this or the Naughty Nurse costume."

Shane sent me a miserable look. "Do you have to say things like that?"

"Guy reaction?"

"You think?" He held out his plate to me, looking so pitiful that I couldn't help but take it. "You just destroyed my ability to get off this couch."

I had to laugh. Shane teased, but he wasn't serious; the two of us never were, and never would be. He was thinking of someone else, and so was I.

I saw the change in his expression when we heard the sound of footsteps upstairs. He looked up and there was a kind of utter focus in him that made me smile. *Boy, you have got it bad*, I thought, but I was kind enough not to point it out. Yet.

Claire practically floated down the stairs. Our fourth roommate— our booky little nerd, small and fragile enough that she always looked like you could break her in half with a harsh word—looked even more ethereal than usual.

She was dressed as a fairy—a long, pale pink dress in layers of sheer stuff, glitter on her face, her hair streaked with blue and pink and green. Soft pink fairy wings. It made her look both younger than she really was, which was still a year younger than me and Shane, and yet also older.

But maybe that was just the look in her eyes that got more mature with every day she spent in Morganville, working shoulder to shoulder with the vampires.

Claire paused on the steps, looking at Shane. Her mouth fell open, ruining her ethereal fairy look. "Seriously? Leatherface? Oh God."

"You were expecting something out of *Pride and Prejudice?*" Shane shrugged and held up the mask. "You don't know me very well."

Claire shook her head, and then caught sight of my own outfit. Her eyes widened. "Holy—"

I sighed. "Don't say it. Shane already did."

"That's really—wow. Tight."

"Catsuit," I said. "Kind of the textbook definition of tight."

"Well, you look . . . wow. I'd never have the guts." Claire wafted over in her layers of pink to sit next to Shane, who gallantly moved his Leatherface mask to make room.

"You look fabulous," he told her, and kissed her. "Oh, crap, now I've got glitter, right? Leatherface does not do glitter. It's not manly." Claire and I both rolled our eyes, right on cue. "Right. Small price to pay for the privilege of kissing such a beautiful girl—what was I thinking? Sorry."

Shane was an idiot, but he was a good idiot, mostly. He'd never hurt Claire intentionally; I knew that. I wondered, though, if she knew that, from the look of concern that flickered across her expression. "Do you like the costume? Really?"

He stopped goofing and stared right into her eyes. "I love it," he said, and he wasn't talking about the costume. "You look beautiful."

That erased some of the worry from her eyes. "It's not too, you know, little girl or something?"

I realized that she was comparing what she was wearing with my Catwoman suit. "It's Halloween, not 'Hello, Slut,'" I said. "You look fantastic, CB. Hot, but not obvious. Classy." I, on the other hand, was starting to think I looked a little too obvious, and not at all classy. "So, are we going, or are we going to waste our amazing fabulousness on this B-movie fool?"

"Hey, Leatherface is an American classic!" Shane objected. Claire and I both smacked him. Then she took the right arm; I took the left. "No fair double-teaming! Don't make me hit you with my rubber cleaver!"

"Speaking of double-teaming, until Michael catches up to us, you're both our dates," I said. "Congratulations. You can be Hefner tonight if you go throw on a bathrobe and slippers."

He stared at me, blinked, and then tossed the Leatherface mask over his shoulder as he bounced to his feet. "Awesome. Back in a minute," he said, and dashed upstairs. Claire and I exchanged a look of perfect understanding.

"They're just so easy." I sighed.

It was the one-year anniversary of the Worst Halloween Ever, aka the Dead Girls' Dance party at Epsilon Epsilon Kappa's frat house on campus . . . and they were throwing it again, although this time it was a rave at one of the abandoned warehouses near the center of town. We'd gotten special invitations. I'd wanted to skip it at first, but Michael and Shane had both assured me that this time things were under control. The vampires of Morganville were working security, which meant that the human frat boys wouldn't be slipping anything into anybody's drinks, and any would-be incoming trouble would be stopped cold, probably at the door.

Not that the EEK boys knew who (or what) they were hiring, of course. Students either didn't know, didn't want to know, or were in the know from the beginning, because they'd grown up in Morganville. I thought there were maybe six guys total in EEK who had insider knowledge, and none of them was stupid enough to talk.

Well, not too loudly. Unless the keg was open.

I parked my big, black sedan at the curb between a beat-up pickup and a sun-faded Pontiac with so many bumper stickers on it I couldn't tell what their actual causes were. Guns, looked like. And God. And maybe puppies.

"House rules," I said, and unlocked the doors. "Stay together. No wandering off. Shane, no fights."

"Aww," he said. "Not even one?"

"Are you kidding me? You've racked up enough medical frequent-flier miles to get a permanent bed in the emergency room. So no. Not even harsh words, unless somebody else throws the first punch."

He was happy about that last part. "No problem." Because somebody else always threw a punch in Shane's direction when trouble brewed. He had a rep, one that he'd worked hard to acquire, as a badass. He didn't look particularly badass tonight, wearing a moth-eaten old tapestry-patterned bathrobe fifty years out-of-date, old-man slippers, silk pajamas—which I know he must have found in a box in the attic—and a classic fifties pipe. Unlit, of course.

He made a surprisingly good Hefner, and as he offered us his elbows, I felt a rush of the giggles. Claire was blushing.

"I am such a stud," Shane said, and swept us into the rave.

As the resident dude, Shane was responsible for the acquisition of party favors, like glow-in-the-dark necklaces and drinks. Nonalco-holic drinks for Claire, of course, because I am a stern house mother even if I suck as a role model. One thing I had to watch out for was the other kind of party favors being passed around, stranger to stranger—white pills, mostly, although there was the light-'em-if-you-got-'em kind, too. I let people pass things to me, then dumped them in the trash. It wasn't because I was Miss Self-Restraint; it was more because I knew better than to trust most people in Morganville.

We'd had hard lessons about that last year. Especially Claire. This year, she was still polite, but fending off the weirdos with much more ease. Of course, having her own personal shaggy-haired Hefner at her side might have had something to do with that.

I started to worry about Michael. Usually, a side trip to the blood bank didn't take up more than thirty minutes, but by the time an hour had passed, he still wasn't in the house.

I went in search of a quiet corner to call him. My mistake was that I didn't tell Shane or Claire, who had their arms wrapped around each other and were dancing their hearts out. No, I struck out on my own.

Hear that sound? It's Eve Rosser and her backup band, the Spectacular Lapse of Judgment.

The warehouse was loud, tinny, and crowded; dark spaces were already filled with the make-out brigade. I kept going, down a narrow little hallway, until the noise was only a thud, not a roar, and took out my phone from its hiding place (yes, in my costume, and I'm not telling you where). I started to dial Michael's phone.

Something touched my shoulder. It felt like an ice-cold electric shock.

"Hey!" I yelped, and whirled around. There was a vampire facing me.

Not Michael.

My heart rate went from sixty to five hundred in two seconds flat, because I knew this guy, and he wasn't exactly Mr. Congeniality. "Mr. Ransom," I said, and carefully nodded. I knew him because he was one of Oliver's crew, but I'd rarely seen him, even at Common Grounds, the coffee shop where the vampires felt free to mingle with the humans according to strict ground rules. He avoided humans as much as possible, in fact.

"Eve," Mr. Ransom said. He was a tall, thin guy with straw-brittle hair and a kind of vague look in his eyes. Tonight, he was dressed in a black jacket, a black shirt, black pants, all straight out of the Goodwill box. Nothing quite fit him.

Mr. Ransom owned the funeral parlor, although he didn't work there. He was kind of a vampire hermit. He didn't get out much.

"Sorry, I'm on the phone," I said. I waved the phone for evidence, pressed dial, and listened. *Come on, come on . . .*

He didn't pick up.

"He will not answer," Mr. Ransom said. "Michael."

I quietly folded the phone and stared at him. "Why? What's happened?"

"He has been delayed."

"And you came all this way to tell me? Um, thanks. Message received." I decided to try to tough it out, and walked right past him.

He grabbed me again. I spun, meaning to smack him good (a superbad move on my part), and he caught my hand effortlessly in his. Now I was face-to-face with a vampire I hardly knew, with my hand restrained, and the noise from the rave had kicked up again to metal-melting levels, which meant screaming would get me nowhere but hoarse, and dead.

"Let me go," I said as calmly as I could. "Now, please."

He raised pale eyebrows, staring right into my eyes. His were dark, like puddles of oil, full of shine, but nothing else. It looked like he was searching for something to say. What he came up with was, "Do you want to become a vampire?"

"Do I—what? No! Hell no!" I yanked, but I couldn't break his grip. "And even if I did, it wouldn't be you doing it, Mr. Creepy!"

"Then do you wish Protection?" he asked, and reached into his jacket. He took out a bracelet, standard Morganville issue—a plain silver thing with a symbol engraved on the front of it. Mr. Ransom's symbol, I guessed, which would mark me as his property. If I took the bracelet, I'd be free from casual fanging by all the other bloodsuckers, but not from him, if he took a notion.

I made a throwing-up sound. "No. Let go, you ice-cold moron freak!"

He did let go. It surprised me so much that I scrambled backward, tottering on my high heels, and bounced into the wall behind me. *Great,* I thought. *The one time I don't wear vampire-killing accessories.* Maybe I could use the shoes? No, wait, that would mean bending over in the catsuit. Really not possible. I settled for sliding against the wall, heading for the safety of the crowds.

Ransom slowly sank down to a crouch, his back to the wall, and put his head in his hands. It was so surprising that I stopped moving away and just stared at him. He looked . . . sad. And dejected.

"Ah—" I wet my lips. "Are you okay?" What a stupid question! And why did I even care? I didn't. I couldn't care less about his bruised feelings.

But I wasn't leaving, either.

"Yes," he said. His voice was soft and muffled. "I apologize. This is . . . difficult. Moving among humans in this way. I thought you wished to be turned."

"Why?"

He raised his head and mutely indicated his face, then mine, which was made up very pale under my Catwoman mask. "You seem to be playing at being one of us."

"Okay, first, I'm Goth, not a vampire wannabe. Second, it's a fashion thing, okay? So, no. I don't. Ewwww." My pulse was slowing down some as I realized that maybe I'd read the situation all wrong after all. Mr. Ransom was a refreshing change from the vampires that tried to eat me first, talk later. "Why offer me Protection?" That was the equivalent of becoming part of a vampire's household. He would have to provide certain things, such as food and shelter, and in return, the human paid part of her income to him, like a tax. Also, at the blood bank, her donations would be earmarked for him.

In short: ugh. Not for me.

"You don't have a bracelet," he said. "I thought perhaps your Protector had died in the late unpleasantness. I was being polite. In my day—"

"Well, it isn't your day," I snapped. "And I'm not shopping for a vamp daddy, so just . . . leave me alone. Okay?"

"Okay," he said. He still looked dejected, like some shabby street person whose bottle of booze had run out.

I thought of something less uncomfortable to ask. At least, I thought it was. "You said Michael had been delayed," I said. "Where? At the blood bank?"

"Near there," Ransom said. "He was taken away."

I forgot all about Ransom and his weirdness. "Taken away where? How? Who took him?" I advanced on the vampire, and all of a sudden the leather catsuit didn't seem ridiculous at all. I was practically channeling the soul of a supervillain. "Hey! Answer me!"

Ransom looked up. "Five young men," he said. "Wearing the jackets with the snake."

Five guys wearing Morganville High letter jackets. Jocks, probably. "Did he want to go?" I asked. Michael had never been part of the jock crowd, even in high school. This was just odd.

"At first, they wanted me to go," Ransom said. "I didn't understand why. Michael told them he would go with them instead, and told me to tell you that he would be delayed." Ransom gave a heavy sigh. "That I have done." In about half a heartbeat, he went from a sad little man crouched against the wall to a tall, dangerous vampire standing up and facing me. Never underestimate a vampire's ability to change moods. "Now I will leave."

I worked it out a second too late to stop him from going. I guess five jocks had been hassling this sad, weird vampire, and he hadn't even realized what they were doing because, like he said, he wasn't out in the human world that much. He hadn't realized the danger he was in—he literally hadn't.

Michael definitely had. That was why he'd stepped in, sent Ransom to find me, and gone off without a fight.

Saving somebody, as usual. Although I wondered why he hadn't just flattened the creeps outright. He could have. Any vampire could.

"Wait, can you tell me where exactly—" But I was talking to the empty hall because Ransom had already beat it. Anyway, my words were just about lost in the thunder of a new tune spinning at the rave on the other side of the bricks.

I hurried out of the hallway, back to the rave, and found Shane and Claire still so into each other they might as well have been dancing at home. I dragged them out of the building, past impassive vampire bouncers, into the cool night air.

"Hey!" Shane protested, and settled his bathrobe more comfortably with a shake. "If you want to leave, all you have to do is say so! Respect the threads. Vintage."

"Michael may need help," I said, and I got their attention, immediately. "You want to come with?"

"I'm not exactly dressed for hand-to-hand," Shane said, "but what the hell. If I have to hit somebody, maybe they'll be too embarrassed to trade punches with Hugh Hefner—guy's got to be about a hundred years old or something."

I was more worried about Claire. Fairy wings and glitter weren't exactly going to intimidate anybody . . . but then again, Claire had other skills.

"You drive," I said to Shane, and tossed him the car keys. He fielded them with a blinding grin. "Don't get used to it, loser."

The grin faded just as quickly. "Where am I going?"

"Around the blood bank. Five Morganville High guys in letter jackets picked Michael up around there. I don't know why, or how, or why he went without a fight."

Shane's face went hard. "You think they lured him off?"

"I think Michael wants to help people. Just like his grandfather." Sam Glass had always put others ahead of his own safety, and I figured

Michael was walking the same path. "It may be nothing, and hell, Michael can handle five drunk jocks, but—"

"But not if they've got a plan," Claire finished. "If they know how to disable him, they could hurt him."

Neither of them asked why a bunch of teens would want to hurt somebody they hardly knew; it was in teen DNA, and we all knew it, deep down. On Halloween, a bunch of drunk assholes might think it was fun and exciting to hurt a vampire. And then, as they sobered up, they might imagine that they'd be better off killing him than leaving him to identify them later. The Morganville powers-that-be didn't look favorably on vampire bashing.

"Maybe they needed his help," Claire said, but she didn't sound convinced.

We got into the huge black sedan without another word, and Shane peeled rubber.

"What do you think?" I asked aloud as we started driving through the more unpleasant parts of Morganville. "Where should we start?"

"Depends on whether Michael's picking the place, or the jocks are," Shane said. His voice sounded low and harsh—Action Shane, not the one who arm-wrestled me for the remote control at home. "The jocks will go someplace they feel safe."

"Like?" Because I had no idea how jocks thought, in any sense.

Shane did. "Nobody at the football field this time of night. No games this evening." Because although Morganville paid lip service to other sports, as in most Texas towns, football was where it was at. To know Michael was with five guys in letter jackets meant football was surely involved, if not at the center of things. "I'd say stadium. Maybe the press box or the field house."

I nodded. Shane took that as permission to hit warp speed. The engine roared as we shot down quiet streets, past derelict houses and empty businesses. Not a fantastic part of town these days. At the end of the street, he took a left, then a right, and we saw the columned expanse of Morganville High School at the crest of a very small hill. To the left and below was the stadium. It wasn't much, not compared with professional arenas, but it was a respectable size for a small Texas town. The lights were all off.

Shane piloted the car into the parking lot and killed the headlights. There were a few cars parked here and there. Some had steamed-over windows—I knew what was going on in there. Kids. I wanted to run over, rap on the window, and take a cell phone picture, but that would have been rude.

There was a cluster of vehicles, mostly battered pickups, at one end of the lot. The windows were clear. Claire pointed wordlessly over my shoulder at them, and we all nodded.

"What's the plan?" Shane asked me. I looked at Claire, but she didn't seem to be Plan Girl tonight. Maybe it was the fairy glitter.

"I'm the one with the stealthy outfit," I said. "I'm going to go take a look. I'll keep my phone on. You guys listen in and come running if I get into it, okay?"

Shane raised eyebrows. "That's stealthy? That outfit?"

"In terms of being black, yes. Shut up."

"Whatever, Miss Kitty," he said. "Call me."

I dialed his number; he answered it and put it on speaker. I slipped out of the car, wondering how anybody could scramble over rooftops dressed like this.

Once I was in the shadows, I felt more at home. Nobody around that I could see, and as I did my best to creep along without being spotted, I felt more and more foolish. There was nobody here. I was skulking without any reason.

I heard voices. Male voices. They were coming from the field house, which contained the changing rooms for the teams, the gym, the showers, that kind of stuff. One of the windows was open to catch the cool night air. This was probably how they'd gotten into the building in the first place.

I sprinted—as much of a sprint as I could manage in the heels— across the open ground to the shadows on the side of the field house, and slid down the wall toward the window. "Shane," I whispered into the phone. "Shane, they're in the field house."

I heard a screech of tires in the parking lot, and retreated to look around the corner. On either side of my big black sedan, two pickup trucks had pulled in, parking so close that there was no way Shane or Claire could open the doors, much less get out. Another truck parked behind them.

They were trapped in the car.

"Shane?" I whispered into the phone. I could hear the drunk jocks high-fiving and *booyah*ing one another in the trucks from here. A couple rolled out of the back and began to jump around on the hood of my car, rocking it on its springs.

"Well, the good news is you drive a damn tank," he said, but I heard the tension in his voice.

"Can you get out of there?" I asked.

"Sure," he said, much more calmly than I would have. "But I think the longer we let them play on the bouncy castle, the fewer of these guys you've got to deal with on your end." He paused. "Bad news: I can't back you up in person if I do that."

I swallowed hard and went back to my original position on the side of the field house. "Stay put," I said. "I'll yell if I get in trouble. Rescue is more important than moral support."

If he answered, I didn't hear him, because just then a big, beefy guy rounded the corner of the field house carrying a case of beer. He dropped it with a noisy crash of glass at the sight of me.

Shane had been right. The costume was not stealthy.

"Look what I found prowling around," my jock captor announced, and shoved me into the doorway of the field house. My heels skidded on the tile floor, and I lost my balance and fell . . . into Michael's arms.

"Oh," I breathed, and for a second, even given the circumstances, being in his arms felt wonderful. He held me close, then pushed me away from him.

"What the hell are you doing here?" he asked.

"Saving you?"

"Awesome job so far."

"Fine, criticize . . . Hey!" Beefy Jock Guy, who'd dumped the case of empty beer bottles outside, had plucked the phone from my hand, peered at the screen, and shut it off.

He looked tempted to do the macho phone-breaky thing, so I snapped, "Don't even think about hurting my phone, you jackass." He shrugged and pitched it into the far corner of the room.

"She's cute," the jock said to Michael. "Bet she likes to party, right?"

I ignored him, and looked around to see what I'd gotten myself into. Not good. Mr. Ransom's assessment had been right. Big guys, all wearing Morganville jock jackets. The smallest of them was twice the size of Michael, and he wasn't exactly tiny.

I still couldn't figure out what Michael was doing here, though. He was just standing there, and he could have wiped the room with these guys, right? But he hadn't.

"What's going on?" I asked. Michael slowly shook his head. "Michael?"

"You need to go," he told me. "Please. This is something I need to do alone."

"What? Kick jock ass? Shane is going to be very disappointed."

Looking into Michael's eyes, I saw the red starting to surface. I blinked. "Did you, ah, snack?"

"No," he said. "I was on my way in when they tried to take Ransom off with them."

"And you just had to get in the middle of that."

Michael's eyes were turning an unsettling color, almost a purple, as the red swirled around. It was pretty. From a distance.

"Yes," he said. "I kind of did. See, they wanted Ransom to come bite somebody."

My own eyes widened. "Who?"

For answer, Michael turned, and I saw a frail young girl sitting on a bench at the back of the room, dressed in a cheap-looking Cleopatra costume. I recognized her after a long couple of seconds. "Miranda?" Miranda was sort of a friend, in that uncomfortable not-quite way. She was about ninety pounds of pure crazy, fragile as glass, and I knew from personal experience that sometimes she could see the future. Sometimes. Sometimes she was just plain nuts.

She'd been under Protection by a vampire named Charles, until recently. I didn't know for sure, but I strongly suspected that Charles had gotten more than just blood out of the kid. I was glad he was dead, and I hoped it had hurt. Miranda didn't need more screwed-up sprinkles on top of her utterly boned life.

"Mir?" I stepped back from Michael and walked over to her. She was very quiet, and unlike most other times I'd seen her, she wasn't bruised, or shaking, or otherwise in distress. "Hey. Remember me?"

She gave me an irritated look. "Of course. You're Eve." Wow. She sounded completely normal. That was new. "You're not supposed to be here." What, according to her visions?

"Well, I am here," I said. "What's going on?"

"They were supposed to find me a vampire," Miranda said, as if it were the most obvious thing in the world. I looked around at the jocks, an entire backfield of muscle, with blank curiosity.

"Why them?" And why, more important, would they be willing to do a favor for a kid like Miranda?

She knew what I was thinking. I saw it in the weird smile she flashed. "Because they owe me favors," she said. "I've been making them money."

Oh God, I could see it now. Morganville had a small, but thriving, betting underworld. What better to put your money on in a Texas town than football? The jocks had used Miranda's clairvoyant abilities to pick winners, they'd cleaned up, and now she was asking them to pay her price.

A vampire? That was her price? Even for Mir, that was just plain weird.

"Why Michael?" I asked, more slowly. Miranda frowned.

"I didn't ask for Michael," she said. "He just came. But it doesn't matter who it is. I just need to be turned."

I refused to repeat that because it would taste nasty in my mouth. "Mir. What are you talking about?"

"I need to be a vampire," she said, "and I want one of them to make it happen. Michael will do fine. I don't care who turns me. The important thing is that if I change, I'll be a princess."

I was wrong. She really was crazy.

For about fifty years in Morganville, none of the vampires had been able to create new ones—except Amelie, who'd turned Michael to save his life. Now . . . well. Things had changed, humans had more rights, and the rules weren't so clear anymore. Why did people want to be vampires? I didn't see the appeal.

Miranda obviously did. And she was going about it in a typically sideways Miranda-ish way. With my boyfriend.

I wheeled on Michael. "Why didn't you just say no?"

He glanced over at the football guys. The defensive line was between us and the door, kicked back with a new case of beer but still looking like they'd love the chance to do a little vamp hand-to-hand.

Idiots. He'd absolutely destroy them.

"I was trying to," he said. "She isn't listening. I didn't want to hurt anybody, and I couldn't walk away and leave her like this. She needs to understand that what she's asking . . . isn't possible."

"I know what I'm asking," Miranda said. "Everybody thinks I'm stupid because I'm just a kid, but I'm not. I need to be a vampire. Charles promised me I'd be one." That last line came out like the petulant cry of a first grader who'd had her crayons taken away. I was willing to bet her vampire Protector (in name only—more like vampire Predator) had promised her a lot of things to get what he wanted. It made me feel even more sick.

"Mir, you're what, fifteen? There are rules about this kind of thing. Michael can't do it, even if he wanted to. No vamps under the age of eighteen. Town rules. You know that."

Miranda's chin set into a stubborn square. She would have done well in Claire's fairy costume. Fairies, as Claire had explained to me in the car, weren't kindly little sprites at all. Right now, Miranda looked like a fey come straight from the old scary stories.

"I don't care," she said. "Somebody's going to do it. I'm going to make sure they do. My friends will make sure."

"Miranda, they can't make me do anything," Michael said, and it sounded like an old argument. "The only reason I haven't blown out of here already is because of you."

"Because I'm so screwed up?" Miranda's voice was dark and bitter. As she moved, I saw scars on her forearms, marching in railroad tracks up toward her elbow. She was a cutter. I wasn't surprised. "Because I'm so pathetic?"

"No, because you're a kid, and I'm not leaving you here. Not with them." Michael didn't even look at the jocks, but they got the point. I saw their beery good humor start to evaporate. Some set down bottles. "You think they're doing this because they like you, Mir? What do you think they want out of it?"

For a second, she looked honestly surprised, and then she slipped her armor back on. "They got what they wanted already," she said. "They got their money."

"Yeah, drunk, bored football types are always fair like that," I said. "So tell me, guys, was this going to be a party night? You and her?"

They didn't answer me. They weren't drunk enough to be quite that cold about it. One finally said, "She told us she'd make it worth our while if we got her a vampire."

"Well, she's fifteen. Her definition of worth your while is probably a whole lot different from yours, you asshole." Man, I was angry. Angry at Miranda, for getting herself and us into this. Angry at the boys. Angry at Michael, for not already walking away. Okay, I understood now why he hadn't. He'd already known he'd be throwing her to the wolves (and the bats) if he did.

I was angry at the world.

"We're leaving," I declared. I grabbed Miranda by a skinny, scabbed wrist and pulled her to her feet. Her Cleopatra headdress slipped sideways, and she slapped her other hand up to hold it in place even as she decided to pull back from me. I didn't let her. I had pounds and muscle on her, and I wasn't about to let her stay here and throw her own vamptastic pity party, complete with dangerous clowns.

Up to that point, Miranda had been all talk, but I saw the look that came across her face and settled in her eyes when I grabbed on to her. Blank, yet focused. I knew that expression. It meant she was Seeing—as in, seeing the future, or at least something the rest of us couldn't see.

The hair shivered on the nape of my neck under my Cat-woman cowl.

"It's too late," she said, in a numbed, dead sort of voice. I drew in my breath and looked at the door. "Oh dear."

The door slammed open, bowling over a couple of football play-ers along the way, and three vampires stood there. One of them was the vague Mr. Ransom.

Another was a particularly unpleasant bit of work named Mr. Vargas, who had the looks of one of those silent film stars and the temperament of a rabid weasel. He'd always been one of the dregs of vampire society. Oliver kept him around—I didn't know why—but Vargas was one of those you had to watch for, even if you were legally off the menu. He was known to bite first, pay the fine later.

The last one, though, was the one who really scared me. Mr. Pen-nywell. Pennywell had come to town with Amelie's father, the scary Mr. Bishop, and he'd stuck around. I knew he'd sworn all those prom-ises to Amelie, but I didn't believe for a second he really meant them. He was old. Really old. And he looked like some androgynous man-nequin, with no emotion to him at all.

Pennywell's cold eyes looked around, dismissed the jocks, and focused in on three things:

Miranda, Michael, and me.

"The boys are yours," he said to Ransom and Vargas.

Vargas's teeth flashed in a white grin. "I've got a better idea," he said, and stepped aside, out of the way. "Run, *mijos*. Run while you can."

The jocks weren't stupid. They knew the odds had shifted. They were severely in trouble. Not a one of them was willing to stand up for Miranda, or for us, and that didn't shock me at all. What shocked me was that they didn't take their beer with them when they broke for the door and stampeded out into the night.

Vargas watched them go, and counted it off. "Twenty yard line.

Thirty. Forty. Ah, they've reached midfield. Time for the opposing team to enter the game, I think."

He moved in a blur, gone. I resisted the urge to yell a warning to the football guys. It wouldn't do any good.

Pennywell said, "You, girl. I hear you want to be turned." He was looking at Miranda.

"No, she doesn't," I said, before my friend could say something idiotic. "Mir, let's get you home, okay?"

Faced with the alien chill that was Pennywell, even Miranda's great romantic love of dying had a moment of clarity. She gulped, and instead of pulling free from my grip, she put her hand in mine. "Okay," she said faintly. I wondered exactly what her vision had shown her. Nothing that she wanted to pursue, clearly. "Home's good."

"Not quite yet, I think," Pennywell said, and shut the door to the field house. "First, I think there is a tax to be paid. For my inconvenience, yes?"

"You can't feed on her," I said. "She's underage."

"And undernourished from the look of her. Not only that, I can smell the witch on her from here." He sniffed, long nose wrinkling, and his eyes sparked red. He focused on me. "You, however . . . you're of age. And fresh."

That drew a growl out of Michael. "Not happening."

Pennywell barely glanced his way. "A barking puppy. How charming. Don't make me kick you, puppy. I might break your teeth."

Michael wasn't one to be baited into an attack, not like Shane. He just got calmly in Pennywell's way, blocking the other vampire's access to Miranda and me.

Pennywell looked him over carefully, head to toe. "I'm not bending any of your precious rules," he said. "I won't bite the child. I won't even swive her."

Leaving aside what that meant (although I had a nasty suspicion), he wasn't exempting me from the whole biting thing. Or, come to think of it, from the other thing, either. His eyes had taken on an unpleasant red cast—worse than Michael's ever got. It was like looking into the surface of the sun.

Miranda's hand tightened on mine. "You really need to go," she whispered.

"No kidding."

"Back this way."

Miranda pulled me to the side of the room. There, behind a blind corner, was the open window through which I'd originally heard the boys partying.

Pennywell knew his chance was slipping away. He sidestepped and lunged, and Michael twisted and caught him in midair. They'd already turned over twice, ripping at each other, before they hit the ground and rolled. I looked back, breathless, terrified for Michael. He was young, and Pennywell was playing for keeps.

On our way to the window, Miranda ducked and picked up something in the shadows. My cell phone. I grabbed it and flipped it open, speed-dialing Shane's number.

"Yo," he said. I could hear the jocks pounding on the car. "I hope you're insured."

"Now would be a good time for rescue," I said.

"Well, I can either ask real nice if they'll move the cars, or jump the curb. Which do you want?"

"You're kidding. I've got about ten seconds to live."

He stopped playing. "Which way?"

"South side of the building. There's three of us. Shane—"

"Coming," Shane said, and hung up. I heard the sudden roar of an engine out in the parking lot, and the surprised drunken yells of the jocks as they tumbled off the hood of my car.

I began to shimmy out the window, but an iron grip closed around my left ankle, holding me in place. I looked back to see Mr. Ransom, eyes shining silver.

"I was trying to bring you help," he said. "Did I do wrong?"

"You know, now's not really the time—" He didn't take the hint. Of course. I heard the approaching growl of the car engine. Shane was driving over the grass, tires shredding it on the way. I could hear other engines starting up—the football jocks. I wondered if they had any clue that half their team was doing broken-field running against a vampire right now. I hoped they had a good second string ready to play the next game.

Mr. Ransom wanted an answer. I took a deep breath and forced myself to calm down. "Asking Pennywell probably wasn't your best idea ever," I said. "But, hey, good effort, okay? Now let go so I'm not the main course!"

"If you'd accepted my offer of Protection, you wouldn't have to worry," he pointed out, and turned his gaze on poor Miranda. Before he could blurt out his sales pitch to her—and quite possibly succeed— I backed out of the window, hustled her up, and neatly guided her out just as my big black sedan slid to a stop three feet away. The back door popped open, and Claire, fairy wings all aflutter, pulled Miranda inside. It was like a military operation, only with one hundred percent less camouflage.

Mr. Ransom looked wounded at my initiative, but he shrugged and let me go. "Michael!" I yelled. He was down, blood on his face. Pennywell had the upper hand, and as Mr. Ransom turned away, he lunged for me.

Michael grabbed the vampire's knees and held on like a bulldog as Pennywell tried to get to me.

"Stake me!" I yelled to Shane, who rolled down the window and tossed me an iron spike.

A silver-coated iron railroad spike, that was. Shane had electroplated it himself, using a fish tank, a car battery, and some chemicals. As weapons went, it was heavy-duty and multipurpose. As Mr. Pennywell ripped himself loose from Michael's grasp, he turned right into me. I smacked him upside the head with the blunt end of the silver spike.

Where the silver touched, he burned. Pennywell howled, rolled, and scrambled away from me as I reversed my hold on the spike so the sharper end faced him. I released the catch on my whip with my left hand and unrolled it with a snap of my wrist.

"Wanna try again?" I asked, and gave him a full-toothed smile. "Nobody touches up my boyfriend, you jerk. Or tries to bite me."

He did one of those scary openmouthed snarls, the kind that made him look all teeth and eyes. But I'd seen that movie. I glared right back. "Michael?" I asked. He rolled to his feet, wiping blood from his forehead with the sleeve of his shirt. Like me, he didn't take his eyes off Pennywell. "All in one piece?"

"Sure," he said, and cast a very quick glance at me. "Damn, Eve. Hot."

"What? The whip?"

"You."

I felt a bubble of joy burst inside. "Out the window, you silver-tongued devil," I told Michael. "Shane's wasting gas." He was. He was revving the engine, apparently trying to bring a sense of drama to the occasion.

Michael didn't *you first* me, mainly because I had a big silver stake and I obviously wasn't afraid to use it. He slipped past me, getting only a little handsy, and was out the window and dropping lightly on the grass in about two seconds flat.

Leaving me facing Pennywell. All of a sudden, the stake didn't seem all that intimidating.

Mr. Ransom wandered in between the two of us, as if he'd just forgotten we were there. "Leave," he told me. "Hurry."

I quickly tossed my whip through the window, grabbed the frame with my free hand, and swung out into the cool night air. Michael grabbed me by the waist and set me down, light as a feather, safe in the circle of his arms. I squeaked and made sure to keep the silver stake far away from him. It had hurt Pennywell, and it'd hurt Michael a whole lot worse.

"I'll take it," Shane said. He shoved the spike back under the driver's seat. "Well? Are you two just going to make out or what?"

Not that we weren't tempted, but Michael hustled me into the car, slammed the door, and Shane hit the gas. We fishtailed in the grass for a few seconds, spinning tires, and then he got traction and the big car zoomed forward in a long arc around the field house, heading back toward the parking lot. Oncoming jocks dodged out of the way.

Pennywell showed up in our headlights about five seconds later, and he didn't move.

"Don't stop!" Michael said, and Shane threw him a harassed look in the rearview.

"Yeah, not my first night in Morganville," he said. "No shit." He pressed the accelerator instead. Pennywell dodged aside at the last minute, a matador with a bull, and when I looked back, he was standing in the parking lot, watching us leave. I didn't blink, and I watched until he turned his back on us and went after someone else.

I didn't want to watch after that.

We'd gone only about halfway home when Michael said, raggedly, "Stop the car."

"Not happening," Shane said. We were still in a not-great part of town, all too frequently used by unsavory characters, including vamps.

Michael just opened the door and threatened to bail. That made Shane hit the brakes, and the car shuddered and skidded to a stop under a streetlight. Michael stumbled away and put his hands flat on the brick of a boarded-up building. I could see him shuddering.

"Michael, get in the car!" I called. "Come on, it's not far! You can make it!"

"Can't." He stepped back, and I realized his eyes were that same scary hell-red as Pennywell's. "Too hungry. I'm running out of time." And so were we, because Pennywell could easily catch up to us, if he knew we'd stopped.

"We really don't have time for this," Shane said. "Michael, I'll drop you at the blood bank. Get in."

He shook his head. "I'll walk."

Oh, the hell he would. Not like this.

I got out of the car and stepped up to him. "Can you stop?" I asked him. He blinked. "If I tell you to stop, will you stop?"

"Eve—"

"Don't even start with all the angst. You need it—I have it. I just need to know you can stop."

His fangs came out, flipping down like a snake's, and for a second, I was sure this was a really, really bad idea. Then he said, "Yes. I can stop."

"You'd better."

"I . . ." He didn't seem to know what to say. I was afraid he'd think of something, something good, and I'd chicken right out.

"Just do it," I whispered. "Before I change my mind, okay?"

Shane was saying something, and it sounded like he wasn't a fan of my solution, but we were all out of time, and anyway it was too late. Michael took my wrist and, with one slice of his fangs, opened the vein. It didn't hurt—well, not much—but it felt very weird at first. Then his lips closed softly over my skin, and I got the shivers all over, and it didn't feel weird at all. Not even the buzzing in my ears, or the waves of dizziness.

"Stop," I said, after I'd counted to twenty. And he did. Instantly. Without any question.

Michael covered the wound with his thumb and pressed. His eyes faded back to blue, normal and real and human. He licked his lips, making sure every spot of blood was gone, and then said, "It'll stop bleeding in about a minute." Then, in a totally different tone, "I can't believe you did that."

"Why?" I felt a little weak at the knees, and I wasn't at all sure it was due to a sudden drop in blood pressure. "Why wouldn't I? With you?"

He put his arms around me and kissed me. That was a whole different kind of hunger, one I understood way better. Michael backed me up against the car and kissed me like it was the last night on earth, like the sun and stars would burn down before he'd let me go.

The only thing that slowed us down was Shane saying, very clearly, "I am driving off and leaving you here, I swear to God. You're embarrassing me."

Michael pulled back just enough that our lips were touching, but not pressed together, and sighed. There was so much in that sound, all his longing and his fear and his need and his frustration. "Sorry," he said.

I smiled. "For what?"

He was still holding his thumb over the wound on my wrist. "This," he said, and pressed just a little harder before letting go. It didn't bleed.

I purred lightly, and nipped at his mouth. "I'm Catwoman," I reminded him. "And it's just a scratch."

Michael opened the car door for me, and handed me in like a lady. Like his lady.

He got in, shut the door, and slapped the back of Shane's seat. "Home, driver."

Shane sent him a one-fingered salute. Next to him, Claire gave me a completely non-ethereal grin and snuggled in close to him as he drove.

Miranda said, dreamily, "One of us is going to be a vampire."

"One of us already is," I pointed out. Michael put his arm around me.

"Oh," she said, and sighed. "Right."

Except that Miranda never forgot a thing like that.

"Hey," Michael said, and squeezed my shoulders lightly. "Tomorrow's tomorrow. Okay?"

"Tonight's tonight," I agreed. "And tonight's good for me."

MURDERED OUT

☾

One of the hard-to-find exclusive stories written specifically for the U.K. editions (which at the time were being published a month or two after the U.S. releases, meaning that die-hard fans rushed to buy internationally), it was offered as an extra to help the U.K. publisher convince fans there to wait for the local edition, and it seems to have worked!

I didn't give Shane his own car early on in the series for a variety of reasons, but mostly because it was fun for him to have to ask nicely for rides. The fact that he couldn't quite earn enough to buy his own said something about Shane's job-related experiences, too. But finally, at this particular point (after *Kiss of Death*, before *Bite Club*), Shane is ready to make the commitment.

I mostly love this story for the small-town details I got to put into it, and the introduction of Rad, the mechanic. Fun factoid: This story was inspired by my getting the rims on my car (a Smart car, which Shane would never drive, but Claire totally would) painted black. The shop salesperson said, "Oh, you mean you're murdering it out." I'd never heard the term before, and loved it.

Normal life in Morganville. As far as normal ever was, Shane Collins thought; nobody was overtly rioting, getting arrested, or killing anyone.

Not on this street, anyway.

Being out in the open around dark was not his favorite survival strategy, but even though the Morganville Multiplex Cinema (three whole screens) tried to cram as many morning and afternoon showings in as practical, it wasn't always possible to avoid getting out later than was healthy for a regular human in Morganville, Texas.

"There's a reason those twilight shows are cheaper than the others," he said to Claire Danvers, who was walking with her small hand in his large one, head down. Claire was thinking, but then, she was always thinking. It was part of what he loved about her. "I wish Eve would have come with us. At least then we'd have had wheels."

"We'll be all right," Claire said. She sounded confident about that. He wasn't, only because he was the guy, and therefore, by his logic, their survival on the way home sort of landed squarely on his shoulders. Claire was his girlfriend. That meant she was his to protect. He knew that if he said that out loud, she'd smack him, and mean it, but it was just how he felt about it.

And he was smart enough not to tell her.

"She and Michael were going out," Claire said. "To that restaurant she likes. And then I guess they were going to the show, so it doesn't make sense for her to see it twice in one day."

"Yeah," he agreed. "It wasn't that good. I mean, don't get me wrong—I am all about the exploding things. But there's a pretty fine line between awesome and explode-o-porn."

Claire laughed, a silvery little thing that made him want to stop, put his arms around her, and kiss the hell out of her, right here in front of Bernard's Best Resale Shoppe. He didn't, only because the sun was scraping the horizon, they had five blocks left to walk to get home to the Glass House, and anyway, kissing her would only make him want to kiss her even more.

Which would make them appetizers for the vampires already getting ready for their nightly strolls.

That was the thing about Morganville. Nice place to visit, but you wouldn't want to live here. And honestly, Shane couldn't exactly define why it was he did live here. He could have left, he supposed. He had, once, and come back to do a job for his father, Fearless Frank the Vampire Hunter. But now he stayed because . . . because at least in here he understood things. He knew the rules, even if the rules were crappy and the game of survival was rigged.

He stayed because there were people here he loved. Claire, for a start, and as much as he felt for her, that would have been enough right there. But then there was Eve Rosser, who was like his annoying/sweet Gothed-out sister. And there was Michael Glass, who was his best friend.

Had been, anyway, before he'd opened the door to the wrong vampire, and now—now it was complicated. Having a best friend with fangs had never been in Shane's life strategy.

One thing about strategy, boy, Fearless Frank had once told him, on one of his more sober days. *It never fails to go to hell once you're knee-deep in the fight.*

"Hey." Claire nudged him. He nudged her back. "You're walking a little too fast."

"What's long, your widdle short legs can't keep up?"

"Watch it. I am proportional."

He waggled his eyebrows. "Just the way I like it."

"Stop that." He loved seeing her blush like that, a creep of hot pink that bloomed from her cheeks and spread all the way down her throat, into the neck of her shirt.

"Stop what?"

"You know what!"

"What can I say? Explode-o-porn. It makes me crazy." He waggled his eyebrows again. She laughed and blushed at the same time. All right, that did it. Sunset or not, he couldn't not kiss her.

He reached down, put his arms around her, and pulled her close. As he bent his head, hers came up, lovely and sweet and beautiful, her dark eyes shining. Her lips shimmered in the slanting orange light, until his were on them.

And oh God, it was good. Good enough to make him forget Morganville altogether, for the space of a long, sweet, damp kiss. And several seconds after, before a streetlight clicked on overhead with a hiss of burning filament, and reminded him why making out on the corner was a very bad idea.

The streets were deserted, except for a few people hurrying by in cars. He and Claire were the only pedestrians. Even so, it wasn't that far to the house, and they had time. Barely.

Until Claire, hurrying to keep up with his long strides, tripped over a crack in the sidewalk and went down, hard. He bent down next to her as she quickly pushed herself back up, hands and knees, gave him a wide-eyed look of shame, and started to rise.

Her ankle folded up under her. "Ow!" she yelped in surprise, and looked down at it. "Ow ow ow!" She took her weight off it, leaning on his arm, and he helped her limp over to a battered old wrought-iron bench. It creaked as they sat down on it, and he immediately slid off to crouch down, take her ankle in both his hands, and carefully probe it. She flinched as he started to move it around, and her face went white, but she didn't scream, and he didn't feel anything broken.

Not that she couldn't have broken one of the smaller bones in her foot. Happened all the time. Nothing they could do about it, even at the hospital, but he thought this was probably a sprain. A bad one. He could already see the smooth matte surface of her slender ankle starting to swell up.

She took out her cell phone and dialed without him saying a word, but closed it up after a moment. "Eve's phone goes to voice mail."

"Try Michael's." She did, and shrugged helplessly when she didn't get an answer. They both knew what that meant—Michael and Eve were having private time, and there would be no rescue coming from that quarter. For once. "Taxi?" Even as he said it, Shane shook his head. "Never mind; he won't get out this close to dark."

They really didn't have time to debate it. What had been sort of theoretically dangerous before, when they were two healthy young people capable of running and fighting, had turned into a calculation. Claire, injured, was going to be irresistible bait. And not every vampire would check whether she had another vamp's Protection before digging in.

Amelie might be furious about it, later, but that wouldn't help Claire right now. And Shane didn't have any Protection at all, except the fact that he was tough to kill.

"Right," he said, and stood up. "No arguments, okay?" He didn't wait for agreement, because he knew he probably wouldn't get it. He reached down, picked her up, and settled her in his arms. She wasn't featherlight, but he'd carried heavier suitcases. And suitcases hardly ever put their arms around your neck, or let their head fall into the crook of your neck. All in all, the kind of burden he was happy to carry.

"You okay?" he asked her. He felt her nod, breath warm against his throat. "All right, you just sit back and enjoy the ride."

She laughed and snuggled closer. "You need a car," she said.

Didn't he just?

They made it home without incident, thankfully, although Shane was almost sure they'd been followed the last block. By that time it had been nearly full dark, and he'd felt stares on him from half a dozen dark spots.

He managed to balance Claire's weight, unlock the front door, and kick it open with a bang as he stepped across the threshold. There was a weird kind of sensation to it, every time, as the house itself recognized him. Welcomed him home.

It meant that no vampire would be lunging in after him, at least.

He didn't trust it, though. He slammed the door shut, jammed a dead bolt home with his elbow, and yelled, "Yo, heads up! Little help here!" Because his arms were about to fall off. He moved forward, trying not to bang Claire's injured ankle against the walls or the furniture, and by the time he'd emerged at the end of the hallway, Michael Glass was just hitting the floor at the bottom of the staircase. He was dressed, but there was something about it that looked like he'd done it on the way down. He took one look at Claire, cradled in Shane's arms, and drew in a deep breath.

"It's not like that," Shane said. "Nobody fanged her. She fell. It's her ankle."

"Couch," Michael said, and shifted aside his guitar, game controllers. "You carried her home? In the dark?"

"Not like you were answering your cell, asshat."

Michael looked up at him, then up at the stairs, where Eve was just pelting down them, a black dragon-printed robe belted around her. From the flash of legs, that was pretty much the extent of the outfit. "Yeah," he said. "Sorry."

The Guy Code ruled the moment, and all Shane could say to that was, "No problem," as he eased his girl down on the battered sofa cushions. She immediately squirmed up to a sitting position and pulled up the leg of her jeans.

Her ankle was swollen, all right. And starting to bruise.

"I'll get ice," Eve said, and ran off to the kitchen. She hesitated in the doorway to call back, "Claire? You need anything?"

"Better balance? Oh, and Angelina Jolie's lips?"

"Cute. Settle for aspirin and a Coke?"

Claire nodded. Eve disappeared through the swinging door.

"Thought you guys were going out to dinner," Shane said. He couldn't resist, really. And it was worth it to see Michael think about lying, because he was just bad at it.

"We were," Michael finally said, which was the truth. "And then we didn't." Also the truth. "We can still make the movie if we hurry."

"Don't," Claire said, and winced as she tried to move her ankle. "It's explode-o-porn."

"What's wrong with that?" Michael looked honestly baffled. Shane really couldn't blame him, and the resulting harassed look from Claire was pretty much fantastic.

Eve came back with a plastic bag full of ice and a couple of towels, and carefully packed it all around Claire's ankle before running back to retrieve the aspirin and Coke. The medical treatment completed, all that was left was to not comment on what Michael and Eve might have been doing to not answer their phones.

That was almost impossible, in Shane's view. Eve and Michael looked so obviously barely out of bed it was crazy. But there was the Guy Code, and then there was the Code of Housemates, which meant he couldn't really say much at all about that unless he wanted to get the hell mocked out of him in return.

So instead, he sighed and said, "I really need a car."

He kind of meant it, and kind of didn't, but over the next few days he found himself looking more and more at the cars for sale in Morganville. There was one car lot that sold a bunch of brands, but there was no way he could afford the shiny new ones anyway. So he ended up looking at the clunkers—the rusting, beat-up models that people wanted to unload cheap. He had a little money saved up, but not much, and after seeing three cars in a row that were barely running and yet still out of his budget, he just about gave up.

Until he came across the little sign in the window of Bernard's Best Resale, which said CAR FOR SALE, BEST OFFER. That was all. No number, no picture of the car, nothing. Which meant it probably was a dog, but he wasn't exactly rich with choices.

Besides, he could use a new shirt or something.

The bell rang as he entered, and the thrift-shop smell hit him immediately—mothballs, and dry paper. Fans turned overhead, stirring the smell and spreading it around, and there was nobody else in the place, except Miss Bernard, dozing off behind the counter. She came awake with a snort as he walked over to the men's shirt aisle, blinked behind her thick glasses, and patted her thin gray hair. "Collins, isn't it? Shane Collins?"

"Yes, ma'am," he said. The *ma'am* was automatic. Miss Bernard had been his second-grade teacher. And his fourth-grade. Not happy memories, but then, school in general hadn't been his greatest time ever.

But it had been better than what had come after, mostly. So there was that.

"Well, Shane, what can I do for you? You need a nice new shirt for a date? Or a suit? How about a nice suit?"

He winced at the idea of him in a suit. Especially a suit from this place. "You've got a sign in the window," he said. "A car? You're selling a car?"

"Oh, that thing? Yes. I didn't think anybody would ever ask about it." She pursed her lips, blue eyes vague and yet somehow calculating. "You want to see it?"

"Sure." He tried not to seem too eager about it.

Miss Bernard led him out the back door, to a shed that leaned precariously in the back. At one time it had probably held supplies, or maybe even horses. Now it was full of junk, and crammed into the middle of the junk . . .

A hell of a car.

Shane blinked at it. Under the layers of dust and cobwebs, it looked like a sweet vintage Charger—big, black, and intimidating. "Uh . . . that's it?"

"Yes. It was my son's. He's gone." Whether Miss Bernard meant dead or just departed from Morganville, Shane couldn't tell, but he thought she meant dead gone. She looked very sad, and those big, vague eyes filled with tears for a moment. "He just loved this car. But I'm not as well-off as I used to be, and I could sure use the money."

He felt very uncomfortable, seeing her like this, so he focused on the car. "Does it run?"

"I expect so. Here." She retrieved a set of keys from a hook on the wall and handed them over. "Start it up."

It took some reconfiguring of the junk pile to even open the driver's side door, but once he was in it, Shane felt something kind of like instant love. The car was old, a little shabby, but it felt right.

The starter ground a little, sluggish from its long sleep, and finally the engine caught fire with a cough and a belch of exhaust, and settled into a low, bass rumble.

Sweet.

Shane stuck his head out and said, "Can I take it around the block?"

Miss Bernard nodded. He didn't ask twice, just backed it out, down the alley, and cruised around, getting the feel of it. It was a hell of a nice car. Little bit of a shimmy on the turns, probably needed some work on the suspension, and a tune-up. But overall . . .

Yeah, it was going to be way out of his range. He could just feel it.

As Shane turned it back to the store, he ended up sitting at a stop-light. A battered old wrecker pulled in next to him, and a voice called, "Hey, that your car?"

"Just test-driving it," Shane called back. The driver was Radovic, the dude from the motorcycle shop; he worked part-time at Doug's Garage. Everybody called him Rad. He looked like central casting's idea of a tough biker dude, all right.

Rad nodded back at him. "Sweet. Hey, you buy it, you bring it by the shop. I can make you a deal on murdering it out."

Shane raised his eyebrows, but before he could figure out what the hell to say to that, the light changed, and Rad charged off with the wrecker, and Shane turned back to the store, where he pulled the car back into the shed, turned it off, patted the steering wheel, and got out to hand the keys to Miss Bernard.

"It's great," he said. "Out of my league, though. Thanks."

"What do you mean, young man, out of your league?"

"Too expensive."

She blinked. "I didn't even tell you how much it would be yet!"

"I know what it's worth."

She waved that aside with an impatient old-lady gesture. "I just want it gone. It reminds me so much of Steve, and I . . . just don't want to see it anymore. And the money would be ever so much help. I need to buy medicine, you know. How much can you pay?"

His turn to blink. "Um . . . I don't know." He had five hundred dollars. He chewed his lip a second, then said, "Three fifty?" Because she'd bargain, right?

"Sold," she said. And he instantly felt like a worm. Before he could try to tell her he was going to pay more, she gave him back the keys. Shane cleared his throat, gave it up, and reached into his pocket. He'd been carrying around the cash for days, just in case, and now he peeled off the three fifty and handed it over. Miss Bernard dug the title card out of the glove compartment and signed it, then thrust it at him. "Don't forget to get insurance. They're really hard on you if you don't have insurance."

"Yes, ma'am," he said.

"And remember to change the oil. Steve was very particular about his oil changes."

"Yes, ma'am."

She patted his cheek with her hard, dry hand. "You always were a sweet boy," she said. "I'm sorry about the troubles your family had."

He nodded, suddenly not able to say anything at all, and slid into the driver's seat. This time, the car started up without a hitch.

He drove it straight to the car wash, a creaking old thing with barely working sprayers and tired old vacuum cleaners. He found spiders in the vents, and an old nest on the engine that was already turning brown from the heat and probably would have burst into flame anytime. He scrubbed off the dust and shined the paint and cleaned the windows, and when he drove it away, glistening in the sun, he felt like he'd made the deal of the century.

And like he'd ripped off a little old lady, too. Which wasn't so great.

He went straight to the garage.

Radovic was there; the wrecker was parked in the front, big hook still swinging from its earlier motion on the road. Shane parked the Charger and went inside, where he found Rad chugging down what looked like a beer and reading a bike magazine.

"What did you mean?" Shane asked. "Murder it out?"

Rad wiped his mouth with the back of his hand. "Get all that chrome off it," he said. "Black it out. Black the wheels. Deep tint. Make it a badass mother—"

"Yeah, I get it," Shane interrupted. "How much?"

Rad shrugged. "It's already mostly there. Three hundred."

"Don't have it," Shane said. "Never mind, I guess."

"Yeah? What you got?"

"One hundred."

Rad laughed. "For a hundred, I could maybe black out the wheels. Do the chrome. Not the tint."

"Okay," Shane said. "When?"

"You got a couple of hours?"

Shane did.

He handed over the keys and walked home, checked on Claire—she was up and walking, though with a pretty significant limp—and made chili dogs for the two of them while she talked about the new weird shit that Myrnin was making her do. It was fascinating, whatever it was. He just liked listening to her talk.

"What?" Claire asked him, stopping in midstream to watch his face. He paused, a chili dog halfway to his mouth. "You're smiling."

"I am? 'Cause I'm pretty sure I'm eating. Which does make me happy."

"That wasn't a chili dog smile. That was some other kind of smile. An I've-got-a-secret smile."

Damn. "I don't know what you're talking about," he said. He didn't want to tell her. He wanted to show her. He was trying not to smile, but dammit, his lips just wouldn't stop with the curving. "Maybe I just like hearing you talk." Which was true, but she wouldn't believe that. Sure enough, she rolled her eyes, let it go, and went back to her Myrnin monologue.

He ate his lunch in silence, smiling the whole time.

Two hours later, he was back at Doug's Garage, and the Charger was parked outside. If it had been sweet before, it was incredible now. There was a kind of gravity to it, a darkness that just sucked in everything around it, and Rad had been dead-on about murdering it out— the Charger went from a car to something like the Car. In a crowd, it would be the only car.

Huh.

Rad had said he couldn't do the tinting, not for a hundred, but not only were the chrome and wheels blacked out; the windows sported a new, heavy tint, black as midnight.

Rad emerged from the door in the side of the garage, the one that said OFFICE, and gestured at Shane. He was carrying a big wrench in one hand, and he was half-covered in grease. Shane walked over, digging out a hundred dollars from his very thin bankroll.

He froze, because inside the office sat a vampire.

"Shane Collins," the vampire said, and stood up to extend a hand. "My name is Grantham Vance. Good to finally meet you." He smiled, no fangs in evidence, which didn't make him one bit less a vamp. "You're getting to be quite a legend in Morganville, you know."

Vance was medium tall, medium broad, with skin that had probably been dark olive when he was alive. It was now sort of a sickly almost-gray, which made his big dark eyes glow even brighter. He had brown hair cut into a kind of Roman style, something antique and weird.

He wore a Western plaid shirt, with pearl snap buttons, a pair of blue jeans, and cowboy boots. Lizard.

In short, he just looked completely . . . wrong.

Shane didn't answer him. He looked at Rad. "What's going on?"

Rad looked uncomfortable. "Mr. Vance, he sort of owns the place," Rad said. "He dropped in, you know, to look around. He saw your car."

"Beautiful machine," Vance said. "I'll give you a thousand dollars for it." He reached in his pocket and peeled off hundreds. Ten of them.

Shane swallowed and said, "It's not for sale."

"No?" Vance peeled off another three. "Really?"

"I just got it!"

"Of course." More hundreds. Shane had lost count. "I've always wanted a car like that. Oh, and I had Rad put on the vampire-quality tinting, so really, it's of no use to you now, is it? You can't even see to drive." Vance lost his smile, and what was left really wasn't good. Not good at all. "Take the money, Collins."

Rad shifted uncomfortably. He was still holding the wrench in one hand, and he was too big a guy to fight, even unarmed. "Just do it," he said. "Sorry, man. I didn't know this would happen. Walk away."

That would have been the smart thing to do. Take the money. Leave the car. Hell, he hadn't even gotten used to having it yet.

"No," Shane said. "Take the tint off."

Rad looked deeply worried now. "Don't play that way. Just let him have it."

"I'm not playing. That's my car. I've got the title to prove it. It's not for sale. Take the tint off."

Vance stopped counting money. Shane tried not to imagine how much there was in his hand. "Really."

"Yeah, really," Shane said.

Vance shook his head. "Stupid, boy. Very stupid. I'd give you the cash to buy any car you liked."

"I like this one."

"So do I. And my wishes rule, in Morganville." Their eyes met, and locked, and Shane felt himself getting dizzy. He braced himself against the wall and held on, somehow, until the vampire looked away first. "You really are a fool," Vance said. "Mr. Radovic."

"Sir?"

"Do you like your job?"

"Yes, sir."

"Then make Mr. Collins leave before I lose my temper."

Rad grabbed Shane by the collar of his shirt and shoved him out into the sunlight. Shane twisted, stiff-armed him, and got some distance.

Rad still had the wrench. In the dusty, hot afternoon, surrounded by the skeletons of old cars, Shane felt like he was ten years old again, getting beaten up for his lunch money by kids twice his size.

Not again. Never again.

"Let him have it," Rad said. "Trust me. Just let him have it."

"Screw you, man, that's my car! I don't just let vampires take stuff away from me!"

Rad grabbed him and hustled him off into the grimy garage. It was large, and filled with cars under construction, destruction, repair. Sparks flew. Machines whined and banged. It stank of old oil and burning metal.

"This way," he said, and dragged Shane around two SUVs, a battered Ford pickup, to the far corner of the garage.

There sat Shane's car. Murdered out. Tint and everything.

Shane turned and looked back outside. A duplicate of the Charger sat in the sun, sparkling. Identical. "What the hell . . . ?"

"That one out front is mine," Rad said. "It's got a blown valve, it drives like shit, and the block's going to crack in the next ten thousand miles, so I've been keeping it in the back. I was going to overhaul it and drop in a new engine. Let him have it. Take the money, man. Don't screw this up and you can walk away with the cash and the car, and Vance gets screwed both ways."

Rad, Shane decided, wasn't as dumb as he looked. He stared at him for a long moment, then nodded, walked back to the office, and looked inside. Vance was still sitting there, counting money. He looked up and said, "Come to insult me again?"

"No, sir," Shane said. "I'll take the deal. For five thousand."

Vance frowned, but Shane had guessed right this time. Five thousand was well within the boundaries of that bankroll, and Vance didn't seem like a guy who particularly cared about the money, anyway.

He counted out the bills and shoved them over, and Shane smiled. "Enjoy the car."

"Oh, I will." Vance smirked. "And they say nobody ever takes advantage of you, Collins. You're not so tough."

"Absolutely," Shane agreed, deadpan.

Then he walked out, handed Rad a thousand bucks, and said, "Hang on to the car."

Rad looked stunned. "What?"

"Your plan, your gain. Keep the car for now. I'll buy it back from you one of these days. Can't afford the insurance right now anyway." Shane shrugged. "Just let me drive it when I want—that's all I ask."

"You're sure?"

"Yeah. I'm sure." They shook hands, and Shane grinned. "But that means you need to let me borrow it right now, okay?"

"Sure."

Shane drove it by Bernard's Resale on the way, and handed Miss Bernard another thousand dollars of Vance's money because, hey, why not?

Then he went home, picked up Claire, and drove her to the movies. A chick flick, this time.

In style.

WORTH LIVING FOR

☽

Another free Web site story, but a late addition—one I'd been kicking around for years before I finally finished it. I wrote it a couple of ways, but this was the best version, I believe. . . . It dates back to the period shortly after Michael turns vampire, and Shane's still deeply uncomfortable about it. He's also still picking fights to work off his rage, which never really helps him.

Warning: There's drinking. And confessions. And secret missions with night vision. Bonus Bishop, and scary battles. Michael and Shane, being heroes together.

Which seems about right.

Fun factoid: For most of my late-college apartment living, spaghetti was the only thing I was good at making. That, and mac and cheese with tuna. But we shall not speak of this again.

When Shane came limping home, he was bleeding all over the place, and even though he was drunk off his ass, he knew that wasn't a good idea. Not with a vampire for a housemate.

The vampire housemate stared at him with a really blank expression, standing in the kitchen doorway, as Shane dropped down on the couch, grabbed a handful of tissues out of the box, and started mopping at his mouth and nose.

"What?" he snapped. Michael shook his head. He was holding a beer in his hand. At least, Shane hoped it was a beer. It had a Budweiser label on it, anyway. "I had a fight."

"No kidding. Looks bad."

"Nah." *Ow.* Shane probed at a sore spot in his jaw and felt a sickening creak in one of his teeth. *Dammit.* The only thing worse than hitting a doctor's office in Morganville was suffering through dental work. Not exactly the best and the brightest setting up shop around here. He was convinced that the jerks had never even heard of novocaine.

Shane spat blood into the tissue, sniffed experimentally, and didn't feel any telltale drippage. Not so bad. Maybe the worst was over.

Michael walked over, but not close. Not close enough to worry about, anyway. "What happened?"

Shane shrugged. "You know, the usual. Couple of vampires got hold of some girl, started dragging her off. Some of us got into it. No big thing. Nobody got hurt bad."

"Was she Protected?"

"College girl, out partying in the wrong side of town. You know the type."

Michael nodded and held out the beer. Shane stared at it, then him.

"Don't be an asshole," Michael said. "It's not blood. And I didn't even take a drink yet."

Shane took it and drank. The beer burned in cuts, but it was a good kind of burn, and it washed the copper taste out of his mouth. He sat back with a sigh and closed his eyes. The room started making loops, so he opened them again. *Really shouldn't be drinking, on top of the drinking I already did.* Yeah, there were a lot of things he shouldn't be doing. Like living in the house with a vampire, for one thing. His dad would have—

His dad. There was a reason to drink. Shane toasted the absent ghost of Frank Collins, Major Douche Bag, and gulped down another mouthful.

Michael sat on the couch, but at the other end. Safe distance, like he knew Shane was still feeling raw about the whole bloodsucking issue. He picked up his guitar and started playing, some Coldplay song Shane half remembered. "Which girl?"

"What?"

"You know, the girl the vamps were trying to drag off. Who was she?"

Shane considered that, rolling the beer between his hands. "Didn't know her. Why?"

Michael shrugged. "Doesn't matter, I guess. She probably never even knew they were vamps. But, dude, you really need to do something about your hero complex one of these days."

"It wasn't just me. There were two other guys who jumped in."

"But you started it."

Oh man, Michael knew him way too well. "Kinda." Shane tipped his head back and laughed, a little. It hurt. "C'mon, man, you would've jumped in, too. I know you. I'm not the only one riding around on a white horse."

Michael studied Shane for a long moment, then said, "You are way too drunk, you know that?"

Shane choked and nearly did a spit take with the beer. "Uh . . . yeah. Not really my fault, though. I was playing poker. Bunch of college guys, easy money. Only they kept buying rounds. The more they lost, the more they bought. Don't blame me. I made almost a thousand bucks tonight. *And* free beer."

"And then you got into a fight with vampires, and walked home. Drunk and bleeding and carrying cash. In Morganville." Michael's face was still, and way too sober. "Man, you really do have a death wish. Why didn't you call? I'd have—"

"I don't need a bloodsucking babysitter," Shane snapped, even though he knew Michael had a big frickin' point. The beer made him feel hot and sick, but he forced down another mouthful. "Weren't you supposed to be out with Eve, anyway? What are you doing here?"

Michael shrugged. "She had to go in to work," he said. "I'm picking her up later. Claire's at Myrnin's lab. She ought to pay rent there instead of here, the time she spends doing his crap."

That gave Shane a bad, even sicker twist in his stomach. "You don't think he's hitting on her, do you?"

"Myrnin?" Michael's fingers went still on the guitar, and Shane got a flash of startled blue eyes. "Jesus. I think she'd have said something. Maybe not to you or me, but to Eve, for sure."

"And Eve would tell you."

Michael smiled. "If she thought Claire was in trouble, she'd tell us both."

That made Shane feel a little better. Just a little. Because when your potential competition was some ancient, occasionally suave dude who dressed in velvet and still looked twentysomething, nothing could make you feel a *lot* better.

Speaking of looking better, Michael was wearing better stuff than usual, probably because he'd been planning on impressing Eve. Blue shirt, blue jeans. Diamond stud earring in his left ear. "Dude," Shane said, distracted. "Can vamps get pierced?"

"What?"

"Your earring."

"Don't know." Michael flicked his earlobe with one finger. "I did this last year. When I was still the old me."

"I never noticed."

"And here I thought you cared."

Shane laughed, a little, and kept on thinking. "What about tats? Do they stay on a vampire?"

"I doubt it. We'd probably heal. Doesn't sound like something I want to try if it isn't going to stay on."

"Sucks to be you, don't it? No pun intended."

Michael looked up and grinned, and all the bullshit faded away. All the bitter anger (it always tasted like blood and tinfoil), all the weird complication of his best friend *drinking blood for God's sake*, all that just up and left, and it could have been two years ago, or three, or more. They could have been twelve years old again, thinking of ways to stick frogs in Alyssa's shoes, worms in her underwear drawer, whatever.

Shane felt the hot sting of tears in his eyes, and looked away. "I missed you," Shane blurted. It felt right to say it, and then it felt stupid because Michael was right there at the other end of the couch, and besides, guys didn't say that crap to other guys. "Whatever."

Michael got real interested in his guitar, all of a sudden. "Yeah," he said quietly. "I missed you, too. How'd we get like this?"

"Well, you vamped out, my dad made me promise to kill you—"

"Seriously."

"That wasn't serious?"

"We used to hang. I miss you having my back."

"I still have your back."

"Do you?"

Shane looked at him in silence for a long few seconds without blinking, and said, "If you don't know that, you don't know shit about me, bro. Do I like it that you're sucking down O neg like it's SlimFast? Hell, no. Creeps me the hell out and it always will. But it doesn't matter. I'll always have your back."

"Then let me have yours once in a while," Michael said, and held out his fist. Shane bumped it, or tried; his coordination was way off. "Next time, don't go wandering around out in the dark, bleeding and wearing a Bite Me sign."

"Oh, blow me," Shane groaned. "I'm *fine*."

"Please. You're so fine you're about thirty seconds from telling me all your deep, dark secrets and crying, or else puking your guts out."

"Yeah, screw you, too, buddy." Shane closed his eyes and leaned his head back on the sofa. The room was doing loop-de-loops, and it was kind of fun at first, and then not so much.

"I worry about you," he heard Michael say very quietly. "I wasn't kidding about the death wish. Jesus, Shane, you keep doing this kind of thing, you'll end up dead in a ditch. Or worse."

"Maybe it's what I deserve." He couldn't believe he'd just said that out loud, but it was true. Maybe it *was* what he deserved. He hadn't been able to protect Alyssa. He hadn't been able to save his mother. The pain—the pain helped, because it was like paying back a debt. Nobody understood that, though. They just thought he was nuts.

He felt a cold hand on his shoulder, and looked up to see Michael standing there, staring at him with so much—*everything*—in his eyes that it made him feel scared. Nobody should know him that well. Nobody.

But at least Michael didn't say it. He just said, "Come on, man. Let's get you upstairs before you puke all over my guitar."

"Don't tell Claire I came home drunk," Shane said.

"Hell no."

"Because I will *end* you."

"If you survive the hangover," Michael said, "we'll see who wins *that* throw-down."

Michael was right about the hangover. Shane woke up with his guts heaving and his mouth tasting like he'd sucked on old sweat socks, and he rolled over in bed and moaned. He hadn't ralphed, but it had been close. He figured he still might. His head was pounding like Metallica's drummer, and he wanted to just make it all go away.

Not an option, though. He got up, slipped on a pair of cheap sunglasses and a ratty T-shirt and jeans that had seen better days, and shuffled downstairs to grab a tall glass of water. There was a pot of coffee on the burner, so he poured a cup of that, too, and took both to the kitchen table. He'd downed the water and was about to start on the coffee when the knocking came at the back door.

Well, not so much knocking as pounding. Which was really *not good* with his head already keeping the beat to a different, sadistic drummer.

Shane groaned, got up, and opened the door without checking to see who it was, mainly because death was preferable to the pain his head was giving him as long as that pounding was going on.

It was two someones, actually. Shane stared at them for a long, blood-shot second, then stepped back to let them in. "Wow, a visit from the mayor," he said. "And it's not even election season. How you doing, Dick?"

Richard Morrell—who was *never* known as Dick, except to Shane—gave him a pained, long-suffering look. For all his faults—and God knew he had a lot, starting with being related to that psycho-bitch Monica—Dick never let the little things get to him. Which was why it was so much fun to try. He looked tanned and fit, and he was wearing an expensive suit, though why he bothered in Morganville was any-body's guess.

"Shane," said the second person, a tall, dark-skinned woman with a scar on her face, tightly cornrowed hair pulled back in a bun, and who was wearing a crisply ironed police uniform, all her brass gleam-ing. She wore the gun like she'd been born with it on her hip. "Sorry for the early visit. I heard you had a late night."

He shrugged, but he was glad he was wearing the sunglasses to hide his expression. And the bloodshot eyes. "No problem, Chief Moses," he said. "Coffee?"

"I never say no to coffee," Hannah Moses said, with a charming, professional kind of smile. Shane got a couple of mugs out of the cab-inet and filled them, brain churning furiously against the numbing fog of the hangover. *Why are they here? What did I do?* Because the chance they could be here for anyone else seemed pretty long, and pretty small. He was *always* the one in trouble with the law.

He carried the mugs back to the kitchen table, which was piled with old, discarded copies of the *Morganville Daily* and flyers for things he never paid attention to; he shoved it all to the side. "Sorry," he said. "Not my kitchen duty day." As Hannah and Richard sat down and started sipping their drinks, he said, "No offense, but we've got a cof-fee shop about six blocks away. Vampire owned. Any particular rea-son you're dropping in on me for your caffeine fix?" *Please say no.*

Richard and Hannah exchanged glances, and then Richard Morrell said, "We need you to do something for us."

Well, that was different. Really different. Shane cocked his head and tried to sort through it, because it wasn't making any sense. "You. Need something. From me."

"Don't make it a thing, Shane."

"Kinda is a thing, though." Neither of them cracked a smile. They both looked very, very serious. "What is it?"

"Michael."

Michael? Shane's eyebrows rose on their own, and he said, "You have *got* to be kidding. *Our* Michael, the Boy Scout? No freaking way. What's he supposed to have done, littered? Jaywalked?"

"No," Hannah said. She sounded regretful, and very sure of what she was saying. "We think that he's hiding a fugitive from justice. A dangerous one, and one who could easily get him killed. And we need to find out why, and where."

Shane didn't mean to, but he sat down, hand cradling the hot ceramic of his coffee cup. *No way.* It wasn't like Michael, not at all. But Hannah wasn't one of those people who went off half-cocked, either. She knew her business, and if her business was Shane's best friend . . . well, that was bad. Real bad.

"Who's he supposed to be hiding?" Shane finally asked, through a throat that felt way too tight. "Osama bin Laden?"

"He's hiding a vampire. I'd rather not tell you who we believe it is."

"What, *Dracula?* Man, that guy gets around." Neither of them smiled. "Kidding. Jeez. Lighten up a little."

Richard reached out and grabbed Shane's wrist as he started to raise the coffee cup. "Lighten up," he repeated. He looked way too pale, and way too angry now. Not the usual Dick Morrell at all. "You stupid punk, you don't know what you're talking about. If you want to save Michael's life, you'd better get your head out of your ass and quit joking around."

"If you want to save *your* life, you'd better take your hand off me, asshole!"

Richard did, sitting back and crossing his arms. Hannah's gaze darted from him to Shane, then back again. "We're all going to just calm down," she said. "Because this doesn't help anyone, least of all Michael. Shane, he's not wrong. This is serious, and if we don't do something, it's going to go bad, especially for your friend, and maybe for the rest of you, too. Please. We need your help."

"To do what? Spy on my best friend? Screw that." Shane felt his jaw muscles bunching up, and his aching hands—still bruised from last night's little scuffle—tightened into fists. "Never gonna happen. Not unless you're straight with me. Who is it you're looking for, exactly? I'm guessing not Dracula, probably."

The house seemed very quiet, to Shane. He knew Claire could feel the house's moods, somehow, but he didn't really. It was just a house. Except it wasn't, and somehow, he knew it was . . . listening.

"I can't tell you that," Hannah said. "And you don't need to know. It's better if you don't."

"Yeah, for you. But for me, trust me, it's better if I believe you when you say I need to stab my best friend in the back."

Another moment of silence, and then Richard made a frustrated sound, like a dog growling, and said, "Fine, Shane. But when I tell you this, it means you are exactly the fifth person in Morganville to know it. You, me, Hannah, Amelie, and Oliver. And guess which one we'll be looking at if it gets out."

Shane was starting to think it really *was* Dracula they were talking about. "All right," he said. "I'll sign a paper, or whatever you want. But I need to know what you're talking about, here."

"Bishop," Richard said. "I'm talking about Bishop."

Shane felt his entire body turn cold. The hangover headache disappeared, just like mist. He slid his sunglasses off and stared at Richard, then Hannah. "You're kidding," he said. "You didn't kill him yet? Or at least keep him in prison?" He *had* to be in prison. Bishop was, hands down, the most terrifying guy that Shane had ever seen in person. He'd never met a serial killer, not a real one, but damn, Bishop was the next-best thing. Shane was willing to bet that Bishop would have intimidated Dahmer, Gacy, and Bundy put together.

And he *lived* to cause destruction. It was his thing. That, and undoing whatever good things his daughter, Amelie, had managed to accomplish.

Not somebody you wanted to have roaming around loose on the streets of Morganville.

Jesus, Shane thought. *I walked home last night, bleeding and drunk. Michael wasn't kidding about the death wish.*

"Bishop was in prison," Richard confirmed. "Amelie had him walled up in a cell. And now he's out. He killed four guards along the way."

"You've got to be—wait, you think *Michael* is hiding him? Why the hell would he do that?"

"I'll be honest with you—we don't *know* that Michael is involved. But there are only a few people in Morganville that Bishop could potentially use, and Michael's one of them—he was under Bishop's influence before. If so, your friend is in deep, deep trouble," said Hannah. "If you can find out where Bishop is hiding, we can take care of this quickly and quietly. Michael never has to be involved. But if you can't, we'll still find Bishop, and we'll bring Michael in as an accessory. Amelie's already said that this time she won't be so merciful—not to Bishop or to any vampire who gives him help. This could save his life, Shane. Help us."

Shane stood up and walked away, arms folded. He was aching

inside now, angry at them for putting him in this position, angry at Michael for . . . for whatever. *If you weren't a bloodsucking leech, this would never have happened.* Not that Michael had asked for it, in the beginning, anyway. He'd been a casualty of war, even at the start.

Even if Michael forgave him for this, Eve never would; Shane just knew that. When it came to Michael, Eve held a grudge like nobody he'd ever seen. And how the hell was he going to explain any of this to Claire? He couldn't tell her about Bishop. No way.

Save his life.

Shane put his sunglasses back on, turned around, and said, "What do you want me to do?"

Following a vampire around was not as easy as it sounded. For one thing, Michael had wheels—a Morganville-issued sedan, with blacked-out windows. The transportation Shane could get was all too obvious—Eve's big black boat of a car, with tail fins, or the murdered-out black Charger he was making payments on with Rad, down at the repair shop. But there *was* a way to do it.

Rad had motorcycles. Lots of them. Most of them were way too flashy—chrome, bright paint, all that stuff. No good for staying anonymous.

"How about this one?" Shane asked, pointing to a dark blue Honda. "That'd probably do."

"Pretty drab," Rad—Radovic—said. "I could maybe put some paint on it if you want." Rad didn't feel that any of his rides were worth much unless they were memorable, which was kind of funny; he didn't have to work to make people remember him. Rad was a big, tough guy, all muscles. He was one of the few Shane would back off from in a fight, because when Rad swung a punch, it broke things. "How long you need it for?"

"I don't know," Shane said. "Hopefully just tonight."

"Twenty-five dollars a day," Rad said. "Friends' rate. I won't ask you if you have a motorcycle license. You don't, that's your problem."

Shane didn't think Hannah was going to quibble about some paperwork, not right now. He nodded. "I need a helmet. Something that covers my face."

Rad nodded. "No problem. You want maybe night vision?"

"What?"

"My own invention," Rad said proudly. "Night vision built into helmet. Very handy for Morganville. You want?"

"How much?"

"Oh, another twenty-five dollars a night for the helmet."

"You're killing me."

Rad shrugged. "Cheap if you can see trouble coming out there. Right?"

Well, Shane really couldn't argue with that. He finally nodded and shelled out fifty from the cash he'd won off the college boys. It was a good value, in Morganville, no question about it.

"You want two?" Rad's lips split in a wide, blinding grin. He had big, square teeth that could have done work in a toothpaste commercial. "One for the girlfriend, eh?"

"Just one," Shane said. "I'm on my own tonight."

As a precaution, Shane parked the bike behind the garage, in the deepest shadows he could find. He'd gotten to know it on the way home, and it was a sweet little ride, not as loud as a lot of motorcycles. That would help, probably. But the important thing wasn't to keep Michael from seeing the bike following him, just that he didn't know it was Shane.

At least, that was Shane's best idea.

When he came in the kitchen, Claire was already there, looking in the refrigerator. She was wearing the same clothes she'd had on yesterday, which meant she'd just gotten back from the lab, and when he started toward her, she held up her hands, looking miserable. "I smell," she said. "No, I'm wrong—I stink. I can't smell it, but I can feel it. I don't want you to smell me right now."

"I love how you smell," he said. "Besides, I didn't take a shower this morning, either. My bad."

She considered that, catching that cute lower lip between her teeth in a way that made him tingle, and then nodded and stepped into his embrace. God, she felt good—small and fragile and warm, soft in all the right places. Her lips were hot and sweet under his, and for a few seconds, at least, he felt all the way better. Kissing Claire did that to him.

He kissed her a second time, lightly, and asked, "Did you eat anything today?"

"I think I had a graham cracker yesterday," she said, and yawned. "I think I'm too tired to eat, though." When she turned her head, he saw the shadow of bite marks on her neck—scars, not fresh. She was growing her hair longer to cover them up. "Where's everybody else?"

"Michael's at the music store. He had a late lesson. Should be back soon. Eve—" Right on cue, the front door banged open. "That'd be Eve."

"Yo, losers, where's my dinner?" Eve yelled.

"Yo, Gothic Princess, your name is on the kitchen duty list today!"

"Is *not!*"

Shane rolled his eyes. Claire was smiling. "I'll help," she said, and started pulling stuff out.

"Not your turn," Eve said, breezing into the kitchen. "You don't have to, Claire."

"I know, but I'm hungry. I think. Maybe." Claire frowned doubtfully at some leftovers. "Is this any good?"

"If you have to ask, the answer is usually no," Eve said, and dumped the bowl into the trash. "Ugh. I don't even know what that was, but it isn't anymore. How about spaghetti?"

It was always spaghetti with Eve, unless someone else stepped in. Today, though, Shane's heart wasn't in it. "Sure," he said, which made her turn and narrow her heavily made-up eyes at him. Mistake.

"Wow. Mr. I Have a Better Idea, stumped? That's crazy talk. Are you running a fever?"

"Spaghetti sounds good." He shrugged and let it go, because he was starting to wonder how he was going to gracefully ease out of here and follow Michael, if Michael left again.

"Not to me," Claire sighed. "You know what? I was right the first time. I'm more tired than I am hungry." She grabbed a can of Coke from the fridge and covered another yawn. She really did look exhausted— dark circles under her eyes, her skin gone paler than it should have been.

"You're working too hard," Shane said. "Promise me you're going to get some rest, okay?"

"Okay," Claire said, and gave him an absolutely beautiful smile. "Promise me you'll wake me up tomorrow?"

He had a flash of what that would be like: sitting on the edge of her bed as the rising sun streamed in, bending over to kiss her awake, seeing her eyes open and that same lazy, delicious smile on her lips. Just for him.

All of a sudden, his pants felt two sizes too small, and he had to clear his throat. "I promise," he said, and meant it. That was something to live for, if everything else failed on him. "Go on. Get to bed."

She kissed him, ran her fingers through his hair, and left, practically staggering. He stood there watching her, not really thinking about anything until Eve smacked him on the back of the head. "You're a good boyfriend," she said.

"Then why did you hit me?"

"No reason," she said, and grinned. "Spaghetti it is. You're in charge of sauce."

"Sauce is most of the work."

"Really? I had no idea."

Shane actually liked being around Eve, mostly, although she could get on his nerves; tonight, when he was anxious and trying not to show it, or think about it, she was perfect company. Her way-too-much-caffeine-powered chatter kept him concentrating just to keep up with her. He made the spaghetti sauce, which mostly involved opening a jar and dumping in more garlic, because it bugged the hell out of Michael, and the time seemed to go incredibly fast.

Michael arrived before the sauce was boiling. "Hey," he said, around kissing Eve's upturned lips. That took a while, and Shane grunted back a greeting that somehow managed to convey both *I'm at the point of gagging* and *Welcome home.* "Shane, the garlic thing? Getting old, man."

"I like garlic," Shane said. "Blame Eve—she told me to make the sauce."

Michael just shrugged. Eve went to the fridge and got out an opaque sports bottle, which she held up. "I already ate," Michael said. Which meant that he'd stopped by the blood bank, which was why his skin was flushed almost to a healthy normal color. The hungrier he got, the paler he got. When you could mistake him for a marble statue, it was time to run for the stakes. "I can't stay," he continued. "I promised I'd do a late lesson thing."

Michael earned his living at the music store—mainly because he refused, so far, to live the way the rest of the vamps did: by taking on a human, or preferably humans, to Protect. What a joke. The only Protecting the vamps did was protecting their own interests. The humans had a choice—pay twenty percent of their earnings into the vampire's account, or make regular donations at the blood bank. Most people chose blood, weirdly enough. Money was tougher to come by in Morganville.

Technically, Shane supposed that his Protector—and Claire's, and Eve's—was the Founder. So far, Amelie hadn't asked him or Eve for anything—no money, no blood, no nothing. Maybe Claire's hard work at the lab for Crazy Mad Bloodsucking Scientist Dude was paying all their bills. That did not make Shane feel more manly.

"Who are you teaching?" Shane asked, trying to make it sound offhand and casual. From the glance Michael shot him, he wasn't sure he'd gotten it right.

"Raoul Garza," Michael said. "Why?"

"Just curious. Seems like you've got a lot of late-night clients. You starting up some kind of undead band or something?" Not that it was a bad idea, now that Shane said it. "You got a bass player, drums, that kind of thing?"

"Not yet. I'm not sure there's a lot of interest in that among the vamps."

"Doesn't have to be all vamps, though. I'm just sayin'."

This was almost a normal conversation, Shane thought. Michael didn't seem paranoid about it, which was good. "Yeah, that's true," Michael said. "I'll think about it. Might be fun."

"Just make sure I get my fifteen percent. It's fifteen for agents, right?"

"Bite me."

"Think you've got that backwards, man."

Michael hugged Eve from behind as she stirred the spaghetti, and kissed the side of her neck. He might have lingered there just a little too long for Shane's comfort, but so far, there weren't any scars on Eve's throat. So far. "I'll be back as soon as I can," Michael said. "You guys have fun."

And just like that, he was gone. Eve looked after him for a few seconds with a sad expression, then turned the heat off under the pasta and started hunting around for the strainer. She didn't talk about Michael's absence after that, just focused on the food.

Shane was hungry, and he wolfed down a bowl, barely stopping to provide *mmm-hmm* commentary to Eve's monologue, which was like a bright, manic soundtrack he barely understood. He was thinking about Michael. About what he'd promised to do. Five minutes after sitting down, he was rinsing out his bowl at the sink.

"Hey," Eve called from the other room. "I know it was good and all, but what's the rush?"

"Got someplace to be," he called back, feeling a stab of guilt at her silence after that pronouncement. "Sorry." That sounded lame.

"I needed some me time, anyway," Eve said. "Where are you going?"

"I'm dating a supermodel on the side."

"Ha-ha, very funny. Is that what you want me to tell Claire?"

Shane stuck his head back into the living room area, where Eve still sat at the dining table in the corner, poking morosely at her half-full bowl. "I can't tell you," he said. "But it's important, okay?"

She raised her head and looked at him, and for all the Goth white paint on her face and the thick black lines around her eyes, not to mention the screaming purple lipstick, for a second she looked just like his mother. Back when his mother was still . . . herself. "You need to say where you're going," Eve said. "It's not safe if you just—take off. You know that. You grew up knowing that."

"Yeah," he said, and avoided her stare. "Well, this time, I can't. I'll be back."

He was out the back kitchen door before she could yell anything after him, and he stuck the helmet on and grabbed the bike and rolled it silently down the drive to the street, where he kicked it into gear. Michael's car was long gone, of course, but that didn't really matter; he kicked the motorcycle into a dull growl, and then into a roar as he rounded the corner. He liked the way it responded to him when he leaned one way, then another, dodging around imaginary obstacles. It was full dark out, and Morganville wasn't big on security lighting, but the night vision built into the helmet was freaking amazing—everything

looked ghostly green, but perfectly visible. There were a few cars on the
street, mostly the dark-tinted variety that Michael drove, but he ignored
them. All the vampmobiles looked alike, especially at night, but Eve had
given Michael a glow-in-the-dark bumper sticker, and it easily distin-
guished him from the rest.

Shane caught sight of the green-glowing death's-head in less than
three minutes, and eased back on his speed. The engine noise faded to
a throb, and he hung back—as much as possible, in Morganville—
and tried to look inconspicuous. Not easy to do, but he was wearing a
black jacket and a black helmet, and the bike's paint blended in with
the darkness.

Michael made some turns, leading him off into the broken-down
industrial area on the south side of the town; they passed up the old
tire factory, for which Shane was grateful because he had bad, creepy
memories of that place. They also passed up the old hospital, shuttered and half-destroyed. There were a bunch of not-very-stable
rusted barns that passed for workshops and storage warehouses.
Again, no stopping.

Michael kept going, heading for the edge of town. Shane started
to worry about that; as a vampire, Michael could conceivably have
permission to go outside the boundaries, but he knew that if he tried
it, somewhere, someone would notice. Plus, he didn't fancy getting
any of the town's memory tinkering, especially now that he knew
who, and what, was doing it. He'd heard way too much on that subject from Claire to feel comfortable. Shane unconsciously backed off
on the speed and watched the sedan's glow-in-the-dark skull begin to
get smaller. He hesitated for a second, then pressed the throttle again,
harder. The engine growled a threat, and he headed for the wrong side
out of town.

But Michael didn't go past the town limits sign. Instead, he took a
left turn into the darkness, down a street that looked as if it had been

built dilapidated, not to mention deserted. Shane pulled far back on his speed, almost coasting. Michael was turning his car right into a dirt yard in front of one of those almost-falling-down tin buildings, streaked with rust like mold.

Shane parked, killed the engine, but kept the cool night-vision helmet on. He crouched down, well aware Michael could see in the dark if he tried, but his best friend's attention was all on the building ahead of him. Michael looked hesitant, even as far away as Shane was; he stood by his car for a long second, then walked forward. Slowly. From what Shane could tell, it was like a man walking to his own execution.

Dammit. Shane realized that he couldn't just . . . wait here. He'd have to follow Mike inside, which was nine kinds of crazy, not to mention suicidal. Michael was into something bad, maybe not by his own choice. It was no place for a human to be, especially without backup.

But he couldn't let Mike go by himself.

Shane moved as quietly as a lifetime of living in Morganville had trained him, toward the dark, sinister-looking doorway through which Michael had vanished. It occurred to him that Eve was never going to forgive him if he got himself killed out here without telling her first.

He didn't want to even think about Claire. Not right now. It might make him turn around and leave.

Shane pulled in a deep, slow breath and stepped into the dark.

A hand closed around his throat and jerked him off-balance, and off into the shadows. The chin strap on his helmet broke, and the whole thing was ripped off, but there wasn't any sound of it hitting the ground, so his attacker had kept it, maybe the better to beat him with it. Shane flailed a little, feet scuffing the broken concrete floor, but he couldn't get any traction. The hand around his throat felt cold, and very strong.

And then Michael said, in a whisper like mist, "Shane?" He let go, and Shane tried to slow his heartbeat down, and breathe without wheezing. "You idiot, what the hell are you doing?"

"Following you," Shane whispered back. "What do you think—I came here for the scenery?"

"You are a fucking moron." Michael was really pissed; he didn't drop the f-bomb very much anymore, not since Claire had moved in. It was probably unconscious. "Seriously, what are you doing?"

"Following. You." Shane said it very slowly, just to be sure. "You're in trouble, man. I got a visit."

"What kind of visit?"

"You want to discuss that here?" Shane waved a hand—which he couldn't see, in the inky darkness—to stress the point. "Now?"

"No, I want you to get back on your little rice-burner and leave me alone," Michael said. "Jesus, did you tell Eve, too? Is she lurking around here?"

"Give me some credit. You know Eve—she's not stealthy. You'd have heard her first, in those damn boots."

Michael made a sound that was not quite a laugh, but should have been. "So you came by yourself. To what, rescue me?"

"Absolutely," Shane whispered. "Now, can we go?"

"No," Michael said. "I have to be sure he's still here."

Shane had a sudden, urgent bad feeling. "Please don't tell me it's who I think it is."

"Mean old guy who nearly killed us all before?"

"Oh man." Shane took in a deep breath. "They think you're helping him."

He didn't need to be able to see Michael's face to imagine his expression—shock, outrage, anger. "What? Who thinks that?"

"Tricky Dick, for one. And Hannah Moses. That ain't good, Mikey."

"No damn kidding."

"How did you get yourself into this?"

Michael was quiet for a second or two, then said, "There was this girl—I knew her back in junior high. She came to see me."

"What, for a booty call?"

"No, asshat, to get me to bite her. Turn her. Bring her over. Give her life eternal. Pick your euphemism."

"I think I liked the booty call explanation better. Wait, this relates to Bishop how, exactly?"

"I was worried about her. I thought she might get herself hurt, so I followed her. While I was following her, she got grabbed." Michael's pause was painful. "She got killed. I couldn't—I was too far away to stop it. I saw it happen. And I saw who did it."

"Bishop."

"I didn't know why he was out, but I knew it was important to find out what he was doing. So I tracked him. He came here, finally. He spends days here, sometimes nights."

Shane swallowed hard. "Is he here?"

"Not right now—I checked. I was planning to wait until I was sure he'd come in, then go get the cavalry."

"Why didn't you turn him in already?"

"The first time, I was going to, but he left again, and I lost him. I figured he'd come back here, so I waited. He did. This is the second time I've been here. I just want to make sure before I get Amelie and Oliver on it."

"You know, I'm not usually the on-the-side-of-caution guy, but I think this is a prime time to call the heavy hitters and get the hell out of the way."

"Probably," Michael said. "But I was afraid they'd think I was with him."

"Guess what? Barn door, horse, et cetera. Come on, let's go drop a safe, long-distance dime on this old bastard." It seemed, to Shane, like the best plan ever. Particularly the part where he didn't get killed, or turned vamp, which for him would be worse. No offense to Michael.

Michael seemed to be torn, but finally, he said, "All right. I just want to make sure he's here when they get here. He's gotten away from them once. It can't happen again, Shane. It can't."

Michael was taking this real damn personally, Shane realized. It wasn't just about Bishop, and general-principles anger at the evil old crow. It was about the girl, the one Michael had refused to Protect, who'd gotten way more than she'd ever bargained for from the next vamp she bumped into.

Shane could understand that on a level so deep it was practically atomic. "Right," he said quietly. "It won't. Let's book."

And they would have, honestly, except that in that moment, as they headed for the front door, something made a sound at the distant, lightless back of the warehouse. It echoed weirdly around the metal, and Shane couldn't decide what it was. A struggle? Someone dragging something? Michael's hand tightened on his arm, pulling him to a sudden, silent stop.

And then Shane heard a child crying.

It was a lost, desperate sound, and it got inside him and pulled in painful places. He couldn't see Michael, but he understood the rigid way his friend was locked in stillness. Michael could hear more, maybe see more.

And it wasn't good.

Shane was trying to decide whether to whisper a question when he heard, very distinctly, a little girl's voice say, eerily calmly, "Please let me go, sir. I won't say a thing. I won't tell anybody."

No wonder Michael was so still, so quiet.

It was happening all over again, like a nightmare.

Shane felt a shiver go through Michael, an impulse, and he knew what it was. "No," he whispered, just a thread of sound. "Don't do it."

"No choice," Michael whispered back. Shane nodded, because he got it—he really did—and he took out his cell phone and texted Claire, mainly because he didn't have any bloodsuckers on speed dial. Claire did. He gave the address, or as close as he could guess it, and added a 911 on the end, just to make it clear this wasn't going to be pretty. If she'd turned her phone off, or left it somewhere . . .

But she hadn't, and seconds later, the screen lit up with a message from Claire. **Sending help. Get out. Get out now.**

Which was a sensible kind of plan, really.

But that left Michael here, all alone, without help. Without anybody. And that ultimately wasn't something Shane could live with. He texted back **Will do**, even though he knew he wouldn't, and in the glow of the cell phone screen looked up at Michael. Michael could see what he was texting, but it was pretty obvious that Michael knew he was lying. Textually speaking.

It was really hard to fold up the phone and lose the light, but Shane knew he had to do it. The darkness fell like a thick, smothering blanket, and for a second he imagined he was drowning in it. Michael had let go of him, and the disorientation was total. Shane stayed where he was, trying not to think about all the things that could go wrong with this non-plan, and almost jumped when he felt Michael's fingers grip his shoulder in warning. He knew what that meant, without any words being said.

Bishop knew they were here.

In a weird kind of way, that was . . . better. The suspense was over. Now it was just about the fight, and the fight was where Shane lived, inside. It was like . . . home.

"Tell me you brought weapons," Michael said. He wasn't trying to hide, either. Shane wondered if he felt the same way; probably not, he thought. Michael didn't run from a fight, but he never seemed to have quite the same thirst for it, either. It was more of a grim acceptance of the inevitable.

"Don't say I never give you anything," Shane said, and reached into his jacket to retrieve two silver-tipped wooden stakes. Guaranteed to leave a mark, even on a vamp of Bishop's age and power. He handed one to Michael, then checked his other pockets. He found a bag of silver nitrate powder, which he handed over, too. "When you throw this, stay out of the way, or you're going to be sparkling, and not in that fashionable vamp kind of way."

"How do you want to do this?"

"You keep Bishop occupied. I save the girl."

"Really? Come on."

"What? You think I've got a better shot at him?"

"No, I think you're better at keep-away," Michael said, "and Bishop likes going after humans first. He likes the easy kills."

"No offense intended."

"I didn't say you'd be one of them."

Shane considered it. Bishop frankly scared the bejesus out of him, but Michael had one thing right—he could get to the girl faster, pick her up, and run her out of danger much better than Shane could. He could be back in seconds to jump in the fight, too.

Shane just had to keep Bishop at arm's length for maybe . . . a minute. Maybe less.

It didn't sound that hard, which was why Shane knew it would be ridiculous. "Sure," he said. "Let's do this thing."

"I'll get the lights," Michael said. "Five seconds." And then he was gone, moving like a ghost through the dark, and Shane was left alone, gripping the stake in one hand, and his plastic bag of silver powder in the other. He counted down in his head, focusing on the numbers instead of all the things that could go wrong.

He was still on two when the lights blazed on in the warehouse, ranks of greenish, flickering things that cast a weirdly alien color over everything—which wasn't much. Piles of debris. Old, sagging cardboard boxes. And over at the far end of the warehouse, some kind of broken-down forklift that was missing its wheels.

And there was Mr. Bishop, holding the wrist of a little red-haired girl about twelve years old. Growing up in Morganville, you knew people by sight, even if you didn't want to have anything to do with them, and he knew that kid. Her name was Clea Blaisdell.

Not that it mattered, whether he actually knew her. He wouldn't have left anybody, even Monica Morrell, to Bishop's nonexistent mercy.

So he stepped out in full view, twirled the stake in his fingers like he actually felt that cocky, and yelled, "Yo, Grandpa, you eating snack sizes now? Trying to lose a few pounds?" He kept walking, closing the distance between them. He couldn't see Michael, but that didn't matter; he knew he was there, working his way around to a good striking distance.

Shane was still twenty feet away, but that was close enough to see Bishop's lips part in a smile like the edges of a knife wound. Bishop was, frighteningly, even more horrible than he remembered—stringy white hair clinging to his scalp like it hadn't been washed, ever; gray, dirty clothes; a face so white and sharp it hardly looked human at all.

"If it isn't the Collins boy," Bishop said. His voice sounded rusty. "I would have thought your father's example had taught you to mind your manners. No matter. I won't waste my time on turning you into one of my own. I'll just settle for having you dead at my feet."

"Nice fantasy," Shane said, and kept walking. His heart was thumping so fast and hard it hurt. "Never happen, sucker. Come on. Show me what you got, you lame old—"

He didn't have time to finish the insult, because Bishop dropped the girl's wrist and flew at him in a blur. Shane took a running step—

not back, but *toward* him—and threw himself flat on the concrete in a slide as Bishop's leap carried the vampire over him. Shane twisted and rolled to his feet as Bishop landed, ten feet too far, and twirled the stake again. He was breathless, and his whole body was screaming at him to run, dammit, but he covered it with a wolfish grin and a *come on* gesture as he twirled the stake. When Bishop let out a low, unsettling growl and lowered his fangs, Shane started backing away. Strategically. Keeping Bishop's back to the red-haired girl . . .

. . . who was caught up by another running blur, which didn't slow down as it whipped through the air toward a gap in the back wall. Bishop's private entrance, most likely. *Go, Mikey,* Shane thought, and then he didn't have time for thinking because he had the world's oldest, meanest vampire on his ass, and Bishop meant business.

Shane tried to keep away, and he dodged a swipe of Bishop's sharp fingernails that would have gutted him; his feet felt clumsy, even fueled by adrenaline and terror. Bishop was fast, very fast, faster than Michael, maybe. Human agility wasn't enough.

As Bishop's hand closed on Shane's arm and yanked him forward, Shane figured he was pretty much already dead. It was only a matter of how it would happen . . . drained and left some dry corpse, or ripped apart in a bloody spree. On the whole, Shane thought maybe the ripping thing was better, but then, he'd never actually had time to give it much thought. His arm would break first, and then . . . then . . .

Then, suddenly, a silver shower of dust exploded around Bishop like fireworks, glittering dully in the fluorescent lights, and Shane blinked and coughed as it hit him, too. About one second later, Bishop's grip on his arm loosened, and the red-rimmed eyes widened, and Bishop's mouth split open in a scream.

His hair caught fire around his head in a weird flaming halo. Shane pulled his arm free and stumbled backward, his brain just catching up with what he was seeing.

Bishop, on fire where the fine silvery powder had hit him. As Bishop whirled to see who'd thrown it, Shane saw Michael standing ten feet behind him, arm still extended from the throw. There were burn marks on his palm.

Now, Shane thought, and as Bishop started to lurch toward his best friend, Shane brought up the stake and lunged, fast. He didn't let himself think about it, or try to direct what he was doing. Sometimes, his body just knew these things.

Sometimes, it was better if the mind stayed out of its way.

The stake hit Bishop in the back on the left side, punched in through the still-burning skin, and slammed straight into Bishop's heart.

Shane fell backward, slapping out the flames that had caught on the sleeves of his jacket, as Bishop screamed and danced madly in place, trying to reach the stake that had pierced his heart . . . and then slowly toppled to his knees, then forward onto his face.

He was too old to die quickly. In fact, Shane wasn't sure even silver would do it—but he hoped. Man, he really, really hoped.

Shane stayed where he was, lying propped on his elbows and watching the vampire, but nothing happened. Bishop didn't pop up, snarling; the silver burned him, but not really very much. It was like a slow, reluctant sizzle around the stake.

Bishop blinked, very slowly.

Not dead. Not yet.

Michael came to Shane's side and offered him a hand.

"We should cut his head off," Shane said, not taking the hand. Michael didn't pull it back.

"Not ours to do," he said. "But promise me something."

"What?"

Michael's face looked so pale, so strange in the greenish glare of the lights. "Promise me you'll do it for me if I become like him."

Shane hesitated, then reached up and took his hand, and let

Michael pull him up to his feet. "You won't," he said, and didn't let go. "You won't, bro. I won't let you."

He let go. They tapped fists, and nodded. It was a bargain.

There was a sound of engines outside, and squealing brakes, and in under five seconds the place was swarming with guys in stark black suits and ties and sunglasses, all with vamp-pale faces and weapons. They surrounded Shane and Michael, and the inert—but not dead—corpse of Bishop.

Nobody said anything.

The newcomers parted ranks, and a woman dressed in white walked through like she owned the place, which technically she probably did. She was carrying the little red-haired girl, who had her chubby arms around the woman's long, elegant neck. The Ice Queen, which was Shane's private nickname for her.

Amelie. The Founder of Morganville.

She was pretty, but in a cold kind of way that made Shane shiver; there was something about her eyes that wasn't quite . . . right. Not even the other vamps had eyes like that.

"You did this?" she asked, and looked at the burning body. There wasn't much of an expression on her face, no hint how she really felt about the whole thing. Shane traded a look with Michael.

"Yeah," Michael confirmed. "Sorry. We had to."

"Oh, indeed," she said. "It's good you did. For his sake. Had I caught him in this situation, I might not have been quite so . . . merciful." She paused, then shifted her gaze directly to Shane. "Who staked him?"

Before Shane could answer, Michael jumped in. "I did," he said. "Shane saved the kid."

Amelie didn't blink. "It's good it was you," she said. "Were it Mr. Collins, I might have to convene a Council meeting and order punishment. Humans don't stake vampires in Morganville, Mr. Collins. Not without consequences. But of course it wasn't Shane at all, was it, Michael?"

"No," Michael said. "It was me."

Shane opened his mouth, got a cold glance from Amelie, and shut it, fast. He didn't nod. He decided that maybe it wasn't a lie, exactly, if he didn't move. Or breathe.

Amelie turned away, toward one of her guards, who leaned toward her expectantly. "Take care of this," she said. "No one finds out about this. See to it that my father goes back where he belongs. And don't be in any hurry to remove the stake."

"Ma'am," he said. He looked over at Michael and Shane. "What about them?" Meaning, Shane realized with a sinking feeling, that they were security risks. Not that they'd hurt Michael. But he was just a breather. Nothing to lose sleep over, assuming Amelie actually slept.

She hesitated a moment, one pale, elegant hand smoothing down the girl's red hair, and then said, "I think we can trust Shane and Michael to understand the importance of keeping this to themselves."

"And the girl?"

Amelie looked down at the kid. "Clea," she said. "Her name is Clea. I'll take her home. I'm sure her parents will also understand how to keep quiet as well." She looked at Shane. "You have something to say?"

He shook his head. "Just surprised. You know her name."

Amelie's pale lips curled into a smile, and there was a shadow of warmth in her eyes. "Of course," she said. "I know all the names."

She didn't look back at Bishop. With a nod to Michael, she turned and carried Clea out of the building, into the night. Probably to a limousine, with a driver. Which beat the hell out of the little motor-cycle Shane had ridden in on.

"We should go," Michael said. "Need a ride?"

"Are you kidding?" Shane asked. "Do you know what Rad does to people who don't bring back his bikes?"

The sun was just coming up when Shane sat down on the edge of Claire's bed. He didn't wake her up, not right at first. . . . She was curled on her side, the morning glow turning her skin gold, making her hair burn red at the ends. Shane curled a strand of it around his finger, and it felt like warm silk.

He let the hair fall away, and moved his finger gently over her cheek, then lightly over her lips. Claire's eyelids fluttered, and she made a soft, vague, pleased kind of sound deep in her throat.

And then she focused on him.

Her brown eyes went all gold in the sun, and he felt golden inside, too. She didn't say anything. Neither did he.

He bent over and kissed her, and her lips were warm and sweet, and he thought, *Worth living for.*

When he finally sat up, she smiled at him, and it was so beautiful he forgot whatever he was going to say to her. Probably something lame, like *Good morning.*

"What did you do last night?" she asked, and scooted over.

Shane slowly lowered himself down next to her, never looking away from her warm, sunlit eyes. And that smile. "You know," he said. "The usual."

She knew better, but she didn't argue. Besides, they had more to think about . . . and none of it involved vampires.

And all of it was . . . good.

DRAMA QUEEN'S
LAST DANCE

☽

This was an important missing scene between books, and for some reason, I ended up selling it as a short story to an anthology: *Eternal,* the follow-up to *Immortal,* also edited by P. C. Cast. I love writing in Eve's point of view, particularly when she's snarky, and there is a lot of that on display here. There are also fancy gowns, jealousy, dancing, Michael in distress, *DANCING OLIVER* (I cannot stress this enough, because I always wanted to write that scene), and, most of all, a spontaneous proposal. So if you haven't read it, here's your chance to see the tale of Michael, Eve, Gloriana, and the last dance of the drama queen.

My name is Eve, and I am a drama queen.

I don't mean like any old garden-variety teen throwing a tantrum, oh no. I am a Drama Queen, with big initial capital letters and curlicues on top. I work hard at it, and I resent anybody lumping me in with a bunch of wannabe poseurs who haven't even qualified in Beginning Pouting, much less Champion Fit Throwing.

So when I had a golden opportunity for launching a big, fat, drama-filled scene, and ended up acting like an actual adult, perhaps you'll appreciate just how important this was to me. But wait, I'm getting ahead of myself.

First, let me explain the drama that is my life—and this is just the background, broad strokes, you know, for I am *epic*, I tell you. I am a Goth, but mainly for the fashion, not the 'tude. I had an emotionally abusive father and a checked-out mom. My little brother turned out to be one step short of either the asylum or federal prison.

Oh, and my boyfriend is a sweet boy, a gifted rock guitarist, and he just happens to have an allergy to sunlight and crave plasma on a regular basis. However, in our hometown of Morganville, this is not really all that unusual, since about a third of the citizens are vamps. Yes, vampires. Really. So you see why my life was generally a nightmare from an early age—the monsters under the bed really existed, and the pressure on all of us growing up was to give in. Be a good Morganville conformist.

Give up our blood for the cause.

Not me. I had a pact with all my other rebel friends. We'd never, ever be part of that scene.

And I mentioned my boyfriend is a vampire, right? Yeah. There's that.

Given all that, when I say that today was a *crisis* . . . well. Maybe you get the legendary scale of which I am speaking.

The saga started out a normal day—don't they all? I mean, surely one morning back there in prehistoric times a dinosaur woke up, yawned, chewed some coffee beans, and thought his day was going to be dead boring, just before a comet slammed into his neighborhood. "Normal day" in my life means that I woke up late, yelled at my housemate Shane to get the hell out of my way as I dashed to the bathroom in my vintage dragon-embroidered silk robe, and spent forty-five minutes doing shampoo, body wash, conditioner, blow-dry, straightening, makeup, clothes, and listening to Shane bang on the door and complain about how he was going to go pee all over my bedroom floor if I insisted on living in the bathroom.

I blew him a mocking black-lipsticked kiss on the way out, checked the time, and winced. I was late for my job at Common Grounds, the best local coffee shop of the two in town. (I also worked at the second best, but on alternate days.) I didn't mind dragging my ass in late to the University Center java store, but at Common Grounds, the boss was a little more of a leg-breaker—probably because he'd been making people show up on time since before the invention of the pocket watch.

I tried sneaking in the back door of Common Grounds, which seemed to work all right; I ditched my coffin purse in my locker, grabbed my long black apron, and tied it on before I went to grab a clipboard from the back. I took a hasty, not very thorough inventory, and toddled out to the front. . . .

. . . Where my boss, Oliver, fixed me with a long, cold glare that had probably been terrifying underlings for hundreds of years. Oliver = vampire, obviously, although he did a good job of putting on a human smile and seeming like Mr. Nice Hippie Dude when he thought it would get him something. He wasn't bothering today, because the counter was slammed three deep with people desperate for their morning caff fix, and his other help, what's-her-name, Jodi-with-an-*i*, hadn't shown up yet. I held up my clipboard and put on my best innocent expression. "I was doing inventory," I said. "We need more lids."

He growled, and I could hear it even over the hissing brass monster of the espresso machine. "Get on the register," he snapped, and I could tell he wasn't buying the inventory excuse for a second. Well, it had been thin at best. I mouthed, *Sorry*, and hurried over to beam a smile at the next harassed person who wanted to fork over $4.50 for his mocha-chocalattefrappalicious, or whatever it was he'd ordered. We made things easy by charging one price for each size of drink. Funny how people never seemed to appreciate that time-saver. I worked fast, burning through the backlog of caffiends in record time, then moved to help Oliver build the drinks once the register was idle. He'd stopped growling, and from time to time actually gave me a nod of approval. This was, for Oliver, a little like arranging for a paid vacation and a dozen roses.

We'd gotten the morning rush out of the way, and were settling into the slow midmorning period, when a door in the back of the store opened, and a girl came strolling out. Now, that wasn't so unusual—that door was the typical vampire entrance, for those who wanted to avoid the not-so-healthful effects of a stroll in the sun. But I'd never seen this particular vamp before. She was . . . interesting. Masses of curly blond hair that had that salon sheen you see in commercials, but which hardly exists in the wild; porcelain-pale skin (without the benefit of the rice powder I was using); big jade green eyes with spots of golden brown. She was wearing an Ed Hardy tee under a black leather jacket, all buckles and zippers. She looked pretty much like any other twentysomething in any town in the U.S., and maybe in a lot of the world. Shorter than most, maybe. She was five feet three, tops, but all kinds of curvy.

I took a cordial dislike to her, on principle, as she meandered her way toward the counter. Oliver, who'd been wiping down the bar, stopped in midmotion to watch her. That seemed to be a male thing, because I noticed pretty much the entire Y-chromosome population, including the table of gay boys, watching her, too. She didn't seem that sexy to me, at least in an obvious kind of way, and she wasn't vamping (no pun intended) it up . . . but she got attention, whether she was demanding it or not.

I wasn't using to being the wallflower, and it kinda pissed me off.

Still, I forced a smile as I went to the register. "Hi," I said, in my best professional welcome voice. "Can I help you?"

"I'll take this," Oliver said, and nudged me out of the way. He was smiling, which normally would be a bad sign, but this one went all the way to his eyes, and all of a sudden he didn't look like a vampire who would kick your ass, *ra-a-a-ar*; he looked like . . . a guy. Just a guy, kind of handsome in a sharp sort of way, although too old for me for sure.

The girl smiled back at him, and *wow*. I mean, it knocked me back a step, and I was (a) not male and (b) not any kind of interested. "Oliver," she said, and even her voice was cute and small and sweet, with some kind of lilting accent that made her sound exotic and mysterious. Well, for Morganville, Texas, but then, we find people from *Dallas* exotic and mysterious. "My dear friend, I haven't seen you in dark ages."

"Gloriana," he said. "I feared the worst, you know. It's cruel to keep us in suspense. Where were you?"

She shrugged and fiddled with the zippers on her jacket, looking coy as she shot him a look from beneath full, probably natural lashes. "After the last great war, I lost track of you, and the rest of our family," she said. "Those I found were—not healthy. I managed to avoid contracting the disease, but I didn't dare take the risk, so I stayed away."

"Where?"

"Oh, you know. Here and there. Europe, Australia was quite nice; I migrated here when they were still traveling by ocean liner. Since then, I've been drifting. I was recently in Los Angeles, where I ran into Bobby Sansome—you remember him?—and he told me almost everyone who was anyone was here, in Morganville. He also said that he'd come here to get the cure. I thought perhaps it was safe."

"It's safe," Oliver said. "But you'll need to present yourself to the Founder. There are rules of behavior in this town, accords you'll have to sign in order to stay. Understand?"

"Of course." Her charming smile got even wider. "Oliver, my sweet, do you really doubt that I know the rules of hospitality and good behavior? I haven't survived this long by preying indiscriminately on the livestock. . . . Oh." Her sparkling eyes flicked to me, inviting me to share the joke. "Not including you, naturally. I meant no offense."

"No?" I raised my eyebrows, and let her know the sweet face didn't impress me. "That 'tude will get you in trouble around here."

Gloriana gave me an honestly puzzled look, then turned to Oliver. "What does she mean?"

"She means that humans have status here." He didn't look particularly happy about it, but then, that's Oliver for you. "You can't expect civility from them. And, unfortunately, you can't punish them for failing to provide it."

I snorted. "Bite me, fanger."

"See?"

Gloriana looked honestly taken aback for a few seconds, and then smiled in what I could only call utter delight. Despite my best intentions, I got a traitorous little impulse to grin back. "Really? But this is *wonderful!*"

"It is?" Oliver's turn to look bemused, as if she'd suddenly started rattling on in a language he didn't recognize.

"Of course! You know I've never been terribly conventional, cuz. I'd be delighted to converse with humans again on an equal basis. Most of them are terribly dull, of course, but this one looks bright enough." Her green eyes swept over me, giving me the female X-ray of appraisal. "And certainly not afraid of controversy." .

"*This one* is named Eve," I said. "And don't check my teeth like I'm your livestock. I bite back."

Gloriana laughed, an honest, full laugh, and I felt a shudder go through Oliver's body next to me. I couldn't tell what had brought *that* on—not fear, surely; the old dude didn't fear anybody that I could tell. "Eve," she said. "I'd like something to drink. Something hot and salty, perhaps in an O negative if you have it."

Ugh, but okay, I served vamps from time to time. I summoned up the professional smile again. "Sure thing. Coming right up."

It was only as I was warming up the blood out of the refrigerator that it occurred to me that she'd named my own blood type.

Hmmmm.

Coincidence. Probably.

Gloriana's visit to the coffee shop was eye-opening, to say the least. I put her blood in an opaque coffee cup, with a lid, and she and Oliver went to sit down together, presumably to jaw about old times, and I mean *old* times. She wasn't standoffish, the way some of the other vampires were—she said hello to people as they passed, gave them the same sweet smile, shook hands with a few.

I was pulling espresso shots for a mocha when my boyfriend came in the vampire entrance and got in the ordering line. I waved, and he winked at me. Michael is a total hottie, always has been: tall, blond, built, and shy, for the most part. He's always been focused more on music than on the people around him, and from what he'd told me about how he'd come to get dead, that had been a real mistake. So he was trying to do a little better about connecting with people, as well as guitar riffs. He's always been my friend, but these days, he's a whole lot more than that.

I don't want to be sick about it, but I love him with my life. It scares me down to the bones to think about losing him—although, in Morganville, it's a lot more likely that *he'll* lose *me*, given the mortality rates among humans here.

Still.

I rushed through the next three orders to get to Michael, and then took my time, leaning over the counter and smiling as our eyes met. "Hi, handsome," I purred. "See something you like?"

"Always," he said, and gave me just a flicker of that devastating Michael Glass grin. "And the coffee looks good, too."

"You are suave. I've always said so."

"And you're strange. But I love strange."

"Mmmm. Want to go take inventory with me in the back?"

"Isn't the boss here?" Michael made a show of looking around for Oliver.

He found him. He also spotted Gloriana, who was leaning her chin on her tiny little hand, looking at Oliver with luminous, big eyes.

"Wow," he said. This was not the thing you wanted to hear out of a boyfriend, believe me. "Who's the new girl?"

"Gloriana," I said. "She's not new. She's ancient." I was hoping that would put an end to it; Michael wasn't interested in hanging around other vampires, although he did it when circumstances required; he liked me, and Shane, and Claire. He liked us a whole lot better than the nonbreathers.

Until now, apparently. I could almost see the word balloon floating over his head: *Should go say hello.* But he was smart enough not to say it. With an effort, he dragged his attention away from Gloriana, and looked at me again. "So, you have plans for lunch today?"

"Nope. I was thinking about a smoothie." In this coffee bar, you had to be sure you were grabbing the pureed strawberries, and not, you know, something else, but the smoothies were pretty awesome. "I could be talked into something non-food-related, though."

"Shane's at work," Michael said. "Claire's at school. House is empty. I could make you something hot."

He said it straight-faced; that was the wonderful, wicked thing about Michael—he could deliver the most outrageous lines with utmost sincerity. It left me wondering if I was the only one with my mind in the gutter . . . until I spotted the amusement in his clear blue eyes.

"I'll bet," I breathed. "Meet you there at one o'clock, okay?"

"Not twelve?"

"I came in late."

"Ah. I'll keep myself occupied."

"Hey!"

He gave me the full, devastating smile, and leaned across the counter to kiss me. His lips were cool and sweet and softer than they had any right to be, but he was gone before I could really savor it.

He'd left $4.50 on the counter—his way of saying that I should have a drink myself. Which I did, making it extra sweet and extra strong, like him.

It was only as I was sipping the drink that I realized Gloriana was staring at the door through which Michael had gone. She finally leaned over and pecked Oliver on both cheeks in a European sort of farewell, and took her cup of O to go . . . following Michael.

I didn't like that.

At all.

One o'clock crawled slowly toward me, to the point where I checked the coffee shop's clock against my cell phone *and* my watch, just to be sure. When the hand finally dragged itself to twelve forty-five, I stripped off my apron and chirped to Oliver, "Lunch!"

"Don't you have time to make up?" he asked, not looking away from the cash he was counting for the bank bag.

"Yeah, I'll stay late."

"I'd rather you worked through lunch."

"Sorry, slavery's gone out of fashion," I said, and hung up my apron on the old coat-tree at the end of the counter. "Gotta run."

He grunted and waved his hand. I retrieved my purse from the locker and dashed out.

It wasn't a long walk home, but it was unexpectedly chilly; rain clouds were rolling in, dark and ominous, and the wind had kicked up. It blew sand and broken bits of grass across the roads, rippled the leaves on the trees, and generally made walking less fun than usual. I was happy to turn down Lot Street and see my big, shiny black hearse parked at the curb. Death's party bus. Holla.

I couldn't wait, and broke into a jog up the walk, up the steps, across the porch, and unlocked the front door as fast as I could. *Yes!* I slammed the door and threw my stuff on the hall table; Michael's keys were already there, in the candy dish. My heartbeat sped up even faster. "Let's get the party started!" I called, and walked down the narrow hallway toward the living room.

On the way there, I passed the formal parlor room, which was basically a furniture museum; we never sat in there. Except this time I registered people in there as I passed. I stopped, backed up, and found Michael sitting in the big red velvet wing chair.

Gloriana was sitting on the settee, her to-go cup on the marble coffee table. She had her legs crossed, and seemed *very* comfortable.

In my house.

With my boyfriend.

"Michael?" I asked. He stood up, looking guilty and nervous, which was new for him. "What's going on?"

"Uh . . . this is Gloriana."

"I know who she is. I told *you* who she was."

"Eve," Gloriana said, all warmth and sweetness and apology. "I only wanted to meet Michael, as he's Amelie's newest child. I am a curious creature, I know. I mean nothing by it."

"Eve, chill," Michael said. "She just came over to say hello."

"I see." My voice sounded flat and pissed, even to my own ears. "That's great. Now she can just say good-bye, too."

"I meant no offense, most surely. Here, I'll be going." Gloriana stood up and extended her hand to Michael, knuckles turned up. "It was charming to meet you, Michael Glass."

He took her hand and looked briefly confused about what to do, then lifted it very formally to his lips and kissed her knuckles. Not *kissed* kissed, more of a brush of his lips, but it still made me feel lightheaded and sick inside. "Welcome to Morganville," he said. "Hope to see you around."

"Oh, I'm sure you will," Gloriana laughed. "After all, the sign says *You'll never want to leave*—isn't that true? I already find much to like about Morganville." She flicked those green eyes toward me. "Eve. Thank you for your hospitality."

"Yeah. Don't forget to take your blood with you."

Michael gave me a look. I gave him one right back. While we were doing the silent stare thing, Gloriana retrieved her cup and headed for the door. Michael moved past me to open it for her, and handed her a big, floppy black coat and hat to throw on. "There's an entrance to the underground a block down," he said. "Look for the glyph. You can bring the coat and hat back later."

"Thank you," she said, and swaddled herself up in the sun-defying garb. She looked like a waif playing dress-up. "You are so kind, Michael." She pronounced it French, like *Meeshell*. "I will return the kindness soon."

He watched her go. I watched him watch her go, and then he shut the door, locked it, and without looking at me said, "So, just how mad are you?"

Without a word, I turned and walked down the hall, into the kitchen, and poured myself a glass of water. I wasn't thirsty, but there was a burning pain in my throat, and besides, it gave me something to do with my shaking hands.

I heard the door open as Michael followed me in. "Seriously," he said. "Eve, I was just being friendly. She's new in town."

"Oh, so the hand-kissing, that's just being friendly? I never see you doing it to Oliver."

"A lot of these older vamp women, it's what they expect. They don't shake hands, Eve."

"Well, they need to bring their undead asses into the twenty-first century, then, because hand-kissing went out with the guillotine, didn't it? And since when do you do what's *expected*, anyway?"

Michael shook his head and leaned back against the counter. "It's not like that."

"Like *what?*"

"Like I want to take her to bed, which is what you're thinking, Eve."

I couldn't believe he'd gone and said that right out loud, even if I *was* thinking it. Not in such polite terms, though. "Then what's it like?"

"Like I'm . . . curious. Look, she's friendly, not like a lot of the others. I can ask her things, about being . . ." There was more color in his cheeks than normal; that was the closest a vampire could come to blushing. "About being what I am."

"What kind of things?" I demanded.

Michael met my eyes. "Like how likely I am to lose control and hurt somebody close to me. That kind of thing. Especially when I'm hungry and we're together."

Oh. That hurt, in all kinds of unexpected ways; these were personal things, and it wasn't just personal for him. *I* was the one who'd drawn the line with him, who'd said I was never, ever going to let him bite me, especially not that way. And it wasn't something we talked about, not ever. Especially not with third parties who might be named Sexy Hell Kitten. "And you thought it was okay to discuss all this with a vamp you met, like, thirty seconds ago."

"We've been talking for an hour, Eve. It wasn't like it was the first thing out of my mouth."

I swallowed. "Did you kiss her?"

"Eve!"

"Did you?"

"Jesus, of course not."

"Did you want to?"

Michael just looked at me for a few, fatal seconds, then said, "She's got that effect on guys, so, yeah, I guess I thought about it. But I didn't do it."

That didn't make me feel any better. Gloriana would be back. At the very least, she'd return the hat and coat, and if I wasn't here, he'd get all cozy with her again, and . . . things could happen. It wasn't that I didn't trust Michael—I did, I really did—but . . . she wasn't just any random chick. She hadn't stopped in just to pay a social call; Gloriana was hunting.

She was stalking my boyfriend.

"Over my dead body," I murmured. Michael looked startled. "Sorry. Talking to myself."

He sighed, straightened up, and crossed to stand right in front of me. He took the water glass out of my hand and put it carefully on the counter, then leaned in and kissed me, sweet and hot and hard. He braced himself with his hands on either side of me on the counter, and *damn*, the white fire of that just about wiped out anything else I had on my mind, including Gloriana's sly, sweet smile, or the way Michael had looked after her when she'd gone.

He was mine. *Mine.*

His hands left the counter and stroked through my hair, down the column of my neck, spread out on my shoulders. My top was stretchy enough to slide down my arms under the pressure of his palms, and I shivered as cool air hit my skin.

Michael picked me up in his arms like I was a bag of air, and for a long second he looked down at my face. His expression left me breathless. "You know I love you," he said. "You know that, don't you?"

"I know," I said. "But I know that can change."

"Never," he said, and kissed me again. "Never."

And for a little while, as he carried me upstairs to his room, I believed that would actually be true.

Always.

Even though I felt the tangle of frustration in him when his teeth grazed my neck, and he didn't bite.

I didn't hear about Gloriana for three days, until Michael told me there was going to be a big to-do in Founder's Square on Friday night to welcome the newest arrival. He had an invitation, of course; all the vampires got them. Some humans did, too, including our bookworm housemate, Claire . . . who, not surprisingly, decided that our *other* housemate, Shane, would be her plus-one to the party. I was kind of shocked that Claire decided to go, though; she wasn't generally the dressed-up party type (or the dressed-down party type, come to that).

I was sorry I asked when I finally did.

"Oh, I met her," Claire said, as we were doing laundry in the basement of the Glass House. She was sitting on the dryer this time while I dumped dirties into the washer; as usual, she was reading, this time one of Charlaine Harris's vampire books. She probably considered it research. "Gloriana, I mean. She seems nice."

Nice? I almost dropped the laundry detergent on my toes, which wouldn't have been as much of an owie as you might think, since my boots are steel-toed. "How'd you run into her?"

"She visited Myrnin."

That was strange, because Amelie was really damn serious that nobody, but nobody, visited Myrnin; those of us who knew Claire's boss at all had sworn under pain of actual, bloody death not to talk about him, ever, to anybody not in the know. Gloriana just strolling into the equivalent of a highly secure facility seemed . . . unlikely.

Except that I'd met her, too. Gloriana seemed like she could charm her way into Fort Knox, and the guards would stand in line to help her carry out the gold. "How'd they get along?" I asked.

"Oh, he was all suave," Claire said, and nearly giggled. "He actually ran off and got dressed up for her. It was cute. Well, I can understand why. She's pretty . . . pretty. They know each other, from olden times. Maybe he dated her once."

"Maybe," I said. Weirder things had happened. "So, you liked her?"

Claire turned her head and looked at me; she'd gotten her shoulder-length hair cut again, shorter, but it was messy from the wind outside.

Still cute, though. Her big, brown eyes were way too smart for either of our good. "You didn't?"

I hadn't told her about Gloriana's visit to the house. I wasn't sure why; I usually come right out with my latest drama, but this had felt . . . more dire than usual. And really personal. Now I just shook my head and focused on adding detergent in the right amounts for the colored clothes. Although I was tempted to bleach the hell out of Michael's stuff. "You ever have that happen where you meet someone and just— clash? We were like a gravel and cream sandwich."

"That is the weirdest thing you've ever said. I suppose you were the cream?"

"Of course I was the cream. Sha."

Trust Claire to not get distracted. "Something happened with her and Michael," she said. Wow. Zero to correct in one-point-nothing second. "Right?"

"Do you really think I'm that shallow that—okay, yes. She came over here. I found the two of them together."

Her eyes widened, and she slipped down off the dryer. "Seriously, *together*? Like—"

"No, not like. Tea in the parlor, or the vampy equivalent. You know. Sitting, talking." I frowned. "But it was way too nice. And besides, here, he's *mine*. You know?"

Claire nodded, not that it made the least bit of sense. She's a good friend. "Did you talk to him about it?"

"Oh, sure. Nothing happened, yada yada. The usual. But my may-dar went off like crazy."

"Maydar?"

"As in, he *may* be thinking about superhot sex with her. Like radar, only not as sure."

Claire rolled her eyes. "Did you *ask*?"

"Yes," I said. "I asked."

"And?"

"And he took me to bed."

"Oh."

"Yeah." I frowned unhappily down at the clothes, slammed the lid, and turned on the washer. "Oh. Exactly."

"Exactly what?"

That was Michael, standing at the top of the basement steps. Claire and I did the guilty dance. She dropped her book, and hurriedly picked it up. "Nothing," I blurted. My cheeks felt warm, and I was glad I was in shadow until I remembered, duh, vampire eyes. "Girl talk."

He nodded, looking at me with a little sadness in his gaze, I thought. "Just wanted to remind you that we're out of milk again. And hot sauce."

"Why are those two always out at the same time? Because those do *not* go together."

"I suspect Shane. He'd put hot sauce in anything," Michael said.

"Ugh," Claire sighed. "So true." Michael didn't leave, and after a second, Claire cleared her throat, closed up her book, and said, "Yeah, I've got something to do. Upstairs. Away from here."

He stepped aside to let her out, then closed the door behind her and settled down on the steps. I had wet whites to put in the dryer, so I busied myself with that, making extra sure that everything was untangled, that the dryer sheet was in, that the timer was just so.

Michael waited patiently for me to get the fidgeting done before he said, "If you don't want to go to the party, just say so."

"Of course I want to go. It's a big swanky dress-up party. How often do I get to go to those, in Morganville? I mean, some of these vampires own their own tuxes, even."

"Eve." His voice was gentle, and very kind. "I mean it. If you don't want to go, we won't go."

"I can't avoid her forever. It's too small a town."

He couldn't argue with that, and didn't try. "That doesn't mean you have to go to her welcome party. And if you want, I'll dress up and take you out somewhere nice."

"*Nice* being a relative term around here," I said, but secretly, the idea that he was willing to put on a suit and take me to the all-night diner made me smile. "Thanks, sweetie. But maybe I should just suck it up and go. What could happen?"

"Oh, plenty," he said cheerfully enough. And he was right. The two of us had rarely been to a party that *hadn't* ended in some kind of disaster, whether it was the senior prom, where Chuck (aptly named) Joris had vomited in the punch bowl, or the EEK fraternity party, which had ended in a vampire attack. And let's not even *mention* Mr. Evil Vampire Bishop's big welcome party, which had been a truckload of trouble.

"I'll be fine," I said, and glared at the clothes tumbling on high heat. "I'll play nice as long as she does."

I turned around. Michael had come down the stairs and crossed the distance between us, noiseless as the air, and I melted into his arms with a sense of real relief.

He kissed the top of my head. "That's my lady."

I really hoped he meant that.

I woke up the next day expecting—oh, I don't know, doom, disaster, and apocalypse; weirder things had happened in this town. But things seemed normal enough, even after I left the house and headed off to the day job. The one not-so-great thing that happened was that when I got to Common Grounds, guess who was there.

Gloriana. Deep in conversation with about a half-dozen admirers. She'd picked one of the tables in the darker section of the room, far

away from the blazing sunlight, and at first I thought all her new group-
ies were vamps, but no, some of them were definitely still rocking a
pulse. A couple of them were college boys, complete with the ubiqui-
tous backpacks. I was pretty sure one of them was Monica Morrell's
future ex-boyfriend, what's-his-name, the football player. Oooh, the
fur would fly if Monica dropped in and saw her current squeeze crushing on the New Girl.

I was kind of hoping for that, but no such luck. Gloriana hung out
for hours, laughing and talking, ordering regular rounds of whatever.

When she finally left, I saw Oliver watching her with a troubled
look on his face. "Boss?" I asked. "Something wrong?"

"No," he said. "No, I don't think so. Not yet, at any rate."

No matter how much extra effort I put into customer service, he
wouldn't elaborate, and that bothered me because (a) Oliver was
pretty free with his criticisms for the most part, and (b) it wasn't like
him to look worried. Ever.

No apocalypse had been declared by the end of my shift, though.
I supposed that qualified as a win.

Gloriana's party was fabulous, from the raised-ink invitations on
paper so soft and thick it felt like skin (but wasn't, thankfully) to the
uniformed vampire doormen on duty at the party building, to the
china and crystal and candles on the round banquet tables inside.
The vampires had turned out in force; I guess they didn't get much
chance to party like it was 1499, either. I was wearing a slinky black
velvet dress, with a train that trailed behind me like a fan. It was cut
low in the back to show off the rose tattoo I had there, and although
I didn't have any really good jewelry, I'd bummed some pretty good
costume stuff off people I knew. I looked fab.

Although in the company of vampires, I looked like . . . lunch. But if there was one thing I knew about Morganville, it was that your risk of being lunch was pretty much the same whether you were dressed like a movie star or dressed like a bag lady. Better to go out in style, if you had to go.

For all that, if Michael hadn't been on my arm, the looks I got coming into the ballroom might have made me turn around and run.

Luckily, Michael stayed steady and whispered, "Easy. They're not going to hurt us." It was the *us* that did it—the fact that we were a unit, and he didn't even try to think about it any other way. I took a deep breath, put on a brave smile, and raised my chin. That put my veins on display, but whatever.

Michael was wearing a nice black suit and a tie that wasn't quite conventional, in this crowd, but he didn't give a damn. Anyway, it was a music tie. They could munch ass if they didn't approve.

There was a line of vampires to meet; some I already knew, and some I didn't. I took my cue from Michael about how respectful to be, but not because I felt particularly humble; many of these old-school vamps took offense easily. When I got to Amelie and Oliver, I breathed a sigh of relief. They might take offense, but I knew what I could get away with.

I shook Amelie's hand firmly. She was wearing white gloves, and I was pretty sure the diamonds around her wrists were real. The gown was ice blue and really beautiful, and probably made by some famous designer I'd never heard about. Oliver was in a tuxedo, with tails. Damn, he James Bonded up really well. He bent over my hand, just a little—more of a suggestion of a hand kiss than anything else.

And then there was Gloriana, in a deep, vivid red gown, laughing and flirting with a whole circle of male admirers, both vamp and human. I saw Richard Morrell, the mayor, right in there, while his sister, Monica, stood off to the side, looking very unhappy. She was used to being the belle of the ball, and she'd certainly dressed for it, but whatever she was wearing, it looked like a knockoff rag next to Gloriana's dress, and she knew it. She also was alone, which was very unusual indeed. Even at a vampire party, she would have expected to draw some male attention, but there was a brand-new queen bee in town.

I felt Michael slowing as we passed Gloriana's group, as if he was reluctant to miss the opportunity, but he kept going. We went to the punch table, which featured two kinds—with plasma and without. He poured mine first. When I looked over at him, his face looked paler than normal, and the pupils of his eyes had gone wide, even in the relatively bright light.

"What?" I asked him.

"Nothing."

Shane squired Claire over to join us, already scanning the edible snacks with the eye of a kid who'd grown up snatching food where he could. He grabbed a plate and filled it until Claire slapped his hand. "You're not starving," she said. "Come on."

"It's been a long time since lunch," Shane said. "So, yeah, I am, Slappy Girl. Do you want one of these or not?" He held up a carrot stick. When she nodded, he fed it to her. Awww. So cute. "All right, you are now a party to the overindulgence. Quiet."

Claire, bless her, had somehow blackmailed Shane into donning a suit jacket, at least, although the pants looked suspiciously like dark jeans. At least he'd left the tuxedo T-shirt at home. The vamps wouldn't have been amused. He was even wearing a tie, though it featured Bettie Page in a lot of provocative poses. I hoped Oliver hadn't noticed.

"Did you see Gloriana?" Claire asked her boyfriend. Shane—big, scruffy Shane, who was cute in a totally different way from Michael, but really, just about as sweet—looked down at her and cocked one eyebrow.

"Am I alive?" he asked, and put his hand over his heart. "Yep, I noticed her. Oh, sorry, Mikey. No offense to the unalive."

Michael would normally have flipped him off—best-friends love—but he just gave Shane a look. Not his normal look, either. "Watch yourself with her," Michael said. "There's something . . . not right about her."

"Dude, she *looks* very right." Shane lost his humor, and started to frown. "Are you okay?"

"I can feel . . ." Michael shut his eyes tightly. "I can feel her from here. It's like a . . . call. A pull."

His hand was tight on mine, so tight it was painful, and I gave a little squeak of pain. When his eyes opened, they were crimson, and his pupils had shrunk down to small pinpoints.

I turned and looked. Gloriana was standing up. The men crowding around her were backing off, making . . . an exit. She smiled at them and glided out, hardly seeming to touch the floor as she went.

She headed straight for us.

For Michael.

She was wearing red gloves, and her diamonds, just like Amelie's, were real. Her smile was brighter than the glitter of the jewels. "Michael," she said, and took his hands in hers. He dropped mine so fast it was as if he'd forgotten I was there, and leaned in. She air-kissed him on both cheeks. He didn't pull back very far, and she didn't let go of his hands. "So glad you came to my party. It wouldn't have been a welcome without you, *mon cher.*" She did let go then, but only to reach up and touch his eyelids to close them. "You're going too far. Control. You must learn control."

He was shuddering very slightly, but when she stepped back, he opened his eyes, and the red was almost gone. Almost. "Thanks," he said. His voice sounded rough in his throat. "Have you met my friends? You remember Eve. . . ."

Somehow, having my name follow the word "friends" didn't make me feel any better at all. I didn't say anything. Neither did Gloriana, who just nodded very slightly. I couldn't tell what she felt about me, if she felt anything at all.

"And this is Claire—"

"Yes, we've met," Gloriana said. Her voice was warm and very sweet. "How is dear Myrnin? I thought he would be here tonight."

"He doesn't do parties, mostly," Claire said. She seemed kind of charmed by Gloriana's make-nice attitude, which was surprising; Claire was usually more levelheaded than that. "Well, neither do I, really. Oh, this is Shane, by the way. My boyfriend."

"Charming," Gloriana said, and extended her hand to him, knuckles up. Shane, who looked just about as overcome as every other guy in the room, took it and shook vigorously. Gloriana looked, just for a moment, taken aback; then she smiled, again. "Very direct, I see."

"I'm not subtle," Shane agreed. "You're very pretty."

Claire dug her elbow into his side. He didn't seem to notice. Gloriana's smile grew wider. "Yes," she said. "I'm afraid I am. It's a bit of a curse, sometimes." She turned back to Michael, who was still treating me like a nonperson, and held out her fingers. "Perhaps you'll save me from this sea of admirers," she said, "and escort me to the dance floor."

I opened my mouth, then closed it, because without a glance at me, Michael walked her past me, out to the open area of the ballroom, and the musicians struck up some kind of a waltz. And that wasn't Michael. It just . . . wasn't.

She was doing this to him.

As I looked around, I saw it on the faces of the guys who'd been hovering around her earlier—a kind of lost longing, as if she were the only girl in the world. I even saw it on the faces of guys I would have sworn knew better, like Richard Morrell.

It was creepy, to the power of actively sinister.

Claire put her arm around me. "Hey," she said softly. "Are you okay?"

I was, surprisingly. "That bitch is going down," I said. "She is *not* taking my boyfriend for a party favor."

"Chill—she's just dancing with him," Shane said. He was watching Gloriana with that same eerie, distracted concentration, and now Claire noticed it, too, with appropriate levels of alarm.

"No, she's not," Claire said, and smacked his arm. "Hey!"

"Oh, sorry," Shane said, and then looked around. "Right. Michael, not a party favor—how exactly are we going to accomplish that? Because she's wearing him like a paper hat right now."

I marched right over to the receiving line, grabbed Oliver's hand, and said, "Dance with me."

He gave me a long, odd look, exchanged a glance with Amelie, who seemed amused, and finally said, "If you insist."

"I do," I said. "Come on."

In my high heels, I was almost a match for Oliver in height. The last thing I wanted to be doing was clutching his undead body and twirling around on the dance floor, but I needed to keep Gloriana in sight, and I needed information. Oliver was a two-in-one.

And surprisingly, my vampire boss could *dance*. Like, reality-show-winning dancing. He whirled me around like an expert, and all I needed to do was pay attention and relax. That was a lot more fun than it should have been.

"Now," he said, about a minute or so into the ballroom display, "what exactly do you want from me?"

"Gloriana," I said, a little breathlessly. "I need to know what her deal is. Now."

Oliver glanced over at Gloriana, who was clinging to my boyfriend like red moss on a tree. Michael looked dazed. She looked delighted. "Ah," he said. "Gloriana doesn't like to be alone. I think she's decided that Michael is her newest accessory."

"He didn't want to go," I said. "She did something to him. I saw it. Some kind of—vampire superpower."

"Glamour," he said. "Most vampires have it, to some extent, though we rarely bother to use it. Gloriana is one of the few that has it in strength, and can use it on her own kind."

"Not cool."

"Not illegal," he corrected. "She'll tire of him soon enough, in a year or two. My advice is to let her have him, rather than risk becoming her enemy. He'll come back to you. Perhaps a bit worse for wear, but—"

"No," I said. My cheeks felt like they were flaming, under the pale makeup. "No way in hell. He is *my* boyfriend, and she doesn't get to play with him. It'd be different if he wanted it, but he doesn't."

Oliver gave me a dark, pitying smile, and bent me over backward. "Are you absolutely sure of that?" he asked. "Because Gloriana can only work that kind of glamour on those who are open to it. Michael's a new vampire. He's never been with one of us. I'm sure he has . . . questions."

He did. He'd told me that, straight up, and now it scared me. "I'm sure," I said. My eyes filled with tears. "He can't just . . . take off with her. He loves me."

Oliver let me up—or rather, snapped me back upright—and glided me backward through a complicated set of twirls. "I'm afraid that love is rarely that simple," he said. "Or that painless. Ah, look, they're leaving."

I caught my breath on a cry and pulled free of him, or tried to; he held on long enough to say, "Don't get into the middle of it, Eve. The pull's strong. Michael may not be able to resist no matter what you do." He smiled, a little sadly. "You may take that from one who knows."

I yanked my wrist free, gathered up my train, and dashed out the door after Gloriana and Michael.

This was the moment when I had a choice to make. I knew what I *wanted* to do—scream, cry, start a slap fight with the undead skank trying to take my boyfriend. But somehow, I knew that fighting for Michael that way would only make me look small, petty, and ugly beside Gloriana's mature poise.

I didn't know what the alternative was, but I was going to have to find it, fast.

They were halfway down the steps when I caught up. The light out here was mostly provided by the white, ghostly moon, and they seemed identically pale as they turned to look at me. I rushed down toward them. "Michael!" I gasped, and came to a halt one step above them. "Michael, please wait!"

Gloriana smiled at me, still maddeningly sweet. I'd been talking to him, but she was the one who answered me. "Oh, don't worry. I'll bring him back," she said. "If he wants to return."

"Go back, Eve," Michael said. "I'll see you later."

"You mean, you'll dump me later?" I felt short of breath. Suffocating. "No. If you want to break up, be a man. Do it now, to my face."

"I don't want to hurt you," he said, and I believed that. I could see it on his face. "I can't do this right now, all right? Just go home. I'm not—"

"Not yourself? Yeah, that's because *she's* leading you around by the—by the nose! Please, *listen!* I love you. I know you don't want to do this to me. Or to yourself."

Gloriana wasn't smiling anymore. I could feel the waves of pressure coming off her, closing around Michael. She was working hard at this, I realized. Harder than she'd expected. I might have taken some satisfaction in that, except that I was terrified that all her effort might actually be enough. "Michael," she said. "Tell her to go away and go back to her *friends*. She's just a child. You need someone . . . more experienced. Someone who understands what you want, and what you need, and isn't afraid to help you through this . . . difficult time."

He didn't say anything. That, in itself, was a victory, but I could see him shaking again, very lightly. Vibrating, really. When she laid her gloved fingers on his hand, I saw his lips part in a soundless gasp.

"No," I said, and took a step down, putting myself on the same level with him. I knocked her hand away, wrapped my arms around him. "No, I'm not going anywhere. You've got a roomful of candidates back there. You don't get him, not unless you go through me first."

Gloriana backed off, frowning. God, even her frowns were adorable, though the anger brewing in her eyes wasn't so precious. I'd surprised her, all right. And now she was starting to realize that she might not be able to hijack Michael as she'd planned . . . and she wasn't pleased. Not at all.

Michael stopped shaking, and I felt him relax against me. Sweet relief. His head came down on my shoulder, and I turned my head to glare at the other vampire. She was expressionless now, not smiling, not laughing, not exuding charm. She looked like a wax doll, and not a particularly pretty one, at that.

"Is that how it's going to be?" she asked.

Michael pulled in a breath and said, "I'm with Eve." Just that. Just three words, but they made me feel faint with relief and love.

I didn't let go of him.

Gloriana slowly, reluctantly smiled, and the prettiness came back. "I apologize," she said. "My mistake, of course. I didn't think you were serious about her, or that she'd be so . . . forceful. I misjudged you both." She put her palms together and bowed—I was almost certain mockingly. "I'm sure we'll see each other again, Michael. Eve."

He didn't answer her. He was frighteningly quiet, I thought. Gloriana looked up, toward the top of the steps, and I saw her face change into something that was momentarily very, very ugly.

Amelie was standing up there, shining in the moonlight, radiantly silver. Beautiful, in a way that Gloriana would never be, for all her charm and good looks.

"Come back to the party," Amelie said. "Your swains are missing you, Glory. I'm sure you wouldn't want to be responsible for any more broken hearts tonight."

She turned and walked away, and I heard Gloriana make a light hissing sound, almost like a snake. She gave Michael one last, sidelong look, and then I felt something . . . snap, as if pressure had broken around us.

As she walked away, Michael tightened his arms around me, almost lifting me off my feet, and whispered, "God, Eve—God, I'm so sorry." He was shaken, and he sounded angry—not at me; at himself. "I couldn't stop myself. It was like being—it was like a dream. But I didn't want to wake up, either."

"Oliver called it glamour," I said. "I can't feel it, though."

"No, not unless she wants you to. She's—narcotic. It's terrible, but it—feels so good."

I closed my eyes for a moment and strangled my inner drama queen before I said, very carefully, "Michael, if you really . . . need her . . ."

Michael Glass raised his head. The moonlight was shining full on his face, and I could read everything there, all the conflict and the love and the desperation. "I want you," he said. "I want to stay with you. I love you. God, Eve, I love you."

The intensity of the way he said it made my heart lurch painfully. I wanted to cry in relief, but I managed to hold the tears back. "Then don't do that again," I said. "Promise."

"No," he said. "You promise *me* something."

I blinked. "I . . . promise never to dance with Oliver again?"

He didn't laugh. "Promise me you'll marry me," he said. "Promise me that you're not going to leave me. I need you, Eve. I've always needed you and I always will. Please. Promise me."

I wasn't sure I'd heard him right, not at first. *Marry.* It wasn't that I hadn't thought about it, dreamed about it, but . . . hearing him say it, right out loud, that was—terrifying. And thrilling. And terrifying, again.

I didn't know what to say, except, finally, "Yes." It came out a whisper, timid and slow, but it seemed to ring like a bell on the still air. I said it again, stronger. "Yes. Oh, God, *yes.*"

He kissed me. It wasn't his normal kind of sweet, gentle kiss— this was full of the same intensity, the same desperate focus. I wanted him in all kinds of ways, with identical ferocity. He was growling, a little, in the back of his throat, and sliding his hands down my arms.

Then he picked me up and carried me down the steps, into the shadows. It was wild, and crazy, and stupid, but neither of us cared just then; we just *needed.*

And that moment came, when his teeth grazed my neck. I thought about Gloriana, about that need inside him she'd used against him. I thought about all my long-held vows to myself, and weighed all that against how much I loved him.

I put my hand on his cheek. "Michael." He licked my skin, just above the veins. "Michael, do it. Go ahead."

For a second he didn't move, and then he slowly pulled away and looked down at me. I couldn't read his expression. "You're sure," he said. "You're really sure."

"I'm sure. Just, you know, don't—" *Kill me,* I thought. My heartbeat was thumping so fast it sounded like war drums. "I don't want to be turned. You know that."

"I know," he said, very softly. "One more time. You're sure."

"Yes." This time, I heard certainty in my own voice, and a kind of peace settled over me. "Yes."

I can't remember what it felt like, not really; it was overwhelming, and scary, and wonderful, and so, so much better than I'd ever imagined. He licked the wound gently, until the bleeding stopped, and then gently kissed it. I felt dizzy and woozy and unbelievably high—vampire bites can do that, if they do it right. If they take the time. Or so I'd heard.

I sank against Michael's chest, and he held me. "Okay?" he whispered. I made a wordless sound of pleasure and snuggled in against him. "Thank you."

I laughed. "It wasn't a gift, Michael."

He kissed my nose. "No," he agreed. "But you are. I don't know what I'd be without you, Eve. But I don't want to find out."

"Not even if Gloriana comes calling?"

"Especially," he said, very seriously. "You were amazing, by the way. You made her look . . ."

"Cheap?" I said cheerfully.

"Immature," he said, and kissed my hand. "You looked like the sexiest woman in the world."

"Well, in fairness, I *am* the sexiest woman in the world."

"And you're always right."

"You are so brilliant."

He helped me to my feet, and got handsy settling my dress back around me comfortably. Then he held me in place and stared down at me for a long moment.

"Am I really sexier than Gloriana?" I asked.

And that got me a slow, *very* sexy smile. "Sorry, don't think I know anyone by that name."

And then he took off his suit jacket, wrapped it around my shoulders, and walked me back up to the party.

VEXED

☾

*Dedicated to Cassie Gilmon for her support
of the Morganville digital series Kickstarter, 2014*

And now, we have our next original short story . . . and another one for
Myrnin, because Cassie wanted it that way! Technically, it's Myrnin
and Oliver, who have a strange affinity, mostly because they're both capable of being utterly weird and cruel when pushed, but also capable of
kindness. Myrnin's kindness is on display here, but so is his weirdness,
and Oliver's cruelty. A little of everything, and a creepy tale of a pursuit
that ends in a sinister house with secrets, ghosts, lies, and monsters.

Some of the monsters, they've brought in with them.

Fun factoid: I borrowed (as I am prone to do, with vampire tales)
from history for this, specifically the gruesome story of the Bloody
Benders, who ran a combination store / traveler's inn, with murder on
the side, in 1870s Kansas. The names I used were correct to that
period, and I have a fondness for bizarre names, having great-aunts
named Pearly Lake and Precious Jewel in my family tree. Rumor says
there was also a relative named Holy Bible, but I can't swear to that one.

"I feel this is all going to come to a bad end," Myrnin said, and clung to the handle above the passenger-side door as the car shrieked around another turn. It was a black and moonless night, and without headlights, a human driver would certainly have crashed by now, but the driver was far from human.

However, Oliver also wasn't a terribly *good* driver, even as a vampire, and the tires jumped the curb. A mailbox impacted the side of the car just behind where Myrnin sat and went flying, spilling a sad scatter of bills and letters.

"Shut up," Oliver said, as Myrnin opened his mouth to comment. Myrnin obeyed, because the tension in the man's voice was on the edge of violence. "I hate these . . . mechanical beasts. No wonder Amelie insists on a driver."

"*I* can drive. Claire taught me."

"Bad luck for all the others on the road, then. Shut up. I'm trying to concentrate."

"You will never catch him like this."

"Why not?"

"He's a better runner than you are a driver?"

Oliver whipped the wheel unnecessarily hard to the left, and Myrnin found himself flung hard against the restraint—the *seat belt,* as Claire insisted on calling it, though clearly it was not a belt at all, and certainly not a seat, but more of a harness. Despite that quibble, he did like the safety measures modern society had imposed. Quite a lot of carriage accidents could have come to better outcomes with the minor addition of such things.

The restraint came into play again as Oliver forcefully applied the brakes, and the vehicle skidded to a loud stop, accompanied by smoke and the smell of distressed tires. "He's off the road," Oliver said. "We'll have to run him down on foot."

"Thank Jesu," Myrnin said. "I'd rather run a thousand miles than endure your substandard mechanized skills again."

"Feel free to bugger off home, then."

"I will not!"

"Then do me the kindness of being silent. I'm *listening*."

Myrnin shut up, because even among vampires, Oliver had a reputation for acute hearing, and one saving grace of Morganville, Texas, was its remote location. Unlike in modern cities of any significant size, the nights here were clear and silent. Easy to hear disturbances, at least with vampire senses. Easy to hear the breathing and heartbeats of potential victims . . . but not so easy to track a fleeing vampire. Vampires were stealthy by nature, sometimes even to one another.

The creature they were tracking was more dangerous than most, and Myrnin was starting to wonder why he, of all the Morganville vampires, had decided to take up this challenge. He was, after all, more of an ambush predator than a stalker. He didn't like the pursuit as much as Oliver; it always felt like far too much effort, and fun as it sometimes was, he often felt so guilty, after.

This was for a good cause, at least, and he *was* operating under orders. Amelie's orders. Or he'd not be voluntarily spending time with Oliver. His issues with the man stemmed back five hundred years or more.

"This way," Oliver said, and was out the driver's side of the car and moving with speed before Myrnin could so much as fumble his way clear of his seat harness. He snapped it in a fit of pique. Useless things, good for nothing but saving humans.

Considering he'd been made vampire as an older man, Oliver was extremely lithe; even with longer legs, Myrnin had to run uncomfortably fast to keep pace. He couldn't detect the man they were following, but keeping track of Oliver would do well enough. The riding boots he wore weren't good for running, but he was somewhat grateful that he hadn't chosen the bunny slippers tonight. They were certainly not made for harsh terrain, and the area in which they'd gone was littered with rusted metal scrap, discarded lumber, and snakes too slow to slip out of the way, but still fast enough to strike at him in the darkness. Dangerous footing, even for a vampire.

He managed to pull next to the still-running Oliver and said, "There are snakes, you know." As a vampire, he had the dignity of not having to gasp it out.

"If a snake bit you, it would die of disgust, and you should die of embarrassment," Oliver said. "He's stopped." Oliver immediately slowed to a walk, and Myrnin fell in beside him, happy for the change. His eyes picked up the starlight and painted a vivid, though shades-of-blue, picture of a leaning old farmhouse with broken windows and a yawning door. Someone had spray-painted slogans on it, layers upon layers of meaningless words. Some things never changed throughout the ages, and graffiti was one of them, from ancient Egypt to modern times. It was as though humanity had a burning need to make a mark, wherever it set its hand—and the mark was all too often an insult.

"How do you want to go about this?" Myrnin asked.

"Keep it simple. You take the back. I'll take the front. We crush him in the middle." A short pause, and then, "Be careful."

Myrnin raised his eyebrows. "I'm touched that you're so concerned for me."

"I'm not concerned for *you*, fool. I'm concerned you'll let him rip you apart and escape. It would be very inconvenient for me to run him down again."

"Ah. It makes so much more sense now."

Myrnin dodged to avoid a blow from Oliver's fist, and moved around to the back of the farmhouse. They were just outside Morganville, and he could feel the difference here. It felt alien, unknown, uncomfortable. He didn't like leaving town anymore. Morganville had become so much his haven, and his home. There, he was protected. Out here he felt small, and vulnerable. Too many memories of being hunted through the streets, hounded in the open. Shut up in torturously small cells. Vampires might be strong and fast, but they were just as vulnerable as all the other mighty creatures that humans had made extinct.

Out here, he was as much prey as predator.

The back door of the house was boarded shut, but he slithered in through a broken window and landed without a sound on the warped wood floor. It was rotten, but he could sense where the fragile spots were, and stepped carefully to avoid any betraying creaks and snaps. There were spiders here, *lots* of spiders, but he rather liked them— elegant creatures, so perfectly suited to their lives. Hard to tell how they felt about him at the moment, though, since they seemed to be scattering out of his way.

One thing he did *not* care for was the scorpion that scuttled out of the darkness to aim its stinger at his booted foot. Clearly, he was *not* amiable. Myrnin bent, picked it up by the segmented tail, and held it up to his face, frowning at it as it snapped its claws toward his nose as it twisted and turned. "Rude," he said to it. "Learn your manners, now." He threw it out the window, and watched it dart across the sand, still jabbing the air furiously with its barbed tail.

Then he sensed something looming over his head, and looked up to see a face staring down at him. Or . . . no. Not a face. In that split second it looked like a face, a formless dark thing watching him, but then it solidified into shadows and an unfortunate pattern of mold.

Still . . . he felt watched.

There was also a corpse in the room, but it was not watching him. It lay in the corner on its back. The young man was clearly dead, and had been for days. Pale and bloodless, he bore neat holes in his throat, and his eyes were closed.

"I've found the missing boy," Myrnin called. "Dead." He didn't really need to say that. Neither he nor Oliver had been deluded enough to believe they'd find him alive.

"Our quarry's moved upstairs," said a voice at Myrnin's side, and he flinched just a little. Oliver had, once again, managed to creep up without drawing his attention. "Amelie's not going to be well pleased with this. We'll need to get the boy decently buried and compensate his family. You retrieve the body and I'll go up and find this . . . I can't properly even call him a vampire."

"The boy's long gone, and he can wait," Myrnin said. "This . . . might take both of us. Whatever this . . . thing may be, he is not quite sane."

Oliver sent him a look. Not the normal look of disdain and dismissal, but . . . something else. Something more serious. "Well, you would know," he said. "But I think you may be right."

Oliver led the way up the steps, and Myrnin was careful to avoid the fragile center of the wood treads; this house, with its alarmingly off-true walls and stench of rot, was ready to collapse in the next strong wind. Surprising that it hadn't already, considering its state. There was threadbare carpet at the top, and some ancient, faded photographs of a posed family lingered on the walls. A bedroom to the right held a tilting four-poster, a decaying mattress with pillows and the type of coverlet unpopular fifty years past. Clothes remained rotting in the wardrobe.

He wondered what had happened to the family who'd once lived here and so evidently vanished without a trace . . . and then decided perhaps it was best not to know. This whole place trembled with fear and tragedy. No wonder their quarry had been drawn to it as a lair.

Oliver tapped his shoulder and pointed down the hall to the other small bedroom. The door was shut, and starlight glinted on the old glass knob. Myrnin steeled himself, and nodded his readiness.

Oliver took hold of the knob and turned it.

The attack came *through* the door with shocking suddenness, smashing the old wood into splinters, and then the vampire was on them, screaming. It was armed with a knife, a sharp, oddly shaped thing that sliced the light as it arced for Oliver's face. Oliver fell back, and Myrnin lunged forward over him and caught the attacker around the chest. His weight and momentum threw it backward, but the dry wood beneath them shattered on impact, sending them both crashing through the floor and down into the room beneath.

It would have stunned a human, or broken his back, but vampires were made of hardier stuff—and this creature was unnaturally fast and strong. Myrnin grabbed for the right hand, the one with the knife, while trying to keep the snapping, ravenous fangs from his own throat. There was no room for fear or strategy. He couldn't plan, couldn't think of anything but simply surviving from one second to the next, until Oliver dropped through the jagged hole from the floor above, grabbed the vampire's head in both hands, and twisted it all the way around to snap its neck with a dry clicking sound.

That didn't kill it, but it effectively rendered it helpless for a while. Oliver slung the thing off to the side and offered Myrnin a hand up, which he accepted without shame. He felt battered and greatly lucky to be alive.

"We need to kill this thing," Myrnin said. His voice, he was surprised to hear, sounded rational and quite precise. "We *must* kill it. Now."

"My orders are to bring him to Amelie," Oliver said.

"Couldn't he just . . . fall and accidentally dismember himself?"

"No matter how much I long for that, no. I follow her orders." Oliver grabbed the prisoner's arm and hauled it up. The head lolled unnaturally. "You did remember the bindings, I hope?"

"Of course." Myrnin searched his pockets, seared his fingers raw on the touch of silver braided wire, and folded a much-abused handkerchief over the flexible length to draw it out. He wrapped it tight around the wrists, then added a silver hook to link that binding to the broken throat. The neck was healing, of course. Slowly, but steadily. It would bear careful attention to make sure the creature stayed helpless.

He tied the ankles with the same length of silver wire, and tested the tensile strength. The bindings seemed solid enough.

The prisoner's shoulders twitched, and he seemed to be staring at Myrnin with wide dark eyes. There was a wild menace in that face, and something far, far worse.

"Careful," Oliver snapped, and kicked at the bound body; the head bounced, but the neck was no longer limp. It recovered shockingly fast. "Look at me with such disrespect and I'll take those eyes right out. Understand, Lucian?"

"It has a name?"

"Unfortunately we all have names. And pasts; his is a particularly unpleasant one. I don't know who had the awful stupidity to make someone like this into one of us, but I hope his maker's long dead, or he'll join this monster's bonfire." Oliver hauled the prisoner—Myrnin refused to use a name for it, even in the noisy privacy of his own mind, because names gave things power—to its feet. It shuffled awkwardly in the silver ankle shackles, which was all to the good, as far as Myrnin was concerned. "Let's go. The faster I have this finished, the better I'll like it."

"What about . . . this place?" Myrnin gestured at the house around them without giving it another look, because once had been truly enough for a lifetime. "It's a certainty there are other victims in here."

"It's a police matter. Something for Chief Moses to deal with, although I suspect most of the victims will be transients. He'd not have gotten away with his killing so long if he'd been preying on Morganville residents exclusively."

Pity poor Chief Moses, then. Myrnin shuddered. "Better to burn it to the ground," he said. "It'll bring their loved ones no peace to tell them how they died."

Oliver stared at him for a second, with a very odd expression. "It's always better to know," he said. "Better haunted by ghosts than always searching for what's not there."

That sounded oddly like experience speaking, and Myrnin almost asked, but all he really wanted was to be out of this oppressive place, with all of the house's evil humors.

Oliver muscled his captive out a broken window, and Myrnin walked toward it to follow . . . and that was when the window disappeared. Between one tick of time and the next, it just vanished, as if it had never been. Instead, there was just a wall, with its skin of wallpaper peeling from the bones of plaster.

Myrnin stopped. He slowly put out a hand, and touched crusted dry paper. It crumbled at his touch.

He moved for the other window, and caught a glimpse of Oliver turning impatiently to find out why he hadn't followed . . . and then that glimpse disappeared as the window filled with old, dry boards in a strange shimmer.

Well. This called for direct action. He punched the wood in a flurry, unmindful of the splinters and shards, and they did indeed break . . . but as soon as they did, more appeared. And more. An endless supply of barriers.

He heard Oliver hammering on the outside of the house, trying to batter a way in, but clearly, the house did not want Oliver.

It wanted *him*.

Shouting Oliver's name at full volume did nothing, except to rain down a tiny storm of dust from the decaying ceiling. Myrnin shut his eyes for a moment, then opened them again. Nothing seemed to have changed. He was used to imagining things, but those always had a certain feel to them; he'd trained himself in recognizing when his wandering mind threw up falsehoods.

This did not seem to be such a case.

He headed for yet another broken-out window, moving very slowly this time. As he stretched his hand forth, the house *shifted* . . . and his fingers touched a barrier, not open air.

This place did not want him to leave.

He could hear it now, a kind of low, lethal hum well below the level of even vampire understanding, but he knew in an instinctive way that it was saying something to him . . . and what it was saying would eat away at him, strip him down to bone and madness, and he could not have that. He was vulnerable here. He'd sensed it even outside, and he'd thought it was only his worry of being away from the safer ground of Morganville, but it was more than that.

This place was alive.

"You want something," he whispered.

Oliver and his prisoner were almost certainly gone by now. Oliver, being Oliver, would have decided that taking his prize back to Amelie would have precedence over any rescue effort—and to be fair, the prisoner he had in chains was too dangerous to leave to its own devices for long.

He'll come back for me, Myrnin told himself, to stem a rising tide of anxiety. *Or he'll send help. I only have to stay calm and find a way to save myself.*

Well, that seemed easy.

He felt in his pockets and found the cell phone that Claire always insisted he carry; it was the simplest possible model, one with only a few numbers programmed and the choice of CALL, END, and EMERGENCY CALL. He decided that this was rightly an emergency call and pressed that button.

Silence.

He checked the small glowing screen. It told him there was no signal. *I knew these things were useless,* he thought, and dropped it to the floor to spin randomly, like a compass pointing toward insanity.

When he looked up again, there was a dining table crouching in the middle of the room. It was entirely out of place, because it seemed new, shining, spotless. There were six chairs around it.

He glanced back toward the wreck of a kitchen, and found it neat and orderly, as though the house itself was going back in time. No ghosts visible. That should have been an improvement. It didn't seem so.

There was now a book on the table—a photograph album, made of old green velvet with fancy celluloid corners. On it, in antique metal script, it said *Our Family.*

There didn't seem much alternative, and it was pointless to try for another exit. He had to follow the path this place set for him, at least for now. The house wanted to tell him something.

He was willing to listen.

Myrnin sat down in the chair in front of the album, and reached out to flip open the latch. There was a space on the left-hand side of the cover for a name, and written in faded copperplate it said *The Vexen Family.*

Vexen. That seemed an ill-omened name.

The right side held a single large photograph—or, rather, a tintype—of a thin, craggy old man in an ill-fitting formal nineteenth-century suit, with a top hat. He was standing in what would have been the best days of this old farmhouse, with a pinch-faced wife half his age in her Sunday-best bonnet and black dress of mourning. A group of children sat at their feet.

But something about the photo struck him oddly, and in a moment he knew what it was: living children, but one dead one in the middle, propped up by his uncomfortable siblings on each side to give the boy a false appearance of life. It was given the lie by his blank stare and lolling head.

A mourning photograph. A Victorian tradition, when only one image might have existed of each person, and a way to immortalize the dead before it was too late. To modern eyes, it was horribly morbid, but for that family, in that time, it would have been a precious thing to memorialize a loved one.

He tried not to read anything into its presence in the album.

The next two pages held clippings of old, yellowed newspaper articles, complete with a not-very-expertly drawn illustration of the very farmhouse in which he now stood. This was, he realized, near the time of Morganville's founding, and well before he'd become sane enough to venture far from his own walls in his new laboratory. The newspaper was the long-dead *Morganville Crier*, and it detailed a murder at the Vexen house. Micajah Vexen, his wife, Virtue, his brother Argus, and his children Trothe and Verily had all been killed. Missing from the home was the middle Vexen daughter, Clemencie. The gruesome scene had been discovered days later by a passing cowboy who'd stopped to water his horse. The Morganville sheriff of that time had been involved. No arrests had ever been made, according to the second clipped article.

The next turn of the page brought photos of the dead. Not in their living years . . . No, the house was not that kind. These were photos taken of them on the spot of their discovery—crime scene photos, they would have been called today. Faded sepia, but vivid enough to be chilling. Likely a profitable morbid sideline for the photographer.

Myrnin stared at them, trying to see what he was supposed to take from them. That it hadn't been a vampire's kill? That much was obvious; the scene was much too chaotic, too enraged, too . . . messy. It seemed to be a very human crime.

"Seems a bit obvious," he said conversationally to the madhouse that was holding him prisoner. "Some family argument that boiled out of control, and the children were in the way of it. Am I right?" He turned the page. Nothing. He turned another, and received blank pages. "If that is your very subtle way of showing displeasure at my lack of comprehension . . ."

He looked up, because there was someone sitting across the table from him. A girl.

"Ah. That's better. Clemencie?" The girl sitting across from him was bone white, eerily so, with hair bleached pale and eyes clouded over. In life, he doubted she'd been so colorless. From the shape of her, she would have been perhaps thirteen or fourteen . . . child more than woman. "Or is your name Trothe?"

The lips parted and shaped a word, but there was no sound.

"Clemencie, then," he said. "If you're meant to terrify me, I'll have to warn you that you won't cause me nightmares. I'm far worse than you. In other words, you'll have to do better."

She smiled. It was a sweet, unguarded kind of thing, and it made her . . . human. And it hurt, to think on this girl suffering. He'd been a predator a long time, but he'd rarely been a monster. Not in that way.

She reached out one pallid hand to him, and turned it palm up.

"You want something, yes. I know that much," he said. "And I must compliment you on delivering a very creditable haunting, but you really must be more specific. I'm a vampire, not a mind reader."

She just gazed at him with those blind eyes, and he finally sighed. He'd been raised believing in many things, ghosts chief among them, and he knew better than to touch one. Especially at the ghost's invitation. In the small Welsh village where he'd been raised, touching a ghost was a direct portal to hell.

But he *did* want to get out of this place, and he sensed very strongly that Clemencie Vexen would be the only doorway through which he could pass.

So he touched her hand . . . and died.

It wasn't *actual* death, physical death, but it certainly felt that way. Not pleasant. Not quick. It was the death of a confused, anguished child who could not understand how her life had gone so badly wrong, or why anyone, *anyone*, would want to wring such pain from her.

He sat back with a sigh, falling back into his own suddenly aching body, and put a trembling hand to his forehead. Where the ghost had gripped his fingers, they felt icy and frostbitten, and were almost as pale as the corpse-girl's. As the feeling came back, they shot through with hot needles of pain, but he hardly even noted it.

He had died once, but by comparison his mortal ending had been much easier. He was not generally given to fits of emotion, but for a long moment he could not speak, nor could he look at Clemencie's still, pale face, which was blankly tranquil, in death as it had not been in the last moments of her life.

"Oh, dear child," he said. "What happened to you here? And where did you go?"

When he looked up, Clemencie was no longer there. No one was there. The book was gone, but the table itself—and the chair in which he sat—were very much in evidence.

"Isn't that what you wanted me to ask? No? Then what do you want from me?" he asked the empty air. There was a terrible feeling in the air, something heavy and grim that made him wonder whether this place would ever release him. *Maybe it's just lonely,* he thought. *Maybe it wants company. It's tired of the dead. It wants the almost-alive.*

He felt hands on his shoulders then. Cold hands. From the corners of his eyes, he saw the bloodless pale fingers, and felt the exhalation of cold on the back of his neck. Vampire or not, he shivered.

"You want me to find you," he said, and drew in a sharp breath he did not need as her cold presence passed *through* him. When he exhaled the breath again, it hung as frozen fog on the air. Clemencie sat again in the chair across from him, staring with her blind, calm eyes. "You understand that it won't bring you back?"

She nodded slowly.

"Are you in the house?" That garnered him another nod, this one more emphatic. *Twenty questions with a ghost.* Well, it was hardly the most insane thing he'd ever done. Or even in the top hundred, if he was forced to be honest. "Upstairs?" No nod. He assumed that meant a negative. "Here, on this floor?" Silence and stillness, again. He heard that buzzing whisper again, pushing at his mind like white static, and it sparked alarm in him. He needed to leave this place. He could almost hear its . . . words, and he sensed that when he did, they would burn him like silver. "Below?"

Not a nod, this time. An explosive movement. Clemencie slapped her ghostly hands on the surface of the table and leaned forward, almost nose to nose with him, and he recoiled. Couldn't quite help it. She bared her teeth and . . . nodded.

Damnation. He *really* needed to leave this place.

"If I go down and find you, will you let me leave here?" he asked her. The spirit stayed frozen in front of him, locked into that aggressive, frightening lean for what felt like far too long, and then she subsided back into a calm sitting position on the other side of the table.

And nodded.

Damnation.

The basement of a murder house, haunted by a very frightening, very sad little girl.

Yes, this sounded like, as Shane would have sarcastically said, *the best time ever.*

It was easy to see how searchers had missed it, he thought; the trapdoor to the cellar was well hidden in the floorboards, much more so than if it had been an ordinary sort of cool room. Someone hadn't wanted this place to be found. Age and rot had sagged the boards, though, and he found the seams and pried it up. The hinges broke loose as it levered away, and the square of rotting wood almost disintegrated in his hands. He stared down into the dark. He'd often said to himself, and to others, that there was nothing in the dark that wasn't also there in the light, but in truth, he knew differently. There was one thing in the dark: fear. Fear that smothered and consumed and twisted.

He'd spent too many years in dark holes like this, and he hesitated for a moment on the lip of the cellar.

Clemencie silently rose from her chair at the table, and the table itself disappeared as she walked through them toward him. Well . . . walked was not quite the right word. Glided, perhaps.

"I know," he told her, and sighed. "I know." Before she could rush at him and surprise him into it, he simply stepped out, and dropped.

It wasn't so deep as he'd expected: ten feet, at most, a minor jump that he hardly felt at all.

But he did *hear* it, because bones snapped and crunched, and for an instant he waited for the pain to hit, but they had not, after all, been *his* bones. The skeleton that lay beneath his feet was dressed in a pale wisp of a dress that matched what the ghost wore.

Clemencie stood now in the cellar's corner, silent and as pale as the dead bones around his feet.

"Ah," he said. "I appear to have found you, Clemencie. And without much effort, it would seem. You didn't escape the terror that found your family after all. . . ."

His voice faded, because he began to pick out the details of the room. Near her stood a row of wooden crates, and in the crates were coins, faded old crumpled paper money, jewels, watches . . . anything of value. Gold teeth had their own special bin. Here and there lying in heaps were mounds of decaying cloth, the glint of tarnished buckles, the withered leather of belts and boots. All carefully sorted.

"What is this?" he asked her. Her head was bowed, and she slowly shook her head. Fine, pale hair had fallen to cover her face like a mourner's veil. But in truth, he did not need her to tell him. He'd seen such a thing before, in terrible places where the dead had been murdered with brutal efficiency, their belongings put into order for later use.

This cellar was a lair all its own, and whatever beast had made its nest here had been red indeed. From the carefully sorted loot, dozens had died here, at the least.

Another chained wooden door led out of the cellar, and he waited to see what she wanted him to do . . . but Clemencie gave him no sign. No sign at all.

No help for it, then. No way out but forward.

He strode forward, grabbed the rusted chain that secured the door, and yanked. It broke apart with a dull thud, and the door sagged on its hinges. Not quite as rotten as the trapdoor, but on its last days.

Beyond was pitch-darkness. Even vampire eyes had trouble without *some* spark of light, but Myrnin could smell the death here. A century on, it had its own powerful stench.

So many bones.

He turned back to Clemencie's broken skeleton, with the dull rags of her hair still spread out on the dirt floor, and shook his head. "It appears to me that whatever fate your family suffered, it was one they well deserved. Still, no one chooses their family, and this is a vile place to call a grave," he said. "I'll take you out of here and bury you in a cleaner spot, if that's what you wish."

He looked at the ghost still waiting in the corner. She raised her head, and she was smiling. Oh, not a smile of thanks, or of relief, or of any sweet thing.

That, Myrnin thought, was an evil smile. A truly, truly evil smile.

"No," Clemencie Vexen said to him, and her voice was full of screams and whispers and pleas and cries. It was the voice of hell given tongue and lips. "You took away my new friend. You will take his place. You will bring them here as my grandfather did, and my father, and my mother, and my uncle. You will sanctify them, and their worldly goods will fund our great works."

I never should have touched a ghost, Myrnin thought. *Never never never. My mother was right.* His mental voice seemed high and strange, and if he had not been through so much in his long, long life, he'd have broken in pieces at that moment and gone utterly mad. Her eyes had taken on a glow; they were not merely blank. They were full of things he most earnestly wished to unsee.

"Very kind of you to offer," he said aloud, "but I already have a job. And that of pet monster has never suited me very well."

She came at him, of course, but by then he was already moving, leaping straight up for the open square of the cellar's entrance, and as he rose, he caught the edges and vaulted up like a tumbler, rolling across the filthy floor and up to his feet and running as hard as he could, because he knew that the little demon wouldn't take no for an answer. He had no idea what kind of harm she could do him, but if she could make the house itself into a weapon, then he imagined it would be quite a lot of harm indeed.

"There's nowhere you can run!" Clemencie shrieked behind him, and then in a flash she was in front of him, a cold wrathful shadow that he only glimpsed before veering away and up the stairs, past the faded photographs of her loathsome family. He ducked as a kitchen knife flew in a steel whirl toward his neck, because while neck *snapping* might be survivable for a vampire, neck *bisection* was not, and he leaped over the yawning gap where he and her last friend, Lucian, had crashed through the floor, and landed catlike in the room beyond . . .

. . . which held another ghost.

Myrnin halted in an instant, because this one was standing facing him not three feet away, and like Clemencie, it seemed to be a soft, sweet girl. Younger, though. And indefinably . . . different.

"Ah, another sister. You must be—Trothe?" Myrnin asked. "Your sister's already made the offer. I've refused."

Trothe held out her hand.

"No," he said. "I think I am quite finished shaking hands with your family of killers."

Trothe gave him a look of utter incredulity, and then *rolled her eyes*, exactly like Claire's friend Eve might have done in similar circumstances. She drew a line across her throat with her finger. Then she pointed past him to her sister, who had slowed and stopped at the entrance to the room . . .

. . . as if she couldn't come into it.

"Ah," he said. "Clemencie cut your throat. And those of the rest of the family, I suspect. Let me speculate. . . . To your parents, murder was only a practical business as a means to robbery. To her, it became less a career and more of a calling."

Trothe seemed to sigh, but she nodded.

"And what do you want me to do about it, girl? You're dead. I'm a vampire. *She's* insane. I don't see this having a positive outcome."

At the door, Clemencie howled. It was the mother of all screams, straight from the pit of despair, and despite himself, Myrnin shuddered.

Trothe just seemed impatient and slightly bored, which was impressive in the face of such madness. It spoke volumes about their home life, when they'd had a life. And a home.

Like Clemencie, Trothe *could* speak when she wished, because she finally found her voice and said, "I want you to *leave*, man." In contrast with her sister, she sounded completely normal for a girl of her apparent age. "I want you to go outside and then burn this house to the ground to be sure it's finished."

That seemed . . . surprisingly sensible. Myrnin raised a hand. "Problem," he said. "Your sister won't let me leave."

"*I* will," young Trothe said, with a grim determination that Myrnin recognized. He'd seen it before, in Claire, who, although she was a bit older than Trothe Vexen, had the same steely resolve. She simply used it in ways that were not so bent on insanity and murder. "Go out this way." She walked to a boarded-up window, and pointed.

He hesitated.

"I told you that he was mine!" Clemencie shrieked in triumph, and the sound was like razor blades on a chalkboard. The screaming seemed to ring in his ears like lost souls, and he wondered for a brief moment if he was as lost as poor bedeviled Lucian, who'd been spelled into carrying on Clemencie's evils. It was possible that the poor devil might not have begun quite so badly as he'd ended. "*He is mine!*"

"You see how she is," Trothe said. "I really can't stay in this house with her anymore. It's unbearable. You need to send us both away."

Myrnin gave Trothe a frown as he said, "You know that likely means sending you both to hell. Assuming you believe in that sort of thing."

"Yes," she said. "I saw my parents there. I was there myself. But Clemencie escaped and came back here to . . . do her work. I had to come to try to stop her. I haven't done very well, though."

"Until now."

"If you don't disappoint me." She looked as if she didn't have much faith in him, which was a bit insulting considering how much he'd already survived in this cursed place. "Promise me you'll do it."

"Oh, I'll do it," he said. "This place deserves to burn."

"So do we," Trothe said. "Don't let her tell you different. We did so many bad things. Don't let her do it to you, too."

Clemencie shrieked again, and the sound drilled at him, clawed bloody furrows in his fragile mind, and he could *almost* hear, *almost* know, *almost* see what she wanted him to become.

Worse, it almost seemed tempting.

No time left. If he intended to survive these bitter ghosts, he had to trust that Trothe could do as she promised.

"Now, go now!" Trothe cried, and he glanced back to see that Clemencie had broken whatever barrier had kept her at bay. She was rushing at him, and this time, he knew that if she touched him, his mind would shatter like a thin glass bowl.

Myrnin took a run at the window, leaped, and hit the boards with a crash that rattled his brain in its bones . . . and the boards broke away, and he soared a bit in cold desert air before arcing down to an ignominious rolling stop in the dirt.

That damned scorpion, or its close cousin, scuttled at him across the sand as he sat up. He didn't bother to warn it this time, just picked it up and threw it hard enough to send it to Mexico, and turned his attention back to the Vexen house.

It was still and quiet and lifeless in the fading moonlight. Dawn was a dull blue edge on the eastern horizon now.

"You took your good time," Oliver said from behind him, and Myrnin managed not to flinch. Somehow.

"I thought you'd be well gone."

"It occurred to me you might need help."

"Thanks for not providing it, then. You did that very well." Myrnin stood up and slapped sand irritably from his clothing. The amount of it that had trickled down into his boots was going to drive him mad. Again.

"What happened in there?" Oliver's face, when Myrnin glanced back at him, was less cynical and guarded than was normal for him. He seemed . . . worried. Perhaps he'd sensed something in that house, too.

And maybe he'd been worried that Myrnin would emerge as mad and savage a beast as their vampire quarry, Lucian.

"Ghosts," Myrnin said. "And I'm about to lay them to rest. Do you happen to have a lighter?"

Oliver raised his eyebrows, but he fished in a coat pocket and brought out an ornate silver thing, engraved with a dragon. "I'll want that back," he said.

"Of course." Myrnin picked up one of the tinder-dry broken boards that had come through the window with him, and searched around for a bit of sun-rotted cloth to wrap around the end of it. It caught on the first flicker of the lighter's flame, and he held it upside down to feed the greedy fire for a moment, then walked back to the house.

Upstairs, in the window he'd exited, he saw Trothe Vexen, smiling down at him.

She blew him a kiss.

"That's unsettling," he told her. "Do give your sister my regards when you see her in hell."

He threw the burning board inside a broken window, and whatever control Clemencie Vexen had over that house, she could not keep fire from seizing hungry hold of all the rotten, ready-burning things in it. In ten seconds the glow was visible at the window, and in thirty, flames were leaping and spreading throughout the structure.

Myrnin withdrew to a safer distance and stood to watch the Vexen house burn. Oliver stood with him, silent, as though he understood this was a necessary vigil.

Trothe stayed in the window staring out until the house collapsed in upon itself in a roaring rush of flames and sparks and ashes, and then it was done. Completely done.

"Whatever did you do with Lucian?" Myrnin thought to ask as smoke rose up in the dawning sky, and the Vexen girls vanished back to whatever fate waited for them.

"He fell," Oliver said. "Tragic dismemberment accident."

"Ah. Pity. How do you feel about a hearty breakfast?"

"I could murder a Bloody Mary," Oliver said.

"Two Bloody Marys sound better."

Oliver fixed him with a long sober look. "Are you sure you're quite all right?"

"As all right as I've ever been," Myrnin said. He was well aware, in fact, that it was not a reassuring answer. But what was one more whispering ghost at the back of his mind? He had a chorus of the wretched things. It was hard for someone to drive him to insanity when he'd already crossed those borders and taken up residence.

Amateurs.

SIGNS AND MIRACLES

⌒

Dedicated to Kelley Armstrong (and her readers) for her support of the Morganville digital series Kickstarter

I was so awestruck that no less than the fantastic urban fantasy / YA author *Kelley Armstrong* helped us get our Morganville digital series off the ground, and she then donated the custom hardcover to one of her readers. She allowed me to choose the characters for this story, and I decided to explore one that I particularly love and have never written in point of view: Hannah Moses. This is a mystery story with Hannah as our detective, unraveling the story of a girl left for dead and a mysterious peddler of anti-vampire drugs, with bonus Monica Morrell, being heroic against her will, mostly. Glimpses inside the Morganville Police Department we've not previously been able to see, too.

I love mystery stories, and getting to write one like this was a total treat. Thanks, Kelley!

A s with most things in Morganville, it started with a body. This one just happened to be alive.

Hannah Moses watched as the paramedics rolled the unconscious young woman away on a gurney, and then turned her attention back to the pavement where the victim had been found. It was dry asphalt, except where blood cast darker shadows. Not much use doing fancy analysis on that; the stains had been smeared around on dirty asphalt, then baked in the sun, and it probably wasn't going to be any help at all. Not like Morganville, Texas, had much in the way of crime scene forensics, anyway.

"Problem?" The unctuous British voice made her stiffen, just a little; she could never get used to the way some vampires could sneak right up on her, even in daytime. Oliver was the worst. He got a hell of a kick out of it.

"You could say so," Hannah said. She turned and put her hands on her hips. It emphasized the gun belt she wore, and she had to use every trick in her intimidation book to deal with Oliver, Morganville's biggest snake and Amelie's—what the hell was he, second-in-command? Boyfriend? God, she didn't even want to know. "Got a resident who was attacked here sometime this morning. Nobody found her for hours."

He stood in the shadows cast by a brick wall, unsettlingly close. He could easily step into the light if he wanted, even without the cover-ups, but she thought he liked the drama. "Quite a lot of blood," Oliver noted. He sounded casual, as if they were chatting about the weather. "Not my work, of course."

"I know. You're so neat when you eat," Hannah agreed. It wasn't a compliment, and from the sharp-edged smile he gave her, he didn't take it as one. "She was bashed in the head. She hung on, waiting for somebody to save her. Paramedics aren't giving her much of a chance at recovery, though."

"Well, you can't save everyone," Oliver said, in the same uninterested tone as before. "In point of fact, you can't save anyone, in the end. Unless you make them immortal, of course."

"That's a hell of a long view you've got there."

"It's practical. I learned long ago not to accept responsibility for things outside my control."

"Then why are you here? Didn't think the problems of regular people-on-people crime were your business."

"Everything that happens in Morganville is my business, Chief Moses, since I am the Founder's . . . What would you call it? Man on the street?" She just stared at him until he shrugged. "The girl's one of mine, technically. I felt obliged."

"You. You're her Protector?" A vampire Protector was, at least on paper, someone who looked out for the humans assigned to him or her—a mutually beneficial arrangement, blood deposited in the blood bank for a guarantee of safety. Problem was, it was too often a one-sided loyalty.

"She was the property of one of my . . . employees," he said. "Said employee was killed by the draug during the recent unpleasantness. I believe I've inherited her."

He said it as if the girl were an old piece of furniture he'd been left in a will. Hannah felt a weary surge of anger. "Didn't do a very good job of it, did you? Protecting?"

Oliver gave her a silent, warning stare, and then he said, "What suspects have you?"

"Have a little patience. This isn't *CSI*. We can't just run a funny-colored light around and find the killer in ten minutes."

"I thought it usually took a full hour for that, although I admit that I am not fully *au courant* on the rules of television dramas these days." When she didn't give him the satisfaction of a comeback, he lifted his shoulders in a lazy shrug. "I want to be kept informed. Send me updates when you have them."

He started to turn away. Hannah took a step toward him—fast, before he could pull his usual disappearing act. "Wait. What do you know about the girl? Friends? Enemies?"

"I know nothing worth telling you. Now get to work."

He was gone almost before the last words reached her ears. Typical vampire nonsense. Morganville was the ultimate in seagull management style: fly in, crap all over everything, fly away. And still, she'd made the choice, for whatever insane reason, to return here to her toxic hometown after her deployment with the military ended. She'd imagined she could make a difference.

Some days, she was still convinced of that . . . but maybe not today.

"Chief?" One of Morganville's uniformed patrol officers at the end of the alley gestured toward her. "I think you should hear this."

She walked toward him, and as she did, she spotted the red convertible parked at the curb, and the girl lounging against the fender. Pretty, spoiled Monica Morrell. She'd gone blond highlights again for the summer. Unfortunately, it suited her, and so did the skintight tube dress she had on. It showed off curves and perfect skin. Even the sunglasses were designer. How she managed all that flash when her family had lost everything . . . but then, she'd probably terrified people into buying all her goodies. It was her life strategy.

"*Chief* Moses," Monica said. She somehow made it sound mocking, as if it were some kind of honorary title she hadn't earned. People like Monica made it hard to hold on to that professional smile. "I didn't know you were still in charge. I thought somebody more, you know, important would have the job by now."

Really tough to hang on to that smile. "You have some information, Miss Morrell? I'd sure love to hear it."

"Fine." Monica yawned and inspected her fingernails, which were a perfect dark blue to match the dress. "I was driving by about noon and saw the body in the alley."

"Body? Last I heard, she wasn't dead."

"Well, she looked it. Anyway, I'm the one who called it in. So I guess I saved her life."

"Probably." Hannah didn't want to say it, but sometimes you had to give the devil his due. "She'd been lying there for hours, bleeding."

"Can't blame me for that. I didn't get the memo." Monica cocked her head to one side. "Huh. You'd think the vamps would have come running to the all-you-can-eat, what with the blood everywhere."

That . . . was actually quite a good observation, and Hannah had to pause to consider it. Under all the hard gloss, Monica Morrell was clever, if not smart. "Did you see anything else?"

"Like some weirdo lurking in a hoodie? Miss Scarlet in the library with a candlestick? Nope. Just the girl and the blood." Monica was quiet for a second. "I know her. Lindsay. I mean, it's not like we're besties, but she wasn't a total loss. I don't suppose you'll ever figure out who did this, though."

"Thank you for the vote of confidence."

"Well, it's Morganville, and she's just human, so why bother, right?"

"It almost sounds like you don't care for that. That's a change, isn't it? I thought the vampires could do no wrong; don't you have that on your family crest?"

"Look, the vampires do what they want—we both know that—so let's not get all Internet rage-aholic about it. Nobody's going to go on strike for better living conditions. So enough already. Am I done?" Monica waved a hand in Hannah's face that she was very tempted to flex-cuff, just on general principles. Too bad she had no real reason.

"Sure," Hannah said. "Get off my crime scene."

Monica got behind the convertible's wheel and pulled away with an insolent squeal of tires that was probably meant as a middle finger, but Hannah didn't much care. She was used to disrespect. When she felt it was necessary, she drew the line, but Monica didn't matter enough to deserve the effort. Hannah had already forgotten her before the smoke faded from the tire scratch.

She walked back to the place where a girl named Lindsay had silently hung on to her life alone, waiting for someone to come save her. All that blood, dried on the pavement. *Vamps must have known she was down and bleeding. Why not check it out?*

It was a really good question. One that deserved an answer.

Hannah documented the scene with meticulous care, took all the necessary samples, and logged the evidence.

And then she went to ask Oliver some questions at his coffee shop, Common Grounds.

Eve Rosser—no, Eve *Glass* these days; hard to get used to that—was on duty, and was her usual Goth-chipper self. Hard to tell under all that dyed-black hair, pale makeup, and abusive eyeliner, but she was a pretty thing. Not delicate, no—strong. Had to be, growing up in Morganville.

She'd taken her fair share of trouble around here, survived, and even thrived; Hannah respected that. As usual, Eve had nothing but a bright smile for her as she approached the counter.

"Chief! Hang on a sec, let me think—how about a *corretto*? I just learned how to make it."

"Doesn't that come with a shot of booze?"

Eve's dimples deepened. "Why, Officer! I think it might."

"Then I'm going to have to pass, and I won't even cite you for attempted bribery. How about just a straight-up coffee?"

"One of these days, I'm going to expand your horizons, Chief— see if I don't." Eve got out a chunky white mug with the Common Grounds logo and poured from a carafe in the back. "Here you go. Hot and black."

"Thanks. I'm going to need to talk to Oliver."

"Don't we all? Because it's payday and he's nowhere to be seen, and I'd really like my sweaty, coffee-scented, pathetically small check."

"He's not here?"

"Nope. Hasn't been in all day. It's weird. He's usually here, or at least calls." Eve shrugged. "Guess he's busy."

Hannah sipped her coffee and thought for a while in silence. Oliver being oddly busy—not to mention being all up in her crime scene business—was something that gave her pause. *Not going to learn anything sitting around drinking Colombian,* she thought. She idly scrolled numbers on her cell phone, considering, and then selected one and dialed.

Three rings. One more than courtesy, but at last, the line picked up, and the head vampire Amelie's cool, calm voice said, "Chief Moses. I'm surprised to hear from you." The implication was pretty clear that mere human cops didn't have the Founder's permission to call up to chat.

"This isn't a social call," Hannah said. "Did you send Oliver to dig around in the assault of a human girl?"

The pause was long, which was suspicious, but it also didn't tell her much. Amelie's silences were never telling, just ominous. "Oliver's business is none of yours," she said. "And I know nothing about this girl."

"Then how about this? The girl was down and bleeding, and no vampires came to check it out," she said. "Must be a good reason why."

"Must there?" Amelie had a gift for sounding completely uninterested; had to give her that. "I'll have to look into it."

"Isn't that what you've got Oliver doing right now?"

Silence. Deep, dark, uninformative silence. And then Amelie said, "Thank you for your call. Do let me know how I may assist you in the future." The same disconnected, disinterested tone, and then dead air.

Hannah wasn't sure if she'd burned a bridge or built one, but either way, she'd taken her best shot. She put the phone back in her pocket and glanced up. Eve was staring at her. She quickly looked away to wipe down the bar.

"So who was it? The girl, I mean."

"Lindsay Ramson."

"Oh *shit!*" Eve put her hand to her mouth in obvious dismay. "I know her. Is she going to be okay?"

"I don't know."

"Was it . . ." Eve mimed fangs in the neck, the universal sign for the most common kind of injury in Morganville. Hannah shook her head.

"I don't know what it was," she said. "But damned if I'm not going to find out. You see Oliver, you tell him to call."

She counted out dollars, and Eve didn't argue; they'd had that battle before over paying for things, and as police chief, Hannah didn't like to be beholden to people like Oliver, even for so much as a free cup of coffee.

She threw in a tip for Eve, which the girl tucked into her shirt with a nod.

"Be safe," Eve said.

Hannah let a snort express her scorn for that thought, and left for the hospital.

Lindsay Ramson wasn't dead, which was a nice surprise. Hannah had gotten so used to assuming the worst that she'd thought the poor girl would kick off. For a moment, as the doctor spoke, it felt like a heavy gray cloud lifted off her . . . and then settled slowly back down as he continued.

"She's alive, which is the good news. The bad news is that there are going to be significant issues," the doctor was saying. "I don't think there's much danger of her succumbing to her injuries at this point; she's proving pretty tough. That makes it all the harder to tell her parents that the injury to her brain is likely catastrophic. She may wake up on her own, or she may never wake up. If she does wake, she'll almost certainly have severe impairments."

Hannah swallowed back the metallic, familiar taste of rage. "Such as?"

"The blows to her head could have any of a range of effects, from loss of language skills to motor skills to vision. Seizures would be likely."

"Or she could recover just fine?"

The doctor—his name was Reed, and he had a good reputation—looked weary. "That's not very likely, Chief Moses. I wish I could tell you that I thought a miracle would happen, but it's not often I see someone that severely injured still holding on. We might have already used up our backlog of miracles. I'm pretty sure that cognitive impairment is going to be part of the landscape." He hesitated for a few seconds. "I know it's not professional to ask, but . . . any suspects?"

"Not any of the usual suspects, anyway. Crime scene was bloody."

"It's not their usual method," he agreed. "So you're looking at . . . the human population?"

"For now," Hannah said, "I'm looking at everybody."

She dropped by Lindsay's bedside. Her parents were there, mother and father, with a couple of siblings hanging back and looking shattered and uncomfortable. Mom and Dad were each holding one of the girl's still, pale hands. The only sound was the steady, slow pulse of the machines. Her head was completely wrapped from the eyes up, but other than that, she looked unmarked. Pretty, in a fragile way that reminded Hannah of Claire Danvers from the Glass House.

One of her brothers broke down suddenly in racking sobs and turned away. Hannah respected the family's grief, but when the brother who'd wept left the room, she followed him to the chapel down the hall.

"Matt?" She'd already done her homework on Lindsay's family. She already knew all their names. "I'm very sorry about your sister."

"Thanks." His voice sounded rough and uneven, but he took some deep breaths and got it under control. "Why? Lindsay was never any trouble to anybody."

"That's what I have to find out. Are you sure there's nobody Lindsay had problems with? Boyfriends? Maybe someone she broke up with?"

"She was a shy kid," Matt said. He was a big guy—Morganville right tackle in high school, she remembered, back in the day. In his thirties now, with the muscle softening to bulk. He worked at the father's used-car place as a salesman. Married, two kids of his own. As the oldest son, he probably still felt responsible for Lindsay even though she was twenty-one and her own person in every legal way. "I know she's had boyfriends, but it's not like she talks a lot about them to us. I guess the most recent one was a kid called Trip. I think his name's James Triplett, Jr. I'd probably want to go by Trip, too, if I was saddled with that."

"Trip," Hannah said, and nodded. "I'll check into him. Were they still together?"

Matt shrugged, a little helplessly. "She doesn't talk about that stuff to me so much. I know she brought him to Christmas dinner. He seemed like an okay guy, pretty laid-back. My dad didn't like him, but she's his little girl. Hell, I've got a daughter, and I'm damn sure going to hate every guy who comes near her."

"Lindsay didn't have any sisters. What about close girlfriends?"

"Sure, a few. I mean, in high school, some in college, but I don't know who she's hanging out with now." That question, curiously, had made Matt uncomfortable. "Why are you asking?"

"Because I'm hoping she might have said something that could give us a lead."

He saw the sense of that, but reluctantly, and he finally gave a shrug. "I guess check her cell phone? I don't know." He did, though. He knew something and didn't want to give it up; his body language seemed off. Hannah let him keep the secret for now, because the cell phone was in Lindsay's effects, and she'd already collected it for processing. She thanked Matt, trying to be gentle as possible, but his gaze was already fixed on the nondenominational stained-glass alcove at the front of the chapel. Lost in his own thoughts, or prayers.

She left him to it.

Lindsay's cell phone was full of contacts; though Matt had described her as shy, she seemed a popular kid after all. Hannah sat at her desk in the Morganville Town Hall building and went through the list methodically, checking off those that she knew about already. That accounted for about half.

She was still studying the list when one of Morganville's two police detectives walked in and took a seat in the chair across from her desk. "Hey, boss," he said, and put a folder in her in-box. "Got the final write-up done on the Garza robbery. The case is going to court next month."

"Slam dunk, Fred?"

"Three-pointer," he said, and made an invisible basketball shot. "Didn't even have to get in close. Crowd goes wild."

She didn't smile. She liked Fred, but she maintained a distance from those she had to manage; besides, he was a vampire. A vampire police detective. Trouble was, he was good at it—too good, sometimes. And she always felt that movie-star smile of his held just a touch too much arrogance for comfort.

Fred always dressed in suits. Today's was a nice gray thing, tailored and elegant, with a bright blue paisley tie and a lightly striped shirt beneath. His hairstyle still seemed faintly antique to her, as if he had to resist the urge to slick it down in 1920s style, but he had fully embraced modern fashion.

Hannah held out the phone list to him. "Anything jump out at you?"

He studied it, and without looking up said, "Is this from your dead girl's phone?"

"She's not dead."

"Okay." He shrugged, as if it really didn't matter to him, and then handed the paper back. "No vampires."

"What?"

"No vampires in her calling list. Not a single one."

Staying well away from vampires was good survival strategy for a human in Morganville, but what was strange was that Lindsay hadn't programmed in her Protector's phone number. In Hannah's experience, Morganville residents *always* kept their Protectors on speed dial.

But Lindsay hadn't. Even though her original Protector had died,

she should have still had the previous number in the list, because people rarely remembered to delete contacts . . . and Oliver's number
should have been in there as her new one.

"Anything else, boss?" Fred asked. "I've got a thing."

"What thing?" she asked, and glanced up to meet his blue eyes. He
had very lovely blue eyes, wide and innocent-looking. He must have led
a lot of victims to their deaths with that friendly look, and she'd long
ago stopped taking vampires at face value. She'd never known Fred to
step outside the lines of vampire good behavior, but she was always on
guard for it.

"One of my people asked me to be there for her daughter's bap-
tism," he said. "That okay with you? Nothing burning a hole on my
desk right now."

Vampires, as Hannah well knew, had religion—often the same
one they'd been born into. There were Catholic vampires, and Jewish
vampires, and Muslim vampires. A couple of religious institutions in
town catered to vampires as well as humans with night services. Still,
it was unusual to see a vampire attending any kind of daytime human
religious ceremony, except funerals. "Sure," she said. "Have fun."

He gave her a smile that showed off even, white teeth—hiding the
fangs—and stood up with an easy grace. "Good luck on that thing,"
he said. "Sounds like human on human to me."

"Maybe," she said. Her gaze followed him out the door. "Maybe so."

Hannah interviewed Lindsay's boyfriend, Trip; he'd been eager to
help, clearly knocked off-balance by what had happened, but he
hadn't had much to offer. She had a pretty clear sense that he was just
what he seemed: a well-meaning guy with no real drama. Lindsay had
good taste in stable guys. That hadn't helped her much, in the end.

Halfway back to the station, her cell rang. She glanced down and saw it was Oliver's number. When she answered, she didn't even have time to deliver her standard *Chief Moses* greeting before his voice was growling at her.

"Let's get one thing crystal clear, Chief Moses," Oliver snapped. "You don't summon me for information. I summon *you*. That is the natural order of things."

She counted to three, just to make sure she didn't sound ruffled. "I need to understand why the vampires avoided that crime scene. You're the one who can tell me."

"Can I?" She waited him out. It was a long wait, one that crawled up and down her nerves, but she was finally rewarded with an irritated sigh. "Very well. She had an unusual scent to her blood. Off-putting."

"Does she make regular blood bank donations?" Because Morganville residents were required to, and as her Protector, Oliver would have first choice of those donations.

"She's running behind," he said. "Two months behind, in fact; she was just added to the list for a visit from our Bloodmobile. Prior to that, her blood wasn't unusual in any way."

"What can cause that kind of change?"

"Illness. Some types of drugs, perhaps." He paused for a second. "It occurs to me that she's not the only one falling behind in the past few months . . . more than normal, I think. Now, I trust that's enough information for you to pursue your investigation. Call me again, and I won't be as welcoming."

He ended the call without another word. She was fine with that, because her mind was busy working. Morganville always had some percentage of people who got behind on blood donations at the blood bank; usually the collectors let it slide at least three months before they started active pursuit, which involved driving the Bloodmobile to the deadbeat's door. She hadn't paid much attention to that; people knew how the system worked, and it ran without much police intervention.

But maybe it was worth a trip to the blood bank just to see what was going on.

The receptionist at the blood bank was Leanna Bradbury; the Bradburys were original town residents, though the family had thinned out through the years, and Leanna was the last of them. Given her charming personality, it wasn't too likely there'd be any more after her.

As Hannah pushed her way through the front door, the electronic bell dinged, and Leanna looked up. She didn't bother putting down her romance novel, and from the expression that crossed her face, she wasn't any too pleased to have a visit from the police. "Help you?" she asked, and then a shade too late to be polite, "Chief?"

"I'm looking for information about Lindsay Ramson's donation record," Hannah said.

"Are you?" Leanna's plucked eyebrows rose up slowly. "Well, I don't know. I think I have to run that by Director Rose before I can let you see any actual records. There are federal regulations about—"

"Leanna, this is Morganville, not Dallas, and you've never so much as set eyes on anybody from the federal government, and you never will. Don't give me bullshit."

"I still have to call . . ." Hannah gave her a steady glare, and the words trailed off into mutinous silence. Leanna's broad jaw set stubbornly. "Fine," she said at last. "Come with me."

She pushed away from the desk. There wasn't anyone in the shabby waiting room; the old magazines fluttered in the cold, dry breeze from the air-conditioning, but that was the only movement in the room except for the broad sway of Leanna's skirt backside as she led Hannah down the hallway, past the slightly murky tank with its lazily swimming fish. The place always smelled sharply antiseptic, but there was some undercurrent of smell to it, too—something Hannah had never been able to pinpoint, and was a little glad she couldn't. She made her donations here, but she never lingered. No one did. There were treatment rooms on either side of the hallway, each with empty donation stations. It had the oddly unsettling look of a movie set, waiting for actors.

At the end of the hall was a closed door with a sign that read NO ADMITTANCE. Before they reached it, Leanna turned left, to another door. OFFICE STAFF ONLY. Inside, a workstation with a fairly new computer and printer, a copy machine, and ranks of filing cabinets. Leanna made straight for the computer, logged in, clicked keys, and began printing pages.

Hannah looked at the labels on the cabinets. On one side of the room, the blue cabinets were marked DONORS. The other side, the red side, had only a single file cabinet marked CONSUMERS.

No mystery about that. The only odd thing was the vampires had allowed those files to be kept. They didn't usually allow that kind of thing from the human population; too much info on individual bloodsuckers made them feel vulnerable. Not that their particular preferences in drinking plasma would make much difference.

"Here we go," Leanna said with false cheer, and gathered up the sheets as the last of them hissed out of the printer. She straightened them with the religious concentration of an obsessive, and then stapled them with a single, sharp rap of her hand on the stapler. She held them out, and Hannah took them. "She's not the only one in that family who hasn't kept up with donations. Her brother—oh, wait. He's got a medical waiver. Some kind of blood disorder."

"Did she have one?"

"It's not in the file. Her results looked like she was fine, up until this last one. Then she fell behind."

"Thanks." Hannah folded the pages and put them in her pocket.

"Those are confidential, you know."

"So's my investigation," Hannah said.

"Investigation?" Leanna really hadn't taken her nose out of her book, apparently.

"Lindsay Ramson," Hannah said. "She's in the hospital."

"Oh . . . I think she was due to get a visit from the Bloodmobile this week. Should I reschedule that, or—"

"She's in a coma," Hannah cut in flatly. "So I don't think rescheduling would be such a great idea right now. I'll let her family know you were concerned."

Leanna looked stricken, then bitterly offended. "Why, I had no idea she was so badly hurt—don't you go saying something like that! Why, they'll think I'm some kind of monster."

"Yeah, Leanna, it's all about you," Hannah said. "Thanks for this."

"I'm telling Director Rose about this!" Leanna called after her as she left.

Not for the first time, Hannah thought it was a damn shame that as the law, she no longer got to flip people off.

The next stop, after a fast lunch at Marjo's Diner, was the Glass House on Lot Street. The old Victorian was ramshackle, but sturdy; the paint was fresh, and the kids were doing a decent job of keeping the place looking nice. Eve had put up a wind chime made of black, shiny skulls that clattered in the hot breeze, and someone had shoved a threadbare old armchair out on the porch, but other than that, it was just the same as always. A mirror of her grandma's old Day House.

Hannah knocked on the door and stepped back to wait. It didn't take long before she heard footsteps, and knew she was being checked out through the security peephole. Locks snapped back, and Claire

Danvers offered her a quiet, calm smile only a little nervous around the edges. "Hannah," she said. "Hi. What's up?"

"I'd like to get your opinion on something technical," Hannah said. "If you've got the time."

"Sure." Claire stepped aside, and Hannah followed her in and closed the door behind her. By common Morganville courtesy, there was no invitation given, and Hannah made sure the lock was fastened. Second nature to folks here in Vampire Town. "What is it?"

"Got some blood analysis that I'd like you to see. I figure you've seen enough working with your crazy vampire boss to be able to spot anything interesting in it."

Claire led the way back through the living room. Shane Collins was sprawled on the couch, asleep, with a comic book covering his face. *Wolverine.* That seemed appropriate. Neither of them commented on him, and Claire led the way into the kitchen, to the table.

"Can I get you something? Coffee?"

"Sure," Hannah said. Her Common Grounds fix had worn off, and she had the feeling it might be a long night ahead. Claire pulled the pot off the burner and filled two cups, then carried them over. Hannah slid the folder over in exchange for the coffee, and Claire sipped as she opened it up to read.

"Lindsay Ramson?" Claire glanced up at her, startled. "She was attacked, wasn't she?"

"Yeah," Hannah said. "Word travels fast, I see."

"If Monica's involved, it does. Do you think she—"

"No," Hannah said. "I don't. She'd never have stuck around to claim credit for finding her if she'd done it in the first place. And she's easily bored. That girl was attacked a whole lot earlier."

Claire nodded and went back to the blood tests. A small frown grooved itself between her brows as she shuffled papers. After a few minutes, she began laying the papers out in a specific order, turned toward Hannah.

"Something's happening to her," Claire said. "See this result, right here?" She put her finger on a particular value. It had an impenetrable chemical code for a name, so Hannah just shrugged. "It means that something was happening to her blood. Just this last entry, though; the rest look pretty normal. I'm not a doctor, though. You'd need to have someone else look at it. She stopped giving blood, though, so I can't tell if it got better, or worse."

"What effect would these changes have had on her blood?" Hannah asked. "What you're pointing to?"

"I'm not . . . really sure. But I think it would have made her anemic. Fewer red blood cells. Maybe it's something like leukemia."

"Maybe," Hannah said thoughtfully, and drank her coffee as she stared at the printed pages. "Maybe."

But in that case, why try to kill someone who was already so ill?

She was so immersed in the thought that she almost failed to hear Shane coming into the kitchen, but her peripheral vision caught the motion and yanked her vividly to attention. She looked in his direction, and it must have been too quickly, because Shane came to a sudden stop, holding up both hands in surrender. One of them still held the rolled-up *Wolverine* comic. "Don't shoot, Officer," he said. "I'm not armed."

"And not dangerous," she said, at which he looked preciously wounded. "Good morning."

"We keep night-owl hours around here. Best to stay awake when the creatures of the night prowl." He advanced on Claire, who was still absorbed in the paperwork, and did a B-movie loom with clawed fingers.

She ignored him, except to say, "Do you want some coffee?"

"Why? Has all the Coke run out?" He veered off to open the fridge and pulled out a frosty can. "Thank God. You had me scared." Shane popped the can's top and slid into the third rickety chair at the table, and ran a hand through his bedhead-messy hair. He gave Hannah a charming smile. "I'm going to be happy you're here, and not get all paranoid about why you're here."

His eyes met Claire's, and held, and so did his smile. She returned it, dimples and all, and reached over to take his hand. "She's asking me to look at something."

"Smart-girl stuff, got it. What's the deal?"

Claire's smile dimmed. "A girl got hurt today. It's her blood tests. Hannah thinks that it might have had something to do with why she was attacked."

"Attacked? Is that 1950s code for . . ."

"She wasn't raped," Hannah said. "She was hit in the back of the head with a blunt object and left to die."

"Oh." Shane sipped cola and fidgeted slightly in the chair, gaze fixed in the middle distance. He seemed to be debating something, and finally he shifted and looked Hannah in the eye. "Look, you're Captain Obvious, and encouraging vampire resistance is kind of your deal with that, so I'm probably not telling you anything you don't already know, but . . . was she one of the guinea pigs?"

"One of the *what*?"

"Oh, man. You don't know, do you?"

"Know what?" When Shane wasn't immediately spilling it, Hannah leaned forward, and he leaned back. "Tell me what *you* know. Now."

He looked torn, and miserable, but he shrugged. He didn't look at Claire, although she was staring directly at him, eyes wide. "I only heard it through the grapevine. I thought for sure you'd already be all into it."

"Shane." She put her impatience and implied threat into it, and he looked away again, focused now on the sweating can of Coke in his hands. "Now."

"Some older guy thought he'd mastered some kind of treatment that was supposed to make blood less tasty to vamps. He was dealing it under the table at a couple of clubs. All I know is it made some people sick, word got around, and he quit selling it. Said he was going to test it out more first."

"Who was it?"

Shane shrugged again, still not willing to risk direct eye contact. "Never met him, Hannah. Sorry."

"That's not what I asked."

"I know. It's complicated. He's a friend of a friend of a friend. You know how it is."

"A girl is lying in a hospital bed with her skull crushed," Hannah said, and stood up. Shane, startled, did look this time. "I don't know if you've lost your courage, or your humanity, but either way, if you find it, give me a call."

Claire took in a deep, startled breath, but said nothing. Shane slowly stood up. It was hard not to be aware of how tall he was, how broad-shouldered, and how still and hard his face had gotten.

"Don't go there," Shane said. His voice had gone deceptively soft. "This isn't my fault."

"It is if you know something that could be vital to finding this son of a bitch."

"Maybe it's a vampire who did it. You going to go arrest him, *Chief*? How do you think that'll go? Slap on the wrist. Hell, if she's in the hospital, she didn't even die. Amelie probably won't even make him pay a damn fine!"

"Are you done? Because I can promise you, not every crime in Morganville is caused by vampires," Hannah said. "And I *will* bring this man—or woman—to justice. You have my word."

"I don't think we've got that in Morganville. Justice."

"We won't if we don't fight for it."

The silence stretched. Claire reached out and put a hand on Shane's arm, and he almost flinched at the contact, so intensely was he concentrating on Hannah. "Shane," she said, in a steady, quiet voice. "Tell her. It's important. Don't make this some us-versus-them issue if it isn't."

"And if it is?" he said, but then shook his head. "You're right. Okay. The word is that the older guy selling the stuff was named Matt. That's all I heard. I didn't ask for details because I didn't want to know. Don't know if that even helps anyway."

Matt. Matt.

For a second, it didn't connect, and then it did.

Then it all made a horrible kind of sense.

Matt Ramson wasn't at the hospital when she stopped there; his mother was, still sitting silently at the bedside of her pale, bandaged daughter. Hannah waited a moment, out of respect, until the haunted woman's eyes rose to meet hers. "I'm sorry, ma'am. How is she?"

"No different," Mrs. Ramson said. Her voice sounded as if it came from far away. "They're saying it'll be a good sign if she wakes up soon. But it'll be a miracle if she's the same girl she was before."

"Miracles happen," Hannah said. "You hold on to that."

Mrs. Ramson nodded slowly. "Father Joe was here. He told me the same thing."

"He ought to know, don't you think?"

"That new Baptist minister was here, too. And some of her friends."

That seemed like a good opening, so Hannah asked, "Did the rest of your family go home?"

"My husband's gone to get us some dinner, but my sons had to go. They'll be back tomorrow."

Hannah thanked her and, for a moment, rested her hand lightly on Lindsay's. She bowed her head. It was partly prayer, and partly promise. *I'm going to see it right.*

Then she left and drove to Matt Ramson's house.

It was dark, so the place was shut up tight, in true Morganville fashion; the street outside was deserted, but most of the houses had brilliant lights burning inside and out. False security, but that was better than none, Hannah supposed. The house was a sprawling seventies-style ranch thing, one floor, and a couple of colorful kid-sized bikes leaning up against the porch railing. She knocked on the thick wood door, and it opened up to show her a tired-looking young woman with a toddler clinging to her leg.

"Can I help you?"

"Chief Hannah Moses. I'm here to see Matt."

"Matt?" His wife looked suspicious, and afraid, and took a long step back. "He's not here."

Didn't have to be any kind of a human lie detector to hear the stress in that lie. "I'm going to step inside," Hannah said. "Is that all right?"

"I . . ." The poor woman didn't know what the right response should be. Vampires couldn't cross thresholds uninvited, and Morganville residents always took it as a sign of respect to enter to prove humanity—it was almost an instinct. And that instinct smashed into her need to cover for her husband, and paralyzed her long enough for Hannah to step across the doorway and ease the door shut behind her. "I don't think you should be here. Matt's not here!"

"Mama?" The little girl tugged at her mother's pants. "Daddy's in the dark place."

Mrs. Ramson froze, eyes going wide, and then looked directly at a plain white door off the hallway.

The dark place. That sounded horror-movie creepy, but Hannah knew what the little girl meant.

The basement.

She walked straight for the door, ignoring Mrs. Ramson's frantic lies, and pulled it open. It wasn't dark. All the fluorescent lights were on downstairs, and she went down fast and quietly, one hand on her sidearm.

Best to be ready.

Matt Ramson was destroying evidence. Too bad, but on the positive side, there was too much for him to get rid of quickly—beakers of chemicals, an entire *Breaking Bad* set covering most of the basement's square footage. He was wearing a protective breathing mask as he poured chemicals into a hazardous materials barrel.

"Matt," Hannah said.

He whirled, saw her standing on the stairs, and she saw it in his eyes. Not just horror. Not just misery.

Guilt.

There were a lot of things he might have done, in that moment. He might have run, or charged her, or gone for a weapon.

Instead, he just put the beaker down, sealed the drum, and removed the breathing mask as he sank down on a plastic chair in front of a table. Defeated.

"I was trying to do good," he said. It might have been to Hannah, or maybe to himself, or maybe he was talking to his sister half the town away. "The first stuff didn't work. Should have worked, but people got sick. I had to test it. I had to."

"So you gave it to your little sister?"

"I told her it would help keep the vampires away. She was happy to do it."

"At first."

He nodded, turning the mask in his hands. "She started feeling sick, and wanted to stop. I told her it was natural, just the body starting to adjust, but she . . . she wanted out. When I asked her to keep

going, she said she was . . . she was going to tell Oliver. Our *Protector*."
The scorn he put into the word was hot enough to burn. "You know
what he'd do."

"Stop you."

"Kill me. Make me disappear. I couldn't let that happen. I have
kids!" He looked up at her then, eyes shimmering with tears. "I just . . .
I wanted to *protect* her. I've got a blood disorder, you know. And a donation waiver. They don't want what I have, and if I can give it to other
people . . . It's not supposed to make her sick. Just . . . not so tasty."

"Why'd you hit her?"

"She was walking away and calling Oliver. I hit her to stop her,
that's all. Just to stop her from calling him. I didn't mean to . . ." He
put his head in his hands and sobbed. "I thought she was dead. I
thought she was *dead*."

Hannah shook her head, walked over to him, and—as kindly as
possible—got him up and handcuffed. She was just snapping the
ratchet on his left wrist when she heard a slight creak on the stairs,
and looked up to see Oliver standing there, watching her.

He wasn't trying to look like anything but what he was now—a
dangerous predator. There was a shine in his eyes that wasn't quite
full-on vampire, but was definitely not human.

"You may go," he said to Hannah, and glided down the rest of the
steps. "This is mine to do."

"Hell if I will," she said, and tightened her grip on Matt's arm. He
was still sobbing messily. "This has nothing to do with you, Oliver.
Or the vampires. It's a human crime, and that makes it totally my
jurisdiction."

He set foot on the cellar's floor, never taking his eyes from her,
and kept relentlessly coming on. "Are you really going to make this so
difficult, Chief Moses?"

She pulled her gun and pointed it at his chest. "I believe I am."

He stopped. Red glowed in his eyes, and she had to suppress that very natural human panic that bloomed inside, that need to fight, to run, to *act*. She had to act calm if she couldn't be calm. She had to remain in charge.

Oliver slowly cocked his head to one side, then shifted his attention to Matt Ramson. An expression of revulsion narrowed his eyes and compressed his lips. "A mewling coward," he said. "With rotting blood. Keep him, and I wish you joy of it. But you, Ramson: Listen closely. If your sister dies, I'll pay you a visit again. Prison bars won't protect you. Neither will our brave Chief Moses."

"Back off," she ordered, and got that eerie stare again. "Last warning, Oliver. Leave this family alone." She shook Matt roughly. "Stop crying and revoke his invitation if you want to protect your wife and kids."

He gulped in enough air to mumble the right words, and Oliver was forced back, as if blown by a wind. He stumbled over the stairs, but went on his own from that point. The look he threw back at her was viciously unfriendly. He hung on to the doorframe long enough to call down, "I'll be seeing you, Hannah."

And then the wind caught him again, to buffet him down the hall. She heard the front door open and slam.

"Keep them safe," Matt said. "Please, keep my family safe."

"I am," Hannah said. "I'm just sorry it has to be from you. Upstairs."

Booking Matt Ramson filled up hours, but she made sure he was safely behind bars, and that her best guys were watching out for any vampire bullshit, just in case. She hated the next part, which would be the toughest, but it was also her job. Serve, protect . . . inform the relatives.

When she arrived at Morganville General, though, she was surprised to see Monica Morrell walking down the hall toward her, clearly leaving Lindsay Ramson's room. Monica hadn't even dressed up for the occasion; she was almost plain in a hoodie, jeans, and flat shoes, with her hair pulled back in a simple ponytail. No makeup.

"What?" she snapped when she saw Hannah's eyebrows rising. "It's a look."

"It is," Hannah agreed. "And it looks pretty good on you, Monica."

"Oh, please."

"You here to visit Lindsay?"

Monica shrugged just enough to make it clear she didn't care enough to put effort into her disinterest. "Figured I should. Seeing as I saved her life and all."

"That was nice of you."

"Well, you know, I'm not a bitch twenty-four/seven."

News to me, Hannah thought, but she kept it to herself. "Any change?"

Monica gave her a blank, disbelieving look. "You don't know?"

"Know what?"

"She woke up half an hour ago and told her parents her stupid brother Matt was the one who hit her in the head. Imagine that? I saved her life, and now I solved your crime. Damn, I'm good!" Monica gave her a wide, superior smile, lifted her chin, and did a runway walk past her and toward the elevators . . . which, of course, opened before she pressed the button. Life just worked that way for Monica. It seemed, sometimes, like God had a terrible sense of humor.

Hannah went to the door of Lindsay Ramson's room. The girl was sitting up, awake—bleary, but talking. She sounded good. More than good. Her parents were holding her hands, and for a moment, there was a sense of peace in Hannah's soul.

Lindsay's father saw her then, and stood up to say, "Chief Moses—"

She nodded. "I know," she said, and saw the relief ease the tension out of his face. "I'm sorry. I've got Matt in custody. We can talk about all that later. For now, I'm just happy you're doing better, Lindsay."

Lindsay smiled. She still looked pale, and in pain, but brave. Brave, and strong. "Is it true that Monica saved my life?"

"She called nine-one-one, so I suppose she helped. I'd say the doctors saved your life, and you saved it, too, by hanging on so tight."

"Bad enough my brother tried to kill me, but now I owe Monica? God hates me." Lindsay moved her head a little, and winced. She reached for the button by her side, pressed it, and the painkillers did their work. "It's not Matt's fault, exactly. He tried to do something good, but he got scared. I shouldn't have pushed him. Mom, I'm sorry. . . ."

"No," her mother said firmly, and patted her arm. "No, honey. You don't be sorry. Matt will be all right. You'll be all right. It's a miracle."

Lindsay smiled and closed her eyes, and drifted off to a drugged sleep. Hannah left them, and on the way out of the hospital, she hesitated, then entered the chapel where she'd originally talked with Matt. It was empty, so she went up front, sat on the pew, and said a prayer of thanks.

"Miracles don't often happen here," said a voice next to her, and Hannah controlled the urge to flinch. It was a quiet, calm voice, not warm but oddly reassuring.

"Founder," Hannah said, and turned to look. Amelie had taken a seat next to her on the pew without a sound or a whisper of disturbed air. She wore a cold white suit, and her hair was done up in its customary crownlike swirl. Beautiful and icy. "To what do I owe the honor?"

"I think you mean that ironically," Amelie said. She continued looking straight ahead, at the nondenominational stained glass behind the altar. "Oliver was investigating reports that someone was tainting the blood supply. The attack on the girl was incidental, but significant, because her blood was contaminated. I am sorry I withheld the information from you. It might have speeded your investigation."

"Might have," Hannah said. "Next time, tell me."

"I will." Amelie was quiet for a moment. "Do you think it was? A miracle?" Almost wistful, the way she asked it.

"I've got no idea. Why?"

"Because I would like to still believe in them. Miracles and signs. An age of wonder and promise, where all things were possible."

"All things still are possible," Hannah said. "Good things and bad. But maybe we've got a clearer idea that we're the ones causing them."

Amelie nodded. "Good work today, Chief," she said. "I'm pleased."

"I didn't do it for you."

"That," Amelie said as she stood up, and her guard seemed to materialize out of nowhere to stand at her back, "is why I'm pleased."

Hannah watched them leave, and then looked back at the altar.

An age of miracles.

Maybe it was, after all.

ANGER MANAGEMENT

☽

It occurred to me, post–*Bite Club,* that Shane might need some counseling for his anger issues. It's common knowledge he has them, but they made an epic appearance in that book, and surely if he didn't seek some help, someone would seek it for him . . . leading to this Amelie-mandated counseling session with Dr. Theo Goldman, who is the closest thing the Morganville vampires have to a mental health professional.

I didn't do right by Dr. Goldman and his family when I introduced them, and I apologize for that; my first attempts were clumsy and awkward and painfully badly drawn, and I hope that their characterizations improved in later books. But this portrait of Theo is, I think, somewhat more flattering, if not where I'd like to take the character someday.

But mostly, it's Shane being Shane, and maybe growing a little bit from his experiences. Baby steps, Shane. Baby steps.

"What do you think makes you the angriest?" my newly appointed shrink, Dr. Theo Goldman, asked. He was puttering around at his desk, straightening papers, adjusting the angle of his pen, not apparently paying much attention to the answer.

I wasn't fooled. The fact was, Theo Goldman was listening carefully to everything . . . words, pauses, the way I took a breath. Vampire senses were a bitch that way. Goldman was probably listening to my heart rate, too.

And why did I come here, again? Well, I hadn't really been given much of a choice.

I shifted uncomfortably on the couch, then stopped and held very still, as if that was going to somehow help me out. Goldman looked up briefly and smiled at me. He wasn't a bad guy, for a vamp: kind of rumpled, a little antique looking, and he never seemed like he was tempted to rip my throat out for a snack. Claire trusted him, and if my girl said that, she'd probably put a lot of thought into it.

"The angriest," I repeated, stalling for time. My throat felt dry and tight, and I thought about asking for some water, but it seemed like that might be weird. "You want that list alphabetically?"

"I mean in all your life, the angriest," Goldman said. "The first thing that comes to your mind."

"There's a lot to choose from."

"I'm sure something stands out."

"Not really. I—"

"Go!"

The sudden, sharp tone of voice hit me like a needle, and I blurted out, "Claire!" I immediately felt sick. I hadn't meant to go there, not at all, but it just . . . came out.

In the silence that followed, Theo Goldman sat back in his chair and looked at me with calm, unreadable eyes. "Go on," he finally said. "What about Claire?"

What the hell had I just said? It wasn't true, not at all. I didn't mean it. I stared hard at my shoes, which were battered old work boots, the better to kick some vampire in the teeth with. In Morganville, Texas, you went with either the running shoes or the teeth-kicking shoes. I wasn't much of a runner.

"Nothing," I said. "It just came out, that's all. Claire's the best thing that ever happened to me. I'm not angry at her. I don't even know why I said that." That was good, that was calm and straightforward, and I checked my watch. God, had it only been fifteen minutes in here, in this nice paneled office, sitting on this comfy Softer Side of Sears couch? "Look, this is great and everything, but I really should be—"

"Why, then, did Claire come to your mind, with all of the terrible things I know you have experienced?" he asked. "You have another thirty minutes, by the way. We have plenty of time. Relax, Mr. Collins. I promise you, I'm here to help."

"Help. Yeah, vampires are known for all their awesome counseling skills."

"Does the fact that I am a vampire bother you?"

"Of course it bothers me! I grew up in Morganville—it's kind of a big deal to sit down and play nice with one of you."

Goldman's smile was sad, and ghostly. "You do realize that just as all men are not the same, all vampires are not the same? The worst murderers I have ever met in my long life were breathing men who killed not for sustenance, but for sport. Or worse, for beliefs."

"Don't suppose we can just agree I'm screwed up and call it a day?"

He looked at me with such level, kind intensity that I felt uncomfortable, and then he said, "There are a surprising number of people who care about what happens to you. The fact that you are here, instead of behind bars, would seem to tell you that, I'd think. Yes?"

I shrugged. I knew it looked like I was the typical surly teen, but I didn't much care what a vamp thought of me. So I kept insisting to myself, anyway. I'd gotten myself in it deep this time—deeper than it looked. Before, they'd let me slide because I was a messed-up kid, and then because I'd managed to end up on the right side (by their definition) of the problem, even against my own dad.

But this time I didn't have any defense. I'd voluntarily gotten involved in the illegal fight club at the gym; I'd let myself get drugged up and stuck in cages to duke it out with vampires. For money. On the Internet.

It was that last part that was the biggest violation of all—breaching the wall of secrecy about Morganville. Sure, nobody on the Internet would take it seriously; it was all tricks, special effects, and besides, to the average visitor who wanted to come poke around, it was just another boring, roll-up-the-sidewalks-at-dusk town in America.

That didn't change the fact that I'd risked the anonymity—the safety—of the vampires. I was lucky I hadn't been quietly walled up somewhere, or buried in a nice, deep grave somewhere in the dark. The only reason I hadn't been killed outright was that my girlfriend had some pull with the vamps, and she'd fought for me. Hard.

She was the reason I was sitting here, instead of taking up a slab in the local mortuary. So why had I said her name when he'd asked me about being angry?

I hadn't answered, even though the silence stretched thin, so Dr. Goldman leaned back in his chair and tapped his pen against his lips a moment, then said, "Why do you feel you need to fight, Shane?"

I laughed out loud. It sounded wild and uncontrollable, even to me. "You're not serious with that question, right?"

"I don't mean fight when your life is in danger; that is a reasonable and logical response to preserve one's safety. According to the records I've reviewed, though, you seem to seek out physical confrontation, rather than wait for it to come to you. It started in school, it seems. . . . Although you were never classified as a bully, you seemed to take special care to seek out those who were picking on others and—how would you say it?—teach them a lesson. You cast yourself as the defender of the weak and abused. Why is that?"

"Somebody's got to do it."

"Your father, Frank Collins—"

"Don't," I interrupted him flatly. "Just stay the hell off the topic, okay? No discussions about my freaking obvious daddy issues, or my mother, or Alyssa dying, any of that crap. I'm over it."

He raised an eyebrow, just enough to tell me what he thought about that. "Then shall we discuss Claire?"

"No," I said, but my heart wasn't in it. Weirdly.

He must have sensed it, because he said, in that gentle and quiet tone, "Why don't you tell me about her?"

"Why should I? You already know her."

"I want to know how you see her."

"She's beautiful," I said, and I meant it. "She doesn't know it, but she is. And she's so—" Fragile. Vulnerable. "—stubborn. She just doesn't know when to give up."

"You seem to have that in common."

We had a lot in common, weird as that might seem; she was from a sheltered, protected place, a family who loved her, a dad who would never betray her, but somehow that had given her an unshakable belief that she could survive anything. I had that, too, but it came from the opposite direction; I knew what it felt like to lose everything, everyone, and understand that it was just me against the darkness.

But it was more than that. Complicated, what I felt for her.

And I didn't want to look too closely at it. "I try to look after her," I said. That was meant to be a blowoff, but Goldman seemed to find it more interesting than I'd intended.

"Does she need looking after, do you think?"

"Doesn't everybody?"

"And your job, the job of all boyfriends, is to protect her," he said. It almost sounded like my own voice, in my own head. "Is that what you believe?"

"Yeah," I agreed. No-brainer.

"What do you think Claire would say if she heard that?"

I couldn't stop myself from smiling, a little. "She'd smack me," I said. "She doesn't think she needs a bodyguard—she's always telling me that." The smile faded too fast, because a cascade of images burned through my brain, uncontrollable and violent: Claire smiling at me. Claire smiling at Myrnin. Myrnin turning crazy on us, as he always did. And Claire just . . . accepting that. Again.

The scars on her neck, pale and small but obvious to me.

"And yet, you're angry at her," Goldman said.

"Bite me," I snapped. The pressure was doing my head in, and I had to get up, move, stalk the room. My fist wanted to punch something; the wild energy in me didn't have any way out except through flesh and bone and pain. "You need to stop pushing me, man. I mean it. I don't want to be paying for repairs around here."

Goldman was unruffled. He sat comfortably and watched me as I paced the room. If he was scared I'd take it out on him, he didn't look it. "Are you angry because I made an observation, or because of what I am?"

"Both," I said. "Hell, I don't know. Look, can we just get this over with? Call it an hour and let me out of here."

"You can leave anytime you like, Shane. I'm not stopping you. But your treatment is mandated by the Founder. If you decide not to follow through on your commitments, she is within her rights to rescind your parole and put you behind bars."

"Wouldn't be the first time."

"I know," he said. There was a world of kindness in those two words, and it derailed the anger train from the tracks. I didn't want to punch him, but I didn't want to answer him, either. He was right; I couldn't just walk out of here, not without consequences. . . . Jail didn't scare me so much, but there was something that did: losing Claire. Going to jail meant not seeing her, and right now, she was the only light in the world shining in the dark where I lived.

Even if sometimes I hated what I saw reflected in that light.

I had my hand on the doorknob of the office. The place wasn't locked; I could just turn my wrist, and step over the threshold, and live with all that meant.

I turned my wrist and pulled the door open. The outer office beyond the door was a little cooler, and I closed my eyes as the soft breeze passed over my face.

One step. That was all it would take. One step.

I slowly closed the door and leaned my back against it. "I'm not a coward," I said.

"I think that is beyond dispute," he replied. "But physical courage is one thing. Emotional courage to look inside yourself, that is another, and many don't possess that kind of will. Do you?"

"Not me. My friends all have it. I don't," I said. I was thinking about Michael, hanging on quietly, alone, ghostly in a house that had been his family's home. Grimly trying to survive as half a vampire, hiding the truth from us, never letting me see his fear or his fury. Eve, always full of acid and fun, with all the fragile terror beneath; she never let Morganville win, even though every day she woke up knowing it could be her last. Claire, sure and steady and calm, somehow coming into our little fraternity of screwups and making us whole, each in our own way. Without her, I'd never have had the courage to defy my dad and side with Michael, even though I wanted to do it.

Claire was all courage, to the core. Just not the kind of courage that hit things.

"I think you are stronger than you know," Goldman said, and leaned forward now, watching me intently as I sat back down on the couch. "And much smarter than anyone gives you credit. I will make you this deal. We can sit for the rest of the hour in silence, if you wish, and I will say that you are progressing with your therapy. Or you can speak. It's your choice. I won't ask you again."

It was a long ten minutes before I finally said, pushing the words out against an overwhelming weight, "It was how she looked at him."

"At who?"

"At her boss. Crazy-ass Myrnin. I saw her looking at him, and he was looking at her, and it was—" I shook my head. "Nothing, it was nothing." No, that wasn't true—I was lying out loud. Worse, I was trying to lie to myself. "She likes him. Maybe even loves him, in a crazy-uncle kind of way."

"You think she doesn't love you?"

"That's not the point. She can't love him."

"Because he is a vampire?"

"Yes!"

"You said before that she loves him like an uncle. Do you believe it is more than that?"

"Not from her," I said. "From him . . . yeah, maybe."

"How did it make you feel, knowing that?"

What a shrink question. "Lost," I said. That surprised me, but it was true. "I felt lost. And angry."

"At Claire."

I didn't answer that one, because it was too scary. I could not be angry at Claire; I just couldn't. It wasn't her fault, any of this; she was a loving person, and that was part of why I loved her, too.

So why did it hurt so much to think that she might smile at Myrnin, love him even a little bit?

Because he's a vampire. No, because you want her to be all yours.

"Have you considered," Goldman said, "that the reason the vampire Gloriana found it so easy to release that anger inside you to make you fight is that you so rarely confront it?"

"What the hell does that mean—is it shrink code for yell and break stuff and act like a douche bag? Because I've already done all that." More often than I liked to admit, even to myself. "I'm all about confrontation."

"Yes," he said, and smiled. It made him look kindly and twinkly and likable, which sucked, because vampires weren't supposed to look that way. "You most certainly have that behavior down. But what about talking honestly with Claire? Have you done that?"

Had I? I talked to her, sure—every day. And sometimes we talked about how we felt, but it was surface stuff, even if it was true. "No," I said. The pressure inside me lightened up, weirdly enough. I no longer wanted to punch something to get rid of it. "I mean, she knows I don't like the guy. . . ."

"Have you told her, explicitly, how you see her relationship with Myrnin, and how it makes you feel?"

That was an easy one. "No." Hell no.

He was still smiling, all grandfatherly and very slightly amused. "Because strong men don't do such things, yes?"

No shit, Sherlock.

"What if I told you that being honest with her, deeply honest, would make her love you even more?"

That was utter crap. If Claire knew me, really knew me, knew all the toxic muck that was sludged up inside me, she'd get the hell away from me, no question about it. I shook my head, not even meaning to do it.

Goldman sighed. "Very well, then," he said. "Baby steps. At least you've admitted it to me. We have at least another two months left together. I consider this a very fine start." He glanced down at his watch. "And I believe that it's time for my next appointment. Very good work, Mr. Collins."

I shot out of the couch like it had an ejection seat, and had my hand on the doorknob when he said, "One more thing, if you don't mind: I'd like to assign you some homework."

"Yeah, 'cause that never gets old," I said, but I was already resigned to doing a searching moral inventory, or whatever psychobabble crap he was about to pull out of his dusty immortal bag of tricks.

He surprised me. "I'd like you to try, for the next twenty-four hours, to solve any problem that arises without allowing your anger free rein. If you're presented with an opportunity to fight, I'd like you to back down. If someone tries to verbally engage you, defuse the situation. If you're insulted, walk away. Just for twenty-four hours. Then you can engage in fisticuffs to your heart's content."

I turned and stared at him. "I have actually gone a whole day without punching somebody, you know. Sometimes even two days."

"Yes, but you channel your anger in other ways, smaller ones you may not even realize. Perhaps by thinking hard about it, you may realize how much you allow it to drive your actions and shape the world around you." He nodded then. "That's all. Just try it, for one full day. I'll be interested to hear how it feels."

I shrugged and opened the door. "Sure, Doc. No problem."

I didn't even make it out of the building before my first challenge came up. It was a big one.

Physically, Monica Morrell was a pretty girl—not as beautiful as she thought she was, but on a scale of ten she was at least a seven, and that was when she wasn't really trying. Today, she was definitely working for an eight point five, and was probably getting it. She had on a short pink dress and looked . . . glossy, I guess. Girls would probably be able to tell you all the technical details of that, but the bottom line was, she turned heads.

And my first impulse, my very first, was to punch her right in the pink lip gloss.

That was so familiar to me that it honestly kind of surprised me when I considered it, in light of Goldman's homework assignment. She hadn't even seen me yet, hadn't smirked or made a snarky, cold comment; she hadn't reminded me of my dead family, or dissed my girlfriend, or done any of a thousand things she was bound to pull out to trip my triggers. It was just a reflex, me wanting to hurt her, and I was pretty sure that most people didn't have that kind of wiring.

I took a deep breath, and as she looked up and saw me getting off the elevator, I held the door for her. I didn't smile—it probably would have looked like I wanted to bite her—but I nodded politely and said, "Morning," just like she was a real person and not a skanky murderous bitch who didn't deserve to breathe.

She faltered, just a little strange flinch as if she couldn't quite figure out what my game was. If I hadn't been looking for it, I never would have seen the odd expression that flashed across her face, and even then, it took me a few more seconds to realize what it meant.

She was afraid.

The flash of fear vanished, and she tossed her shiny hair back and walked past me into the elevator. "Collins," she said. "So, did you rig it to explode?" She said it like she was unimpressed, and stabbed a perfectly manicured finger out at one of the floor buttons. "Or are you just going to throw paint on me before the doors shut?"

I considered saying a lot of things—maybe about how she deserved to die in fire—and then I let go of the door, stepped back, and said, "Have a nice day, Monica."

She was still staring at me with the best, most utterly confused expression when I turned and walked away, hands in my pockets.

Frustrating? Yeah, a little. But oddly fun. *At least I can keep her guessing,* I thought. And it felt like a little victory, just because I hadn't done the first thing that popped into my head.

Walking toward home, I nodded to people I knew, which was pretty much everybody. I didn't hit anybody. I didn't even say anything snide. It was kind of a miracle.

I decided to test my luck a little, and stopped in at Common Grounds.

If I'd been relatively unpopular around Morganville before, I'd taken things to a whole new level. Down a level. I walked into the coffee shop like I had a thousand times before, and this time, conversation pretty much stopped dead. The college students ignored me, as they always did; I was a townie, unimportant to their own little insulated world. It was the Morganville natives who were reacting like Typhoid Mary had just sailed in the door. Some got real interested in their lattes and mochas; others whispered, heads together, darting looks at me.

Word was out that I was on probation with the Founder. Somewhere, some enterprising young buck was taking bets on whether I'd survive the week, and the odds were not going to be in my favor.

My housemate Eve was behind the counter, and she leaned over it and waved at me. She'd put some temporary blue streaks in her coal black hair, which gave her some interesting style, particularly when paired with the livid blue eye shadow and matching, very shiny shirt. Over her outfit, which was probably more cracked out than usual, she wore the tie-dyed Common Grounds apron. "Hey, sunshine," she said. "What's your poison?"

Knowing Eve, she meant that literally. "Coffee," I said. "Just plain, none of that foo-foo stuff."

She widened her eyes, and leaned over to stage-whisper, "Honestly, men do sometimes have cream in their coffee. I've seen it on the news. Try a latte sometime—it's not going to reduce your testosterone level or anything."

"B—" I was about to automatically say *Bite me*, which would have been right and proper and comfortable between the two of us; it wasn't an angry response, just the usual thing I said when Eve snarked on me. I loved her, but this was how we talked. Probably wasn't covered by Goldman's rules, but I thought that maybe, just maybe, I'd try to change it up. "Okay," I said.

That got me a blank stare. "I'm sorry?"

"Okay," I repeated. "I'll try a latte, if you think they're good."

"You'll—" Eve cocked her head slowly to one side, her blunt-cut hair brushing her shoulder. "Wait, did you just say you want me to make you a drink that isn't something you get at a truck stop?"

"Is that a problem?"

"No. No, not at all," she said, but she was frowning a little. "You feeling okay?"

"Yeah, good," I said. "Just trying something different today."

"Huh." Eve studied me for a few long seconds, and then smiled. "It's kind of working for you, boy." She winked at me and got busy doing complicated things with espresso and steamed milk, and I turned to look at the crowd sitting around the tables. A few local business types, cheating a few minutes away from the office; the college kids with their backpacks, headphones, and stacks of textbooks; a few pale, anemic people sitting in the darker part of the room, away from the windows.

One of them rose and walked toward me. Oliver, owner of the place, who redefined the term "hippie freak"—he had tied his long graying hair back in a ponytail, and was wearing a Common Grounds apron that made him look all nice and cuddly. He wasn't, and I was one of those who knew just how very dangerous he really was.

He also wasn't my biggest fan. Ever, I mean, but especially now.

"Collins," he greeted me, not sounding too thrilled to be taking my money for caffeine. "I thought you were due for therapy." He didn't bother to lower his voice, and I saw Eve, who'd overheard, wince and keep her attention strictly on the drink she was mixing.

"Already been," I said. I couldn't sound cheerful, but I didn't sound angry, either. Kind of an achievement. "You can check with the doc if you want."

"Oh, I will," he said. "This needless charity toward you is not my idea, and if you fail to meet the conditions of your parole . . ."

"I'll be in jail," I said.

Oliver smiled, and it was a scary thing. "Perhaps," he said. "But I wouldn't count on it. You've had too many chances. Amelie's patience may be unlimited, but I promise you, mine is not."

"Back—" . . . *off, man. I'm not impressed with the size of your* . . . Yeah, that wasn't playing by Theo's rules so much. I bit my tongue, tasted blood, and really wanted to toss off a few incendiary rounds in his direction. Instead, I took a breath, counted to five, and said, "I know I don't deserve the break. I'll do my best to earn it."

His eyebrows rose sharply, but his eyes remained cold. "It was given over my objections. Again. You needn't waste your sudden change of heart on me."

Well, I'd tried.

Eve cleared her throat, loudly, and pushed my drink at me. "Here," she said. "Hey, is Claire meeting you?"

"No, she's got classes. Thanks for this." I passed over a five, and she made change. Oliver watched the transaction without commentary, thankfully; I'd just about used up my entire reserve of polite vampire-appropriate conversation that didn't involve the words *drop deader.*

I carried the drink over to an open table and sat down. I had a good view of the street, so I people-watched and surfed my phone. The latte, surprisingly, wasn't bad. I saw Eve watching me, and gave her a thumbs-up. She did a silent cheer. *Score so far: Shane three, temper zero,* I thought, and was feeling kind of smug about it when a shadow fell across me. I looked up to see three Texas Prairie University jocks—which wasn't saying much, in the great athletic world—looming over me. They were big dudes, but not that much bigger than I was. I automatically did the precalculations. . . . Three to one, the one in the middle was the ringleader, and he had a mean look. Sidekick one was vacant-looking, but he had a multiply broken nose and was no stranger to mixing it up. Sidekick two was unmarked, which meant either he wasn't much of a fighter or he was ridiculously good.

Eh, I'd had lots worse matchups. At least none of them had fangs.

"You're at our table," the center one said. He was wearing a Morganville High cutoff muscle tee, with the school mascot—a viper; go figure—and I finally placed him. He was a native son, and he'd been just starting to get a rep as a decent defensive lineman before I'd left town. He'd been a bully back then, too. "Move it, loser."

"Oh, hey, Billy, how's it going?" I asked, without actually moving an inch. "Haven't seen you around."

He wasn't prepped for chitchat, and I got a blank look from him, then a scowl. "Did you hear me, Collins? Move it. Not going to tell you again."

"No?" I looked up at him and sipped my latte. "Common Grounds, dude. You really going to start some shit here, with him staring right at us?" I nodded toward Oliver, who had his arms crossed and was watching us with so much intensity I was surprised some of us weren't catching fire. I sipped my latte, and waited. This nonviolence thing was kind of fun, because I got to see Billy squirm without breaking a sweat.

Only problem was, Billy wasn't all that smart, and he punched me in the face. Just like that, a sucker punch to the jaw.

I dropped my latte and came up out of my chair in a single surge of muscle, my fist clenching even before the news of the pain hit my brain like a sledgehammer. Counterattack was instinctive, and it was necessary, because nobody, nobody got to hit me like that and not have a comeback.

I was pulling back for a real serious hit when I heard Theo Goldman's voice say, clear as a bell, *Twenty-four hours.*

Hell.

I gulped back my anger, opened my fist, and blocked Billy's next punch. "You owe me a latte," I said, which was something I hadn't exactly expected to say, ever. The table was a mess, spilled coffee and milk dribbling off the edges of it. My heart was pounding, and I wanted to punch all of these guys until they were too stupid to move. This time, holding back didn't feel good; it felt like losing. It felt like cowardice. And I hated it.

But I sacked up and walked away. The table was theirs. Now they had to clean up their own mess.

Outside, the air felt sharp and raw on my skin, and I leaned against the bricks and breathed deeply, several times, until the red mist that still clouded my vision started to clear up. My fight-or-flight reaction had just one setting, I was starting to realize; that wasn't smart. It was fun, but it wasn't smart.

Eve came running out, still in her apron. She saw me standing there and skidded to a stop. "Hey!" she blurted. "Are you okay?"

"Fine," I said. "He's too wimpy to break anything except his own hand. Doesn't throw from the shoulder."

"No, I mean—Jesus, Shane, you just..." Eve stared at me for a second, and I thought she was going to say something that would make me feel a hell of a lot worse, but then she threw her arms around me and hugged me hard. "You just did something totally classy. Good for you."

Huh.

She was gone before I could explain that it wasn't really my choice.

Classy? Girls are weird. There's nothing classy about getting sucker punched and walking away.

But I guess today was about fighting myself, and God help me, I was kind of winning.

I had a date late afternoon to walk Claire home from campus; she didn't really need the escort, but I enjoyed pretending she did, and spending time with her was always a plus. I had a lot to make up for, with Claire; I'd lied to her, and when things got dark on me with the fight club, I'd gone dark on her, too. She hadn't deserved that, or any of the terrible things I'd said, or thought. It was going to take some real effort to get back to where we were, but I was determined to make it happen.

And normally, I wouldn't have let anything interfere with that, but as I was passing the empty house on Fox Street, the second from the corner, with the broken-out windows and the ancient, peeling paint job, I heard something that sounded like muffled, frantic crying. *It's a cat,* I told myself. The place was a lifeless wreck, and the yard was so overgrown that just getting to the barred-over front door would have meant a full-blown safari, with the added benefit of thorny weeds, possible snakes and poisonous spiders, and who knew what else. I'd feel really damn stupid if I ended up snakebit to save a cat who wasn't even in trouble in the first place.

But it didn't really sound like a cat.

In Morganville, the principal survival rule was always keep walking, but I've never been one for that strategy; it's soul-sucking, seeing people hurt and doing nothing to help. Goldman was right—I did have a savior complex—but dammit, in Morganville, people sometimes did need saving.

Like, most probably, now.

I sighed and started pushing through the tangle of waist-high weeds toward the house. The front door was a nonstarter; I could see from here that the padlock was still intact. Whoever had found a way in had done it with at least a small bit of stealth.

The windows were still full of jagged glass, so even if someone else had gone in that way, I wasn't about to try it—and I didn't need to, because the back door was standing wide-open, a not very inviting rectangle of blackness.

I could hear scuffling now, and the crying was louder. Definitely being muffled. It was coming from upstairs, and from the thumps, it sounded like there was a fight under way.

The stairs creaked and popped, alerting anybody who was paying the slightest attention that I was on the way, and I wasn't surprised when a girl of about fourteen appeared at the top of the steps, gasping and sobbing, and plunged past me toward the exit. She looked relatively okay, if panicked.

The boys—two of them—at the top of the steps weren't much older than she was. Sixteen, seventeen, maybe. Local kids, but nobody I had on my radar.

They looked real surprised to see me.

"Hey," I said, and stopped where I was, halfway up, blocking the way down. "You want to explain what just happened?"

One of them opted for bravado. Not a good look for him. "None of your business, jackhole," he said, and flipped me off. "We're not doing anything."

"You mean now," I said. "Here's a pro tip, kids—when the girl's crying, she's not that into you." I was angry now, angrier than I'd been at dumb-ass Billy with his sucker punch. That would have been a meaningless fight. This one, on the other hand, had some meat to it. "You know who I am?"

One of them had some sense, at least, and he nodded. "Collins," he said, and tugged at his friend's arm. "Dude, let it go."

The friend wasn't that smart. "You can't prove nothing," he shot back at me. I shrugged.

"Yeah, I might really care about that if I was some kind of cop, but I'm not. I'm just a guy who gets pissed off a lot. So here's the deal. I'm going to give you one chance to promise me you'll stop being giant douches. Do that, and you can get the hell out of here." My voice went cold for the next part. "You break your promise, you touch any girl in this town again who doesn't sincerely beg you for it, and I'm going to rip off any parts that dangle, you got me?"

"Who died and made you Batman, dickhead?" the bigger one asked.

"For the purposes of this discussion, let's just say my dad," I said. "Because he'd already have left you room temperature on the floor. I'm the kinder, gentler version." Not quite true; my dad hadn't possessed any real moral compass. If these fools had been vamps, he'd have been all over it, but regular human idiots? He'd shrug and walk away.

They didn't need to know that, though.

"Dude, let's just go already!" said Lesser Douche Bag, and didn't wait for his friend to make up his alleged mind; he held up both hands in surrender and edged by me down the steps. When he hit the ground floor, he ran.

The remaining guy reached in his pocket and flicked open a fairly serious-looking knife. I respect knives. It raised him a notch or two in my threat levels, though he wasn't yet even breaking orange. "Bad idea," I told him, and began climbing the stairs toward him. "Real, real bad idea."

He started backing off, clearly spooked; he'd thought just having a knife meant he won. I hit the top step and lunged, knocking his knife hand out of the way, twisting it, and catching the weapon before it hit the floor.

Then I put a forearm against his chest, shoved him against the wall, and showed him the knife. "Bad idea," I repeated, and drove it into the wall next to his head, close enough for him to feel the passage of it. He went really, really pale, and all the fight bled out of him as if I'd actually stabbed him. "You just got upgraded. You no longer get a full pass, jackass; you get to look forward to seeing me a lot. And I'd better like what I see, you got me? Any girls crying, even if it's at a sad movie, and we're going to finish this in a way that's not going to look real good on you."

I wanted to punch the little bastard, but I didn't.

I just stared at him for a long few seconds, and then pulled the knife free, folded it, and put it in my own pocket. Then I let him go. "Scat," I said. "You've got a ten-second head start."

He made use of it.

I sat down on the steps, toying with the knife he'd left behind. I hadn't lost my temper, but I hadn't exactly been nonviolent, either. I called that one a draw.

I hadn't heard him, but all of a sudden I realized that someone was at the bottom of the steps, looking up in the gloom. Pale skin, curly wild hair, out-of-fashion old man's clothes. Small wire-framed glasses pushed down on his nose.

Dr. Theo Goldman.

"You following me?" I asked. I felt surprisingly relaxed about it.

"Yes," he said. "I was curious how much effort you would put forward. I'm pleasantly surprised."

I gestured with the knife. "So, how does this count?"

He smiled, just a little. "I've never really been a fan of the teaching that you should turn the other cheek," he said. "Evil must be fought, or what does it matter if we're good? Goodness can't be weakness, or it ceases to be good." He shrugged. "Let's call it a draw."

I could live with that. "You were right," I said. "It doesn't have to be all fight, all the time. But I'm going to miss it. Kind of a lot."

"Oh," he said cheerfully, "I'm quite sure there will be plenty of chances for you to indulge yourself. It's Morganville, after all. See you tomorrow."

He was already gone when I blinked. I shook my head and started to pocket the knife.

"Leave it," his voice drifted back. "I trust you better when you're not armed."

I grinned this time, and dumped the knife through a crack in the boards. It was swallowed up by the house.

It wasn't twenty-four hours yet, but somehow, I felt like I could probably make it the rest of the way.

Probably.

AUTOMATIC

☽

Another anthology tale, written for the *Enthralled: Paranormal Diversions* collection, edited by Melissa Marr and Kelley Armstrong. That amazing anthology is the result of Melissa and Kelley inviting a bunch of their author friends along for a road-trip signing tour called the Smart Chicks Kick It event, and it was a huge success and blowout fun. To help fund the tour (because all of us pitched in for costs), they put together this anthology, which also allowed us to give back a little to our readers.

This stand-alone story is set late in the series, but before the Day-lighters show up, and it deals with something I've always wondered about. . . . We have vending machines for snacks, cold drinks, even hot drinks. Why don't the vamps have one for blood?

Well, this examines why it might not be such a great idea, by way of Michael's experience. A sweet little love story, too, in an unexpected way.

Fun factoid: I was addicted to soft drinks in college (not coffee) and if I couldn't find a working machine that served Dr Pepper, my day was bound to go almost as badly as Michael's is about to in this story. Physics class without the sweet relief of soda? Unthinkable!

There was a new vending machine at the Morganville Blood Bank. In the withdrawal area, not the deposit area. It looked like a Coke machine, only instead of handy ice-cold aluminum cans, there were warm cans labeled *O Neg* and *A* and *B Pos*— something for everybody. The cans even had nice graphic logos on them.

My girlfriend, Eve, and I were standing in front of the vending machine, marveling at the weirdness, and wondering a lot of things: First, what the hell did they tell the can manufacturers about what was going in those containers? And second, would the blood taste like aluminum? It already had a coppery tone to it, like licking pennies, but . . . would it be any *good*?

There were twelve vampires in the room, including me, and nobody was making a move to get anything out of the shiny new machine. The Withdrawal Room itself was clean, efficiently laid out, and not very friendly. Big long counter at one end, with staff in white lab coats. You took a number; you got called to the counter; they gave you your blood bags. You could order it to go, or drink it here; there were some small café-style tables and chairs at the other end, but nobody really liked to linger here. It felt like a doctor's office, someplace you left in a hurry as soon as you could.

So it was odd how all the tables and chairs were full, and the sofas, and the armchairs. And how there were vamps standing around, watching the machine as if they expected it to actually DO something. Or, well, expected me to do something.

"Michael?" Eve said, because I'd been a long time, staring at the glossy plastic of the machine in front of me. "Uh, are we doing this or not?"

"Sure," I said, resigned. "I guess we have to." I had actually been *asked*—well, ordered, really—to lead the way on this particular new Morganville initiative. Morganville, Texas, is—to say the least—unusual, even for someplace as diverse and weird as our great state. It is a small, desert-locked town in the middle of nowhere, populated by both humans and vampires. A social experiment, although the vampires really controlled the experiment. As far as I knew, we were the only place in the world vampires lived openly—or lived at all.

I was on the side of the vamps now . . . not through any plan of my own. I was nineteen years old, and looking at eternity, and it was starting to look pretty lonely because the people I cared about, that I loved . . . they weren't going to be there with me.

Somehow, the machine summed up how impersonal all this eternal life was going to get, and that made it so much more than just another Coke machine full of plasma.

I was still amazed that eleven other vamps had shown up today for the demonstration; I'd expected nobody, really, but in the end, we weren't so different from humans: novelties attracted us, and the blood dispenser was definitely a novelty. Nobody quite knew what to make of it, but they were fascinated, and repelled.

And they were waiting.

Eve nudged me and looked up into my face, concerned. She wasn't too much shorter than I was, but enough that even the stacked heels on her big Goth boots didn't put us at eye level. She'd gone with subdued paint-up today: white makeup, black lipstick, not a lot of other accessories. We were so different, in so many ways; I wasn't Goth, for starters. I wasn't much of anything, fashion-wise, except comfortable. And she seemed okay with that, thankfully.

"Swipe?" she said again, and tapped my right hand, which held a shiny new plastic card. I looked down at it, frowning. White plastic, with a red stripe, and my name computer-printed at the bottom. GLASS, MICHAEL J. My dates of birth and death (or, as it was called on the vamp side, "transformation"). The cards were new, just like the vending machine—issued just about two weeks ago. A lot of the older vampires refused to carry them. I couldn't really see why, but then, I'd grown up modern, where you had to have licenses and ID cards, and accepted that you were going to get photographed and tracked and monitored.

Or maybe that was just the humans who accepted that, and I'd carried it over with me.

It was just a damn glorified Coke machine. Why did it feel so weird?

"So," Eve said, turning away from me to the not-very-welcoming audience of waiting vampires, "it's really easy. You've all got the cards, right? They're your ID cards, and they're loaded up with a certain number of credits for the month. You can come in here anytime, swipe the card, and get your, uh, product. And now, *Michael Glass is going to demonstrate*."

Oh, that was my cue, accompanied by a not-too-light punch on the arm.

I reached over, slid the card through the swipe bar, and buttons glowed. A cheerful little tone sounded, and a scrolling red banner read MAKE YOUR SELECTION NOW. I made my selection—O negative, my favorite—and watched the can ride down in a miniature elevator to the bottom, where it was pushed out for me to take.

I took the can, and was a little surprised to find it was warm, warm as Eve's skin. Well, of course it was: the signs on the machine read TEM-PERATURE CONTROLLED, but that just meant it was kept *blood* tempera-ture, not *Coke* temperature. Huh. It felt weird, but attractive, in a way.

They were all still watching me, with nearly identical expressions of disgust and distaste. Some of them looked older than me, some even younger, but they'd all been around for centuries, whereas I was the brand-new model . . . the first in decades.

Hence, the guinea pig—but mainly because I'd grown up in the modern age, with swipe cards and Internet and food from machines. I trusted it, at least in theory.

They hated it.

I rolled the can indecisively in my hand for a few seconds, staring at the splashy graphics—the vampire fangs framed the blood type nicely. "How do you think they got away with getting these made?" I asked Eve. "I mean, wouldn't somebody think it was a little strange?"

She rolled her eyes. "Honestly, Michael, don't you pay attention? Out there"—meaning, anywhere except Morganville—"it's just a big joke. Maybe they thought it was for a movie or a TV show or a new energy drink. But they don't think about it like we do."

I knew that, even though, like Eve, I'd been born and raised in Morganville. We'd both been out of town exactly once in our lives, and we'd done it together. Still, it was really tough to realize that for the rest of the world, our biggest problems were just . . . stories.

As hard as Morganville was, as full of weirdness and danger, Out There hadn't been a walk in the park, either. Though I wished I'd been able to go to a really big concert. That would have been cool.

I was still turning the can around, stalling. Eve grabbed it from me, popped the top, and handed it back. "Bottoms up," she said. "Oh, come on, just give it a try. Once."

I owed her that much, because the black choker around her neck was covering up a healing bite mark. Vampire bites healed quickly, and usually without scarring, but for the awkward three-day period, she'd be wearing scarves and high necks.

It was typical Eve that she was also wearing a tight black T-shirt that read, in black-on-black Gothic-style lettering, GOOD GIRLS DON'T. AWESOME GIRLS DO.

She saw me looking at her, and our eyes locked and held. Hers were very dark, almost black, though if you really got close and looked, you could see flecks of lighter brown and gold and green. And I liked getting close to her, drawn into her warmth, her laughter, the smooth hot stretch of her skin. . . .

She winked. She mostly knew what I was thinking, at moments like these, but then, as she'd once told me, smugly, most guys really aren't that complicated.

I smiled back, and saw her pupils widen. She liked it when I smiled. I liked that she liked it.

Without even thinking about it, I raised the can to my lips and took a big gulp.

Not bad. I could taste the aluminum, but the blood tasted fresh, just a bitter streak that was probably from the preservatives. Once I started drinking, instincts kicked in, and I felt the fangs snap down in my mouth. It felt a little like popping your knuckles. I swallowed, and swallowed, and all of a sudden the can was light and empty, and I felt a little shaky. I don't usually drink that much blood at one time, and I'm more of a sipper.

I crushed the can into a ball—vampire strength—and tossed it across the room into a trash can, basketball-style. It sailed neatly through the narrow circle.

"Show-off," Eve said.

I felt great. I mean, *great*. My fangs were still down, and when I smiled, they were visible, gleaming and very sharp.

Eve's smile faltered, just a little. "Really. Showing off now."

I closed my eyes, got control, and felt the fangs slowly fold up against the roof of my mouth.

"Better," she said, and linked arms with me. "Now that you're all plasmaed up, can we go?"

"Yeah," I said, and we got two steps toward the door before I turned back, got the card out of my pocket, and slid it through the machine's reader again. Eve stared, blinking in confusion. I chose another O negative ("This Blood's for You!") and slipped the warm can into the pocket of my jacket. "For later," I said.

"Okay." Eve sounded doubtful, but she got over it. She turned back to the crowd of vamps watching us. "Next?"

Nobody was rushing to swipe their cards, although one or two had them out and were contemplating it. One guy scowled and said, "Whatever happened to organic food?" and went to the counter to get a fresh-drawn bag.

Well, I'd done what Amelie had asked me to do, so if it didn't work, they couldn't blame it on me.

But I did feel great. Surprisingly, the canned stuff was better than the bagged stuff. Almost better than when Eve had let me have a taste, straight from the tap, if that's not too sick.

I felt them watching us. Eve and I weren't the most popular team-up in town; humans and vampires didn't mix, not like that. We were predator and prey, and the lines were pretty strictly drawn. In vampire circles, I was looked at as either pitiful or perverted. I could imagine what it was like on Eve's side. Morganville's not full of vampire wannabes—more a town full of Buffys in the making.

Our relationship wasn't easy, but it was real, and I was going to hang on to it for as long as I possibly could.

"What do you want to do?" Eve asked, as we stepped outside into the cool Morganville early evening.

"Walk," I said. "For starters." I let her fill in what might come after, and she smiled in a way that told me it wasn't a tough guess at all.

Later, it occurred to me that I felt jittery, and it was getting worse.

We were strolling out in Founder's Square, which is vampire territory; Eve could come and go from here with or without me, because she had a Founder's Pin and was pretty much as untouchable as a human got, in terms of being hunted—by vampires who obeyed the rules, anyway. But it was nice to walk with her. At night, Morganville is kind of magical—bright clouds of stars overhead in a pitch-black sky, cool breezes, and, at least in this part of town, everybody is on their best behavior.

Vampires liked to walk, and jog, along the dark paths. We were regularly passed by others. Most nodded. A few stopped to say hello. Some—the most progressive—even said hello to Eve, as if she was a real person to them.

I had a wild impulse to jog, to *run*, but Eve couldn't keep up if I did, even in her practical boots. Holding that urge back was taking all my concentration, so while she talked, I just mostly pretended to listen. She was telling some story about Shane and Claire, I guessed; our two human housemates had gotten themselves into trouble again, but this time it was minor, and funny. I was glad. I didn't feel much like charging to anybody's rescue right now.

Up ahead, I saw another couple approaching us on the path. The woman was unmistakably the Founder of Morganville, Amelie; only Amelie could dress that way and get away with it. She was wearing a white jacket and skirt, and high heels. If she'd stood still, she'd have looked like a marble statue; her skin was only a few shades off from the clothes, and her hair was the same pale color. Beautiful, but icy and eerie.

Walking next to her, hands clasped behind his back, was Oliver. He looked much older than her, but I didn't think he was; she'd died young, and he'd died at late middle age, but they were both ancient. He had his long, graying hair tied back, and was wearing a black leather jacket and dark pants. He was scowling, but then, he usually was.

Weird, seeing the two of them together like this. They were usually polite enemies, sometimes right at each other's throats (literally). Not tonight, though. Not here.

Amelie glowed in the moonlight, ghost-bright, and when she smiled, she didn't look cold at all. She inclined her head to us. "Michael. Eve. Thank you for doing the little demonstration today. It was much appreciated."

"Ma'am," I said, and returned the salute. Eve waved. We would have kept on walking, but Amelie stopped, and Oliver was a solid block in front of us, so we stopped as well. I said, "Hope you're enjoying the walk. It's a nice night."

Lame, but it was all I had for small talk. I was aching to keep moving. I couldn't keep still, in fact, and I drummed my fingers against the side of my leg in a nervous rhythm. I saw Oliver notice it. His scowl deepened.

"It's turned quite cool," Amelie said. Like Oliver, she was zeroing in on my trembling fingers. "I heard you sampled the new product today."

"Yeah, it's great," I said. "I got another one to go." The can was heavy in my pocket, and I'd been thinking about it the entire evening. I'd found myself actually wrapping my hand around it inside my pocket, but I'd managed to stop myself from pulling the tab. So far. "Very convenient. You ought to think about selling them in six-packs."

"Well, the modern age seems to demand convenience." Amelie shrugged. "But we'll see how the single-can sales go. So many wanted access at odd hours to the blood bank that automation seemed the most logical solution. You don't mind the taste of the preservatives?"

"No, it's good stuff," I said. I remembered that I hadn't liked it at first, but now, for some reason, it seemed like that memory was wrong—as if it had actually been delicious but I hadn't been ready for it. "It tastes better than the bagged stuff." I almost said *and better than from the vein,* but Eve was right there, and that would embarrass her on two levels, not just one. First, that I was telling people she was letting me bite her, and second, that somehow her blood wasn't good enough. I was able to stop in time, barely. "Has anybody else tried it?"

"Really, Glass, do you think we put it out for public consumption without testing?" Oliver snapped. "It's been tried, analyzed, and tested to death. I cannot imagine a more boring process. Two years, from concept to actual delivery. Half the vampires in Morganville have been involved in taste tests."

"Have *you* tried it?" I asked him. "You should. It's really—" I didn't know how to finish that sentence, once I'd started it. "—fierce," I finally said. An Eve word. I wasn't sure I even knew what it meant in the way she used it, but it seemed right.

Evidently, Oliver didn't really understand the usage, either, because he gave me a long stare, one that could have melted concrete. "Our major difficulty seems to be in convincing the elders to use it," he said. "Most of them are not familiar with the concept of identification cards, much less credit cards, and machines confuse them."

"I'll bet," Eve put in. "Not much call for Cokes among the fang gang, I guess."

"Well, I like Coke," I said. Amelie smiled, very slightly.

"As do I, Michael. But I fear we're in the minority." There was something guarded in her eyes, a little worried. "Are you feeling all right?"

"Great," I said, probably too quickly. "I feel great."

Oliver exchanged a fast glance with her, and gave an almost invisible shrug. "Then we should be going," he said. "Matters to discuss."

It was dismissal, and I was happy to grab Eve's hand and walk on while the other two headed the other way. Oliver always bothered me; partly it was his eviler-than-thou attitude, and partly it was that I could never quite shake the memory of how I'd met him . . . how he'd come across as a nice, genuine guy, and turned on me. That had been before anyone in Morganville had known who he was, or how dangerous he could be.

And he'd killed me. Part of the way, anyway; he hadn't left me much choice in becoming what I was now. Maybe he thought of that as a fair trade.

I still didn't.

A tremor of adrenaline surged through me—hunting instinct. It took me a second to realize that there was a complicated mixture of things happening inside of me: hatred boiling up for Oliver, well beyond what I normally felt; hunger, although I shouldn't have been hungry at all; and last, most unsettlingly, I felt the steady, seductive pulse beat of Eve's blood through our clasped hands.

It was a moment that made me shiver and go abruptly very still, eyes shut, as I tried to master all of those warring, violent impulses. I heard Eve asking me something, but I shut her out. I shut everything out, concentrating on staying me, staying Michael, staying *human*, at least for now.

And finally, I fumbled in my pocket and popped open the aluminum can of O negative, and the taste was metal and meat, soothing the beast that was trying to claw its way free inside. I couldn't let it out, not here, not with Eve.

The taste of the blood silenced it for a moment, and then it roared back, shockingly stronger than ever.

I dropped the can and heard it clatter on the pavement. Eve's warm hands were around my face, and her voice was in my ears, but I couldn't understand what she was saying.

When I opened my eyes, all I saw was red, with vague smeared shapes of anything that wasn't prey. Eve, on the other hand, glowed a bright silver.

Eve was a target, and I couldn't resist her. I *couldn't*. I had to satisfy this hunger, fast.

I gasped and pushed her backward, and before she could do more than call my name in alarm, I spun and ran through the dark, red night.

I didn't know where I was headed, but as I ran, one thing took over, guiding me more by instinct than by design. When I saw the shining, warm targets of human beings out there in the dark, I avoided them; it was hard, maybe the hardest thing I'd ever done, but I managed.

I stopped in the shadows, not feeling tired at all, or winded, only anxious and more jittery than ever. The run hadn't burned it off; if anything, it had made things worse.

I was standing in front of the Morganville Blood Bank. This was the entrance in the front, the donation part, and it was closed for the night. Blessedly, there weren't any people around for me to be a danger to, at least right now.

I turned and ran down the side alley, effortlessly jumping over barriers of empty boxes and trash cans, and came around the back. Unlike the front, this part of the building was hopping with activity—human shapes coming and going, but they didn't have that silvery glow I'd become so familiar with. All vampires, this side, and none of them were paying attention to me until I got close, shoved a few aside, and made it to the waiting room.

The vending machine stood there in the center of the room. A few people were doubtfully studying it, trying to make up their minds whether to try it, but I shoved them out of the way, too. I swiped my card; when it didn't immediately work, I swiped it again and randomly punched buttons when they lit up. It took forever for the mechanism to work, and the can to be delivered.

Working the tiny pop top seemed impossible. I punched my fingers through the side and lifted it, bathing in the gush of liquid. It no longer tasted like metal. Warm from the can, it tasted like life. All the life I could handle.

"Michael," someone said, and put a hand on my shoulder. I turned and punched him, hard enough to break a human's neck, but it didn't do much except make the other vampire step back. I grabbed my card again and swiped it, but it was slippery in my fingers, damp with the red residue from the can, which had gotten all over me. I wiped it on my jeans and tried it again. The lights flashed. Nothing happened. "Michael, it won't work again. You used all today's credits."

No. That couldn't be true, it couldn't, because the rush hadn't lasted, hadn't lasted at all this time, and I felt bottomlessly empty. I needed more. I had to have *more.*

I shoved the other vampire back and slammed both hands into the plastic covering of the vending machine. It held, somehow, although cracks formed in the plastic. I hit it again, and again, until the plastic was coming apart. I shoved my hand through, heedless of the cuts, and grabbed one of the warm cans.

That was when someone behind hit me with an electric shock, like a Taser, only probably five times as strong, and the next thing I knew, I was limp on the floor, with the unopened can of AB negative rolling on the carpet beside me.

I tried to grab for it, but my hands weren't working. I was still reaching for it, fumbling for the fix, when they picked me up and towed me out of the waiting area, into a steel holding cell somewhere in the back.

Days passed. They took me off the canned stuff and put me on bags again, and finally, the frenzy passed. I won't lie—it was awful. But what was worse was slowly realizing how bad I'd been. How close I'd been to becoming . . . a thing. A senseless monster.

I wasn't sure if I ever wanted them to let me out, actually.

Music was the only thing that helped; after they got me stabilized, the woman who delivered the blood also delivered my guitar. I didn't feel myself until I was sitting down with the guitar cradled in my lap. The strings felt warm, and when I picked out the first notes, that was good; that felt right. That felt like me, again.

I don't know how long I played; the notes spilled out of me in a frantic rush, no song I knew or had written before. It wasn't a nice melody, not at first; it was jagged and bloody and full of fury, and then it slowly changed tempo and key, became something soothing that made me relax, very slowly, until I was just a guy, playing a guitar for the thrill of the notes ringing in the air.

From the doorway, a voice said, "You really do have a gift." I hadn't even heard him unlock it.

I didn't look up. I knew who it was; that voice was unmistakable. "Once, maybe. You took that away from me," I said. "I was going somewhere with it. Now I'm going nowhere."

Oliver, uninvited, sat down in a wooden chair only a few feet away from me. I didn't like seeing him here, in my space. This was my personal retreat, and it reminded me of how it had felt when he'd turned on me in my house, in my *house*, and . . .

. . . and everything had changed.

He was looking at me very steadily, and I couldn't read his expression. He'd had hundreds of years to perfect a poker face, and he was using it now.

I kept on playing. "Why are you here?"

"Because you are Amelie's responsibility, and it follows that you're also mine, as I'm her second-in-command."

"Did you take the machine out?"

Oliver shook his head. "No, but we changed the parameters. The testing was done on older vampires, ones who'd had centuries to stabilize their needs. You are entirely different, and we'd forgotten that. Very young, not even a full year old yet. We didn't anticipate that the formula would trigger such a violent response. In the future, you'll only receive the unprocessed raw materials."

"So it's because I'm young."

"No," he said. "It's because you're young *and* you refuse to acknowledge what you are. What it means. What it promises. You're fighting your condition, and that makes it almost impossible for you to control yourself. You need to admit it to yourself, Michael. You'll never be human again."

Last thing I wanted to do, and he knew it. I stopped playing for a few seconds, then picked up the thread again. "Fuck off," I said. "Feel free to take that personally."

He didn't answer for a long moment. I glanced up. He was still watching me.

"You're still not yourself," he eventually said. "And you're speaking like your scruffy friend."

He meant Shane. That made me laugh, but it sounded hollow, and a little bit desperate. "Well, Shane's probably right most of the time. You are an ass."

"And even if you think it, you rarely say it. Which rather proves my point."

"I'm fine."

"Are you? Because you've not asked a thing about your girlfriend, whom you left on her own in the middle of a vampire district, at night."

That sent an electric jolt of shame through me. I hadn't even *thought* about it. I hadn't spared a single thought for Eve all the time I'd been in here; I'd been too wrapped up in my own misery, my own shame. "Is she okay?" I asked. I felt sick, too sick to even try to keep on playing. The guitar felt heavy in my hands, and inert.

"She's becoming annoying with her repeated demands to see you, but yes, otherwise, she's as well as could be expected. I made sure she got home safely." Oliver paused for a few seconds, then leaned forward with his elbows braced on his knees, pale hands dangling. "When I was . . . transformed, I thought in the beginning that I could stay with those mortals I loved. It isn't smart. You should understand this by now. We stay apart for a reason."

"You stay apart so you don't feel guilty for doing what it is you do," I shot back. "I'm not like you. I'll never be like you. Best of all, I don't have to be."

His eyebrows rose, then settled back to a flat line. "Have it your way," he said. "The canned blood had an effect on you, yes, but not as much as you might believe. That was mostly you, boy. And you need to find a way to control that, because one day, you may find yourself covered in blood that doesn't come from a punctured can."

The way he said it chilled me, because it wasn't angry; it wasn't contemptuous; it was . . . sad. And all too knowing.

I let it drop into the silence before I said, "Eve wants to see me."

"Perpetually, apparently."

"I think I'm ready." Was I? I didn't know, but I ached to see her, tell her how sorry I was.

Oliver shrugged. "It's someone's funeral, if not yours." He moved fast, out the door before I could make any comeback, not that I could think of a good one anyway, and I clutched the guitar for comfort. My fingers went back to picking out melodies and harmonies, but I wasn't thinking about it anymore, and it didn't feel comforting.

I was afraid I wasn't ready, and the fear was a steady, hot spike that made my throat dry and, horribly, made my fangs ache where they lay flat. I didn't know if I was ready to see her. I didn't know if Oliver would care to stop me if I went off on her.

But when Eve stepped in the door, the fear slipped away, leaving relief in its wake. She was okay, and back to her fully Goth self, and what I felt wasn't hunger, other than the hunger anybody felt in the presence of someone they loved.

The shine in her eyes and her brilliant smile were the only things that mattered.

I had just enough time to put the guitar aside and catch her as she rushed at me, and then she kissed me, sweet and hot, and I sank into that, and her, and the reminder that there was something else for me other than hunting and hunger and lonely, angry music in the night.

"Don't you do that again," she whispered, her black-painted lips close to my ear. "Please, don't. You scared the hell out of all of us. I didn't know what to do."

I relaxed into her embrace, and breathed in the rich perfume of her hair, her skin, the subtle tingle of blood beneath her skin. I didn't like to think about that last part, but maybe Oliver was right. Maybe I needed to stop denying it, or I'd end up in an even worse place, in the end.

"I didn't know what to do, either," I whispered back. "I'm sorry. I could have—"

"Stop." She pulled back, staring at me fiercely. "Just stop it. You could have hurt me, but you didn't. You didn't hurt anybody, except that stupid machine. So relax. That's not you, Mike. That's some B-movie monster."

But I was the B-movie monster, too. That was what Oliver meant, in the end; I was exactly that, and I had to remember it. It was the only way any of this would work.

I forced a smile. "I thought you liked B-movie monsters," I said. My girlfriend punched me in the arm.

"Like, not love," she said. "You, I love."

I held out my hands, and she twined her fingers with mine. Warm and cool, together. "I don't know how to do this," I said.

She laughed a little. "Dating? Because, news flash, big guy, we've been doing it awhile."

"Being this. Being me. I don't know who I am anymore."

She stepped closer, looking up into my eyes. "I know who you are. More importantly, I know *what* you are," she said. "And I still love you."

Maybe she didn't know. Maybe she'd never looked into the heart of the red and black tormented *thing* that lurked deep inside me. But looking at her now, at her utter sincerity and fearlessness, I couldn't help but think that maybe she did, after all. Know me, *and* love me.

Maybe, in time, she'd be able to help me understand and love my monster, too. Because, in the end, it was always Eve. And always had been.

And I bent close, put my forehead against hers, and whispered, "You make me real."

From the doorway, Oliver cleared his throat, somehow managing to make it sound as if he wanted to gag at the same time. "You're free to go," he said. "Congratulations. You've passed."

"Passed what?" Eve asked, frowning.

"They wanted to see if I'd hurt you," I said. I focused past her, on Oliver. "You were my test. And I won't hurt her, not ever. You can count on that."

He raised his eyebrows, without any comment at all, and left.

The vending machine suffered another accident the next day. And then the next. It wasn't just me. My best friend, Shane, took to the idea of vandalism with frightening enthusiasm. So did Claire (surprisingly), and Eve . . . but it wasn't just the four of us sabotaging the damn thing, because at least twice when I went to enact some mayhem, I found it was already nonfunctional.

The last time, I saw someone walking away from the machine, which had a snapped electrical cord. He was wearing a big, flaring coat, but I knew him anyway.

Oliver paused at the door, looked back at me, and nodded, just a little.

And that was the last time they fixed the machine. The next day, it was gone. I felt a little tingle of phantom hunger, of disappointment . . . and relief.

Because some things just aren't meant to come out of a can.

DARK RIDES

☽

It was probably inevitable I'd get around to writing about carnivals and Morganville, right? Yeah. I thought so, too. But this one is unique, even so, in that I have Michael and Eve off on a mission together, from Amelie. Hijinks and life-threatening danger may ensue. Also, a brand-new vampire character that I really need to explore more, because I liked him a lot.

Fun factoid: I used to work in a haunted house—not a carnival but one of those seasonal death traps that was set up fast and taken down faster, run by virtual amateurs. Working as a character in them is fine for me, because I'm in on the mystery and the joke, but I am completely unable to handle haunted houses any other way as "fun." They really do creep me out. Also, I got stuck in one of the secret passages of that seasonal haunted house once, and nobody notices or cares if you're banging on the door and yelling for help when everyone is screaming already. (Yes, I intend to write that murder mystery someday.)

There's something deeply creepy about an unlit Ferris wheel in the dark. It looks like the skeletal remains of something large that once rolled across the earth scooping up screaming victims in its buckety jaws. Or at least, it looked like that to me, but I naturally have a pretty macabre imagination. "Wow," I said, looking up at the outlines of the black girders against the fading dark blue of the sky. "You take me to the nicest places. I am so lucky to have a guy like you."

"Eve! Shhhh," whispered Michael, my significant sweetie, as we crouched down between a blown pile of trash and the iron-shuttered side of some kind of cheesy win-a-toxic-stuffed-animal booth. This one specialized in rabbits. They all looked manic and a little diseased. I couldn't help but fill in the old-time Elmer Fudd voice in my head. *We're hunting wabbits.* It made me giggle a little breathlessly, with a nice knife-edge of terror, because we were in a closed amusement park, looking for a vampire, and hey, who doesn't get the giggles now and then under those circumstances?

Don't answer that.

Michael was giving me his *I'm concerned and a little disturbed* look, which was adorable. I'm not a fragile flower. Hell, I was born and raised in Morganville, Texas, which is likely the only place vampires can call home; if you grow up human there, you learn how to deal with life-threatening danger the way other, luckier people learn to deal with those annoying telemarketers. I don't eat danger for breakfast, because it's really just a tiny little bite-sized snack in hometown terms.

Michael, meanwhile, was the same . . . but different. He'd also grown up human in Morganville, but unlike me, he'd had the seriously bad misfortune to actually be bitten, almost two years ago. It hadn't gone well for him, and now, my all-time best guy ever was . . . well, fanged. But fighting to stay the Michael I'd always loved, which was nice, because we were, well, married now. Fangs and all.

He couldn't have looked less bloodsucker-y, really. Gorgeous blond hair, clear blue eyes, the face that in earlier ages they would have put on a really hot marble angel—not vampire material, generally. He even dressed as if he were a regular dude who was looking forward to being of legal drinking age. . . . I wondered if he ever lamented the fact that he was going to be carded for all of his immortal life. *Probably.*

Me, I looked like I was aspiring to be what he actually was, what with my Goth black hair (temporarily streaked with electric blue, because, why not?), and the baggy black cargo pants and stomp-'em boots. My shirt was tight, sheer, black over black, and had a particularly cool dark-blue-on-black embossed skull on it. Fighting clothes, although Michael had just shaken his head when he'd seen what I decided to wear for our middle-of-the-night tour of the scary carnival grounds. He just didn't know what was stalking-appropriate, obviously. Men. No fashion sense.

"Over there," Michael whispered, and nodded toward—of course—the haunted ride. It was what the carnies called a dark ride, which I thought was awesomely appropriate, especially tonight, what with all the creepy skulking around. The structure featured an absolutely gigantic Grim Reaper leaning over the top of it, gripping his scythe in one bony hand as the other reached down for the would-be riders. It probably looked super cheesy in the daylight, but tonight, I could practically see those black, flowing robes ripple in the cold wind.

If I believed in omens, that would probably be a really bad one.

"We're looking for Death? Found him," I said. I got another look, but also a smile. "Right. Stealth mode, engaged." I made a zipping motion across my mouth. He did me the favor of not quite rolling his eyes.

We crept from the cover of the toy shed to that of a greasy-looking shack that dispensed hot dogs of doubtful meat content (oooh, but they had funnel cakes!), and then made it to the shadows next to the dark ride itself. The roller coaster was making a thin, high, creaking sound in the wind, and across the way, a shadowy carousel's painted horses leered at me with wild eyes.

God, I loved this place. I wondered how Michael would feel about running away to join the circus.

Michael had paused, listening, doing that vampire-senses thing; I was content to wait for him to get back to me with a plan. I was just glad he'd asked me to come along as his backup. Usually our mutual buddy Shane got that job; to be fair, Shane was big, strong, and built for quality mayhem, but he was trying to cut down on the fighting, and I was happy to help that along. I'd seen all of us wearing sporty black and blue too much lately. Not the Goth kind. The bruise kind. Much tougher to accessorize.

We were operating on a bona fide secret mission, dispatched by the Founder of Morganville herself, the vampire Amelie—an ice-cold queen of a lady, and I was not on her list of Most Favorite right now, but I was incidental to this plan. Michael was her agent. Hmmm, he'd looked so nice in a James Bondian tuxedo at our wedding. . . .

I had to shake myself and put away the hot mental image for later. We—or he, more precisely—had work to do. This carnival was two towns over from Morganville, so we had to be on serious best behavior. This wasn't home, with its peculiar rules and dangers. It was the real world, which was in many ways more dangerous for us, because whatever the rules might be, we probably didn't fully understand them.

This was one of those no-name traveling shows that still honored the old tradition of "novelty acts" . . . or, more properly, freak shows, which I'd read about in books. Books that responsible adults frowned upon, but I'd lapped up as a kid. Said "novelties" usually included ancient mummies that were usually fakes or so badly mauled it'd take that dog-headed Egyptian god a week to put it back together . . . and, of course, the usual set of human oddities. Real tall, real short, real fat, fake facial hair, fake shape-shifting acts . . . and this one had one actual, real vampire, locked in a cage just like the mangy tiger and the totally depressed lion. That was a "special" freak show, only for high-rolling customers who got off on seeing what they assumed was a guy in makeup biting the neck of a partner in crime . . . only he was a real vampire, and those were real victims, and Amelie wanted it stopped, immediately.

She wasn't concerned about the human lives being lost, of course. That was never going to be any vampire's primary concern. She wanted to rescue the neck-muncher, and make sure nobody ever caught a clue that there was such a thing as a real, genuine vampire in their midst. Oh, the carnies knew, of course—if they hadn't known before grabbing said bloodsucker, they certainly had by the time they started feeding him victims.

If Michael had received instructions on what to do about that situation, he didn't tell, and I didn't ask.

Right now, we were paying attention to one of the carnies making the rounds, checking to make sure everything was locked up and turned off. He was a big, burly guy—a roustabout or a strongman—and he was carrying a flashy knife on his belt, plus a wooden baseball bat, the better to beat you with, my dear. From the look on his face when he came out of the dark ride, it didn't seem that security was his favorite job in the world when nothing happened. He looked more like he hoped to find an excuse to use the bat on something that would beg him to stop.

Michael suddenly cocked his head. In the moonlight, his eyes still had small pupils, like I would have had in full sun. Great night vision, vampires. One of the many depressing advantages they had over the breathing version of humanity. He squeezed my hand, gently, and nodded toward the ride that Batty McMurder was just leaving. Oh, great. Perfect.

No, I really meant that. Perfect! I practically wiggled with excitement. I loved haunted house rides, because, hello, mechanical scares, nothing actually dead and lurching in there. Well, normally. Tonight might very well be an exception.

We hurried across the open ground. Michael didn't make any noise, and I tried to minimize mine, but the thump of my combat boots still sounded way too loud. He stopped me before I jumped up on the deck of the ride, urgently making a shushing motion; I eased up carefully, and immediately saw why—it creaked . . . a lot. Moving slowly made the creaking sound more like the general creepy noise made by the wind, and less a neon *We're up in your business, sneaking around* sign.

Michael kept hold of my hand, and led me under the leering glare of the Grim Reaper into a darkness that smelled like mold and engine oil. And boy, I mean darkness. It was a close, claustrophobic kind of inky emptiness, and except for the tight grip of Michael's cool hand on mine, I wouldn't have been able to tell it from space. No, I lie. At least in space, there are stars.

From the feel of the floor under my boots, we were on some kind of raised wooden walkway—probably a maintenance area. I felt a rising panic as we kept walking. What if something fell on me, like a giant hairy spider? It was Texas, after all, home of all kinds of stinging, biting, poisonous creatures. I wanted to hold up my free hand and sweep the air in front of me, but that was kind of useless; Michael was going first. He'd keep me safe.

It was a bit of a shock when I saw that the darkness was going a little gray, and at first I thought there was something wrong with my eyes, but no. There was a thin strip of light up ahead, on the left, like what would escape under the bottom of a door. It revealed an upright coffin with—appropriately enough—a cheap-looking mechanical dummy dressed in vintage Dracula drag, which would probably launch out at the creaking, trundling carts when the power was on.

There was a hidden door behind Dummy Drac.

We crossed the tracks, and I stepped carefully to avoid tripping any switches or getting my boots caught in the rails. I was glad I'd worn the heavy things, because a rat ran out of the dark and raced over my laces, heading for cover on the other side. I managed not to squeak, though there might have been a dry rattling in my throat. Might.

Michael took hold of the knob of the door and lightly turned it, then shook his head. Locked, obv. That posed no serious issues for him, but it'd make some noise; the glow of the light under the door made me less of a blind human liability, so I pulled my hand free of his and pulled the snub-nosed revolver out of my belly pack. I didn't like guns, particularly, but they were real useful around humans who meant me no good. I had a knife, too, but if it came to hand-to-hand with Mr. Batty out there, it wasn't going to be an even match, and I liked advantages.

Michael twisted, hard, and broke something metallic inside the door with a harsh snap. The knob slid out, and he reached into the hole and manipulated things until there was a click and the door yawned open, letting loose a flood of what seemed like a five-hundred-watt spotlight . . . but it was just one bulb, not even remotely bright. My eyes adjusted quickly, and I shut the door behind us. Without the lock, it wasn't going to do much good, but I followed Michael's lead and reached into the empty hole where the knob had been to push on metal until the tongue slipped back in place. It'd slow them down, at least.

When I turned to look, I saw we were in a plain metal room. The one bulb was on a swinging chain hanging in the middle of the open space. There was a miniature viewing stand of seats that would hold maybe twenty people, if they were really friendly, and then there was the cage. It was the size of something you'd use for a lion or tiger act, big enough to move around in; it held a cot with a blanket and a pillow, and some kind of pot under the bed I assumed was their version of a portable toilet. Apart from that, it was just iron bars coated with silver, and a single stoutly built wooden chair that was bolted to the floor at the center of the cage.

There were stains on the floor around it, and a few soaked into the wood. Dark stains. I told myself it was chocolate, and left it at that. I was too busy staring at the vampire in the cage.

Because he was just a kid.

I mean, a *kid*. Maybe twelve, thirteen years old at the most—a thin boy with long legs that he had tented up as he lay on his back, staring at the ceiling of the room. He must have heard us coming, but he hadn't moved, not an inch. From the still way he lay, I'd have thought he was regular dead, but he was the special kind. The kind that could still get up and kill us.

"Hey," Michael said softly. "You need out of there?"

That made the kid sit up, with a sudden fluidity that made me glad there were bars between him and me; Michael didn't move like that. Most vampires in Morganville didn't, because they were trying to fit in, be less alarming to the people they farmed for money and blood. (To their credit, most of the blood donations are voluntary, through the blood bank. It's sort of like the Mafia, but with fangs.)

Seeing a vampire move like the pure predators they are . . . that was a bit scary. So was the emptiness in this kid's eyes, the utter lack of interest or emotion. He could have been the lion the cage was meant for, only at least a lion would have more of an opinion.

"Open it," the kid said, and rattled the door. It was extra sturdy; he couldn't hold it for more than a second before the silver began to burn him. He was wearing only a ratty, dirty pair of khaki shorts that was two sizes too large for him—no shirt, and his thin chest was as pale as ivory. Veins showed blue underneath the skin, like one of those see-through anatomy dolls. "Open it." He didn't even sound angry, or hopeful, or desperate. The words were just as emotionless as his eyes. Most vampires were faking it, to some extent or other, but this kid—I had the eerie idea that he might never have been human at all.

Michael was considering him thoughtfully, although he was putting on the leather gloves he'd brought along in the event of silver. Unlike with the kid, I could read emotion in my honey's expressions . . . and he looked just as startled and worried about what we were facing as me. "In a second," he said. "What's your name?"

The kid blinked, a slow movement like he'd learned it from observation, not nature. "Jeremy," he said. "My name is Jeremy."

"Okay, Jeremy," Michael said, in a soft, calming voice, the way you'd speak to a particularly dangerous-looking wild dog. "Are you hurt?" He got a headshake. "Hungry?"

That got a flat stare for a second, and then Jeremy turned it on me. "Let me have her, and I'll be fine."

"Uh, no, creepy kid, really not happening," I said. "I'm not your lunch."

Jeremy didn't even bother to blink this time. Honestly, the kid was scarier than anything I'd seen out there in the carnival.

"Jeremy," Michael said. He sounded colder now, with an edge; it got the kid's attention in a flash. "I'm here to get you out, but you so much as look at her again, much less touch her, and I'll walk away and leave you to rot. Understood?"

Jeremy tilted his head a little to the side, considering Michael, and then said, "If that's what you want, then I won't touch her."

"Swear," I said. "Pinkie swear."

He shrugged. "I swear." I didn't hear any particular meaning in it, which wasn't good, but we didn't have a wealth of choices. Amelie's instructions were to bring the weird kid back with us, not leave him here. Michael was doing his best.

"Go watch the door," Michael said to me, and I nodded and backed off to stand next to it. That not-so-coincidentally put a lot of space between me and Jeremy, with Michael in the middle between us. I watched as Michael put gloved hands on the bars, got a firm grip, and applied pressure. He was strong, but the bars just groaned and held. Jeremy watched with interest but no emotion as Michael panted, shook off the strain, and tried again. I winced when I saw the pain on his face; the stuff was burning him even through the gloves.

"Michael," I said. "Did you see any tools out there?" Because this crew didn't seem like the type to be neat about putting things away. He took a step back from the cage, stripped off his gloves, and I saw that beneath them his hands were swollen and pink with burns. Ouch. Very high silver content.

"Maybe," he said. "Look, this silver's pretty soft, but I can't get a grip even with the gloves. I'll go get the tools. It'll just take a second."

"A second," I repeated. "Promise?"

Our eyes locked, and he smiled just a little. "Cross my heart," he said. "Jeremy, you back off and sit on your bed. Eve's going to stay with you."

Jeremy said nothing, but he walked back to his cot and stretched out, looking bored with the whole thing. I considered him for a second, then nodded. "I'll be fine. Go."

Michael was a blurred flash that paused to get the door open, and then it swung shut behind him with a soft thump. I took a deep breath and wished I'd worn something warmer—all of a sudden, it seemed much colder with him gone. I walked over to the cage and examined it.

It didn't look so hard. The silver was wire, and it was wrapped around the bars tightly, but when I found an end of the wire and grabbed it, it bent easily enough—high-content silver, pretty soft. I was concentrating so much on unwinding it that I didn't realize Jeremy had moved until I glanced up.

He was standing only a few feet away, staring at the point where I was unwinding the silver. *Not* at me, which I supposed fell under the letter of the law. I swallowed and said, "Michael told you to stay on the bed."

"No," he said. "He told me to go to the bed. He didn't tell me to stay there."

Wonderful, he had a kid's built-in ability to parse orders and find loopholes. That was just great. "Yeah, well, why don't you just sit down over there? It'll take a little time to do this."

He didn't move. Evidently, I didn't have the same kind of authority as Michael wielded. Up close-ish, Jeremy's eyes were not black; they were a very dark brown, with a central ring of amber. They'd have been nice if they'd been in a face that moved like a human being's, but as it was, they reminded me of glassy dolls' eyes. I like a good creep-out as much as any self-respecting Goth, but this kid was giving me a serious freaking.

"You smell nice," he said.

"As long as I don't smell like dinner," I muttered, and unwrapped another length of silver. Michael was taking an awfully long second to get back here with the tools. I had to ask myself what was going to happen when I stripped the last of the silver away and Jeremy decided that I had a fabulous aroma of roast beef, blood rare. Okay, I didn't really have to ask. Nothing good.

Jeremy suddenly moved, and his cold hands folded over mine, waking an instant, instinctive shriek that I just barely managed to check to a weak little chirp—but it wasn't an attack. He leaned forward, pressed his forehead against the iron bars, and said, "They're coming in. You need to hide now."

Crap. I yanked back and stumbled backward, pulling the last of the silver free on that one bar; it snapped into a tight coil like the world's most expensive Slinky as I looked around for someplace to go. The only obvious place was under the bleachers, and it was a tight squeeze to get by, but better hurt than dead was my motto. I jammed myself through the narrow opening and crouched down in the darkness beneath. *Michael,* I was thinking, *where are you?* Because this didn't bode well, not at all.

I heard the voices first. The words were muffled, but the music was clear—they were upset about the missing knob on the door. I heard metal scrape as they pushed their way inside, and moved around a little to find a good vantage point to peer through the slats between the bleacher seats.

Mr. Batty was one of the men, which somehow failed to surprise me; he was still carrying around the baseball bat, swinging it like a nightstick. Next to him was a sleek, thin man in a black turtleneck sweater and dark pants; he had a *GQ* look going on, and under other circumstances I might have thought he was eye-worthy, but not now. Not when I saw him rattle Jeremy's cage, testing the lock, and say, "You've had visitors, haven't you, Jeremy?"

Jeremy didn't say anything, just stared at Mr. Slick with cold, dead eyes. Mr. Slick didn't seem nearly as bothered as he should have been, and he shrugged and turned to Batty. "Harry, make a thorough sweep. I want everybody on their feet and checking every corner. If they see anybody who doesn't belong, I want any intruder's body dumped right here, dead or alive, clear?"

"Clear, boss," Harry said. He sounded happy with the assignment, and strolled off swinging his big stick. As he left, another guy came in . . . and man, he was massive. This was undoubtedly the carnival's strongman-slash–big guy. . . . He was seven feet at least, and broad as a truck. Wearing a wifebeater tee assured that everyone could see the steroid-thick bulge of his muscles. He had a shaved head, lots of tats that seemed to feature overly endowed women, and nasty little beady eyes. Not too smart, but plenty mean, and from the state of the T-shirt, personal hygiene wasn't high on his list.

I reached into the pocket of my cargo pants and pulled out my cell phone—sensibly on silent—and frantically texted Michael. **Whr r u? Trbl!!** I shielded the screen with one hand, in case someone noticed the unearthly glow coming from under the bleachers, but nobody was looking my way except Jeremy.

Skinhead walked up to the bars and slammed a giant forearm into them. Jeremy didn't flinch, and he didn't back up, which made Skinhead laugh. He had a voice that didn't match his exterior at all—high as mine, sounded like. "Your pet rat looks hungry, boss," he said. "Got anybody to feed it?"

"Later," the boss man said. "Right now, we've got a bigger problem, because Jeremy here has had some friends drop by, haven't you, Jeremy?"

Jeremy stood there staring at him for a long, silent few seconds, and then he smiled, and swear to God, I felt ice forming along my spine in sharp little stabby crystals. That was not a vampire's smile, as awful as those could be—it was something else completely, something I didn't get at all.

And then Jeremy said, "She's under the bleachers," and I couldn't hold back a gasp. I backed away, but that wasn't going to help . . . not like there were any secret exits back here, and Skinhead was grinning and heading my direction. God, why had he done that? Did that idiot not understand that we'd come to help him?

No, of course he did, I realized . . . but he just didn't give a damn. He was on fire, and he liked to see everything else burn.

I texted Michael again with a lightning-quick 911!!!!!, which might not matter since he hadn't responded yet to my first text for help anyway. Something was wrong, and not just with Jeremy—this whole thing felt utterly bad. Drastically wrong.

I had the gun, and it felt heavy in my hand. Shane hadn't just given the thing to me; he'd forced me to go to the range with him many times, practice target shooting, practice loading and unloading it in the dark. He'd even tested me (with an empty gun) in a deserted house where he'd popped out of a closet at me to see what I'd do.

I'd screamed and shot him six times, theoretically, in the face. He'd approved.

All well and good, but now I was facing firing that gun into actual flesh and bone. Into Mr. Skinhead, who looked like he could chew small-caliber bullets and spit armor-piercing ones back; this was not his first pistol rodeo, for sure. One good thing: he wasn't going to fit through that narrow opening I'd wedged myself into. . . . But he was more than capable of pulling the entire bleachers out, which he began doing, with harsh metallic shrieks of protesting, creaking metal. He paused and shone a flashlight into the gaps, playing it around until it spilled over my pale face.

He grinned, or at least I thought he did, behind the glare of the light in my eyes. "Hello, girl," he said. "Let me help you get out of there. Lots of scary things under there, you know. Black widows and brown recluse spiders, snakes, scorpions . . ."

I hadn't even thought about it, but now it sounded sickeningly likely. . . . The very poisonous spiders he was talking about liked the shadows, the scorpions were badass and went anywhere they wanted, and the snakes would crawl in here to cool off. Damn. Now I didn't even want to back up. Vampires, I can deal with. Creepy-crawlies in the dark, not so much. "Back off, gorgeous," I said, and tried to make myself sound tough and mean. "I'm armed and dangerous."

He giggled, high as a little girl. "Do your best with that toy," he said. "I've been shot before—it don't scare me." For proof, he yanked aside the neck of his wifebeater tee, and I saw star-shaped scars in his skin right below the collarbone. Wow. He wasn't kidding. I had the weapon in my hand, but my hand was shaking, and I knew I'd miss if I fired. Better to wait and make it count. . . .

He pulled the bleachers out at an angle with a final yank, leaving a narrow space against the wall that he could squeeze through—but didn't. He bent and looked through it at me. No smile now, nothing but serious menace. "You put that popgun away and come on out of there," he said. "I'm not going to hurt you unless you do something stupid, like pull the trigger. Got me?"

Shane had told me before, a gun is not a magic shield, it's not a bulletproof vest, and it's not a defense. It's an offensive weapon, but I'd never really appreciated how true that was before. If you're going on offense with someone like Mr. Skinhead, you'd better put him down hard, and I was shaking too badly. He was careful not to give me too good a target, either.

Hell.

I took a deep breath, holstered the gun in my pants, and held up my hands. Probably useless effort, but I tried to look harmless now as I walked toward him. He grunted in satisfaction and squeezed himself under the bleachers a little more, ready to grab me as I got close. In the process, he pretty much immobilized himself.

And that was what I'd been hoping he'd do. As he wedged himself in solidly, I pulled the silver-edged knife from the sheath on my wrist, under my shirt, and leaped forward to slam him against the hollow wall of the metal room. He hit with a resonating thud, and I got my forearm against his Adam's apple with my knife resting just off to the side, over his fast-beating veins. "Hey," I said. "I put the gun away, just like you said."

He laughed, a thin and kind of crazy sound. Up close, he smelled sour and damp, as if he'd worn the same clothes for weeks without so much as going out in the rain. Ugh. "I'll break your arm, little girl. For starters. I'll bet I can get real creative with you. . . ."

I let the knife slip a little and gave him another scar. "Whoops," I said. "Sorry about that." I kept the knife steady on his throat as he froze, and pulled out the gun with my left hand. "I'm not a great shot with this hand," I said, "but you know what? Good enough to hit the broadside of a piece of barn like you." I shoved the muzzle against his chest. "Back up."

He did, moving slowly, and his massive muscle-bound arms rose as far as they could. I'd impressed him, at least this far. He might not take a .38 seriously, but he knew I couldn't miss if I fired it into his heart from that distance. He could have grabbed my arm and broken it in two shakes, but that left the knife at his throat.

So we did the dance, moving backward, until we were out of the bleachers . . . and that was when Michael said, from behind Mr. Big, "Need any help?"

I grinned tightly. "Well, I think I've got this, but sure. I wouldn't want you to get bored."

Michael grabbed the guy by the scruff of the neck and swung him around like a bag of cotton balls, slammed him face-first into the cage bars with stunning force, and Mr. Big dropped to the dirt floor limp as overcooked pasta. (I know about overcooked pasta. I am so not a cook.)

That left Mr. Slick, but he wasn't just standing around, as it happened.

He'd unlocked Jeremy's cage, and stepped back to pull the silver bars of the door in front of him as protection from attack. I decided, from the way he moved, that he was the local lion tamer. Or, more likely, lion-abusing a-hole. "This is your chance," he said to Jeremy. "Kill them and go."

Jeremy looked at him through the bars, close range, and said, "What if I want to start with you first?"

You'd think Mr. Slick would be freaking scared, but this was—unfathomably, to me—a guy who'd managed to capture a sociopathic machine like Jeremy and keep him under control for what looked like quite a while. He didn't seem scared, or even ruffled. "You won't," he said. "You can keep the girl. I know you like to play with them first."

"Hey!" I said, and pointed the gun at Slick. "Standing right here!"

Jeremy hadn't moved his gaze away from his—I guess?—jailer, but somehow, in less time than it took for me to register the blur, he was moving toward me. I didn't have time to get the gun or knife up in my own defense; he was just that fast.

And then, he was past me.

Jeremy came to a sudden stop next to the unconscious bruiser Michael had left lying on the floor, picked him up like a rag doll, and—before even my vampire husband could stop him—had his fangs buried in the man's neck.

Michael tried. He grabbed Jeremy by the shoulder and yanked hard, trying to separate victim from predator, but it was useless; the kid's wiry strength wasn't going to give, and anyway, it was over fast.

When Jeremy dropped the corpse formerly known to me as Mr. Skinhead, it was paper white and drained of every drop of blood.

Mr. Slick didn't move for a second, clearly stunned, and then as Jeremy licked his lips clean of the thin smear of red that remained, he dashed around the cage door, threw himself inside, and slammed it behind him. Then he cowered in the center of the cage, eyes as big as headlights and just about as shiny. He'd thought he'd broken this lion he'd caged, but he'd just discovered that was completely wrong.

Michael was looking spooked, too, but he spoke gently. "Hey, man, Amelie sent us. She wants you to come with us, back to Morganville."

"Morganville," Jeremy repeated, without so much as a flicker of emotion. He'd just killed somebody, and he didn't seem to have really cared at all, beyond looking a little less pallid. "Never been there."

"You'll be safe there. No one will hurt you." Michael was being unaccountably gentle; maybe he hadn't seen the flat, shark-worthy shine of the boy's eyes as he drank up Mr. Skinhead. "Trust me, man. Please. We need to leave here."

"You forgot something," Jeremy said, and pointed one long, skinny, dirty finger at Mr. Slick cowering inside the cage. "He just heard where we're going. Can't be safe if he knows. Got to get rid of him."

"No, we don't," Michael said. He moved to the bars and crouched down, and when he spoke next, I heard that scary vampire tone in his voice. He didn't use it often, but when he busted it out, he had real power. "Look at me."

He waited, and after a long few breaths, Mr. Slick uncovered his face and met Michael's eyes. I couldn't see them, but I knew how they would look—glowing, red, terrifying if you weren't drowning in that pool of crimson and unable to feel anything at all.

Michael had one of the most powerful forget-about-me abilities Amelie had ever seen, apparently, and he proved it now, because he said, in low, measured tones, "Poor Jeremy starved to death in this cage. Say it back to me."

"Poor Jeremy starved to death in this cage," the man repeated in a dull, calm voice.

"And you're feeling very bad about that."

"I'm feeling very bad about that." I watched Mr. Slick's eyes suddenly fill up with wet, hot tears that spilled over and down his cheeks in messy trails. "Oh God . . ."

"You feel so bad that you're never going to run this kind of show, ever again. Not with anyone who doesn't sign up and get paid. And there are no such things as vampires. No real ones."

"No real ones," he echoed. His voice was shaking now, and so were his shoulders. Wow. Michael had really rocked his world, and not in a good way. "I'm sorry. I'm so sorry. . . ."

"How many others knew about Jeremy?"

Mr. Slick named them, but it was a small, tight circle of insiders—himself, Mr. Dead Skinhead, and one other woman named Isis, who was asleep in her trailer near the Ferris wheel.

"Do you have a key to this cage?" Michael finally asked. When the man nodded, he said, "Throw it out to me."

Mr. Slick tossed it, and Michael effortlessly shagged it out of the air. He dropped it on Skinhead's body and frowned down at Jeremy's handiwork. "We need to make it look less—vampire," he said.

I slowly held up the gun and the knife. "Man, I'm going to regret this," I said, "but I think I've got that covered."

Best to skip what came next, except to say that I made Mr. Skinhead's body look like he'd been attacked with a knife to the neck, then shot. A decent coroner—like the ones on TV, say—would have figured out the wounds were postmortem, but it was doubtful that this little burg would have anything like a coroner, much less a good one. If the carnies actually reported the death, which I thought was doubtful.

It'd pass. I felt faint, after, and Michael grabbed me when I staggered while trying to get up. He put his arms around me and held me tight for a few long seconds, and then whispered, "Eve—"

"I'm okay," I said, and swallowed the nausea that threatened to bubble up. "Just another frakking day in Morganville."

"You watch way too much TV."

"Yeah, probs. So? What about this Isis lady?"

"I'll take care of it," Michael said, and loosened his hold just enough to put some air between us, but he didn't let me go. I loved him for that, for knowing just what I needed, and when. "I love you."

I managed a grin. "Back atcha, stud. You only love me for my body-mutilation skills."

His smile disappeared, and there was no trace of vampire in his blue eyes, none at all. He looked just like the boy I'd fallen so hard for in high school. An avenging angel, this one. And not a fallen one at all. "No," he said. "I love you for you. Always."

I kissed him, which was probably weird, given the circumstances, but I needed to feel his arms around me again, and the solid, safe weight of his body, and the cool, sweet taste of his lips. I needed to know it was okay.

He said, without words, that it was.

Then he stepped back, looked at Jeremy, and said, "I'm here to help you, but I swear to God, if you lay a finger on her, I'll rip you apart. Are we clear?"

Jeremy shrugged, which I guessed was his version of a yes, and Michael glanced back at me. The silent exchange went something like this: *You okay? Yeah. Love you. Love you, too.* Etc. Oh, and somewhere in that glance, he also warned me to keep the knife and the gun handy, which I wasn't about to give up anyway.

"We should go," Jeremy said, as Michael blurred off through the open doorway. "Don't want my boss man here to remember anything."

He was right, but I felt bad leaving—Michael hadn't said to stay put, but I was uncomfortable with the idea he might not be able to immediately locate me if I got into trouble. Because Jeremy was trouble. He gave off a kind of dark smoke around him—something shadowy in my peripheral vision, as if he clouded himself with it. I had to concentrate and watch him straight on to feel he was there at all. Useful skill, probably, but really scary when I felt like the warm-blooded prey to his cold-blooded, hungry predator.

He kept his word, though. He didn't touch me, and he walked about three paces ahead, knowing I didn't want him at my back. Once we were out of the room, though, I stopped, because I'd totally forgotten that this was a dark ride . . . that I'd only found this room in the first place because of Michael's dark-adapted eyes.

I couldn't see a damn thing.

I heard Jeremy's faint, whispery chuckle from a few feet away, and I saw a flash of something that might have been his eyes. Creepy.

"No flashlight?" he asked. "Should be one on the dead guy."

I went back for it, and didn't look at the corpse's face while I pilfered it out of its holster. It was a heavy Maglite, which was good—one more weapon, though I had to put away the gun to hang on to it. The knife was of more use against Jeremy, anyway.

The Maglite had a brilliant beam, and it revealed all the monsters in their tacky glory—Dracula, in his threadbare cloak and dusty coffin; the Wolfman, whose fake fur was molting away; a large spider overhead made of Styrofoam and cloth and real spiderwebs, recently woven by some very ambitious arachnid. The place was filthy, and full of rats and cockroaches, and I was real glad of my stomping boots, again.

The worst, most real monster in here was Jeremy, who looked the color of exposed bone, and whose eyes were as alien as anything you'd find on earth. His smile was something he'd learned, not something he felt, and even though he was small and wiry and looked pathetic in his baggy khaki pants, I was so afraid of him it was hard to breathe.

But he kept his word.

We made it out, into the cold, sharp wind; overhead, the rusty Grim Reaper creaked as he swayed. I saw nothing moving outside except some rolling tumbleweeds and blowing trash.

Jeremy walked off a few feet, then stopped, staring up at the sky. He closed his eyes, and took in a deep, slow breath, as if he wanted to drink in the world around him. For that moment, he looked his physical age—I had no idea how old he really was, but he looked maybe a growth-spurt thirteen, maybe fourteen. Really young to become a

vampire, but depending on when that had happened, thirteen or fourteen might have been adult, pretty much.

But my heart went out to him, anyway. He'd been locked away in a
cage for people's entertainment, for God's sake. No matter how scary
he was, how divorced from human emotions, he didn't deserve that.
Nobody did.

Jeremy said, without opening his eyes, "You're wondering how old
I am."

Well, *that* was uncomfortable. "Yeah," I said. "Kinda."

"I died when I was fourteen," he said. "But that was a really long
time ago. I'm not a kid."

"I guessed."

"You know I could kill you and be gone before your boyfriend
could catch me, right?"

"Husband," I said, and held up my left hand, because I knew that
even in the dark he could see the ruby wedding ring. "Newlyweds."

I'd managed to surprise him, a little, because it looked like his
eyebrows rose up just a touch. "Huh," he said. "So you're one of those
who thinks vampires are some kind of sex gods, right?" He coupled
that with a creepy laugh.

"No, I'm someone in love with a guy who happens, unfortunately,
to be a vampire," I said. I'd had lots worse hazing from lots worse people than him, especially after marrying Michael. "Personally, I think
vampires are the opposite of sexy, mostly. Being dead and all. But he's
my guy, and he's different."

"We're all different," Jeremy said. "And deep down, we're all the
same. We're alive because we didn't want to die and we were ruthless
enough to make it happen. Your man's a killer, too. Sooner or later,
he'll realize it, and so will you. Probably be kinder just to kill you now."

"Try it," I invited softly, and made sure I had the knife in a firm
grip. "I grew up in Morganville, sonny. I'm not Bambi."

That made him smile enough to show teeth. Wow, so not an improvement. "Even wolves get eaten," he said. "Especially when they're away from their pack. Ah, he's back." He sounded a little disappointed, but in the way that someone might be at a restaurant when he learned the kitchen was out of his favorite dessert. I didn't hear Michael coming back, but all of a sudden he was there, staring at Jeremy with flickering red eyes. Wary.

"Eve," he said, and held out his hand. I went over and took it, and his fingers felt cool and strong as they closed over mine. "He's got the ability to cloud himself. Most vamps do, to a certain extent, but he's really strong. You'd never see him coming."

"You, either," Jeremy said. He took in another deep breath and held it, as if he was enjoying the smell of the desert air. He let it out slowly, and said, "Tell Amelie I'll be by when I feel up to it. Got to get some space around me right now. Not fit for friendly company." He looked sharply at Michael, suddenly. "Don't you even think about stopping me. Got no reason to hurt you, but I will if you get in my way. Did you make Isis forget?"

"Yes."

"Good. Better get going, then."

Michael frowned, and pulled me closer. "Jeremy? What are you doing?"

"I'll go to Morganville someday," he said. "Not now. Tell her. Now leave unless you want to lose your wife. She's a pistol, and she'd taste real good right about now."

Michael had made Amelie a promise, but he wasn't about to risk that. "We're going," he said. "I'll tell her what you said."

"Good." Jeremy walked back to the dark ride, to the Grim Reaper with his cheap tin scythe looming overhead. He looked weirdly at home there, and even though I was watching him, focusing in, he seemed to just . . . blend into the darkness. "I'll be around."

He must have pushed a button, because suddenly the creepy organ music boomed out of the speakers, and lights flashed on and off, making the Grim Reaper look like he was all raved out. Cars began to shuttle forward, all empty.

He was waking up the whole carnival with the racket.

"Let's go," Michael said, and we ran for the car. I didn't ask any questions until he'd put it in reverse and raised a cloud of dust around us as he drove for the farm road access, made the turn, and headed for Morganville. Not for safety, but at least for familiar territory. I didn't breathe easier until I saw the white glow of the Glass House, our home, in the headlights, murky through the vampire-thick tinting.

I don't think either of us wanted to know exactly what Jeremy had in mind, but I Google-flagged articles with the name of the carnival. There was an eerie silence for a few weeks after we got back, and then the mentions started appearing, slowly.

The haunted dark ride. Missing people. Investigations finding nothing.

He was out there, moving with the carnival, haunting it like a hungry ghost.

It was pretty selfish, but frankly, I hoped he'd stay out there.

I didn't want him in Morganville.

Ever.

And that was the last time I'd ever take a chance on one of those rides, however cheesy, however safe.

"Hey," Michael said from behind me. I shut the lid on the laptop, and Jeremy's latest missing person, and leaned back as he put his hands on my shoulders and bent to kiss my neck—not in a vampy way, just in a sexy way. "You've been on there for hours. Ignoring me?"

"Never," I said, and stood up to face him. "Real life's so much better than Internet life."

He agreed with a kiss, a long one, sweet and cool, hot in ways that had nothing at all to do with body temperature, although his mouth took on heat from mine the longer they touched. I loved that, seeing the effect I had on him. I could change him, at least briefly; sometimes, when I woke up in bed with him, my body heat had transferred to him so effectively that he felt alive again. He loved that, too. It made him feel connected, alive, and . . . human.

"Bed," he said, in a whisper that vibrated against my skin. "You and me. Now, Mrs. Glass."

"Right now," I agreed.

And I left all the dark rides behind for something much wilder and better.

If you're smart . . . you will, too.

PITCH-BLACK BLUES

$\smile$

Dedicated to Jennifer Stangret for her support
of the Morganville digital series Kickstarter

Another brand-new offering!

Jennifer, bless her, wanted a Shane/Myrnin story as part of her Kickstarter contribution, and I was happy to oblige. So here is Shane, and Myrnin, and a tie-in to a story earlier in this collection: "Nothing like an Angel." If you read them back-to-back, you'll see why I say that; events in this particular story feed into events in that one, though it might not be obvious without a closer look. We get graveyards, corpses, mysterious alchemical machines, time travel (maybe), and the payoff on a romance that I built between *Bitter Blood* and *Daylighters*. This story occurs after the end of the series, so you may think of it as an epilogue of sorts.

No matter how many times I destroy Myrnin's lab, I always want to rebuild it and bring it back as a setting, because it so perfectly reflects the state of the inside of his mind. "Pitch-black" refers to many things in this story, not the least of which is the state of Myrnin's mind at various times in his history.

I don't know what I did to deserve this. I mean, I'm relatively nice to old ladies. I've never been mean to animals. Sure, I've had my occasional dives into punk-ass behavior, but who doesn't sometime in his life? Hey, I'm only twenty. It isn't like I can't learn better.

Which is why this was so damn unfair. "Why me, God?" I muttered, as I shoveled another heavy load of dirt out of the hole in the graveyard. "Why am I the one who always gets the crap jobs?"

"Well," my supervisor said as he sat on a tombstone, sipping on what looked like a Bloody Mary, and which almost certainly had a whole lot more blood in it than most drinks, never mind the ornamental celery. Come to think of it, it might have had someone named Mary in it. "I didn't know you were a serious student of philosophy. That gladdens my heart. However, your question does confuse me. Expound, please."

"It was rhetorical," I shot back. The hole was up to my neck, but I could still glare out of it at him as I leaned my weight on the shovel and dug it into the damp, wormy soil. "And I don't know shit about philosophy."

"So much clearer now. However, I hope you realize that using the word *rhetorical* means you are also a student of philosophy, even if ill taught." He saluted me with the drink. In honor of the refreshment, I guessed, he'd put on a loud Hawaiian shirt and board shorts, which at least went together, though where he'd found the Liberace-quality sunglasses I had no idea. Also, I wondered if I should clue him in that the flip-flops he was wearing were meant for girls. Probably not.

If you're wondering why I was in the graveyard doing minion work for Myrnin the Crazy Vampire, well.

So was I.

Hi, my name is Shane Collins, and I hate vampires. I have ever since I was old enough to understand that (a) there were vampires in Morganville, Texas, and (b) they were the boss of me, no matter what I wanted. My goal was to be a fearless badass vampire hunter, and sometimes I have been that, but the reality that I've come to reluctantly accept is that not all vamps are terrible people. Selfish, sure. Annoying, definitely. But I can't support my original stake-'em-all theory any-more, because—well, case in point was sitting on a tombstone watch-ing me get covered in dirt while he had a cocktail. Myrnin was a lunatic, he dressed funny, and he was as annoying as an ingrown toe-nail, but I'd seen him do kind things, and brave things, for no better reason than a real person lurked somewhere in that vampire body.

It just spoils the fun when you realize that your *kill all monsters* cru-sade actually includes real people as collateral damage.

"Are you resting?" Myrnin asked, then took a loud sip through his straw. "I don't think I'm paying you to rest."

"It's hard work."

"Not for a vampire."

"I'm not a vampire."

"That would seem to be a pity."

Myrnin took another gulp of his drink, probably just to irritate me, and I jammed the shovel in once more . . . and hit something solid. Instantly, he was off the tombstone, drink abandoned, and he was leaning over the grave to look down in it. "That's it," he said, and gave me a quick, commanding look. "Out. Now."

"Don't have to tell me twice," I said, and managed to claw my way up and out of the hole. Of *course* he hadn't brought a ladder. Vampires could do Olympic jumps, straight up, so they hardly ever felt the need for one. By the time I was collapsed on the thin grass of the Morganville Pioneer Cemetery, I was sweaty and filthy, and I ached all over. Also, I wanted to strangle the little rat, but only in an abstract kind of way. Mostly, I just wanted a shower. "Want to tell me why we're digging up a dead guy from olden days?"

"We aren't," he said. "Well, I suppose we are, in a sense, but the bones aren't what I'm after. . . ." His voice trailed off, and I heard scraping, as if he was clearing dirt away, and then a sharp snapping sound. A heavy, groaning creak. Yeah, that was some serious ghostly soundtrack, and it said something about my experiences in Morganville so far that it didn't even make me nervous.

Silence then. Pardon the pun, but . . . dead silence.

"Hey," I finally said. "Everything okay down there?"

No answer. *Perfect.* I tried to get up and my aching muscles put up a fight, but I won and rolled up to look over the edge of the hole.

Into . . . darkness.

The lid was up on the coffin, but there was no body. It was just . . . black. Kind of disorienting, and I sat back a little because it almost felt like it was trying to suck me in.

"Hey, Myrnin? Stop screwing around. You down there?" No answer. I flipped a rock over the side, expecting it to hit the bottom of the coffin, but it just . . . disappeared. "Come on. I'm getting paid to dig a hole, not haul your ass out of one!"

Myrnin had been mostly a giant pain in my neck since I'd first met him. He'd been suspiciously nice to my girl, Claire, for one thing, and

I knew he had feelings for her. . . . Of course, what those feelings actually *were* was a different story, because Myrnin didn't exactly follow normal rules of behavior. For instance, he'd once intended to kill her and put her brain in a computer, and to him, that didn't even seem all that unfriendly. He'd gotten a little less crazy over the past few years, but honestly? Still pretty nuts.

Not something you really like to see in a guy who's capable of ripping you limb from limb if he's in a bad mood.

But also . . . unlike most vampires, Myrnin did care. He cared about pretty much *everything*, including people. He protected puppies and little kids. He had a spider for a pet. He'd practically adopted Claire, and personally saved her life (and mine, sad to say) more than a few times.

So I kind of owed the crazy bloodsucker.

"Dammit." I sighed and grabbed the shovel, because I was not doing this unarmed. I had an LED flashlight clipped to my belt loop, and I turned it on and aimed it into the grave. Whatever that was at the bottom of the coffin, it just ate the light whole. "Why me, God?"

I didn't wait for the answer, because I already knew it.

Because you can.

I jumped.

I felt my feet hit the bottom of the coffin with a thump, and then crack right through the rotten wood into soft, damp dirt. I won't lie—it smelled pretty foul, and my skin crawled, because there was no way that it ought to be this dark down here; I'd just been in this hole, and the moonlight had been bright enough for me to see up top. Now it was like being trapped inside a black velvet bag.

I still had the flashlight in my hand, and I smacked it against my thigh, hoping that it would turn on and somehow this was all just some big misunderstanding, but it stayed pitch-black.

And then a pair of cold, too-strong hands grabbed me in the darkness. Yeah, I might have yelped. A manly sort of yelp, obviously.

"Calm yourself," Myrnin said. He sounded annoyed, not unnerved, which would have been interesting if the sane part of me hadn't been kind of freaking out. "It's perfectly normal."

"Normal?" My voice came out high enough to have been mistaken for my friend Eve's. I cleared my throat and tried again, and got it into a more usual range. "What the hell is normal about this?"

"It's a bit difficult to explain, but clearly, the item I was hoping to find is here. . . . Now stand very still, boy. And try not to make noise."

I stood still. It wasn't easy, because after Myrnin let go of my shoulders, I felt like I was drifting in the dark, pulled out into space. Nothing seemed real. I finally reached out and put my hand on what felt like rough, solid dirt to the side, and that reminded me that I was standing at the bottom of a grave. Weird that it should make me feel better.

"I think I said *stand still*," Myrnin said, but he didn't sound too angry. I could hear creaking, and then a sound that seemed like snapping bones, and then he let out a pleased sigh. "Perfect. Brace yourself."

I didn't know what he meant, and then there was a soft click, and light poured in. After that complete darkness, it seemed like somebody had a flashlight pointed directly in my face, and I gasped and blinked and realized that, hey, someone *was* shining a flashlight directly in my face, and that someone was me, because the thing hadn't been working before and now it was. Probably because of something Myrnin had done.

I switched the beam off, blinked a few times, and saw Myrnin crouching down, examining what looked like some ancient, boxy camera held in the hands of a grinning skeleton. I'd managed not to step on him, whoever the dead guy was; my feet were braced on either side of the corpse.

Suddenly, I *really* wanted out of this grave.

"Don't move," Myrnin said absently, and carefully moved one of the skeletal hands. I expected the thing to come apart, but the hand held together. That seemed weird, because I thought skeletons this old fell apart. I didn't see any muscle connecting the bones.

"I'd really like to go now," I said.

"Oh, I wasn't talking to you," Myrnin said, and moved the other bony hand. It suddenly turned and wrapped around his wrist like a living thing. "Damn."

The skeleton sat up and wrapped its other bony hand around Myrnin's throat. Its fingers tightened fast, and I saw them sink in deep; it probably would have killed me, or anybody still human, but it didn't seem to hurt him much. Benefits of being a bloodsucker. Myrnin grabbed hold of the skeleton's neck and twisted, which only seemed to piss the thing off. Myrnin was left holding a skull that snapped its dry teeth at him, trying to bite, and the hand around his throat didn't let up at all.

I didn't know what to do, but I figured getting rid of the skull might help, so I grabbed it out of his hands and pretended it was a gross, snapping football. I threw it long and up, aiming for the next county.

As soon as the head left the grave, the rest of the skeleton collapsed into dust and bones. The hand around his neck clattered in pieces back to the coffin's wood. Myrnin's throat looked like he'd been hanged by an old-time Western sheriff, and he coughed a little, shook his head, and bent down to pick up the old black camera thing from the litter of bones. Then he jumped, straight up, out of the grave, and left me standing there like an idiot.

"Hey!" I yelled. "Little help, since I just saved your life?"

No answer. I swore under my breath, tried not to step on any bones as I pulled my feet out of the rotten wood. Hard to see how I was going to climb out, since when I scrambled up, the sides started to collapse in on me. *Great,* I thought grimly. *I'm going to suffocate in a grave because Claire's boss forgot about me.*

Myrnin's face appeared over the top of the grave, just as another avalanche of dirt piled in on me, raising a choking cloud. "Oh," he said, as if he was surprised to find me still down there. "Can't you get out?"

"Sure, I'm just staying down here because it's so damn comfy." I spat out a mouthful of dirt, and God only knew what else. "Little help?"

He extended one bone-white hand down to me. I grabbed hold, and he pulled so hard that he almost dislocated my shoulder. "Come along, Shame," he said. "We have work to do."

I was technically working for him, true, but no way did that mean he could call me that. "My name is Shane," I said. "With an *n*. Dickhead."

"Sorry," Myrnin said. I saw the thinnest, fastest ghost of a smile. "I'm just very forgetful."

Like hell he was. "Speaking of that, you paid me a hundred to dig up a coffin for you. Not to follow you around the rest of the night and battle dead guys. I think a little evil-skeleton-demon hazard pay might be a good idea."

"He wasn't evil," Myrnin said, seizing upon exactly the wrong thing, of course. "Keep up, then; there isn't any time to lose. I must get this camera obscura to my lab."

I didn't know what a camera obscura was, but it sounded like trouble. "Oh no, you don't. If you want me to tag along, it's an extra hundred."

Myrnin was notoriously cheap, or at least, utterly oblivious to the concept of fair pay, but he didn't hesitate to raise my bluff. "Two hundred, plus what I already pledged," he said. "I suppose you want to be paid in those paper bills. You may count them out yourself. I can't be bothered."

I should have known that if he was willing to double my asking price, it was going to be a bad, bad night, but then again, *three hundred bucks*. I'd done some terrible things for less than that. Hell, I'd done them for free.

"Deal," I said. "But we're taking my car."

My car was a sweet, sinister ride . . . deep black, with murdered-out wheels and chrome. Ninja black. Since I wasn't a vamp like my passenger, I had to keep the headlights on, which spoiled the stealth effect, but image wasn't worth dying over.

I half expected to argue with Myrnin about how to ride in a car like a human, but he got in, fastened his seat belt, and seemed perfectly at home. I eyed him suspiciously while I started up the engine. "Where'd you learn to buckle up?"

"Claire has explained to me the rules for riding in a motorized vehicle," he said. "Also, I understand not to attempt to drive from this position. She got very upset when I tried it last time."

"Touch this wheel, and swear to God, I'll kill you."

"I see what she likes about you," he said. "How long have you been wedded now?"

"Coming up on a year," I said. It still felt weird, *really* weird, to say that. I'd never thought past having the wedding—it seemed like the biggest possible goal there was in the world, and I hadn't bothered to think about what would happen after.

And the wedding day came, and the fear and pride and rush of something so big I couldn't even define it. Love, I guess. So much love.

Then the world turned, the sun came up, and . . . we were *married*. And that was weird, because it turned out getting married wasn't an achievement so much as a level-up, play-on kind of deal. Life was more different now than I'd ever imagined, because there was this other person entwined with me who was there *every day*. Not in the boyfriend/girlfriend I-can-leave-if-I-want way, but in an I'm-never-leaving-you way. Took time to figure out how to live with that, for both of us. We had amazing times and stupidly bad times and days where nothing happened at all, because . . . life. Life was happening together now, not separately. And it was only just beginning to dawn on me how incredibly wonderful that really was.

Every morning when I opened my eyes, I was still amazed she was lying in the same bed with me. But I didn't want to say any of that. Not to Myrnin, anyway.

"She seems happy," Myrnin said. He was looking out the window as I drove, and he sounded quiet. Thoughtful. Not the usual thing for him. "I thought she would be more . . . restless."

I guessed he was meaning to be nice and make small talk, but talking about Claire was creeping me out. I knew he'd had some kind of feelings for her—what they were exactly was a mystery, because he wasn't even as normal as most *vampires*, never mind regular human guys. When he said he loved Claire for her mind, I think he meant it, and from him, that was equally creepy.

"How's Jesse?" If we were talking about girls all of a sudden, it seemed only fair we should talk about his . . . though it was hard to figure out exactly what attraction crazy, wardrobe-challenged Myrnin had for hot, funny, savage Jesse, except they shared a liking for plasma.

"Lady Grey is . . . indescribable," he said. "But then, she always was. She rescued me twice, you know, from a particularly awful kind of hell. And she was very kind to me in my recovery. I've missed her."

"Uh-huh. And?"

"And what?"

"Seemed like the two of you had a thing."

"A thing?"

"You know."

"I do not know, and I might prefer not to know."

"Let me put it another way: Do vampires . . . ?" I left it right there, filling in the blanks with raised eyebrows. He sent me an irritated look.

"Do we *what*? Your generation's infelicity with verbs fills me with despair."

I didn't even know what *infelicity* was, but I guessed it meant we were bad at them. So I spelled it out. "Do vampires have sex?"

He seemed shocked. That was pretty funny, because I could swear he was about a thousand years old, and surely someone had mentioned sex to him before. If not, *holy crap*, this was going to be awkward.

"I . . ." He clearly had no idea what to say, and flapped his hands as if he was shooing the whole subject off. "That is far too personal a question, Shame, far too personal!"

"Yeah, the name's still Shane."

"No, I believe I had it quite right this time. It suits the moment much better."

It was pretty great, watching him squirm. "Are you actually a virgin? Because I don't think I've seen this much nervous fidgeting from anyone out of grade school."

"I come from an age when what happened behind closed doors was kept there. And since you clearly will not abandon the subject, vampires are fully capable of . . . such things. Just not as driven by them as humans, since we are not constantly hounded by the shadow of death. And we do not . . . procreate in the same way."

That almost made sense, I guessed. "You skated by my other question. The virgin one."

Myrnin gave me a frosty silence, so I guessed he wasn't going to answer . . . until he did. "I've had lovers," he finally admitted. "Ada was my last. Since her . . . death, I've not been moved to attempt it again."

I'd met Ada only in her last incarnation—a crazy, disembodied brain in a jar powering Myrnin's machine in his basement. I knew, because Claire had told me, that he'd killed the girl. Hadn't meant to, but she'd died, and his answer to that had been to try to make her live on as a brain in a jar. She hadn't cared much for it, and then she'd tried to kill us all. I guess in relationship terms, yeah, that kind of thing might put you off dating for a hundred years.

I know he regretted it. But that didn't change the fact that Claire had worked side by side with him for *years*, and every single day I'd wondered if he'd suddenly turn on her, too. And of course, he had, but Claire was ready for it. She was tough, my girl. My *wife*.

Wow. Still weird.

"So," I said. "Changing the subject . . ."

"Thank you."

". . . what exactly is that thing you pulled out of the grave, anyway?"

"A kind of camera obscura. Oh, but I suppose they teach you nothing in school these days. . . . That is the earliest type of camera, invented in perhaps the sixth century. This one has been enhanced with certain properties that make it project something else."

"What?"

"Darkness," Myrnin said. "Or, more accurately, the complete absence of light. It can create an area of darkness in which things that prefer darkness can be studied."

"Yeah, that doesn't sound creepy at all."

"Humans have an irrational dislike of darkness. Really, there's nothing in it that isn't also there in the light."

"I like to be able to see what's biting me, thanks."

"Does that really help?" Myrnin sounded honestly interested. "It's all well and good *knowing*, but *stopping it*, ah, that's the real challenge. Things that bite are rarely easily discouraged."

He ought to know, I guessed. "What exactly is it you're researching?"

His tone turned cautious, all of a sudden. "I can't say, really."

I made the last turn down a dark cul-de-sac. His lab was off to the right, at about two o'clock on the circle, next to the imposing loom of the newly refurbished Day House. Gramma Day was still up, or she'd left some lights burning. The alleyway that led to Myrnin's lab entrance was still dark. Of course.

"Can't say why?"

"I believe I'm paying you not to ask."

He was. I parked the car, killed the lights, and grabbed his arm as he popped the passenger door open. "Hey," I said, and he turned to look at me. There were red glints in his dark eyes, like sparks coming off a fire. "Tell me you're not cooking up something dangerous."

"Now, why would you think something like that?" Myrnin effort-lessly broke my grip and got out and dashed like the spider he was down the dark alley.

Me, I locked the car doors behind me, got out my flashlight, and followed at the pace of just another human.

An armed and dangerous one, at least.

Claire had equipped Myrnin's lab with motion-activated lights, mostly for her own benefit because Myrnin, damn him, could see just fine in the dark. The rising glow helped me not to break my neck on the steps leading down into the main room, because he'd spilled something all over the stone again. Sticky or slick, no way was I going to step in it. No telling what it was, but it looked biological.

Myrnin was already at one of the lab tables, which had been cleared of its usual litter of crazy stuff . . . cleared because he'd just shoved it off on the floor, of course. Claire had tried to educate him about trip hazards and keeping the place cleaned, but he just couldn't get there, and she'd finally given up and resigned herself to picking up after him. I left the stuff on the floor. Wasn't being paid to clean.

"So explain it to me. Why am I here exactly?" I asked him, as he fitted on a pair of weird-looking goggles. He flipped a switch on the side, and they were bathed in an eerie blue glow inside. The glass magnified his eyes.

"You're here to protect me, of course," he said.

"From what?"

"Ah, that's the question, isn't it? *From what.*"

This wasn't sounding too great. "Can't help you if you're not more, you know, specific."

"You're here to protect me from getting lost," he said, as he hooked up the cemetery camera to something that looked like a vacuum hose straight off a Hoover. It didn't quite fit. He duct-taped it together with way too much tape, and then jammed the other end into another box. . . . This one was polished wood, decorated with ornate little gold letters applied in neat rows all over it.

"Wait, getting lost?" I said, as he worked. "Are we going somewhere?"

"We are," he said. "Come here." I put the flashlight down on the table and came around to join him. He pushed a button on the wooden box, and grabbed my hand to slam it down on top of the switch as he slipped his own hand away. "Now, don't let go of it," he said. "Not until I tell you. And no matter what you see, stay still."

"I don't—"

My voice choked off, because darkness crashed in with the thick weight of midnight, and there was *nothing.* My mouth dried up; I flinched and almost pulled my hand back but managed to hang on. Myrnin gripped my arm and held tight.

"You'll see things," his disembodied voice whispered. "Bad things.

But they won't harm you. But one thing is *very* important: Don't let me stay here. You can't let me stay, no matter how much I want to do it. Don't let go of the button until I tell you, and when you do, you have to be touching me. Understand?"

I couldn't *see* a damn thing, and almost said so, and then something moved at the corner of my vision. Not like a light, exactly—more like a disturbance of the darkness. I turned my head that direction, and saw a very small wisp of gray that moved, got brighter, and took on form.

A ghost, at first. A woman, from the form, wearing an old-fashioned long, full skirt like something from a documentary on Victorians. She took on more color, though she stayed pale in skin. The dress was dark red, like drying blood, and it had a high collar and long sleeves. She had her dark, glossy hair up in a complicated bun thing.

It took me a second, but then I realized who she was. Ada. Myrnin's former lab assistant, a vampire who'd gotten on his bad side and ended up as a brain in a jar. I'd only known her as a crazycakes hologram thing, but she looked real enough here, as she glided up toward us.

Myrnin took on form and color, too, but not the Myrnin who was holding on to my arm. That one never let go, never moved. The one walking toward her was the *old* Myrnin . . . and he was dressed out of the same period closet as Ada was, with some kind of fancy tight black trousers and high boots and a white shirt with lace under a long black coat. The only color on him was a bright bloodred ruby he wore as a pin on the front of his shirt.

That old-school Myrnin lunged at her, slammed her into the invisible wall behind her, and as she screamed, he bit at her throat. Tore it open.

Drank.

"No," Modern-Day Myrnin whispered. He sounded shaky. Horrified. "*No. No*, this is not what I want. Not what I need. Stop. *Stop.*"

The Myrnin acting out Ada's murder in front of us never paused. She was dying, and it was pretty horrible. I looked away and swallowed hard. I've never been good with just bystanding.

Myrnin—the one next to me—took in a deep breath and let it out, slowly. The scene vanished, just melted on the air as if it had never been there. His voice, when it came, was hesitant. "It is an inexact science, and that . . . nightmare is rarely far from my mind. Bide a moment."

I guessed that was another word for *wait*, and I did, as more shadows moved and whispered and crowded, all unseen in the dark. Some talked. One or two screamed, and I flinched. I could almost feel them brushing over me, like damp breezes. It felt sickening.

"There," Myrnin whispered. He sounded different. More focused. "*There* it is."

This time, a storm of gray appeared, swirling like clouds, and then parted to show a confusion of bodies, men, dressed in those same period clothes, all wrestling and shouting, though I could hear it only in a muffled kind of way. It looked like they were clustered in around something.

Someone screamed. A woman. High and thin and terrified. In pain. Myrnin's hand closed hard on my arm, hard enough to bruise, but I didn't mind. It felt like I was falling into that crowd, or that it was rushing up on us, and suddenly I was standing surrounded by all those guys yelling and striking out, and in the center was a woman crouched on the ground, screaming as clubs came down on her. She was bloody and one of her arms was broken, but she still kept putting it up to try to protect her head.

I wanted to let go of that button and help her. I didn't know who she was. Didn't matter. Bunch of bullies beating somebody—my natural impulse was to jump in.

And then I realized she was *protecting* someone who was lying on the ground senseless underneath her. A man in dirty rags, curled into a shaking ball, bleeding in the street.

The woman raised her head, and I saw her flame red hair slipping free of pins, and her eyes caught fire and she snarled, showing fangs, and leaped for the man whose club was coming down toward her. She snapped his neck, picked up his club, and effectively beheaded a couple of guys with it.

I knew who that was.

Jesse. Lady Grey. Myrnin's current girlfriend, if that was the right word for two vampires who were kind of hooked up, or not. But this must have been a couple of hundred years ago, and the man lying on the street, trying to get up and slipping in his own blood . . . that was Myrnin. A crazier version than the one I knew. He looked pretty terrible.

And he had a book clutched in his grimy, shaking hands.

As Jesse killed people with claws and teeth and clubs, defending that babbling crazy man on the ground, the Myrnin I knew let go of me and moved into view. He took on solidity and color as he did, and the contrast was pretty harsh. I hadn't appreciated how relatively sane he was now, until I saw the before picture. That trembling wreck wasn't anybody I would have normally recognized, except for the eyes and the chin.

"Give it to me," Modern Myrnin said, and bent to grab the book. Ancient Myrnin snarled at him and held on, looking feral. "Give it to me, fool! You're going to destroy it, and I need it!"

I guessed Ancient Myrnin wasn't too keen on it, because he dropped the book and launched himself at Modern Myrnin's throat, and *damn*, that was some vicious killer instinct at work. Jesse was scary, but that old, crazy hobo was something way, way worse. And it was pretty clear that Modern, Mostly Sane Myrnin wasn't about to win that fight *at all.*

At least until he called out to Lady Grey. "Please!" he shouted. "Help me subdue him!"

She turned, teeth bared, and blinked in shock. Two Myrnins. Yeah, that might have done it. "Who are you?" Jesse demanded. She back-handed some street thug who tried to grab her. "What sorcery is this?"

"Science, they call it now," Modern Myrnin said. "Assistance!"

He blurted that last part out, and it choked off because Old Crazy Myrnin had seized hold of his throat. Jesse didn't hesitate. She flashed forward, grabbed Crazy Myrnin, and made him let go. She held on to him, stroking his matted hair as he shook and stared and made weird noises. Modern Myrnin stared at them with a look I hoped I'd never see again . . . kind of like looking back into hell and seeing yourself.

"I need the book," he told Jesse. "Please. He'll take it from here and destroy it, and if I don't have it now, where I am . . ."

"I don't understand how this is possible," she said. She had the same fire as the Jesse I knew, the same challenge, and she shook her broken arm in annoyance. Bones slipped back together. It must have hurt, but she ignored the pain. I didn't see any sign of the mob now, except for the dead ones that still littered the ground around them. Didn't really blame them for running; I might have backed down, too, faced with that look in her eyes. "Are you *Myrnin*? But he is here."

"That me is broken," he said. "I'm much better now. But, Lady Grey, I must have the book. I must. Please. Do this for me, for the care you take of me in this moment. It will make no difference to him, because all he longs for is your touch, your kindness. Books are mean-ingless to him, and will be for some time."

"But not to you. Does he improve?"

Modern Myrnin spread his arms and bowed. "As you see."

"You hardly dress any better," she said. "But I see spirit in your eyes that is absent in him now, and that . . . that is what I would hope to see."

She reached out and gently tugged the bloodstained book free of Crazy Myrnin's grip. He made a croak like a crow, not words, just distress, and grabbed for it, but she eased his hand away, and he let it go. Instead, he just grabbed for her, and held on.

It was her broken arm, but she didn't flinch. She held the book out to Modern Myrnin, and as his fingers touched it, there was a spark of light between them, almost like static electricity. She gasped and let go of it. Myrnin shoved it in the pocket of his coat, but he was staring at her, and I knew that look. Hell, I felt it every time I looked at Claire. Hunger. Longing. Fever.

"Take care of me," Myrnin said. "You're the only reason I lived, my lady. Or continue to live, even now. Remember me, I beg you."

For a lady who'd just killed a lot of men, she looked kind of vulnerable right then . . . and sort of sweet, under the blood.

"It isn't every day I see a man from the future," she said. "I can scarce forget."

He smiled, and he bowed to her again, deeper, and stepped back toward me. Close enough to grab. "Shane," he said. "I believe I'm ready to—"

Lady Grey was right there, all of a sudden, and she reached for his hand. He let her take it. "You'll not go anywhere," she said, "until you explain yourself, Myrnin of the future. You know what will happen, yes? Tell me. *Tell me.* Shall I follow Amelie to the New World? Or stay here?"

"I can't," he said, very gently. "I can't tell you what to do, my lady. You must choose it on your own. I've done enough."

She looked back at the crazier, dirtier version of him, huddled now in a crouch on the ground, and said, "I love him, you know. He has . . . vision. And freedom."

"He's quite mad," Myrnin said. "But I suppose you know that, too."

"I know. But I can't let him be slaughtered in the streets. I'll see him safe."

"Yes. You will."

She turned again, facing him, and I figured that was the end of it . . . but she didn't let him go. "If you know me, you'll know that I've never been much for propriety," she said. "I do what I like."

"It is your very best quality—"

She cut him off by planting a kiss on him. Not a little peck on the cheek, oh no—a full-on press of her lips on his, with her arms slipping around him and holding on, and wow, that was a *kiss*. He seemed shocked at first, and then he got into it. Well, I could understand that, although I really didn't need to see it; his hands traveled up her sides, her arms, cupped the sides of her head, and she moaned and pressed up against him, and he didn't seem to mind that *at all*. In fact, he gave it right back, to the point where I was starting to wonder just how far this was going to go, because—*damn*.

And then Jesse pulled back, lips red and eyes wild, and whispered, "Stay. Stay with me. I need you to stay."

"No," Myrnin said. He didn't sound too convinced. "I can't."

"I've been alone for so long, and this—this *you* is more my patient than anything else. I love him, but he's broken, and will be so long in healing. Just bide with me a day. Only a day."

"I . . . can't . . ."

Yeah, that sounded like a man who was seriously thinking about it. And he hadn't let her go. He brushed hair back from her pale face and kissed her again. Hard. This was *not* a side of Myrnin I'd ever really imagined seeing. I was starting to hope I never saw it again, because I couldn't help but see Claire in Jesse's place, and that was an *oh, hell no* kind of experience.

"Hey, man," I said to him. "Gotta go. Come on."

He didn't listen. I reached for him at the extent of my stretch, not letting go of the button, and got him. I grabbed hold of the back of his coat, and dragged him a step back to where I could get a good grip on his collar.

Lady Grey turned on me, snarling, and the frustrated anger in her eyes made me remember all the men she'd just laid out dead on the street. Whoa. There was wanting, and then there was *wanting*. This lady wasn't used to being told no.

He hadn't told me so, but I figured it must be time to bail. Myrnin hadn't made it clear whether I needed to be touching skin or just his clothes, but I grabbed the cold back of his neck before I let go of the button.

And the darkness cut off like . . . well, like somebody had flipped on the lights. And Myrnin and I were standing there in the same place, next to the lab table, and the only difference was that he had a book in the pocket of his coat, and he was shaking like a leaf. He put his hands to his face. To his lips.

"Sorry to be your anti-wingman," I told him, "but you said don't let you stay. Looked like you were tempted to me."

"Tempted," he repeated faintly. "Yes. She is very tempting. She was . . . different in those days. Less in control. More . . . feral."

"*Sexy as hell* is the phrase you're looking for."

He glanced at me and turned away, bracing his hands on the lab table, head down.

"So, you got what you wanted? This book thing?"

"Yes," he said. "With it, I can rebuild many of the systems on which I based Morganville, but better. More powerful. So why do I feel that I've . . . lost something? Left something?"

"Because you didn't get to have the wild sexy night with Victorian Jesse?"

"She was *not* Jesse. Not then. She was . . . Lady Grey. And Lady Grey only. But she never . . . We have never . . . It was more that I idolized her. She saved me. She brought me out of the dark and back from the dead, in many ways that matter. And I feel . . . robbed of knowing more of her now."

"Good thing you told me to pull you back," I said. "What would have happened if you'd stayed and I let go of the button, anyway?"

"I'd have died. More importantly, I suppose, I would have never existed. Two of the same cannot exist in the same space and time. The only reason this was possible was my tether, using the box, to this time. There are calculations, if you'd care to see them. . . ."

"Pass," I blurted. "And if you'd have never existed . . ."

"Morganville would never have existed," he said. "Or at least, not in this form. The world would change. You might not be here. Claire might not. Things would be . . . quite different."

I didn't want different. I shuddered to think about it, actually. "Thanks for warning me about that up front, man."

"I didn't!"

"Sarcasm. Look it up."

"Oh. Well, you see, I didn't tell you because I knew if I had explained the stakes, you'd have not allowed me to go."

Suspicion struck me. "That's why you didn't get *Claire* to do this. She'd have figured it out. Right?"

"Right," he said. "Whereas you're not as . . . ah . . ."

"It's okay to say I'm not as smart. Not many people are."

"Very true. And I'm sure you have other sterling qualities. Sports, perhaps. Something like that."

I kind of wanted to kick his ass, but he did look like he'd had some part of his heart ripped out, so it probably would have been mean. Also, he'd have killed me if I'd tried.

"So, am I done?" I asked him. "Because I need twelve kinds of showers."

He was looking off into the distance. "Yes," he said. "I suppose we're done here."

"Not until I get paid, man."

He shook his head, pulled open a drawer, and pulled out a wadded fistful of money. I grabbed for it before it could start falling to the floor, where something might eat it in the chaos. Wow. All hundreds. "Um . . . I think that's too much."

"Is it? Oh, never mind; take it and go."

I didn't argue about it. I headed for the stairs, and the lights came on to guide my way . . . and lit up the modern, leather-clad Jesse, Lady Grey, sitting halfway down the steps in what would have been the darkness until I'd triggered the motion detectors.

She looked . . . strange.

"Hey, Jess," I said, and she nodded to me, but her eyes were fixed past me, on Myrnin. "How long have you been there?"

"Long enough," she said. "I'd forgotten. Isn't that odd? To forget something like that? So much time. Or maybe I wanted to forget."

Yeah, no doubt, she'd seen it all. From this spot, she'd have had a balcony view of Myrnin's past, I guessed—and of her own. She was rubbing her arm as if she remembered it being broken.

"Well . . . see you," I said.

She nodded and stood up as I passed.

Across the room, Myrnin raised his head to meet her eyes, and he straightened, as if wary of what she was going to do. I'm not going to lie—I paused at the top of the steps, and watched.

Jesse crossed slowly to him, and silently held out her hand. He took it.

"Too long," she said. "Too long. The girl I was then is long gone, you know. I've changed."

"I've changed, too," he said. "Well, I bathe now. And I'm less insane. But yes, it's been too long. We can't go back to . . . what never was. It's for the best."

"Oh, my sweet fool, that's not what I meant at *all*."

And she kissed him. Same kind of kiss. Same kind of unexpected flash of passion. And Myrnin, caught by surprise, just stood there . . . until he put his hands up, traveling slowly up her sides, her arms, to cup her head as he kissed her more deeply, more fully.

Yeah, I knew how that felt. And I knew where it was heading.

So I left.

What? I'm not a perv. Much.

I parked the Murdermobile out front, next to Eve's black hearse— they made a hell of a curbside statement—and jogged up the walk to the front door, keys in hand. Nobody tried to eat my face, which was nice. I got inside, slammed the locks, and turned to see Claire standing in the hallway. She gave me a look that was half-resigned, half-appalled, and all hers.

"Really?" she asked, and sighed. "Wow. And also, you smell."

"Wow," I agreed. "Blame your boss. Also, you really need to teach him about money. But maybe not until I do a few more jobs."

"Funny. How about you go straight upstairs and take at least one layer of dirt off? I guess there must be clothes under that, so maybe throw those in a garbage bag and I'll do the laundry."

"Laundry?" Eve popped her head around the corner, and her Goth-rimmed eyes widened. "Holy *shit*, did you crawl out of a sewer? Because I can smell you from here, and that is a whole world of gross."

"Hey, nice to see you, too, Vampirella. What did you want?"

"Well, I *was* going to say that I'd put some stuff in the laundry, too, but again, oh, hell no to that. Try not to get whatever is on you on anything I have to touch, okay?"

I was too tired to give her the finger, but I did it anyway. She winked and pulled her head back around the corner.

I wanted to kiss Claire, but I knew better; there was no way I'd want to kiss me. So I trudged upstairs, trying to keep my grave dirt to myself, and grabbed a garbage bag on the way to bundle my clothes in.

I brushed my teeth to get the taste out. I needed a *Silkwood* shower, to be honest, something with fire hoses and wire brushes wielded by guys in hazmat suits, but at least the hot water held out long enough for me to use soap and shampoo about four times, until I couldn't feel the phantom wriggle of worms anymore.

I shut the water off and dripped for a minute, leaning against the wall, before I slid the curtain back ... and found Claire standing there, holding up a towel. Poker-faced.

"Well," I said. "This is nice."

"It gets better," she said, and when I took the towel, she held out a beer in her other hand. Ice-cold. I dried off fast and reached for the beer, but she pulled it out of reach. "Uh-uh. Not until you tell me you missed me."

Stepping forward put me solidly against her, and pushed her back against the tiled bathroom wall near the sink. I grabbed the beer from her upraised hand, started to drink, and then put it down on the window ledge.

Then I picked her up and sat her on the bathroom counter and kissed her. Sweet and hot and slow, lots of tongue, and she tasted like heaven to me. Heaven, and home.

"I missed you," I whispered in her ear, as I trailed kisses down her jawline and up to nibble on her lobe. I felt her gasp and shiver. "Can you tell?"

"I'm convinced," she said. I liked that she had a shirt with buttons on the front. They opened nicely. She'd also switched to front-hook bras, which was extra fun and convenient. "What are you doing?"

"Getting ready for bed," I said. "How about you?"

"I should . . . do the . . ."

"Laundry?" I nipped at her neck, licked lightly at the barely visible scars where Myrnin had once bitten her. Bastard. "Really?" I unzipped her jeans. "You should probably put these in, then."

"Probably," Claire said, and helped me slide them off. "Probably should put my panties in, too."

"Seems logical."

From that point on, there wasn't much talking, really.

A WHISPER IN THE DARK

This one is a late addition to the Web site's free stories; it's another one I started, restarted, edited, and abandoned for a while, only to return to it with fresh eyes and a new story line. I loved the interplay between our gang, especially with Michael still odd-vampire-out at this time in the universe. I really loved the idea that Eve's background and family tree end up being the central focus of this story, too.

It has a bit of a horror story twist to it, but I think it's still firmly within the Morganville county lines!

Fun factoid: I also hate cleaning out my fridge. I do it, but I have to force myself. Also, I hate leftovers. You have to forget them in the back only once to have nightmares forever.

Michael Glass leaned against the kitchen counter and thought about the end of the world. Had to be the end of the world, because his best friend, Shane Collins, had on a pair of latex *CSI*-style gloves and was . . . cleaning.

"Dude, what's with all the crap in the refrigerator?" Shane asked. He held up one sports bottle after another for his housemate Michael's benefit, because they were all Michael's. "Can't you write an expiration date on these or something?"

Michael snatched one out of Shane's hand, sniffed it, and said, "It's good. What's your problem?"

"My *problem*? Our fridge is full of bottles of human blood and I can't find any place to put a Coke. *That's* my problem. And what the hell, are you binge eating now? How many of these do you actually need?"

"How many Cokes do you need? I know you're trying to work up to a diabetic coma, but still, give it a break, man." Michael kept the bottle he was holding, popped the cap, and took a healthy swig. Shane shuddered, shoved two cans of Coke into the open space, and swung the door shut. "What crawled up your ass and made you worry about housekeeping, anyway?"

Shane gave him one of his classic *Keep talking* looks, grabbed a bag of chips off the counter, and sank into a chair at the kitchen table. It was a mess, piled with dirty dishes, half-full glasses, and junk mail. "Check the schedule," he said. "You're on kitchen duty. I'm supposed to do laundry. Eve said if we didn't get our shit together before she got home, she was going to get extreme. I've seen her get extreme. It's not pretty." He stripped off the latex gloves, popped some chips in his mouth, and said, "Besides, man, she's right. This place is a sty. I think I saw a roach crawling into the Lysol bottle this morning. It's your house, too. Have a little pride."

"Trade you for laundry," Michael said. Shane gave him the universal sign for *Blow me*, and Michael had to grin. "I'll take that as a no."

"Unless you want to be explaining that to both our ladies, real good idea." Shane tossed him the bag of chips, and Michael took a handful. No garlic, thank God. "Not that I wouldn't pay good money to see you try."

Michael threw the bag back at him, hard, but Shane got it before it attached itself to his face. Had to give it to him, the boy was quick, for somebody who wasn't vampire-enhanced. "Don't you have to go sort some underwear or something? Because if I have to do the kitchen, you're up in my way. Get your chip-eating ass out of the chair."

"File the attitude, bro. I'm going." Shane ate more chips as he stood up, then froze in midchomp. Michael was way ahead of him, turning toward the door as he put his sports bottle carefully down on the counter. Shane's tone, when it came, was way different this time. "Guests?" he asked.

Michael nodded. "I heard. Maybe you ought to let me take the lead."

Shane didn't say anything. On this, at least, they didn't argue much anymore. . . . Michael was better equipped to take the hits, if the hits were coming, and Shane was a wicked backup for anyone, vampire or not. They were both natives of Morganville, Texas, and had grown up with stress, trauma, and vampires . . . not necessarily in that order.

Shane was right behind him on the way to the front door, and Michael had his hand on the doorknob just before the brisk knock hit the wood.

He knew, before he opened it, that there was a vampire standing on the other side of the door. That vamp was wearing a hat, a coat, a muffler, gloves—he wouldn't have been out of place in Chicago in the winter. The problem was that it was a million degrees of heat outside in Texas, but to a vampire, that didn't much matter. Not as much as experiencing fatal sun combustion, anyway. Michael had never met a vampire who'd thought the Texas sun was actually too hot.

Maybe, he thought, because at heart, inside, vampires were always cold. Always. He felt the same brittle chill inside himself, all the time; chill, and silence. Silence where his heartbeat used to be. Blood still moved through his body, slow and thick, but he wasn't sure how that happened; he wasn't science-minded like Claire, and he just accepted that it worked, against all natural laws that he'd ever understood. Being a vampire, he'd learned almost immediately, wasn't about science. It was about something less measurable. Souls, maybe.

But the important thing was that the vampire was staring out at him from under the shrouding muffler and hat, and those icy blue eyes seemed familiar. Not Amelie; the Founder of Morganville didn't bow to anyone, including the sun.

"May I?" the vampire asked. The two words were tinted with a musical foreign accent.

Shane was looking at him for a clue, and Michael finally shrugged. "Come on inside," he said, and stepped back. The vampire entered, and the vampire pulled off his hat and muffler and handed them to Shane with the thoughtless arrogance of someone who'd lived his entire life with servants around him.

Michael stifled a laugh at Shane's expression, but he couldn't help the smile as Shane dropped the items to the floor and kicked them into a dusty corner.

"Sorry," Shane said. "I'm all out of hat racks."

The vamp took off his coat and—with a pretty good-humored display of cooperation—tossed it to the same corner, and then added the gloves. Michael knew him by sight, because the Morganville vampires were a small community, and he likely knew the name, but didn't know how to match them up. He was blond, short haired, and blue eyed, with an unexceptional round face. In fact, nothing about him, except the eyes, would make him stand out in a crowd.

He directed his attention to Michael, which felt like a laser between the eyes. "I am Kiril Rozhkov. Hello." He offered a slight nod of his head, and a calm smile. His accent held a strong hint of cold Russian winters.

"Hello," Michael said, because he felt like one of the Glass House residents ought to be polite, and it damn sure wasn't likely to be Shane.

"Excuse me," Rozhkov said, "but I have a matter to discuss with you in privacy, Mr. Glass."

Mr.? It was a weird sound, and disconnected from the way Michael thought about himself; he saw Shane give him a look that threatened to make it all way too funny. Laughing in the face of a visiting strange vampire wasn't generally a good idea.

Michael surrendered. "Follow me."

He led the vamp into the parlor. It was an old-fashioned name for an old-fashioned room; when the house had originally been built, it was an age when neighbors dropped around for tea and lemonade, stiffly formal visits conducted in a room set aside just for that purpose. He and his housemates never used it except to pile boxes and coats and bags in it. The boxes had been shifted out recently, but Claire's backpack leaned against the leg of one wing chair where she'd abandoned it, and one of Eve's skull-themed umbrellas flopped on the floor, dusty and dispirited. Not much call for umbrellas out here in West Texas, unless you were using them for sun relief. Rain was rare.

Kiril Rozhkov took in the layers of dust and disuse, and then sat on the broken-down Victorian sofa with an ease and a grace Michael recognized as weirdly foreign. A lot of vampires moved that way—as if they'd been trained from an early age to be graceful and correct. Not a skill people learned anymore.

"I am sorry to intrude on your home, Mr. Glass——," Rozhkov began.

Michael held up a hand. "Michael. Please."

"Very well, Michael. Named for an angel; that is a lot to live up to, yes? I myself am named for a saint, and the father of the Russian alphabet. Our fathers expected much from us. I wonder if they were satisfied." Rozhkov shifted slightly. "You may send your man away. I am no threat to you."

"He's not my man," Michael said, and wondered exactly how Rozhkov meant that. Probably in the antique sense, as if Shane were some soldier in service to a feudal lord. "He lives here. Housemate."

The other vampire shrugged, as if all these fine distinctions were too much for him to bother with. "It is no matter. I only meant that these matters were for our kind, not his."

Shane was hovering near the doorway, openly staring; Michael gave him a frown, and Shane ignored it, lounging against the wall. If a vamp told him to go away, he was absolutely going to stay. It was just Shane's basic nature.

"He's fine," Michael said. "What do you want?"

Rozhkov's pale gold eyebrows twitched just a bit, surprised by what he probably perceived as rudeness; he composed himself almost instantly into an expression of patience. It was irritating. "I wish to meet the girl."

Claire. They always wanted to meet Claire, sooner or later; for a quiet, somewhat shy girl, she tended to have rock-star status in vampire circles. That was probably because she had the cachet of being the first human to manage to survive working with her bipolar vampire boss, Myrnin, in ages—or that she had Amelie's good favor. Rare for the Founder of Morganville to take such an interest in a human.

"You don't have to ask my permission," Michael said. He was genuinely grouchy now. "Claire lives here. I don't own her."

"Ah. I see we are misunderstanding one another. I do not mean that one." Rozhkov dismissed Claire with a tiny wave of his hand. "I mean the one blood-bound to you."

Eve? Michael sat back. So many ways to respond to that, none of them adequate to the rush of anxiety he felt. Vampires didn't come asking about Eve. They were almost unanimously content to ignore her and hope she would go away. Claire was accepted by them as a valuable resource; Eve had been seen as an oddity when he'd begun to date her, a temporary thing of no real importance. But since he'd married her, all hell had broken loose. The humans didn't trust her. Neither did the vampires.

So having a vampire show up specifically to meet her was . . . unsettling.

"Let's get a few things straight. She's not my *girl*," Michael said. "She's not blood-bound, whatever that means to you. She's my wife, but that doesn't mean I own her."

"I have heard you are married," Rozhkov said. He didn't seem moved at all. "Blessed by the sacraments of the church and by our Founder. To no one's pleasure but yours, it would seem. It will all end badly."

Michael took a second to remember why he shouldn't punch the man right in the superior, thin smile. "Why do you want Eve?"

"That is my business, and not yours, since you so plainly do not—as you put it—own her."

Shane coughed. It sounded like *asshole*. No way to tell if Rozhkov caught it at all.

"Eve's not here," Michael said. "Sorry. Want to leave your number?"

He got that faint, superior smile again. "No, I do not," the man said, and rose from his sitting position. "I will try again. Informative to meet you, Michael Glass."

"Same here."

It was not quite dangerous, the look they exchanged, but enough to run a shiver down Michael's spine, like the lightest brush of death-cold fingers. He held the stare. However young he was—human age, and vampire—he knew coming from Amelie's bloodline gave him power . . . perceived and real. He had some abilities he'd never tried to use. They were there, like boxes on a shelf he'd never opened. He opened one now, and felt a new, strange sensation slide chilly through his nerves. He felt his body shift balance, just a little, and suddenly he could sense Rozhkov's essence, like a thin shimmering cloud around him. Blues and pale yellows.

Rozhkov was weak. Something was wrong with him. Badly wrong. It lasted only a moment, and then the vision faded.

One thing was certain: Michael didn't want Eve anywhere near him.

"Thanks for coming," Michael said. It was insincere, and he knew Rozhkov could hear it. Rozhkov gave him a tiny, strange shrug in response.

"It is nothing," he said. "I only attempt politeness out of some minor respect for your sire."

That was . . . ominous. There was something extremely unsettling about Rozhkov's confidence, too; Michael knew that many of the vamps treated him well not so much because of any status of his own, but because Amelie loomed over everything like a severe, sometimes benevolent shadow. Rozhkov didn't seem to care that much about Amelie's wishes.

"Get out," Michael said. "And stay out. The house won't let you in again."

He felt the Glass House waking up around him; the place had a sentience to it, and loyalty, and it responded to him and Claire even more than Eve and Shane. It would defend him if Rozhkov was stupid enough to try to force the issue.

Which Rozhkov wasn't. He walked straight to the front door, donned all his protective gear, and left without another word.

"Well, that was interesting," Shane said. "What's up with that guy?"

"He's sick."

That got Shane's immediate attention. "Sick? Sick how?"

"I don't know," Michael said, "but if he's five hundred years old, why is he wearing that much sun protection if he isn't?"

Michael locked the door and exchanged a look with Shane.

"You going to tell me what he wanted now?"

"Eve," Michael said. "He wanted Eve. And we have to make sure he doesn't get her."

"I don't know," Eve said as she painted a henna tattoo on Claire's left arm. "I think I'm taking it as a compliment. You know, I'm not the one the vamps are always calling. That'd be you, CB. Makes me feel all special."

"You're special, all right," Shane said. "Extra points if you think coming to the notice of some creepy ancient bloodsucker is a good thing. They give you shock treatments for that kind of special."

"Hey, let me bask in my spotlight for a minute." Eve put the finishing touches on the tattoo and sat back, tilting her head to consider it. Michael tilted his head, too, trying to see what it was she'd drawn. It looked like a skull with all kinds of ornate flourishes and a way-too-cute bow on top. Girly Goth. It did kind of fit Claire, he had to admit. "Okay, basking's over. What the hell does he want with *me*? Because I am the very definition of not useful to them. It's been kind of my mantra."

Eve wasn't kidding. She'd spent her life since the age of about sixteen trying hard to piss off the vampires, mock them, and be utterly uncooperative. It was why she was steadfastly Goth in her look; the vampires found that whole trend distasteful and downright disrespectful. Right now, she was rocking a complex confection of braids that curled and stuck out at odd angles around her head. She'd tinted her midnight-black hair with dark blue in streaks. Between the careful pale makeup, dark eyeliner, pale blue lipstick, and skull-and-spike clothes, she looked intimidating to anyone who didn't know her.

Of course, if you did know her, Michael thought, you probably loved the holy hell out of her. Eve was just like that.

"I don't know what he wants," he said, and reached out to take her hand in his. She gave him a quick, warm smile and leaned in to fit her warmth against his side—sunlight in flesh, his own portable sun that heated but never burned him. "I just know that whatever it is, it can't be good for you."

"Well, yeah, that's kind of a given. I've never known a vamp to drop in to make it rain fun. I just can't figure out . . . me. Why me? Claire's the one who usually gets that honor."

"Trust me," Claire said, inspecting her henna tattoo with a mixture of bemusement and delight. "I'm happy to share that." She held her forearm out to Shane, who ran his fingers over the ink. Michael saw her shiver, and heard the faint whisper of her heartbeat speed faster. "Do you like it?"

"Is it a training tat?"

She laughed. "Kind of."

"Then I like it. Hey, want to see my new one?"

"Where is it?" Michael, Eve, and Claire somehow managed to say it in unison, and they all dissolved into laughter at Shane's wounded expression.

"My *back*, jackasses. C'mon. Do you think I'm that desperate for attention I tattoo my—"

"Let's just leave it right there," Eve interrupted. "Because I'm really afraid I might have to think about that one way too hard." She looked up at Michael, and for a second he lost himself in the shine of her dark eyes, the intoxicating, exotic spice of her scent. "Michael doesn't have any tats."

"Michael doesn't like needles," he told her.

"Ironic, coming from a dude who bites people for a living," Shane said.

"Why do you think I don't like needles?"

Michael was sitting in his comfortable armchair, with Eve snugged against him like a happy cat, and Shane and Claire had the sagging, much-abused sofa. Not for the first time, Michael considered that they'd really have to start taking better care of the place. Home improvement never seemed to get high up on the priority list, though. Or, at least, not as high as staying alive in a town that wanted to kill them at least twelve hours of every day. Tonight, though, it seemed quiet. Gentle. Normal. The TV was playing silently in the background; Shane had turned it on, which meant he was going to be loading up a game anytime now, and soon they'd be taking turns shooting zombies and trash-talking each other.

But Michael's mind kept worrying at the problem of Kiril Rozhkov, and what the vampire wanted with his wife. For all her attitude and toughness, she was still human, and fragile. And precious to him.

"Claire," he said. "How do you feel about asking Amelie for a favor?"

"Not so good," she replied. "Why can't you?"

It was a fair question. He was, after all, her creature; she'd made him a vampire, and he was part of her own bloodline. That entitled him to certain privileges, normally. "She's keeping her distance," he said. "We had a—difference of opinion."

By which he meant she was still cold toward him because of his marriage to Eve. She still didn't approve, though she hadn't actively stopped him from doing it; it had nothing to do with Eve herself, but more with the principle of humans and vampires making those kinds of commitments, and the general attitude of vampires (and humans) about it. Amelie needed to stay above the fray, and right now, he *was* the fray.

"I guess," Claire said. "You want me to ask her about Rozhkov?"

"Yes. I just need a clue about the guy—how dangerous he is, how worried I should be."

"We," Eve said, without raising her head from where it rested against his chest. "How worried *we* should be."

"We," he agreed, and looked at Claire. "Please?"

She grinned. Even though she'd grown up over the years he'd known her—grown into a capable, calm, intimidating young woman, really— she still looked like she was ten when she smiled like that. "Since you said please," she said. "Thanks for the tat, Eve. It's supercool."

She excused herself and went upstairs to make the call, and Shane (as Michael had predicted) loaded up Dead Rising and went to work slaughtering the undead. Eve uncurled herself from her place at Michael's side and took up the other controller, and before a minute had gone by, they were insulting each other nonstop, in colorfully hilarious ways.

Michael's fingers itched to pick up his guitar and play, but he also knew it was probably the wrong time. Instead, he went upstairs and knocked softly on Claire's closed bedroom door.

She opened it. Her cell phone was in her hand, but she put it on her dresser and walked back to her bed to sit down.

"Rozhkov is bad news," she said to him.

"Kinda got that already."

"Amelie wouldn't say much. She just said not to let him inside."

"I wish she'd imparted that wisdom a little earlier. Like before we let him inside."

Claire smiled a bit, but she looked pale and serious as she stared at him. "She didn't say it in so many words, but Eve's in danger. I could read between the lines. I don't know why he wants her, but if he does, it's not for fashion tips and henna tattoos."

"She's not going to like being guarded."

"Nope," Claire said, and the smile grew wider. "She's not going to like it a bit. We should probably take turns so we all get the blame equally."

"She's not going out after dark."

"You're going to have to tell her that yourself, because I am not sticking my hand in that wasps' nest."

It wasn't going to be a pleasant conversation, for certain. "I guess it's my job. Thanks for helping watch out for her."

"We look out for each other. We're family. It's what we do. Is that the door?"

Michael had heard it, too—the doorbell was broken, so it made a weird buzzing sound that was sometimes hard for human ears to hear, but Claire had found a way of attuning herself to it even from up here. To him, it sounded like a fly buzzing in his ear—annoying, and alarming.

Even more alarming when Eve yelled out, "I'll get it!" from downstairs.

Michael didn't think; he just moved. It was rare he engaged the speed vampire life had given him, at least here in the house; he'd grown so used to mimicking human behavior around his friends and with Eve that it came almost naturally. But just now, with the prickling awareness of danger seeping into him, he didn't even consider appearances.

Shane yelped when Michael passed by him, but Michael was gone and down the hallway before the sound even registered. Eve was at the end of the hallway, cracking the door open. She wasn't as careful as she should have been, but the fact that Rozhkov was a vampire, and the house was on alert about him, had probably lulled her into a false sense of security.

It wasn't Rozhkov out there. It was a human—a scared one. Michael recognized him as Mr. Lockhart, from down the block. "Please," the man said, as Michael joined Eve at the door. "Please, you've gotta help me. *He's in my house.*"

"Who?" Eve asked. "What's going on?"

"We'll call the police," Michael said. He was pulling out his cell.

"No!" Lockhart shoved at the door, and Eve let him open it wider so he could thrust his desperate, sweaty face closer. "No, please, he said—he said he'd kill my wife if you did. He said you know what he wants. Please. You've gotta help."

They all went still and silent. Lockhart wasn't lying; his distress hung in the air around him like a white-hot electric cloud, and Michael could smell the adrenaline flooding through his bloodstream. Claire sent him an anxious, pleading look; Shane had gone tense and unreadable.

It was Eve who punched Michael on the shoulder, swung the door open, and said, "We can't let this happen. You know that."

His hand flashed out without any real planning, grabbed her shoulder, and pulled her back across the threshold when she stepped outside. "No," he said, when she opened her mouth to yell. "Eve, it's you he wants. It's you. And you can't do this."

She gave him a blackly miserable look, one that chilled him in places he hadn't know he could still feel the cold. "Do you think he'll do what he says?"

Yes, Michael thought, but he kept himself from saying so. He tried not to project what he felt for Eve onto Lockhart, desperate to save his own wife, but he couldn't help it. He'd always been way too soft-hearted about these things for a vampire—he knew that. But falling in love with Eve—falling more in love with her every day, it seemed—he couldn't *not* know what Lockhart felt.

Eve was still pinning him with that bleak stare. "Michael. We can't let her die. *I* can't."

"And I can't let you go."

"Dude," Shane said, "what makes you think you *let* any of us do any damn thing?"

And he shoved past, out the door, and down the steps, with Claire fast on his heels. That left him and Eve standing together, with Lockhart looking at them in silent, tormented distress.

"He's right," Eve said. "What makes you the boss of me? Are we partners, or not?"

He didn't like it, but he let go. "Partners," he said. "Which means what you do affects us both. All right?"

She kissed him. It was a quick, warm, sweet thing, and it made him crave her in too many ways to comprehend, and then she was gone, heading after Claire and Shane toward the Lockhart house.

Michael closed and locked the door behind them, because . . . Morganville.

Lockhart's front door was wide-open, throwing a warm, buttery glow of light down the cracked front steps and shimmering on the shiny wood floor visible inside. As Michael approached with Eve, Claire and Shane stopped at the foot of the steps, and Claire looked back at them. "How do you want to do this?" she asked. Lockhart pushed past them into the house, stumbling in his eagerness, and disappeared around the corner. Like the Glass House, this house was basically a square, but it was about half the size. They'd taken good care of it, Michael could tell; what he could see inside looked clean and neat, and on the walls were framed photos of a happy family. There were kids. Two of them.

Eve took a deep breath and said, "Well, it's me he wants, so let's see what happens. Michael's got my back."

"He's not the only one," Shane said. "I'm on Mission Protect the Goth, too."

Claire didn't need to add that she was, too. They all took that for granted.

Michael fought an almost overpowering urge to hold Eve back, to keep her safe, and let her walk ahead of him up the steps and down the polished wooden hallway. He felt Shane behind him, solid and steady, and knew Claire would be analyzing everything, thinking through the possibilities. Nobody better to have going into a bad situation than Claire, even if she looked deceptively fragile.

Eve, on the other hand, looked badass, and she knew it. And as she turned the corner, he saw her put on attitude like armor as she stopped, set her feet in a battle stance, and sent the man seated on the sofa across the room a cocky tilt of her head.

"You wanted me? You got me," she said. "Now let her go."

Kiril Rozhkov had Mrs. Lockhart sitting close against him, a position she obviously hated. He had his arm around her shoulders, but every muscle in her body was tensed and quivering, and the look in her eyes was one step away from madness. She didn't look hurt, and Michael smelled no spilled blood. So far, so good.

Rozhkov took his time looking Eve up and down. "You are not as I expected."

"No? Goody. Get your damn hands off her."

"I think I will wait," he said, apparently not bothered at all by Eve's tone of utter disrespect. "Your great-grandmother was named Ulyana, yes? She was born in Minsk?"

"My *great-grandmother?*" Eve shook her head. "No idea. I never knew her."

"But your mother's family is Russian."

"I guess, yeah. Mostly we're just Morganville. Why? You feeling nostalgic for the Old Country?"

Rozhkov smiled. It was chilling, and the cold light in his eyes had an edge like broken glass. "In a way," he said. "Come, child. Sit." He patted the sofa on his other side. Eve didn't move. He patted again, the way someone would encourage a pet dog. Michael gritted his teeth against an urge—a very real one—to go at the guy with his teeth. "Sit and I will allow this woman to go." Eve still didn't move, and Rozhkov's patience visibly frayed. "Or, by all means, stand and watch as I rip her apart for my entertainment. You may choose."

It wasn't even a choice. Eve let out a slow breath and walked to the sofa, but didn't sit. She stood, looking down at the vampire. "Let her go and I'll sit."

He hesitated, just to draw out the moment, and then took his hand from around Mrs. Lockhart's shoulders; the young woman— not that much older than Eve herself, Michael realized, maybe twenty-five—launched herself off the couch and ran to throw herself into her husband's arms.

"Get out of here," Shane said, without taking his eyes from what was happening with Eve. Michael didn't spare the two a glance as they left, either, rushing upstairs to what was probably the kids' room, bunkering down their family as best they could.

The living room was profoundly silent after that, and Michael's vampire senses—on high alert—heard every click of the clock on the wall, the low hum of electronics, the heartbeats of his friends, the subtle whisper of their breathing.

"Sit," Rozhkov said again, staring up at Eve.

She did.

Michael shivered from the barely controllable impulse to rush forward. He felt the displacement of air like needles on his skin as Shane stepped off to his left, out of the way, ready to make a move when needed. He felt immersed in his senses in a way he rarely did, an entirely vampiric dimension of the world that *hurt*; it pressed on him in so many intimate ways.

"You know," Rozhkov said—not to Eve, but suddenly to Michael, driving it home with a shift of his focus—"you would not feel so discomforted if you didn't keep the world pushed so far away. You fight what you are, and it makes you weak, Michael. We all know that. All except you, perhaps." He laughed a little. It sounded sad, but it had the flash of fangs behind it. Rozhkov was disconcertingly contradictory. He shifted back to Eve. He hadn't tried to touch her, which was good; Michael wasn't at all sure he could hold back if that happened. "Your great-grandmother, we were speaking of her. Ulyana. I knew her."

"You kidnapped a lady and threatened to kill her so you could ramble on about old dead people?" Eve asked. "Get help."

Rozhkov's faint smile disappeared, and there was something about his face that seemed like all the life had drained out of it—a corpse's face, except for the living fire in his blue eyes. "Careful," he whispered. "Your blood only takes you so far."

Eve had a finely tuned sense of danger, thankfully, and she shut up and went still. Michael met her gaze and held it steady. *I've got you*, he told her. *You're safe.*

Her faint smile said, *I know.*

"What do you mean, her blood?" Claire had been very quiet, but now she spoke up, and Michael sensed her moving forward on his right. "What do you want with Eve? Or rather, *from* Eve?"

"Clever girl," Rozhkov said. "I'd heard as much about you. It's gratifying to know that gossip can convey truth, occasionally. I'd heard much of the four of you. It seems it's all true."

"Answer the question," Shane said.

Rozhkov made a motion that wasn't quite a shrug, wasn't quite a headshake. It was something that came from some earlier time, and a distant land, and it had the feeling of disinterest to it. "There is power in some bloodlines; even you untutored children must know that. Power handed down, life to life, generation to generation. Yes?"

"I'm not some witch," Eve said. "I might wear the look, but—"

"Not witchcraft," he said. "But your blood holds a secret that you do not know, and cannot use. I can." He turned toward Eve, and Michael took a step forward, fists clenching in a sudden rush of dread and fury . . . but the other vampire only touched her hand very gently, with fingertips as pale as snow. Traced the blue lines of veins in her wrist. "Therefore I ask that you donate your blood to me."

"Wait, back up," Eve said. *"What?"*

"You give blood, as part of your taxes in Morganville, do you not?"

"Well . . . yeah . . ."

"Then I only ask you to give it to me."

Michael's urge to hit the man was only getting more pressing. Asking for Eve's blood was personal. *Way* too personal. In vampire terms, it was like sex, and he was doing it *in front of her vampire husband.* He knew Shane and Claire might not get the distinction, but he knew Eve did.

She pulled her hand back and folded it into a fist. "I'm spoken for, in case you hadn't gotten the memo."

Rozhkov studied her for a moment, then nodded and sat back. He seemed different now. Thoughtful. "I suppose I must tell you the truth, then," he said. "I am ill, you see. You may ask Glass if you wish confirmation of it."

Michael unwillingly nodded.

"It is an affliction that strikes old vampires, sometimes. We . . . begin to lose our essence, which is diluted by so much borrowed blood in our veins. We lose touch with who we were, and when that happens, we lose . . . too much. So from time to time, the oldest of us must find one who shares that blood with us, to remind us of who we are."

Claire, of course, worked it out first. "Wait. You mean you're *related* to Eve?"

"Distantly, through many, many generations," Rozhkov said. "Your great-grandmother Ulyana granted me this favor, once. I only need a single small amount from you. Just enough to reconstruct my own— what do you call it, the chains of life?"

"DNA," Claire said. "You need Eve's blood to fix your broken DNA?"

"I suppose that is as good an explanation as any," he said. "So yes. I could take it by force, of course, but I would prefer not. You are, after all, family."

Eve stared at him, a frown deepening between her brows. "Family," she repeated. "Yeah, that's rich. I kind of loathed my family, you know."

"All families are full of good and bad. But I ask you, for blood's sake, to do me this favor. This honor." He met Michael's eyes once more. "I ask that it be allowed, just once. I take no more than a taste."

"It's Eve's decision," Michael said. He wanted to make it for her, but he knew how she'd take that, and he also knew, deep down, that she'd be right to be angry. "Ask her, not me."

"I have," Rozhkov said. He returned that unsettling stare to Eve's face.

She didn't meet it. She was looking down at her hands. "I don't know you," she said. "All I know is that you're desperate enough, or cruel enough, that you'd threaten the life of an innocent person just to get my attention. If it's desperation, then maybe I should do this, or you'll do worse. If it's the other thing . . ."

"I *am* cruel," Rozhkov admitted. "I am old. Not as old or as powerful as Amelie is, true, but I know the world in old ways." He gave her a sudden, strangely sweet smile. "One would also say I have learned this *new* world, because I did not resort to violence."

"Yet," Shane said.

"Yet, yes." Rozhkov's gaze remained steady on Eve. "I do not beg. If you tell me no, I will go. Perhaps I will sicken. Perhaps I will do terrible things as my senses twist in on me. I do not know, as I have never let my—debility grow so strong. But is your decision, as Michael said."

Eve's shoulders rose and fell in a shrug. "Hell." She suddenly lifted her wrist and held it out to him, and her eyes squeezed tightly shut in anticipation. Her whole body was clenched, rebelling against the decision, and Michael knew he looked just the same—*felt* just the same. He wanted, with every cell of his being, to pull her away from Rozhkov, get her safe from him . . . and it took every single ounce of will he possessed to hold still as the other vampire raised Eve's arm, then parted his lips, and the fangs came out.

"Mike?" Shane's voice was sharp with tension, and his friend was practically vibrating with eagerness to get into it. Claire was quiet, but she was looking at him, too, from the other side. If he lost it, they'd go with him.

It's Eve's decision. Eve's decision. The mantra beat in his temples like a hammer, loud and just as painful, and he almost lost control as he saw the pain sheet across her expression as Rozhkov bit down. *No no no no no . . .*

And then it was over. He was true to his word. A single quiet mouthful, and then Rozhkov pressed a pale hand over the wound, sealing it. Eve pulled free and clamped her own hand over the bite mark. It wouldn't bleed much, Michael knew. Part of the vampire's bite was a healing agent that flooded the wound as the fangs withdrew. He smelled the blood, but not for long.

Rozhkov closed his blue eyes and slumped against the cushions of the sofa. The relief on his face was as intense as suffering. "Thank you, *devushka*. I am in your debt. In return, I will make you a promise. Never will I threaten you or those near you again. And should you need me, you may call upon me for a favor, yes?"

He got up and walked toward the door, but Shane stood in his way. From the hard set of his face and ready stance, he was still ready to fight if he had to.

"Shane," Eve said faintly. "Let him go."

Michael nodded. Shane didn't like it, but he backed off.

"An excellent decision," Rozhkov said, as he walked down the hall—silent on the hardwood floor. "One must trust family."

Michael felt the other vampire's presence fade into the night outside, and let himself finally relax. "What do you know? We didn't have to fight anybody," he said. "Interesting."

"I'm just a little bit disappointed," Shane said, and made a space of about an inch between two fingers. Claire walked over to him and compressed the space to a minuscule amount. "Okay. Maybe not so much."

As Shane put his arm around his girl, Michael went to Eve and extended her a hand. She looked up at him, then let him pull her to her feet and into a hug.

"Did I do the right thing?" she whispered to him. The heat of her breath, her body, was like summer against him, a whole beautiful season made manifest.

"I don't know," he said. "I hope so."

He kissed her, and the kiss held, sweetened, and when their lips gently parted, she said, "So. Now you've met my family. What do you think?"

He laughed. "I think everybody's got embarrassing crazy uncles, *devushka*."

"What does that even mean?"

"No idea." He dropped his voice to an intimate whisper against her ear. "But it sounds as sexy as you."

"Shhh!" She was blushing under the Goth makeup now, and he felt the heat curl up from her skin in invisible, sweet tendrils. "Somebody should tell the Lockharts that they're safe. And we should, ah, go home. Right?"

He liked the plan.

In the coming days, they forgot about Rozhkov; he didn't return, didn't so much as show up in the distance, and whatever he was doing seemed far away and very much not their problem. Eve's wrist healed without even a hint of a scar. Life went on, turbulent and calm in spurts.

Michael had never slept soundly since becoming a vampire—too aware of the world around him—but he'd learned to lie still and savor the warmth of Eve next to him as she murmured and dreamed. It was a kind of comfort and peace that he'd never really understood, until he had it.

So he was instantly aware when it started to change.

The first time, it was minor; Eve stirred, murmured something, and sat up in bed. He sat up, too, thinking she'd heard something, but her heartbeat was the same slow, steady rhythm, and though her eyes were open, they were dark and sightless, staring into dreams.

"Eve?" he asked her. She didn't respond. He watched her, worried, but after a long few seconds, she drifted back down to the pillow, rolled on her side, and was instantly still and quiet again, still breathing softly and regularly.

She'd never woken up.

The next night, she got out of bed. She didn't walk; she just stood, staring at the wall blankly, and then, with the slowness of dreams, climbed back into bed and snuggled up tight against him. He folded his arms tight around her, holding her safe. The next morning he asked if she knew she'd gotten up; she didn't remember.

"Guess I'm a sleepwalker," she said, and flashed him a carefree smile.

He smiled back, but didn't feel it. It worried him. Eve had always been a sound, peaceful sleeper before—and the blank distance in her when she'd risen had seemed wrong. Very wrong.

The next night, she rose and walked to the window. She tried to open it, but the latch was stiff with age, and after a few tries, she came back to bed.

Michael got up and went to look outside. He saw a dark shape in the shadows by the trees in the yard, but it was gone before he could even begin to identify who it was.

The next night, Eve tried to kill him.

She rose at three in the morning, wandered toward the bedroom door, and went out into the hallway. If she fell down the stairs . . . He followed after her, hovering and unsure whether he ought to try to wake her up, and as she turned, he realized she was holding the silver knife she kept under the bed. Her movements up to that point had been slow and dreamy, but the knife slashed at him with deadly purpose and speed, though the blank, black distance in her eyes never changed.

If he hadn't been gifted with vampire speed, he would have been gutted. He closed with her after avoiding the slash, gripped her hand, and took the knife away. "Eve? *Eve!*" He shook her, hard, but she didn't wake up. She didn't resist.

When he let go, she drifted back into the bedroom, got in bed, and went promptly back to sleep, leaving him with the cold knife in his hand.

God.

Something was wrong. Very, very wrong. And the next morning, she remembered none of it. What if she'd gone to Claire's room? Or Shane's? What would she have done?

He had to find out. Quickly.

———

Amelie refused to see him. She was, according to her assistant, very busy, and unavailable for the foreseeable future. Michael had the strong, and unsettling, feeling that she'd put him on the no-admittance list to emphasize how deeply angry she still was about his refusal to push Eve away. She'd allowed the wedding, but that didn't mean she was pleased about it.

Oliver, on the other hand, was right where Michael expected to find him: behind the bar at Common Grounds, pulling espresso shots for an impatient, texting college student who obviously had not the slightest idea he was disrespecting one of the oldest, most dangerous vampires in the world. Oliver appeared to shrug it off, but there was a chill light in his eyes that made Michael wonder about that student's future longevity.

Michael put a five-dollar bill on the counter, ordered a drink— the vampire standard, Red Bull and blood—and as Oliver mixed it and capped it, he said, "Rozhkov."

There was just the slightest hesitation in Oliver's smooth, practiced movements, but it was enough to let Michael know he'd hit the jackpot. Oliver put the cup on the counter between them and said, "In my office. Terrell, take the wheel." He stripped off his tie-dyed Common Grounds barista apron and hung it on a peg as he flipped up the passthrough on the bar.

Oliver's office was dark—just enough low light to be comfortable for vampires, not enough for humans to make out details. Michael sat in the guest chair as Oliver took the desk side; it was just a plain task chair, nothing special, yet Oliver always made it seem like a throne. He had the presence of a ruler. Like Amelie.

"Rozhkov," Michael repeated. "Tell me about him."

"What business is it of yours?"

"It's not. It's Eve's."

Oliver sat back, eyelids coming down to hood his gaze; he steepled his fingers together and was quiet for a moment before he said, "Tell me why."

"Eve's sleepwalking. Last night, she did it with a knife. Rozhkov took blood from her, and I think he's doing this."

"Why in God's holy name did you allow that to happen, Michael?"

"I didn't *allow* anything," Michael said. "Eve did. He said he was family, and he was sick, and she could help."

"Family." Oliver's voice sounded heavy on the word. He fell silent again, gaze gone far into the past, and then finally blinked and straightened again to put his hands flat on the desk. "Yes. I thought we'd restrained him better than this."

"You—knew about this?"

"Not about Eve. Rozhkov has a certain—mental instability. He believes that if he eliminates all human members of his family, he will become the most powerful vampire on earth. It's not true, of course. It's nonsense. But he believes it. He's been hunting down and destroying his family for generations."

"You could have warned us about him!"

"Why would I?" Oliver's look at him was irritated and impatient. "She is no more related to him than she is to me. Rozhkov killed his bloodline off long, long ago. But since his prophecy of great power failed to come true, he conceives these notions—delusions. If I'd known he had fixed himself on Eve, I would have warned you."

"You said you thought you'd restrained him. What did you mean by that? He was walking around free."

"He's under the care of Dr. Goldman, who gives him drugs to lessen his abilities. You might have noticed that he seems . . . different."

"I thought he was sick. He was drugged?"

"It should have been enough to free him from his delusions. Evidently not. How far has it gone?"

"She's been sleepwalking. Last night, she almost stabbed me."

Oliver looked away, drumming his fingers on the desk. "Then he has her," he said. "She's in his power. There's no breaking that, Michael. It's how he destroys—not by his own hand, but by taking control of his victims. He's destroyed many families this way—silently, in the night, without bloodying his hands."

Michael swallowed, though his mouth and throat felt dry and clenched with aching thirst. "How do we stop him?"

"How do you think?" Oliver shook his head. "No human platitudes, boy. This is vampire business. We've tried the soft approach to him; it's time for the sword. Rozhkov is a threat to your wife. If you want to protect her, it's your right to face him."

Oliver's look was long and measuring; he wanted to know, Michael realized, that he'd step up. That he *could* step up. "Do I really have to prove myself to you? Again?"

"No," Oliver said, and leaned forward to busy himself with a folder of paperwork on his desk. "You see, I know very well that you loathe being a vampire, in your heart. You cope well enough; you let very few of us see your conflict. But in this particular case, you have to prove your convictions to yourself, or stand aside, because what you are fighting for is a great deal more than your childish feelings. Now leave."

"Not until you tell me where to find him."

"Are you ordering me?" The question was calm and a little amused, but Michael wasn't fooled. There was steel underneath it. Steel with a sharp, sharp edge.

"Yes," he said, and slapped his palms on the desk to lean into Oliver's space. "I am." He felt that warm tingle in his eyes, and knew they were flushing bright, threatening red.

"Better," Oliver said, unperturbed. "Save your aggression for the one who needs it. You may find him at his shop in Founder's Square."

"He has a *store*?"

"Did you think he simply haunted graveyards? He owns a shop that sells flavored teas. He won't be at the counter; he is not as . . . hands-on as I. But he will be in the rooms above." Oliver flipped a hand at him. "Go."

Michael did, pushing his anxiety and fury back until his eyes were blue and normal, and he could force a smile for the people outside in the coffee shop.

Then he went to find Rozhkov.

The tea shop was something he'd never paid any attention to before. It was closet-sized, just big enough to serve two or three at a time. Shelves of dusty jars of product, and a very bored woman behind the counter who barely looked up from her copy of *Romantic Times* when he came in. The clean, flowery scent of the teas was overwhelming. Then she came back for a second look, folded the magazine, and brightened up. "Oh, hello," she said. "How can I help you? We have a special on Earl Grey and some of the Tazo flavors. I can brew you up samples, too."

He didn't have the heart to go full vampire on her; she seemed so happy to see a customer. "How about"—he picked one at random— "Blueberry Bliss Rooibos?" He had no idea what it was, but it sounded like something Eve would like.

"Sure!" she said brightly, and grabbed one of the dustier glass jars. "I'll just make you up a cup to taste. Wait right here."

She went through a beaded curtain to the back, and Michael quickly scanned the shop again. *The rooms upstairs*, Oliver had said.

He took hold of the shelves on the right, and pulled. They swung out. Behind them was a door—locked, but he snapped it easily enough and pushed it open. There was a handle on the shelf from the other side, and he pulled it to behind him as he entered.

Stairs. It was utterly dark, but he could make out silvery outlines, enough to find his way. Michael took them quickly, knowing that Rozhkov would have heard the lock breaking, and was at the top in only a second.

It was still long enough for Rozhkov to be ready.

Michael ducked the swing of a sword that would have easily decapitated him, and lunged forward, connecting hard with the bony, sinewy body of the other vampire. It would have overwhelmed a human, broken bones, but it hardly rocked Rozhkov back a few steps, and he kept his balance to drive a fist hard into Michael's chest. It pushed Michael back, and he swayed back to avoid the next slash of steel.

Rozhkov looked strong, and cocky, and he gave Michael a broad, fanged grin. "Boy," he said. "How long have you been in our life? You're hardly more than an infant to me. Give up. I don't need your life."

"You don't need Eve's."

"Ah, but I do. It's destiny. She was drawn to me."

"You came to *us.*"

Rozhkov shrugged. Logic didn't matter, of course. "Her blood is true, and when she dies, I will take her energy. It is how I live. How I grow greater."

"You're insane," Michael said. "Last chance. If you let Eve go, we can end this peacefully."

"Why in the world would I desire such a thing?" Rozhkov put the tip of the sword against Michael's throat. "*Peacefully.* You threaten me? You're nothing. Nothing but a whisper in the dark."

"No," Michael said. "I'm the dark."

He let go.

The thing he hadn't said to Oliver, the thing he hadn't said to anyone, was that the reason he fought his vampire nature so hard, the reason he loathed it so much, was that it was so incredibly *easy*. As easy as relaxing, and falling, and being . . . something else.

He grabbed the sword's edge, ignoring the pain of the cut, and twisted the weapon out of Rozhkov's hand, snapping the man's wrist with the crisp sound of breaking twigs. Part of him—the small, trapped human part—screamed for it to stop, but the vampire didn't listen. Rozhkov was prey. Rozhkov was enemy.

Michael tossed the sword into the air, grabbed it with two hands as it fell, and swung with all his might, aiming cleanly for the vulnerable, narrow throat.

It hardly gave any resistance at all.

Rozhkov was saying something, or trying to, when he died. Michael didn't bother to listen. He stared down at the man's face as it went still, then slack, and the malice in the eyes faded into nothing.

There wasn't that much blood, and what there was trickled out dark and thick.

Michael reached into the inside pocket of his jacket and took out a silver-coated stake that he'd swiped from Shane's stash, and buried it in Rozhkov's heart, just to be sure. Then he put the sword down and closed his eyes.

The dark was a storm inside him, a force like a whirlwind, stirred and excited by the violence. *Yes*, it said. *Yes, this is you. This is how you are. How it will be.*

He stood perfectly still, willing the darkness back into its carefully locked little box, forcing it with every ounce of what was left of his humanity. It was harder than ever before. So hard he was afraid that if he ever let it out again, no box would hold it.

That's not me, he told himself. *I'm not that. I can't be that.*

The terrifying thing was that he so, so easily could be. Oliver knew it. That was why Oliver had sent him, instead of doing it personally. It was the old vampire's way of teaching him a lesson.

Not this time, Michael thought.

But he couldn't really be sure about the next time. Not at all.

The whole thing seemed to take a lifetime, but when he went back downstairs, the little shop was still empty. As he pushed the shelf back in its place and heard it click closed, the beaded curtain rattled, and the shop clerk bustled out holding a steaming cup of tea.

"Here you go." She beamed, and held it out to him. "I think you'll just love it."

It tasted of ashes and blood and fear to him, but he bought two bags anyway.

That evening, Michael found Chief Moses standing on their porch. Behind her, twilight had fallen, and the sky was a rich dark blue, painted through with the fading orange of sunset. She was bathed in the yellow glow of the bug light. Her hat was off and tucked under her arm in a strangely official way.

"I have some news," she said.

"Bad news?" he asked her. She shrugged.

"Depends," Hannah said. "Can I come in?"

She was human; she didn't really need an invitation. He nodded and stepped back to let her cross the threshold. She sighed, as if this was something she *really* didn't want to do.

"Can you get Eve?" she asked him.

"Sure. Why?"

"Just get her, Michael."

He didn't need to; he heard the clump of her boots on the stairs, and knew she'd heard the knock. Claire and Shane were gone off on their own somewhere, so it was just the two of them in the house. Eve arrived breathless and flushed, still adjusting her top from where she'd pulled it on. "Oh, Hannah. Hey. What's up?"

Hannah nodded without any change in her poker-faced expression. "I need to show you a picture and see if you recognize the man in it." She didn't pause; the photo was on her phone, and she clicked it on and turned it to show it to both Eve and Michael.

It was Kiril Rozhkov.

"What's he done?" Eve asked. She sounded resigned.

"He went and got himself decapitated and staked," Hannah said. "From what I hear, not much loss from anybody."

"You think we had something to do with it?" Michael asked.

Hannah shook her head. "Nope, but in his coat pocket I found this." She reached into her own pocket and took out a plastic bag sealed with red tape. Inside was a photo of the two of them, the one that had been in the local paper announcing their marriage.

"I know what you're thinking, but it wasn't Shane," Eve said. "Or Claire."

"I know that, too. They're not the only ones in this town willing to stake a vampire now and again."

"Then who do you think did it?"

"Doesn't matter," Hannah said, still expressionless. "I'm not likely to get to arrest anyone."

She knew. Her gaze settled on Michael, and stayed, and he felt a momentary chill. "Well," he said. "I guess someone thought it had to be done."

That earned him a very small, tight smile. "Guess so. I had a word with Oliver. He says it's finished." Hannah returned the photo to her coat pocket, along with her phone, and nodded to them both. "Have a good day, you two."

She left without another word. Eve stood where she was, lips parted on questions she obviously couldn't quite voice, as Michael shut the door behind her.

"Are you all right?"

Eve stared at him for a few long seconds. "I guess," she said. "It's just—he said he was family."

He took her in his arms and kissed her, very gently, lips and forehead. "Family takes care of its own."

He stayed awake all night, haunted by the memory, the darkness, the violence, but she slept soundly cuddled against him.

And as dawn came, and he knew she was all right, he closed his eyes and slept with her, in the light.

AND ONE FOR THE DEVIL

☽

*Dedicated to Martha Jo Trostel for her support
for the Morganville digital series Kickstarter*

We end the collection with another brand-new look at Morganville, courtesy of Martha Jo, who wanted a story from Claire's point of view . . . and I just happened to have one lurking in the back of my mind. Claire and Myrnin (with bonus Eve) are always a dynamic combination for me; I love that his sometimes rash ideas balance out with her native caution. Mostly. This time, it isn't Myrnin putting Claire in danger so much as Claire being forced to figure out a puzzle he's put into motion, then been caught within.

If we've learned anything from our time in Morganville, it should definitely be *Don't go in the creepy building*, but then again, in Morganville . . . they're all creepy, to some extent. When you mix in Myrnin's proto-time-travel technology, anything is possible.

Fun factoid: I got the idea for this story because weird things sometimes happen when you're on a book tour. You get tired. You come in late at night. Often, there's no thirteenth floor in a hotel, but sometimes there is; sometimes there's a thirteenth floor but no room thirteen on that floor.

I had room number 1313 one evening, and then the next day at a new hotel, when I was also given a room on the thirteenth floor, my brain told me to look for 1313. It didn't exist. I was convinced that the room had disappeared, until I reasoned it out, but I didn't forget that out-of-body weirdness of looking for something that no longer existed.

When Myrnin was in one of these moods, it just didn't pay to argue with him.

Claire sat calmly in his wing chair, near the far back corner of his laboratory, while he whizzed around at vampire speeds, tinkering with this, muttering at that, flipping through ancient tomes and flinging them across the room when he didn't find what he was looking for. She'd asked him what he was doing. He'd given her a wild, distracted look, and she'd decided that maybe it was time to feed Bob the Spider some flies, and sit and read for a while.

She was two chapters into her book when she realized he was looming over her. Without looking up, she said, "You're in my light."

"Are you or are you not my assistant?" Myrnin demanded. "I can't find *anything* in here! What have you done, rearranged things? Again?"

"No, I haven't," she said, and put her bookmark in place before she closed the volume and looked up at him. Myrnin had a black smudge along one side of his cheek, and his hair was sticking up at odd angles, as if he'd rubbed grease into it and forgotten about it. "You move things, and you forget you move things, and if you'd tell me what it was you were looking for—"

"I'm looking for something that isn't here, or I wouldn't be in quite such a state, now, would I? Up. Up up up."

Claire rose and stepped aside, and her vampire boss flung himself into a boneless slouch in the chair, frowning at nothing. After a moment, he said, "It's warm."

"What?"

"The chair. It's warm."

"I was just sitting in it."

"Ah. I forget, that's a side effect for people with pulses."

"What are you looking for?" Sometimes, with Myrnin, the patient repetition of the question worked better than anything else.

Like this time, because he suddenly looked at her. His dark eyes widened, and his mouth formed a surprised O, and he bolted up out of his chair and hugged her. It was a vampire-speed hug, which meant that she didn't have time to object or respond before he was away, flashing toward a bookcase in the other part of the lab. He tossed out at least ten books, then found a slim volume and held it high. "Found it!"

"Could you please *not* leave books all over the floor?"

"Bother," he said, and came back to throw himself into the chair with great enthusiasm. "I haven't the time for that nonsense. Shelving, reshelving, picking up, cleaning . . . Everything tends to entropy and it's just fighting the inevitable. But please, by all means, pick those up."

"I will," Claire said. "What is that?"

"This?" He held up the book, and she read the faded title. It wasn't some ancient dusty Latin thing, which was what he was most fond of collecting; this was printed in the 1960s, by the weird type style and strangely quaint illustration. The title was *A Traveler's Guide to Haunted Places*.

"Seriously?"

"Oh, I am dead serious. Well, dead and serious, you understand. I stored some things many years ago at a place I built, and I need them back. What time is it?"

"Time . . ." She pulled her phone and glanced at it. "Um, almost midnight. Why?"

"Because we'll need to get there before sunrise," Myrnin said. "Most important."

That made zero sense, because Myrnin was fully capable of going out in the daylight when he wanted to, vampire or not. He was old, older than Morganville's resident vampire queen, Amelie; that gave him a certain invulnerability to sunlight that younger undead didn't have. Besides, a coat and hat usually did fine for protection.

"Where are we going, exactly?"

"The Morganville Traveler's Rest," he said. "Come along, then. Bring everything."

Claire rolled her eyes and texted her husband—*husband*; she loved thinking that so much—Shane, to let him know where she was going. It was an established thing, when Myrnin was in his crazycakes moods. Just insurance. Not so much that she thought he'd hurt her; they were long past that kind of fear. More that he'd forget and abandon her someplace. That happened *way* too much.

Shane texted back that he wished she were coming home. She wished she were, too. But sending Myrnin off unescorted seemed like a bad plan. He was in a manic phase, and that almost never went well . . . but she could keep him from doing something really crazy.

Hopefully.

Take everything. Right.

Claire grabbed what she thought she might need, bundled it into a bag older than she was, and followed Myrnin out into the night.

She had no idea where the Morganville Traveler's Rest might be; she'd never heard of it, and Morganville, Texas, wasn't that big of a town. So she wasn't too surprised to find that it was one of the many dilapidated, shuttered buildings around town . . . the crumbling ruins of places that weren't worth keeping up or renovating. Home of rats, cockroaches, and vampires too derelict or damaged to play by Amelie's rules of good behavior. Or those who just enjoyed a good scary place to haunt.

It was definitely scary. Definitely. Morganville's nights were clear and cold, and though she'd wrapped up in a thick jacket and a scarf and gloves, her breath fogged white as she struggled to keep up with Myrnin. He wasn't vampire-speeding away from her, at least; he was clearly impatient, but keeping more or less to a human pace.

A fast human pace.

"Slow down!" she finally gasped. He didn't slow; he stopped, and then he turned and looked back at her, sighed, and came to take the heavy bag from her.

"Better?" he asked.

"Not if you keep acting like it's a race!"

"Well, it is, a bit," he said. "I would have asked you to drive me, but you seem to have such trouble with the windshield."

"It's a vampire tinted windshield, Myrnin."

"Just as I said. Ah, good. This way."

They were at the corner of Oh-Hell-No and You're-Gonna-Die, as Eve would have put it, and *this way* looked like it was definitely worse. The silver wash of moonlight on sagging wood and leaning buildings turned it all into a Gothic nightmare, and except for the occasional streetlight, there wasn't any sign of life here. Old, old buildings, mostly built of brick with concrete ornaments on them. There was one across the street that looked like it had once been a hotel, six or seven generations back; above the boarded-up door, a gruesome-looking gargoyle leaned down. Up near the top, letters in the concrete read EST. 1895.

Definitely not the place Claire wanted to be urban exploring at this time of night. Or, actually, at all, ever, the end, but what was worse than urban exploring at this time of night was that Myrnin might actually leave her *alone* doing it.

She hurried after him when he darted for the EST. 1895 building. The front door was boarded over, but the plywood hadn't weathered the tough Morganville sunshine and heat too well, and besides, vampire strength was enough to rip even sturdy plywood like tissue paper. All Claire needed to do was stand back—well back, because sometimes Myrnin forgot where he was throwing stuff, and that didn't end well. The shredded board skidded past her, out into the street, where she doubted anyone would be running over it for a couple of days, at least. Still, she trudged over, grabbed the wood (it was surprisingly heavy), and towed it back onto the sidewalk.

Myrnin had already shoved open the door, which leaned on rusty hinges like a drunk. Beyond, it looked scary-black, but Claire sighed and turned on her very bright little LED flashlight. She never left home without it, for precisely this kind of reason. It lit up an ancient hallway, a ceiling that looked bulging and precarious from some leak long ago, and wallpaper that she couldn't imagine had ever been pretty. There was a front desk up ahead, which had survived fairly well, and a honeycomb of wooden boxes behind it, most with dusty keys still in them. *Lots of vacancies,* she thought, and shuddered. She imagined most of them weren't vacant at all. It was every horror movie Eve had ever forced her to watch, come to life.

Myrnin leaned over the dusty counter and grabbed a key from a box, then hurried up the sagging, none-too-safe-looking stairs. Claire tried to see which key he'd grabbed, in case he (inevitably) left her behind.

Number thirteen. Of course.

She went up after him. Carefully. The safest part of the step was at the edges, so she went slowly, testing each for her weight and holding to the rickety banister in case something gave way. Nothing did, surprisingly. At the landing, she saw a sign in old-timey block lettering that pointed to her right for rooms one through ten, and left for eleven through twenty.

When she turned left, Myrnin was standing there, waiting for her. He snapped his fingers in that restless, manic way he sometimes got, and said, "Hurry, hurry, the moon will be down soon. Come on, Claire!"

He stalked off down the dark hall, and she lit it up with her flash, for safety. Good thing she did, because a grandfather clock had tipped over at some point, and lay flat across the path like a dead body. Myrnin had skipped right over it, but she had to be more careful.

"Ah!" Myrnin sounded gratified, and when Claire looked up, she saw him standing in front of a doorway. Number thirteen. "And one for the devil. Good. We're in time."

"In time for *what?*"

"I told you, the moon will be down soon." He inserted the key and turned it carefully; the lock gave a groaning, rusty scrape, but the door swung open with a horror-movie creak. "Hurry, please. Speed is safety."

That sounded . . . ominous. He was gone in the next second into the room, and she had to make a decision. Fast.

She stepped into the room.

It was, slightly to her disappointment, just an old, dilapidated hotel room, with a leaning bed on a rusty metal frame, one of those funny wooden wardrobes people used to use for their clothes instead of a closet, and a wooden stand with a cracked bowl and jug on it. Turn-of-the-century equivalent of running water, she guessed. It looked . . . depressing.

The glass was still intact in the window, and through it, she could see the moon glowing on the horizon. It was just touching the flat desert landscape, casting an icy blue glow into the room. Bright, though. Bright enough to see without the flashlight, so she clicked it off.

Myrnin opened up the old wooden wardrobe.

"What did you mean?" Claire asked him. "You said, *And one for the devil.* What does that mean?"

"Old expression," he said. "Sometimes people would spill a drop of their wine and say it—one for the devil—so he'd not be angry at being cheated out of his due. But have you ever noticed that hotels of this age never have a room thirteen?"

"I know sometimes hotels skip the *floor* thirteen," she said. "Because it's unlucky, right?"

"Oh no, not at all. It's the devil's number, thirteen, and a number of great power from an alchemical point of view, which is not at all the same thing, whatever the churches may say. Ah! Perfect." He rummaged in the cabinet, throwing out decaying old boxes, one of which held something that scuttled. Claire switched on her flashlight, and recognized the shiny black shell of the spider that hurried across the floor. That wasn't Bob or his friendly cousin the house spider; that was the sleek Porsche edition of spiders: a black widow.

Claire took a couple of steps back to let it hurry past to the shadows in peace. Black widows weren't attackers, generally, but you still didn't want to piss one off. Myrnin kept searching the closet. There must have been a lot in there, because she heard him opening chests and slamming them shut again, tearing open boxes, muttering to himself.

The room was getting darker. She was glad she had the flashlight.

"Claire?" Myrnin's voice came muffled from the closet. "Check the moon. Is it still up?"

That seemed like a nonsensical question, but she edged toward the window and looked out again. The moon seemed to be shivering on the horizon now, as if it were clinging to the thin edge. Just a sliver of it remaining now. Sunset—and moonset, Claire guessed—came fast out here on the dusty prairie. "Not much of it," she said. "Wait—there it goes."

Suddenly, Myrnin was beside her, staring out the old, warped glass. "Damn," he said. "He's coming." He was holding a thing in his hand, but she couldn't tell what it was, other than large and metallic. He dropped it to the floor with a heavy crash (and she hoped it wouldn't break right through), and before Claire could draw breath, he grabbed the sash of the window and yanked it upward.

It shouldn't have opened at all, because it probably hadn't for close to a hundred years, but vampire strength forced it up with a rending shriek. Glass broke. "What are you—?" Claire started to ask, but broke off into a startled cry when Myrnin grabbed her by the arms, and swung her *out the window.*

She had time to register that she was dangling out in the cold, sharp air, with stars turning overhead, and that Myrnin had leaned far, far out the window, holding her hands.

"Pull me in!" she yelled.

He shook his head, and said, "I need to get you out of here. It isn't safe." His face looked grim and as serious as she'd ever seen him.

Then she felt his strong, chilly fingers release hers, and she was falling.

It was a long fall, and she hit hard and rolled. She'd landed on a rotting sofa abandoned on the sidewalk, which explained why she hadn't broken bones, but the bounce to the street's harder surface left plenty of bruises.

Myrnin hadn't followed her down.

Claire rose to her feet, shaky and disoriented, and stared up at the window. Myrnin was still up there, but he'd pulled himself back into the window. "What are you doing?" she yelled up at him, and heard the angry, unsteady edge to her voice to match the pump of adrenaline through her veins. "Are you *crazy*?"

"Well, yes," he said. "Get me out before he—"

He never finished the sentence, because the window in front of him warped *in*, toward him. No, not just the window—a whole vertical piece of the building sucked inward, about ten feet of it.

And then it was gone. The window, the ten-foot column of brick building—all *gone*. But it wasn't as if there were damage or a bomb or something.

A part of the building had sucked in on itself and vanished without a trace, without a seam, as if it had never been there at all.

Claire stood staring upward for a long moment, then dashed for the open front door. She pounded up the rickety stairs, not concerned anymore for the condition of the steps, and turned left. *Room eleven. Room twelve.*

Room fourteen.

Claire stopped in her tracks, breathing hard, and slowly backed up.

Room twelve.

Room fourteen, right next to it.

There was no room thirteen.

Not anymore.

It had vanished into thin air, and it had taken Myrnin with it.

"That's . . ." Eve's dark-rimmed eyes were wide, and she sat very still on her chair, hunched over her cup of coffee. They were sitting together in Common Grounds, at way-too-early o'clock. Eve had the morning shift, and though she'd opened the shop, there was nobody here yet. Just Eve, and her morning cup. "That's just crazy."

And Claire, with her problem. "I know," she said. "I spent hours in that hotel, looking all over the place. It only has twenty rooms. Number thirteen is just . . . missing."

"So it has to do with moonlight? As in, it's only there when the moon shines? That's beyond regular crazy, girl. That's restraining-order, straitjackets, and men-in-white-coats crazy."

"I know! Believe me, I know. But I was *in* that room, Eve. I was there. I saw it. Myrnin . . . saved me, I guess. But he's trapped in there, and I need to get him out."

"Um, so . . . moonrise? Or just a really nice spotlight with . . . a moon bulb, I guess? Look, what's the harm? He's a vamp. A day hanging out in a hotel room won't exactly kill him, right?"

"Right," Claire said, but she was unconvinced. Eve had made her a mocha, and she sipped at it but didn't taste a thing. Her brain was still racing faster than her senses. "But he seemed scared, Eve. I don't think it was just a matter of waiting around. There's something else. Myrnin said *he* was coming."

"He? What the hell does that mean?"

"I don't know," Claire admitted. "I only know that he was worried enough to throw me out of a second-floor window to get me away from *him*, whoever that is."

With a sudden chill, Claire remembered Myrnin saying, *And one for the devil.* He couldn't mean the literal devil, though, horns and tails, pitchfork and all . . . could he?

She honestly didn't know, with her crazy vamp boss. But she did know that he was scared. And Myrnin didn't frighten easily. He'd taken a vanishing thirteenth room in stride, but it was what was *inside* the room that frightened him.

Or what was inside the room when the moon wasn't there.

It made her head hurt. She compensated by drinking the rest of the mocha in gulps, and asking Eve, "Where's Oliver?"

"In his hidey-hole," Eve said. "Doing ninja accounting, I guess. I don't ask. Why? Are you going to seriously ask him for help?"

"Who else can I ask? Amelie?" Claire shook her head. "I need backup."

"What am I, *chica*? I've got skills. Mad ones, even."

"Fair point, but neither one of us have, you know, *vampire* skills. And I'm pretty sure that would come in handy at some point, seeing as we're not dealing with a human problem, exactly."

"It's a Myrnin problem, not a vampire problem. I think they're just as badly equipped as we are, sweetie." Eve patted her hand and bounced out of her chair. In fact, she kept bouncing up and down on the balls of her feet, which was a neat trick in those heavy black boots. "You said it had something to do with alchemy, right? Well, you're the resident Morganville alchemy scholar. So *you* are our secret weapon. See?"

"No," Claire said. "I don't. I mean . . . yes, I probably know more about alchemy than anybody else here except Myrnin, but . . ."

"But what? Suit up, Alchemy Girl. We're going to hero."

"I really don't think this is a good idea," Claire said. Eve stopped bouncing and looked at her with a long, level stare, until she finally sighed and said, "But we're going to do it anyway."

"Yes." Eve held up a fist to be bumped. "Yes, we are."

First stop was, of course, Myrnin's lab, because it was the place Myrnin kept . . . things. Claire didn't honestly know what some of them were, but she had a good enough guess at a few, and she could decipher his scribbles well enough to infer the rest. Eve took one look at the place, shuddered, and said, "I'm fine here, thanks. I'd rather not explore the fun house of horrors."

"I'd have thought the fun house of horrors would be your kind of scene," Claire said, but she left Eve sitting on the steps that led down to the lab proper, and started making her way over and around the piles of debris that always seemed to collect around Myrnin. She was looking for something in particular. Myrnin had a system; she'd finally recognized what it was, and it had less to do with the placement of things than groupings of them. He mounded things together into more or less coherent subjects; once he started moving them around, he moved the piles, not just single items.

So she was looking for the pile that had to do with the alchemical influence of the moon. It was a big subject, because the idea that the moon's light held very different properties from sunlight was central to a lot of alchemical theory; things that worked in the sun didn't always work in the moon, and vice versa. She personally thought it was a load of nonsense, but Myrnin liked to keep an open mind, and after seeing the magically disappearing room thirteen, she was prepared to cautiously admit that maybe he was on to something.

The mound of things loosely grouped together under the general heading of *moon* was staggering. She started combing through the books and setting aside what might come in handy, but what she was really looking for was a particular gadget that Myrnin had shown her, once upon a time. As with most things he invented, she doubted she'd gotten the full story of what it did, but it had *sounded* like the alchemical equivalent of an ALS, an alternative light source.

It looked like a cross between a flamethrower (because of the giant backpack) and a flashlight (connected to the backpack with a flexible copper tube), as imagined by someone with lots of steampunk flair. Claire found it under the table, in a box marked DEADLY AND FRAGILE, which didn't bode all that well, but she was pretty sure that the box belonged to something else entirely anyway.

"Really?" Eve said from the stairs. "You're joining the Ghostbusters now? Because that looks like a movie prop."

Claire avoided the obvious *Who you gonna call?* joke—too easy—and slid the leather straps over her shoulders. It was heavy, this thing, but it balanced okay. The flashlight-ish part had a simple on/off switch, and she took a deep breath, pointed the light at a dark corner of the lab wall, and switched it on.

A pale blue-white glow bathed the lab's textured stone. It didn't look much different from moonlight.

"Got it," she called to Eve, and grabbed up a random assortment of other things that might come in handy, too—weapons, mainly. Myrnin had a lot of weapons lying around, everything from modern guns to ancient clubs. All that went into a black nylon bag with a sports logo; she doubted Myrnin even knew the brand, but he probably liked that the name came from Greek.

"I'll take that," Eve said, and grabbed the bag. "Anything else? Do you have to feed the spider or anything?"

"Bob's fine—Myrnin fed him yesterday," Claire said. "And I didn't think you liked spiders."

"Ugh, I don't. But he's weirdly cute, I guess. For a spider. Whatever, this place is creeping me out."

"Wait until you see where we're going," Claire said. "Maybe we should call Michael?"

"Michael's teaching today. What about Shane?"

"He opened the restaurant for the day, and he's kind of, you know, in charge."

"Heavy lies the assistant manager crown. Okay, then, it's girl power all the way." Eve grinned, and bounced on her toes again. "Lead the way, Ghostbuster. I'm ready."

"You're really not," Claire said, "but here goes."

Eve had grown up in Morganville, and left it only once in her entire life, and even *she* didn't come to this area of town. "I thought they'd torn it down," she said, as she pulled her big black hearse to a stop about a block

from the hotel. That was as close as she could get, given the stuff litter-
ing the street ahead . . . trash, but also boards with rusty nails sticking up
and broken bricks. It looked like the aftermath of a riot, but it could just
as easily have been the last big storm that had swept through, about the
time the water-vampire draug had attacked the town. Morganville wasn't
real big on civic services. Or civic pride, in these parts of town.

"They should," Claire said. "But maybe the vampires don't want it
torn down."

"Prime lurking territory," Eve said. "Can't imagine they get a lot
of wandering victims, though. Even meth cookers go more upscale
than this."

Claire had to agree with that. There was a totally creepy vibe to
this place, and suddenly she wished she'd called Shane, or Michael,
even though they had work to do of their own. *This is my job*, she told
herself, and put the steampunk moonlight on her back while Eve gathered up the weapons. Eve added a shotgun from the back—probably
Shane's—and locked up the car. Claire looked around. In the daylight,
she'd have expected this place to seem more sad than scary, but nope.
Still scary. The shadows were too dark in the bright sunlight, and with
the warming wind hissing sand through the streets, it seemed like an
alien, empty world.

"Which one?" Eve asked. She didn't sound worried; she sounded
steady, and Claire needed that just now.

"The hotel," Claire said.

"With the creepy gargoyle? Awesome. Take point, fearless leader.
I've got your back."

Eve might sometimes seem fragile, but she wasn't; growing up in
Morganville either broke people or gave them a core of strength that
wouldn't bend. Eve was solid steel where it counted, and having her
on hand made Claire feel steadier, sharper, *ready*.

She adjusted the dragging weight of the—moonlight?—and led

the way through the still-open door, down the molding hallway, to the silent, dusty check-in desk. The key for thirteen was still missing. She supposed that Myrnin had held on to it. *Could be a problem*, she thought, and went behind the counter to rummage around in the drawers. Carefully, of course; she was mindful of the shiny black widow spider that Myrnin had discovered upstairs. There were decades of dead insects in the drawers, but under a desiccated old beetle, she found a ring of keys.

The master set for the rooms.

"So," Eve said, in an appropriately quiet voice for the venue, "just how scary is this going to be?"

"Well, how do you feel about disappearing rooms with vampires trapped inside?"

"When you put it that way, it *is* a moot point," Eve said. "Right. Let's do this. Oliver said I could have the morning off, but it's already nearly ten. If I'm not back on the clock at noon, he'll want blood. I mean, literal, actual blood."

Claire nodded and went up the stairs. She remembered running them before, but that seemed desperately unwise again, because they really were pretty rickety from dry rot and just plain old time. Nothing gave way, but the groaning was horror-movie loud.

The landing was just as she'd left it . . . silent, forbidding, and dark. Claire turned down the hall and switched on the special moon-flashlight. It cast an eerie bluish glow onto the wallpaper, and the wallpaper seemed to . . . crawl. For a shocked instant she thought she'd surprised bugs, but no, that was just the wallpaper moving, all on its own.

This place was definitely not what it seemed.

"Stay close," she said to Eve. Eve was staring hard at the crawling wallpaper, too.

"Not a problem, sister," Eve said. "I plan to be so close we might have to get married. Seriously, does the creepy ever stop in this town?"

Claire didn't answer that, because she honestly had no idea. She concentrated on running the light slowly over the door to Room Eleven. It looked dusty and normal. The wallpaper crawled like ants between that door and the next, but again, Room Twelve looked sane.

The wallpaper didn't just crawl after that; it pulsed and heaved and pushed, and as she passed the light over the center section, a door appeared. It shoved up *out* of the wallpaper, first in a thin line, then expanding like something drifting up out of black water. A closed door, with the number thirteen in tarnished brass on it.

Claire reached out and touched it. Cool, painted wood. She ran her fingers across and onto the wallpaper. Different texture.

Just as an experiment, she moved her hand back to the door, pressed it flat, and switched the cold blue light off. Instantly, the texture changed from paint and wood to the brittle, dusty feel of wallpaper.

Eve made a little sound of distress as the dark closed in. Claire switched the light back on, and there was the door, impossible but present.

She fumbled with the keys, tried them one after another, and finally, one turned in the old, rusted lock.

The door swung open.

"Claire," Eve said. "You can't go in there. If you do, you can't keep the light on the door, and that means . . ."

"That means it seals up behind me," Claire said. "Yeah, I get it. So . . ."

"So that's me, volunteering," Eve said. She stepped up next to Claire and swallowed hard; the shotgun was in her hand. Not enough to stop most vampires, but enough to slow them way down and make them think twice. In terms of Morganville's vampire population, a shotgun was the equivalent of a Taser—nonlethal force, as long as it wasn't aimed at their face. "I go in first, right?"

"You can't," Claire said. "Step in front of me."

Eve did, and the second she blocked the light, the doorway just . . .

disappeared, in the shape of Eve's body. No matter where she moved, if she blocked the artificial moonlight, the whole room disappeared. "Well, this is awkward," she said. "So, how about we just stay out here and nicely ask Myrnin to please come out? Hello, crazy dude? Anyone?"

There was no answer. Nothing. Claire swallowed hard and said, "Put your arm around my neck, Eve."

"Um . . . okay?"

Claire stepped in closer and changed the light source to her left hand. Her right went around Eve's waist. "We have to move together," she said. "Don't let go."

"I won't," Eve promised. "So, left foot first?"

They took each step together, edging carefully through the doorway. Without looking, Claire knew it had sealed behind them. She pinwheeled Eve to the left to sweep the light through the darkness, and purely by luck, she managed to shine it directly on the window opposite.

Sunlight poured in, bright and cheery . . . and for a second it lit up the entire room. The wardrobe, both doors shut now. The small chest with the old-fashioned bowl and pitcher.

The bed.

And Myrnin, lying on it, still as death.

It was only a glimpse, because as soon as the sunlight poured across the room, Claire's light ceased to function at all—or, more accurately, it just became completely useless. She quickly averted the beam toward her feet, away from the window, and plunged them into darkness so thick it seemed to wrap around them like black cotton.

Eve made a little squeak of protest.

Claire carefully lifted the blue beam again until it rested on the bed. On Myrnin. Together, she and Eve twin-walked toward him. He didn't look hurt, just motionless. His hands were folded together on his chest, over what looked like the same device he'd retrieved from the wardrobe the night before. His eyes were open. Claire risked poking him. No response.

"This isn't good," Eve said. "What now?"

"Drag him out, I guess," Claire said. "But you'll have to put the shotgun down if you do."

"I do not like this plan."

"Got another one?"

"Not so much. Okay. Hang on." Eve leaned forward and pulled the round device from Myrnin's arms; she stuck it inside the pocket of the vest she was wearing, where it made a big, awkward bulge. Then she leaned her shotgun against the wall and grabbed Myrnin by one arm to pull him toward her. He slid like a dead man, slack and empty, and it was awful to see. Eve kept pulling until Myrnin thumped off the bed to the floor, and then she grabbed the back of his shirt. "Right. Now what?"

"We back up toward the door and never take our eyes off of him," Claire said.

That plan lasted one step, and then they both stopped, because of a sound that shouldn't have been there . . . the sound of the wardrobe door creaking open from behind them . . . just off to their left.

And a slow rustling.

"Claire?" Eve whispered. Her voice was shaking. "Might want to, ah, light that up."

Something told Claire that whatever was coming out of that cabinet, she *really* didn't want to see it. She had the strong feeling that the reason Myrnin was in this state might have something to do with it. So instead of turning and looking directly, she took the light, reversed it, and pointed it straight behind them where she thought the room's door should be.

"Step back," she told Eve. "Fast. One, two, three . . ." They moved in an awkward, but fast, backward scuttle, dragging Myrnin along with them, and Claire's arm bumped into the wooden doorframe. "Squeeze!"

Eve pushed hard into her, and somehow they both got through the doorway. *Myrnin,* Claire thought suddenly, and swung the light in a smooth curve upward as they passed through the doorway to keep it open for him.

His feet had just passed the boundary when she saw the thing from the wardrobe.

It was a vampire. Ancient, bony, bitter white, with mad pale eyes and rags for clothes.

And it was staring at them.

At freedom.

Claire didn't think; she lunged forward, grabbed the doorknob, and slammed the door shut an instant before the vampire moved. The keys were still dangling in the lock, and she twisted them, and then switched the light off.

Just before she did, she heard the thing whisper something.

She backed away, and Claire felt herself shuddering beyond any possibility of control.

"Oh God," Eve whispered. "What did we just do?"

"I don't know," Claire said. She pulled in a deep, shaking breath. "Let's get him out of here."

Myrnin woke up slowly in the hearse. Blinks first, then moans, then twitches. But finally, he turned his head to look at Claire, and said, "Out?" He said it as if he wasn't entirely sure he could trust his eyes.

"You're out," she said, and touched his hand. She wasn't sure he could feel it, but it seemed like the right thing to do. "What happened to you?"

"He—" Myrnin tried to put it into words, then shook his head. "It doesn't matter. The device?"

"Got it," Eve said. "Whatever it is. Also, please tell me it isn't a bomb or radioactive or something."

"It isn't, Shreve."

"Still Eve, man."

"Apology."

"Accepted, I guess, and what the hell was that thing in the room with you?"

Myrnin closed his eyes. For a long moment, Claire didn't think he'd answer Eve's question, until he finally murmured, "Someone I thought long dead. In a sense, he *is* dead. Time still passes in that room, but he can't leave it."

"But doesn't moonlight reveal the door? Can't he open it tonight?"

"It only reveals itself during one *particular* configuration of moonlight. Last night was the only opportunity for the next one hundred years . . . unless you use that device. Clever girl, Claire. I didn't even tell you to find it."

"What are you going to do about . . . him? Just leave him?"

Myrnin's dark eyes fixed on the horizon for a moment. His expression didn't change. "Yes," he said. "Yes, I will leave him."

"And one for the devil," Claire said. "You *were* talking about him."

Myrnin sighed and leaned his head back against the plush upholstery. "Maybe I was," he said. "What time is it?"

Eve checked her phone. "Eleven thirty, which, wow, I'm cutting it close. I'm dumping you off at the lab, guys, and then I'm out. It's been super fun. And you owe me a shotgun."

"I do?" Myrnin didn't open his eyes.

"Also therapy sessions, because, wow. But here you go. Have fun." She handed Claire the device from her vest pocket. It was about the size of a baseball, heavy and slick. "You going to be okay?"

Eve pulled the hearse in at the curb. Claire looked down at the narrow, dark alley that led to Myrnin's lab, and nodded.

"We'll be okay," she said.

Then she grabbed her boss and helped him into the dark.

And one for the devil.

At least she'd picked the devil she knew.

"Claire?" Myrnin's voice sounded still and quiet and small. He was just barely walking, and it was all she could do to keep him upright as they struggled down the steps to the lab. The motion lights brought up the visibility, at least. "I need to tell you something."

She stopped and looked at him. He seemed sincere, for once. And not crazy in the least.

"It was me," he said. "It was me, in that room."

"I don't . . . I don't understand. Of course it was you. I mean, I got you—"

"What we left in that room is the me of the future," he said. "The me that I would have become, starving and mad, if you hadn't returned for me. In that room, times blur. Worlds blur. The creature was me . . . a *me* that won't exist now, because of you. Thank you, Claire."

That explained it, Claire realized. What the creature had said right at the end.

It had whispered, "Thank you, Claire."

She couldn't speak. Couldn't tell him. But she thought that he might have understood anyway.

"Well," he said, "don't make too much of it—it isn't as if we haven't encountered far worse in our time together. Besides, we have work to do! This, for instance. We need to work on this." He took the baseball-sized device from her hand and tossed it into the air. Weak as he was, it was a minor miracle he caught it.

"What is it?" she asked.

"Not the vaguest idea," he said. "I just remember putting it in that room about a hundred years ago. Let's find out, shall we?"

She put the moonlight device down in the spot she'd found it, and smiled, just a little. "Let's find out," she agreed.

And they did. Eventually.

AFTERWORD

So ... am I finished with Morganville? No, I'm not. I don't know how, or why, I'll be returning to this special little place, but I know that it still holds secrets and wonders for me, and I will most certainly return for visits, or even long stays. I don't know when, but I hope that when I go back to Morganville, you'll come along for the ride. It's always best to have friends in a place like that.

Until next time, then, we wave good-bye to Morganville in the rearview mirror. But remember what the sign says: YOU'LL NEVER WANT TO LEAVE.

I certainly don't. Not quite yet.

Thank you to my wonderful friends at Penguin USA and Allison & Busby UK for encouraging me to put this collection together, and thanks especially to my Kickstarter backers of every level, who helped us take a run at Morganville in an entirely new way. But most of all, thanks to my hundreds of thousands of loyal Morganville residents. You rock.

Until next time,
I remain your friend,
Rachel Caine

Photo © 2013 Robert W. Hart

Rachel Caine is the *New York Times, USA Today*, and international best-selling author of more than forty novels, including the Weather Warden series, the Outcast Season series, the Revivalist series, and the Morganville Vampires series.

COPYRIGHT